BUSTED!

Arresting Stories from the Beat

An Anthology

Edited by
Verena Rose, Harriette Sackler
& Shawn Reilly Simmons

Trade Paperback
ISBN-13: 978-1545252895
ISBN-10: 1545252890

Manufactured/Printed in the United States of America
2017

TABLE OF CONTENTS

Introduction

BYGONES
     by Bruce Robert Coffin....................1
FALL IN NEW HAMPSHIRE
     by Sharon Daynard...........................9
SENSITIVITY TRAINING
     by Albert Tucher.............................20
GET ALONG LITTLE DOGIE
     by C.C. Guthrie...............................32
THICKER THAN WATER
     by Micki Browning...........................39
AFTERNOON DELIGHT
     by Steve Liskow..............................45
JUSTICE DUE
     by Jack Bates...................................55
CHAINS
     by Claire A Murray..........................61
DEADLY DISCOVERY IN DALLAS
     by Sanford Emerson.........................66
ANNIE GET YOUR GOAT
     by LD Masterson..............................76
NO SAFE PLACE
     by Harriette Sackler........................85
LAST CALL FOR BUFFALO
     by Randall DeWitt...........................93
THE LETTERS OF PATRICK BUSHELL
     by Gavin Keenan.............................101
CHRISTMAS SHIFT
     by Dale T Phillips...........................113
THE RUNNER
     by Steve Roy...................................120
THE CATTLE RAID OF ADAMS
     by Keenan Powell............................128

THE PROGRAM
    by Cyndy Edwards Lively................140
IDA MAE BUYS A CROWN VIC
    by Kate Clark Flora............................150
THE DRIVE-BY
    by Alison McMahan..........................161
THE OWL AND THE PUSSYCATS
    by Verena Rose..................................173
MOST EVIL
    by Peter DiChellis............................189
BECKY'S FILE
    by Ruth McCarty..............................196
NO MULLIGANS
    by Leone Ciporin.............................208
GOLDIE
    by KM Rockwood.............................218
THE WOMAN IN WHITE
    by Tracy Falenwolfe.........................224
PLAY DEAD
    by Shawn Reilly Simmons................231
THE MAN WHO WASN'T MISSED
    by Brenda Seabrooke.......................244
BURNING BRIGHT
    by Vicki Weisfeld............................256
TRUTH, GRACE AND LIES
    by A.B. Polomski.............................268
PET PEEVE
    by Kari Wainwright.........................279
BAD FRIDAY
    by Martin Edwards..........................285

INTRODUCTION

For as long as societies have existed, there has been a need for law and order. A unified force of brave individuals sworn to protect the people and uphold the laws of the land is essential to any community, from the smallest wide-spot-in-the-road with a single sheriff on duty to the largest cities where police forces numbering in the thousands are charged with protecting millions.

The first American police force was established in 1838 in Boston, followed by New York City in 1845, then Chicago in 1851, Philadelphia in 1855, and Baltimore in 1857. It wasn't until the 1880s that every major American city had a centralized police force in place. Prior to that time, community volunteers and command watch systems were the norm, resulting in varying degrees of success in maintaining justice and keeping the peace.

To maintain a fully-functioning free society and marketplace where laws could be uniformly enforced to protect citizens and trade, an organized and accountable police force was created, which has evolved into the network of law enforcement agencies and professionals we know today.

Fictional police officers have long been popular heroes (and sometimes anti-heroes) in crime fiction. Their stories allow readers a unique look into the investigation of crimes, from uncovering clues and gathering evidence to questioning suspects, studying forensics, and piecing all of the information together to solve the case. The pursuit of justice and insight into the lives of those who enter law enforcement professions as their career are what keeps fans of the genre coming back, story after story, case after case.

For this anthology we had the pleasure of reading and selecting stories by and about law enforcement professionals. The editors received close to ninety submissions for the project, which were read blindly. The result is this collection of stories which is as varied and original as the authors who wrote them, all with police work as the central theme.

Busted! Arresting Stories from the Beat features five period pieces. The old west is the setting for "Justice Due" by Jack Bates, the story of one family's search for the truth. New England in the 1890s is the backdrop for Keenan Powell's "The Cattle Raid of Adams" about a family finding their way after the loss of their father. "Fall in New Hampshire" by Sharon Daynard takes place in the 1940s, and features a glamorous movie star who for better or worse is the talk of the town. "The Letters of Patrick Bushell" by Gavin Keenan is an epistolary tale detailing one police chief's experiences during labor unrest and mill worker strikes in early twentieth century New York. And "Get Along Little Dogie" by CC Guthrie, takes place during WWII and features a one-armed special ranger in Oklahoma trying to stay one step ahead of the town's local cattle thieves.

Female officers assume the primary role in several of the stories, proving that women who wear a badge are tough as nails. In "Chains" by Claire A. Murray, an officer fights to save an abused woman's life, as well as her own. "Truth, Grace and Lies" by A.B. Polomski delves into the investigation of one of the worst crimes imaginable, the death of a child. And in "Burning Bright" by Vicki Weisfeld, a policewoman works to stop a group of reckless people from staging a very dangerous event involving a wild bear and a tiger.

The modern-day issue of gang violence is explored in the stories "The Program" by Cyndy Edwards Lively, about a youth group whose members keep falling victim to violence; "The Drive By" by Allison McMahan, which highlights the dangerous dealings between different gangs and alliances that can sometimes be formed; and "Thicker than Water" by Micki Browning, about a cop who finds herself in the middle of a completely unexpected and dangerous situation.

Gang life with elements of voodoo and the supernatural are featured in "Most Evil" by Peter DiChellis, and the supernatural is also a big part of Steve Roy's "The Runner," an original take on living in Hell. And Tracy Falenwolfe's eerie, don't-turn-off-the-lights tale "The Woman in White" might make you reconsider your next nature walk.

The issue of homelessness, especially that of returning veterans, is touched on in "No Safe Place" by Harriette Sackler. And good old fashioned bad deeds and human frailty spark the investigations in Leone Ciporin's "No Mulligans," featuring the suspicious death of a well-liked and successful golfer; Randall Dewitt's "Last Call for Buffalo," which poses the question of why someone would open a bar commemorating Buffalo's Super Bowl XXV loss right in that very town; and Brenda Seabrooke's "The Man Who Wasn't Missed" about a lawyer who vanishes into thin air, leaving behind a number of suspects, none of whom have much to gain from his being gone.

Small town cops have to go it alone, and do it well in several stories included in this anthology. "Deadly Discovery in Dallas" by Sanford Emerson, is the investigation into how a hired hand got impaled by a piece of farm equipment. In "Becky's File" by Ruth McCarty, the new police chief looks into a cold case involving her best friend from school. And in "Christmas Shift" by Dale T Phillips, a lonely cop has to solve the case of who stabbed Santa Claus. In "Ida Mae Buys a Crown Vic" by Kate Clark Flora, a woman with ambitions of her own strives to forge a new path in life.

Sometimes cops partner up to catch the bad guys like the detective teams in "Play Dead" by Shawn Reilly Simmons, where a wealthy businessman's dog appears to be the only witness to his murder, and "Afternoon Delight" by Steve Liskow, where two cops try and find out who killed the beautiful wife of the local television news anchor.

Several stories in the anthology feature animals. "The Owl and the Pussycats" by Verena Rose, starring two rag doll kitties who fall victim to a catnapper, "Goldie" by KM Rockwood, featuring a working police dog whose specialty is sniffing out drugs and contraband in a prison, and "Pet Peeve" by Kari Wainwright about a dead guy and a missing cat all prove in very different ways that animals can be the key ingredient to solving police investigations. "Annie Get Your Goat" by LD Masterson, about two rival goat breeders, illustrates how far some people will go to attain their own ambitions.

Unique settings are featured in Albert Tucher's "Sensitivity Training," which takes place in Hawaii, and in "Bad Friday" by Martin Edwards, in which a crime is uncovered on a busy commuter train to Liverpool. Bruce Robert Coffin's "Bygones" takes the reader on a scenic boat ride to the middle of a large lake in New England, where we're reminded you can't always get away from it all.

Busted! Arresting Stories from the Beat has something for every fan of crime fiction, especially those who love police stories. So pour yourself something to keep you warm and get ready for your ride along. We hope you enjoy it as much as we do.

Verena Rose
Harriette Sackler
Shawn Reilly Simmons

BYGONES

Bruce Robert Coffin

It was six o'clock in the morning as I made the turn from Route 35 into the nearly deserted lot of the Standish town boat-launch. The headlights of my SUV illuminated Stanley Rouselle's blue pickup, already backed up to the ramp. I slid the Land Rover in between the painted lines of a parking spot to my right. The rays of a crimson sunrise danced through the silhouette of trees lining the lot in front of where I'd parked. I tried recalling the phrase used by ancient mariners, something about red skies in morning. It escaped me.

My name is Phillip Timmons. I am a general practitioner with a modest-sized practice in the nearby village of Raymond. During twenty-odd years as a physician, I've cared for many local families including the Rouselles, their children, and grandchildren. The Rouselles, in particular, have always treated me like a part of their family, even mailing Christmas cards to my wife and me.

I hadn't seen Stan in more than two years, not since his wife passed. He hadn't even been in for his annual checkup. So I was elated when he called last week and invited me to go fishing.

I stepped out of the SUV onto the pavement. Fallen leaves carried by a crisp October breeze skittered around my feet. I closed my eyes and inhaled deeply, basking in the intoxicatingly earthy aromas of lake water and decomposing foliage. There's nothing quite like autumn in Maine. I grabbed my cooler, slammed the door, and hit the alarm button on my key fob, causing the horn to beep twice.

I headed across the lot, waving. "Good morning, Stan."

"Mornin' yourself, Doc. Easy with that horn. You'll scare 'em all away."

Stan was a big man with an easygoing demeanor and an infectious smile. White hair spilled out from under his cap. A weathered and ruddy complexion chronicled the life of man who'd made his living in the out-of-doors. A registered Maine Guide for more than forty years, he'd lead all manner of folk into the wilderness. If it could be climbed, sailed, hunted, or trapped, Stan had been there and done that.

"Need a hand?" I asked.

"Nope," he said. "Been doin' this myself for fifty years, ever since I could drive."

Stan unlocked the trailer winch and began to hand-crank the boat into the water.

1

"Think they'll be biting today?" I asked.

"Ayuh, reckon they'll be hungry now the damn tourists are gone. Most of them folks can't fish a lick. Don't do much more than feed 'em really," he said with a wink.

"You sure you don't need me to do anything?"

"If you wanna toss your stuff in the boat, you can pull my truck outta here after I get her in the water."

"Fair enough."

He tipped his cap back and gave me a quizzical look. "How are ya with backin' a trailer?"

I looked at the pickup and the long trailer hitched behind it. "Can't be that hard, can it?"

"Maybe you'd better let me get that, Doc. Tell ya what, you tie off to that piling so ol' Betsy here don't float away, and I'll park the truck."

"Deal," I said, taking the rope from Stan and following his instructions to the letter.

Stan jumped up into the driver's seat and fired up the big F-250's engine. I watched in awe as the old veteran whipped the trailer around and backed smoothly into one of the vacant spots.

Stan approached the boat carrying a large metal object attached to a short length of chain.

"I guess it's a good thing you didn't let me try that," I said. "We'd have been here all day."

"All's it takes is practice."

"Whatcha got there?" I asked.

"New anchor. Thought we'd try her out."

"Wow. That's a big one."

"Ayuh, big boat. Don't want her getting away." Stan climbed onto the boat and set the shiny new anchor on the rear deck. "Gonna need anything else before we set sail, Doc?"

"Think I'm all set," I said.

"Good. Here, put these on," he said, passing me an old pair of rubber boots. "They'll save your shoes."

I examined the grungy footwear, turning my nose up at the prospect of wearing something so nasty. "Do I really need to wear these?"

He fixed me with a knowing grin. "Nope. Long as you don't mind your shoes smellin' like fish."

"Right." I sat down and removed my shoes then slipped on the ancient galoshes.

"Whatdaya say we go catch us some fish, Doc? Why don't you sit up in the bow? You'll be able to see a whole lot better."

"Sounds good to me," I said as I made my way to the front of the boat.

Stan started the motor and untied us from the dock. "Hang on," he said.

In a matter of seconds the launch was well behind us, and we were headed toward the choppy open water of Sebago Lake. I did my best to hang on

2

to the seat using both hands, trying to steady myself as the boat plowed through the waves. A fine spray of icy water misted my face. It was hard to believe that I'd been swimming in this very lake just over a month ago.

I looked west where Mount Washington, shimmering with the day's first light, rose majestically in the distance. Not wanting to lose my new Red Sox cap, I spun it around backward and pulled it down tight on my head. I glanced at Stan. The sparkle in his eye and the grin on his face said it all. The old man was happy again. I knew he'd taken the death of his wife hard and it was good to see him like this.

The motor was too loud for normal conversing. I let go of the seat long enough to give him a thumbs up. He returned the gesture then pointed to the sky, slightly to the right of where we were headed. I turned and looked up, squinting my eyes until finally I saw what he was looking at. A bald eagle was circling high above the lake. Illuminated by the sun, the feathers of its white head stood in sharp contrast to its brown body. Something had the bird's attention. Suddenly it dove straight down, gaining speed as it went, hitting the surface of the water with a tremendous splash. We were at least two hundred yards from the eagle but still close enough to see what it was after: a fish, large enough that the eagle struggled to resume flight.

I heard the engine slow as Stan cut back on the throttle.

"What's he got?" I asked.

"Salmon. Son-of-a-gun beat us to that one."

I watched in awe as the impressive winged creature took to the sky, gripping the fish tightly in its talons. The salmon struggled for a few more seconds then grew still. The eagle adjusted its grip, turning the prey parallel to its body.

"Why does he hold it like that?" I asked.

"Makin' himself aerodynamic. Tough to fly with a sideways fish," Stan said, chuckling.

"I guess it would be at that."

He throttled up the motor again, continuing on his northwest course to the middle of the lake.

Twenty minutes later he powered down the boat, then killed the engine.

"This the place?" I asked.

"This is it," he said, reaching into his cooler and pulling out a beer.

On unsteady legs, I joined him at the back of the boat. "One of your secret fishing spots?"

Stan winked. "Trust you won't tell no one?"

I crossed my heart. "Not a soul."

He held a can out toward me. "Want a cold one?"

"No thanks," I said. "Never drink before noon."

"Suit yourself," he said, frowning.

Gradually, the air began to warm. It was mid-October but the sun's rays were still strong. I peeled off my windbreaker and turned my hat back around so that the brim would shield my eyes from the glare.

"Saw you wearing your cap backwards. Thought maybe you were hoping for a rally, Doc," Stan said. He picked up one of the rods and began to bait a hook.

"No," I said. "Just trying not to lose it. What are you putting on there?"

"Smelt."

"What's a smelt?"

"Bait fish. Salmon love 'em. Gotta set the hook just right so it cuts straight through the water. Drive one into each end of this little feller. After I get 'em baited, we'll troll."

"Troll?"

"Ayuh. We let a little line out then just go slow ahead, pulling the lines behind the boat."

"Ah. Okay," I said, feeling like a fool. "Learned something new there."

Stan tipped his cap back and scratched his head. "Hard to believe you ain't never gone fishin' before."

"Sad but true."

"How can you be from Maine and not fish?"

"Actually, I'm from Massachusetts. Didn't move up here until after my residency."

Stan nodded and began to bait another hook.

"Just never had the time, I guess, not with college, medical school, family, and now holding down a full time practice. Maybe someday I'll get to slow down a bit. Do more stuff like this."

"Gotta stop and smell the roses, Doc."

I looked to the west. An approaching front of dark storm clouds had swallowed up Mount Washington, leaving me with only its memory. "Those clouds look kinda ominous, Stan. Think we're okay out here?"

"Ayuh. We'll get a few good hours in before the weather gets here. Here you go, Doc," he said, handing me a one of the poles.

"Thanks. So what do I do?"

"You hang on a minute. I'll show ya."

I studied the waves and the distant shoreline. "How far you figure we are from land?"

"Lake's about a mile across and we're smack dab in the middle. Ya know it's almost three hundred feet to the bottom."

I felt my knees buckle. "Shouldn't we be wearing life vests or something?"

"Ha," he cackled. "I got a couple under the bow seats, if you really want one. Look kinda silly though."

"Don't you ever wear one?" I asked.

"Nope, not since I was a tot. Want me to fetch one for ya?"

I thought his offer through. I couldn't help but think about how goofy I already looked in the fishing boots he'd given me to wear. Stan was a real man's man and I didn't want to appear as fearful as I was unknowledgeable. "No, guess I'm okay."

4

"Good for you."

Stan fired up the boat again, tapping the throttle until we were barely moving forward.

"Kay, Doc, what you wanna do is let out enough line so the bait's behind us, but still in the wash."

I was wondering what the hell a wash was, but before I could open my mouth to ask he explained.

"Stuff the motor's churning up."

"Okay, I gotcha." I watched as he let out about forty feet of line and followed suit. "Now what?"

"Set the rod in the holder beside ya and have a seat."

"That's it? We just wait?"

"Ayuh. Relax and have another drink."

Stan cracked open a fresh 'Gansette.

"Sure you don't want one?" he asked.

I thought about the flavored seltzer water my wife had packed for me, and how that would look to this seasoned Maine outdoorsman. "Thanks," I said, accepting the beer. "Getting kinda rough out here."

"Ayuh. Winds bring'n the storm in. That's good."

"Why is that good?" I asked, looking up at the darkening sky.

"Salmon love the waves. Makes for good fishin'."

I looked at my line, trailing from the end of the pole out into the lake. "So what do we do if we get a bite?"

"Whatcha wanna do is keep a close eye on the end of your rod. Wait for the fish to tug on the line and take the bait."

"How will I know?"

"You'll know," he said with a nod. "That rod'll bend. Soon as he's on there, you set the hook."

"Set the hook?"

"Ayuh. Yank the rod up and back, hard." Stan pantomimed the act with his own pole. "Drive the hook right into him, then just keep working the reel. Don't give him no slack. Keep tension on the line and keep reeling. Nice and easy. Do it right and he won't get away."

"You make it sound so easy," I said.

Stan winked again. "Easier than you think, Doc." He finished his beer then cracked open another.

"So, how you doing, Stan?" I asked, trying to make conversation with a man I had very little in common with.

"No worse than the next feller, I expect."

"Doris and I were real sorry to hear about Betsy's passing," I said as delicately as I knew how.

He stared out the water thoughtfully. "Ayuh. Cancer took her right quick. Guess you just never know."

"No, I guess not," I agreed. "Cancer's a tricky thing."

"Course, you bein' her doctor and all, she trusted you."

5

I knew sooner or later we'd be having this uncomfortable conversation. It was part of the grieving process.

"I did all I could for her, Stan. You know that."

"Ayuh, I remember you sayin'. Funny thing though, I talked to the specialist down in Boston. He said if they'd caught it sooner, my Betsy mighta lived."

"That's the thing about cancer, Stan. There's so many different types. It's not always easy to diagnose."

I hoped my words didn't sound as hollow as they felt. The truth was, I'd misdiagnosed her condition the first time. It wasn't until Betsy had come back to see me six months later, complaining of pain, that I'd sent her to Maine Medical Center for additional tests.

"There are a number of other things that can manifest the same signs and symptoms as cancer," I said.

"That so?" Stan guzzled the last of his beer and grabbed another.

"Maybe you should slow down a bit," I cautioned. "I don't know a thing about driving a boat."

He grinned at me. "And there's something else you don't know."

"What are you talking about?"

"You got one."

I followed his gaze to the end of my pole and saw that it was bent over sharply.

"Holy shit, you're right," I said, jumping up and grabbing it from the holder.

"Now stay calm, Doc. Don't get so excited that you lose him. Remember, set the hook like I showed ya."

I whipped the rod up and back and felt resistance from the other end of the line.

"I think it's in," I said.

"Alright now, keep tension on the line. Reel him in, slow and steady."

The salmon broke through the surface of the lake, arcing three feet into the air before diving back into the water with a splash.

"Did you see that?" I yelled.

"That's a keeper, Doc," he said, patting me on the back. "You'll have a story to tell for sure."

"He's a monster." I could feel the excitement coursing through my veins and I fought to maintain my composure. My hands were shaking.

"Steady now," Stan said. "Don't give him no slack. Don't wanna lose him."

I continued reeling, fighting the salmon until it had almost reached the boat. The fish was so close that if it jumped again, it would land right on top of us.

"Kay, now hand me the rod and take this net," Stan said.

"Don't lose him," I said as I traded items with him.

"Get the net right down in the water, Doc, and I'll lift him to the surface."

I leaned over the side of the boat and dipped the net under the water. The dark shape of the fish was just out of reach.

"Just a little more," Stan said as he reeled the salmon ever closer.

I pushed the net under the water as far as I dared. My torso was hanging entirely over the side when I felt something catch my leg. Before I could react I plunged face-first into the icy water. Sputtering and coughing, I resurfaced and flailed for the boat, just managing to grab hold of the chrome rail attached to the hull.

"Hang on," Stan yelled. "I gotcha, Doc."

I let go of the net and clutched the railing with both hands. "I can't pull myself up," I said. "Hurry."

Waves swept over my head, filling my mouth with water. I felt the icy fingers of panic closing around me.

"It's them damn boots, Doc. They're filled with water, weighin' ya down. Give me your hand."

I reached up and gripped Stan's outstretched hand.

"Here we go," he said, lifting me by the arm like a rag doll.

I felt something click around my wrist. I looked up, unable to believe what I was seeing. Stan had handcuffed me.

"What the hell are you doing?" I yelled.

"Just settin' the hook, Doc."

He let go and stood upright, leering at me.

"Stop fucking around," I demanded. "Help me back onto the boat."

He shook his head. "'Fraid I can't."

"Come on, Stan. This shit isn't funny."

"Jeepers, almost forgot," he said.

Stan disappeared from sight. A moment later he returned, holding the anchor.

"Remember when you asked about my new anchor, Doc? Well, the other half of that handcuff is hooked to the chain on this thirty pound beauty."

"Please," I pleaded with him. "We can talk about this."

"Just hope she's big enough to do the job. Whatcha think, Doc?"

"For-the-love-of-God, please stop this. It's not too—" My words were cut off by yet another wave, another mouthful of water.

"You gotta keep the line nice and taut, Doc. That's the trick. Once you get 'em on there, ya can't give 'em any slack."

The cold water had numbed my fingers. I struggled to maintain my grip as I felt my strength slipping away. "Please," I begged. "I won't tell a soul."

"Nope, I don't suppose you will."

Horrified, I watched as he tossed the anchor over the side. It splashed into the lake beside me with a loud *kerplunk*, yanking my hand off the wet rail and down into the water.

7

Stan looked down at me and grinned. "Whatdaya think of fishin', Doc? Some days it's so good I never wanna leave the lake. How 'bout you?"

Bruce Robert Coffin is a former detective sergeant with more than twenty-seven years in law enforcement. At the time of his retirement, from the Portland, Maine police department, he supervised all homicide and violent crime investigations for Maine's largest city. He is the bestselling author of the Detective Byron Mystery Series from HarperCollins. His short stories have been featured in several anthologies including the *2016 Best American Mystery Stories*. He lives and writes in Maine.

FALL IN NEW HAMPSHIRE

Sharon Daynard

Little Harbor, NH
October, 1942

True to the adage there's no such thing as too early when showing up for rummage sales and wakes, locals had been claiming their spot in line for the six o'clock viewing at Krueger's Funeral Parlor since four. By five, the line of mourners stretched from under the red awning, along the matching runner, and down Main Street to the village common. Everyone who was anyone from Broadway to Hollywood, family and friends, shutterbugs, fans, and rubberneckers had descended upon the picturesque village nestled along the coast of New Hampshire to pay their respects to retired broadcast legend David Engle, and to catch a glimpse of Claudia Carlisle, the Hollywood starlet he'd married.

It was going on five-thirty when Effigy Price commandeered a window seat at the Blue Bird Diner and ordered the Patrolman's Special. She craned her neck from left to right, taking in as much of Main Street as possible for a woman of her advanced years, then focused her binoculars on Krueger's Funeral Parlor across the way, only pausing from her task when the diner's owner, Dot Brinkman, deposited a mug on the table and filled it three-quarters of the way to the brim with coffee.

Effigy looked from the mug to Dot and let out an exaggerated sigh. "Give it a break, Dot. I'm working a stakeout here. It's bad enough you're stretching the coffee with chicory, but this is nonsense. It's not saving you anything. All it does is have you coming back sooner for refills."

"Not anymore." Dot pointed to a new sign on the diner wall that read DUE TO RATIONING, WE ARE UNABLE TO SERVE MORE THAN ONE CUP OF COFFEE PER GUEST.

"One cup," Effigy scoffed. "But I'm a deputized member of the police department."

"And I'm Elliot Ness. Enjoy your coffee."

Effigy pursed her lips, biting back a less than Christianly comment. A smile forced itself across her face as she reminded herself why she was there. "Dorothy Jean Brinkman, did you color your hair? I swear you look ten years younger." It was a lie. Dot, like so many women who'd taken on the role of breadwinner after their husbands had been drafted, looked haggard.

9

"You think so?" Dot scrunched up her nose and filled Effigy's cup to the brim. "It's my lipstick—the same shade Claudia Carlisle wears."

"Claudia Carlisle," Effigy repeated, struggling to keep her smile from backsliding to a scowl. Claudia Carlisle was everything she imagined a transplanted Hollywood diva to be: conceited, pampered, and pretentious. Her husband, David Engle, on the other hand, was a gentleman through and through, earning a spot in the hearts of millions as one of America's most respected broadcast journalists. How he married a conniving trollop twenty-five years his junior was beyond her. "It's stunning. *Blood On My Hands* from the Lady Macbeth Collection?"

"Max Factor's *Chinese Lantern*."

"And Claudia told you that herself, did she?"

"Well, no. I asked her husband the last time he was here." Dot took a seat across from Effigy and looked out the window. "Another delivery truck. There's been a steady parade of them since we opened this morning. What I wouldn't give to own a florist shop instead of a greasy spoon. I still can't believe David Engle's dead. The two of them falling down those stairs, I don't know how Claudia didn't break her neck."

"Neither do I."

Dot turned to Effigy and patted her hand. "I forgot...you were there with the Ladies League for a luncheon when it happened, weren't you? It must have been awful. Vidia Weston said she'll never forget ringing the doorbell and Claudia's bloodcurdling shriek followed by the horrific *thump, thump, thump* of their bodies hitting one step after the other down the staircase. It's given her nightmares."

Effigy rolled her eyes. "You know what gives me nightmares? Claudia Carlisle getting away with murder."

Dot's jaw went slack, her eyes opened wide. "Effigy Price, you can't be serious?"

"As serious as a boil on the Queen Mum's bum," Effigy mumbled as a lone, black Packard limousine pulled up to the front of Krueger's. Despite Dot's objections, she stood on her chair for a better view as the limo driver opened the passenger door and Claudia Carlisle emerged wearing a sleeveless black velvet cocktail dress with a matching chiffon wrap. Even from across the street, the bruises on her arms and legs were visible. Effigy let out a groan as Claudia steadied herself on the driver's arm, stumbled, and was helped inside.

Safely inside the funeral director's office, Claudia requested a brandy to calm her nerves and a few minutes with the only man she'd ever loved. Snifter in hand, Winston Krueger helped her to a viewing room spilling over with floral arrangements, funeral wreaths, and potted plants. At the head of the mahogany casket were David's golf clubs and a portrait of him waving from the Swilken Bridge at St. Andrews in Scotland.

"It's perfect. All of it." Claudia brushed a tear from her cheek and smiled down at her husband. "David could've retired to anyplace in the world and golfed, but he fell in love with your precious little town." Her voice dissolved into sobs as she ran her fingertips over the clubs and placed one inside the casket.

Catching a glimpse of herself in a nearby mirror, she cringed. She'd worked her hair into a French twist. David had preferred it parted off-center and pooled about her shoulders. Somehow it didn't seem right for the wake. Neither did makeup. She barely recognized the woman staring back at her in the mirror. Her signature shimmering platinum hair had dulled to a dishwater blonde. Hints of laugh lines and whispers of crow's feet, once scarcely discernible against her near-flawless porcelain complexion, were unmistakable in the crevasses that cut deep into her ashen skin. And the dark circles that seemed to have taken permanent residence beneath her bottle-green eyes were nearly as black as the dress she wore. Friends told her it was nerves.

Nerves were the least of it. It was Effigy Price.

Six months earlier, Little Harbor's police chief, Bobby Coffey, deputized twelve female residents to serve as The Ladies League Auxiliary Police. The women patrolled the streets of their neighborhoods from 9 PM to 4 AM, enforcing blackout laws and the seacoast dimming-of-automobile-headlights mandate. Eleven of those women performed their duties flawlessly. The twelfth, seventy-two-year-old Effigy Price, made Coffey's life a living nightmare. She patrolled the streets like a cat on the prowl, handing out citations for even the most insignificant of infractions, and brandishing her 20-inch "billy" like a sidearm. On more than one occasion she'd used it to knock out a car's headlight as a warning.

Not that it ended there. Effigy considered herself a duly noted detective on the Little Harbor PD. What she was was a pot stirrer, a busybody, and all-around annoyance. She meddled in police business, invented crimes where none existed, and occasionally stumbled upon the real thing. David Engle's fatal fall down a flight of stairs was her latest preoccupation.

Before anyone murmured "He's dead," before the doctor arrived, even before the three bean salads, baked beans, and creamed carrots dropped from the hands of the Ladies League biddies that horrible afternoon, Effigy was inserting herself with her measuring tapes, notepads, and Brownie box camera, making a nuisance of herself and declaring the entire first floor a crime scene.

Condolence casseroles and pity pies in hand, Effigy paid surprise visits to Claudia in the days leading up to the wake. She stopped by under the guise of collecting bacon grease and tin cans for the war effort. She phoned at all hours of the day and night with quick questions and veiled intimations. She hinted at a lighthearted nudge, alluded to a playful push, and ratcheted it up to a deliberate shove that sent David Engle to his death.

Claudia's demands to have Effigy locked behind bars until after the funeral fell on the deaf ears of Little Hampton's police chief. Effigy was harmless, Bobby Coffey assured Claudia. In a couple of days her fascination

11

with David's accident would wane and she'd latch onto something else. It wasn't so much a lie as it was wishful thinking. Coffey knew from experience once Effigy Price set her mind on something even a restraining order was useless.

When Effigy wasn't busy "getting the goods" on Claudia, she was running her theories past Coffey. She didn't buy into Claudia's teary-eyed catchall "It just happened so fast." So fast she couldn't remember if David lost his footing first or if she did. So fast she couldn't remember who was walking on the inner part of the staircase and who on the outer. Or who grabbed onto whom and dragged the other down with them.

And as was typically the case, Coffey feigned genuine interest, offered raised brows and pensive nods, and wished he'd taken his mother's advice and entered the priesthood.

Effigy Price elbowed her way through the crowd at the door into the packed viewing room and planted herself in front of the guestbook. She scanned the hodgepodge of who's who, locking eyes with Claudia. In what promised to be a standoff, all it took was an impish smile and enthusiastic wave to turn the widow's eyes away.

"Amateur," Effigy muttered, flipping back to the first page in the guestbook. She ignored the exaggerated sighs and stage-whispered complaints, taking her time to peruse each page, reading every name and comment. She looked back at poor, devastated, guilty-as-hell Claudia Carlisle, scribbled her sentiments and moved on to pay her respects.

She buffed out a smudge on the mahogany casket's lower lid, lifted it, and let it drop with a bone-jarring *bang*! Mouthing a feeble "sorry" to Claudia, she knelt at the casket and peered inside.

She'd probably attended a hundred wakes in her lifetime and never once could conjure up what words of wisdom, consolation, or faith she could impart to the deceased to make whatever lay ahead more palatable. She usually counted to fifty, patted their arm, and took her place in the procession line. But today, she leaned into David's casket and whispered, "Claudia won't get away with it."

Effigy waited until she was within earshot of Claudia to announce to the woman in line behind her, "I waked three of my husbands here and put down a dollar deposit should my fourth and final *faux pas* stagger back into my life. Of course, it was so much easier to rid oneself of a man back then. Rat poison in his hooch, water hemlock roots mixed in with his carrots, a do-it-yourself brake job, and *poof*! These days, a gal's got to be creative what with J. Edgar Hoover and the boys down at the FBI looking to make a name for themselves. Let's face it, not every woman can throw her husband down a flight of stairs and get away with murder." She turned to Claudia and offered a pout. "You poor, poor dear." Effigy took Claudia's hands in hers. "I hardly know what to say that would be of comfort. Winston did a wonderful job with David."

12

"Yes, he did," Claudia mumbled, trying to pull free from Effigy's grasp.

"You'd never know there was a dent the size of the Grand Canyon in the back of his head. I swear it had an echo." Effigy gave a knowing nod to the woman behind her before resuming her conversation with Claudia. "My, but that dress looks stunning on you. I wore the exact same one last New Year's to the VFW. Bought it at the five and dime up in Portsmouth."

Claudia jerked her hands free and looked to the next person in line. "Magda, darling, I can't believe you're here."

"I can't believe Claudia didn't snap her neck tumbling down those stairs." Effigy jockeyed for Magda's attention. "The angels themselves must have floated her to the bottom on a marshmallow cloud. I was there. Not for the elbows over teakettles part, the crumpled in a heap at the bottom part." She pulled a photograph from her purse and handed it to Magda as if offering up Exhibit A. "For a woman that lives for the camera, it's far from flattering."

"Mr. Krueger!" Claudia ripped the photograph from Magda's hands.

"Did you have a stand-in or did you do your own movie stunts, Claudia?" Effigy asked. "You know, the horseback riding, swan dives off cliffs, falling down a flight of stairs, that sort of stuff?" She turned to Magda, scrunched up her nose, and confided, "To be honest, I prefer stage theater. It's amazing what a few well-placed props, the right sound effects, and a motivated actor can have the audience believing."

"Get out," Claudia hissed, "or I'll have you dragged out in handcuffs."

Effigy rolled her eyes and turned to Magda. "I doubt it. The chief's sweet on me. It'd be embarrassing if he weren't so damned handsome. He could pass for Clark Gable's better looking, baby brother."

"Mr. Krueger!"

"Lower your voice, Claudia," Effigy reminded. "You'll be waking the dead and lord only knows the tales they'll tell. Here in New Hampshire deathbed testimonies and those from beyond the grave carry the same weight in a court of law. Ouija boards on the other hand..." Her voice trailed off as she spotted Bobby Coffey cutting a path in their direction.

"Sorry to interrupt, ladies," Coffey apologized. "I'm afraid Mrs. Price is needed elsewhere."

"Who is it this time?" Effigy sighed. "The district attorney or that baboon of a doctor you call a medical examiner?"

"Ladies." Coffey offered a nod before leading Effigy away by the elbow. "Any idea who Udi Dit is?"

"Sounds Scandinavian."

"Seems Udi's signature took up the better half of a page in the guestbook," Coffey confided.

"A child, maybe? Was it scribbled in crayon?"

"Could be I'm pronouncing it wrong. Udi Dit, U-di Dit, U-did-it."

"You did it!" Effigy slammed a palm off her forehead. "There you have it. Even a child can see Claudia murdered David Engle."

13

"Are you insane?"

For a second or two Effigy paused as if contemplating the question, then asked, "Care to buy an old broad a drink?"

Effigy wondered what was inside the Pyrex pot Bobby Coffey deposited on his desk. It looked like coffee, but smelled like burnt hair. Taking a seat across from her, he grabbed two once-white ceramic mugs from his bottom desk drawer and offered her one. She figured it to be about eight-years-old, based on the number of brown rings she counted inside.

"Something wrong?" Coffey asked, filling his mug.

"Nothing a charcoal biscuit can't cure."

"Tell me when," he said, pouring the brew into hers.

Guesstimating the cutoff point as an inch of what had to be the incubation medium for the next great plague, she muttered "Enough." She pulled a flask from her handbag and topped it off. "Too much caffeine gives me the jitters."

"And too much whiskey makes you think you're sitting on this side of the desk. I'm warning you, Effigy, one more stunt like the one you pulled tonight and you'll be off the force and rooming at the county jail."

"She killed David Engle."

"Doc Cargill says otherwise." Coffey slid a folder across his desk. "He says it was an accident."

"Accident my Aunt Millie's bloomers." Her jaw went slack when she opened the folder. "You're going to let a man who can't even spell intracranial right have final say on what was and wasn't a murder?"

"Let it go."

"None of this makes any sense," she argued. "There wasn't a single bruise on David Engle's body and yet Claudia is covered in black and blues."

Coffey shrugged. "Engle's feet went out from under him, his head slammed down on the edge of a stair, his body went limp, and he rag-dolled it to the bottom. Claudia nailed every step on the way down."

"And all she sustained were bruises? No fractures, no head trauma, no internal injuries. If nothing else, you'd have expected a dislocated shoulder."

"She got lucky."

"It was a pratfall," Effigy countered.

"It was an accident."

Effigy turned the folder to face him and tapped a finger to the middle of the page. "Cargill didn't even get the time of death right."

"Engle was dead when he got there."

"David Engle was dead long before Cargill got there. His hand was cool when I touched it."

"It's fall in New Hampshire, Effigy. There's a chill in the air. A body tends to cool—"

14

"One point five degrees per hour until it reaches ambient temperature," she finished his sentence. "Per hour, not minute. And FYI, it wasn't even close to cool that day. We were enjoying a bit of Indian summer. Are you listening to any of this? His hand was cool, his pupils were dilated, and his skin had already taken on a bluish hue. David Engle had been dead for hours."

"Not according to Vidia Weston and the rest of the Ladies League. They heard Claudia and David Engle talking right before they heard 'em fall."

"I was there. The only person anyone heard talking was Claudia. David didn't say anything. David was dead. Claudia killed him, dumped his body at the foot of the staircase, and then flung herself down those stairs when Vidia rang the bell, guaranteeing herself twelve witnesses that would swear on a stack of bibles that it was all a tragic accident."

"That's pure conjecture and you know it."

"I'll show you conjecture." She pulled a handful of photographs from her purse, shuffled through them and handed one to Coffey. "Notice what he's wearing?"

"Pants and a shirt."

"He's wearing his golf clothes."

"He was golfing that morning with Vern Shepherd."

"And according to Vern they finished around 12:30. Vidia rang the front doorbell at 2:00."

"So?"

"So why didn't he change his clothes?"

Coffey handed her back the pictures. "The doc's ruling holds."

"David Engle didn't fall down those stairs. He was laid out for me and the rest of the Ladies League to get an eyeful. Claudia staged the whole thing."

"What possible motive did she have for murdering him?"

"He was worth millions."

"She has money."

"She hates living here. That big old house has been a prison for her these last two years."

"She gets furloughed every other weekend to their Manhattan penthouse. Anything else?"

"She killed him, isn't that enough? I just proved it to you."

"Because she didn't dislocate her shoulder and Engle didn't change his clothes? This whole Nancy Drew turns seventy-two nonsense ends tonight. You're not a detective. You're an auxiliary policewoman. You're supposed to be enforcing blackout laws, period. I'm going to drive you home, walk you to the door, and wait out front until I see your bedroom lights go out. Tomorrow morning, you're taking up knitting or jarring jams and jellies or whatever women your age do to keep themselves out of prison. And you're going to stay clear of the funeral service. Understood?"

"Can I at least visit David's grave and apologize for letting Claudia get away with murder?"

"There isn't going to be a grave." Coffey helped Effigy up from her seat. "He's being cremated."

"Cremated? Well isn't that convenient."

Effigy wrapped a strand of pink yarn counterclockwise under the knitting needle in her right hand and behind the one in her left, pulled the yarn through the loop, and pushed the stitch onto the right needle. Her face screwed up into a knot as she examined her handiwork. It looked like something a pink cat hacked up. How anyone in their right mind considered knitting a calming and productive hobby was beyond her. The needles were cumbersome, the yarn cost a fortune, and the "easier than ever" directions might as well have been written in Chinese.

"Around, under, over and through. Around, under, over and through," she repeated to herself as the front door opened.

"Is that you, Claudia?" Effigy called from a tartan wingback.

Claudia's jaw clenched as she stormed into the den. "How did you get in here? The front door was locked."

"Was it?" Effigy shrugged, struggling with another stitch. "I've been beside myself ever since I woke up and realized I've lost one of the genuine rhinestone earrings I was wearing last night. I tried calling Krueger's in case it dropped into David's coffin when I whispered my goodbyes into his ear, but Winston was setting up the chapel for the funeral service. I tried calling you, but your phone was busy."

"Get out," Claudia hissed.

"By the time I dressed, did up my hair, and drove to Krueger's, the service was over and the place was locked up. Everyone was over to the White Caps Inn for the funeral brunch. Personally, I would have gone with the Blue Bird Diner."

"Get out!"

"I didn't want to be a bother so I let myself into Krueger's and checked the coffin myself. I checked under the pillow, inside David's suit jacket, and down by his feet. I even emptied the dustpan in the broom closet and came up empty. I checked with the pawnshop, but nobody remembered waiting on you. I came by here on the chance that you're one of them finders-keepers-losers-weepers kinda gals."

"I said get out!"

"I hate knitting. One dropped stitch and the whole damn thing unravels, much like your story."

"I'm calling the police."

"Don't bother. I already called to tell Chief Coffey I was knitting him a pair of socks. Not that he cared," Effigy griped, dropping the ball of pink yarn into the knitting bag at her feet. "That's a striking shade of green on the walls. I can see why David would've wanted it on the collar of the golf shirt he was wearing for the Ladies League luncheon that afternoon. It must've brought out the blue in his eyes. The photograph I have hardly does it justice. Of course by

16

now, a smart cookie like you would have disposed of the clothes David was wearing. Much like you thought sending the murder weapon off to the crematorium would destroy it."

"What?" Claudia followed Effigy's gaze to the golf club on the coffee table.

"That was a cruel joke, putting that five iron in the casket with him," Effigy chastised. "Sort of like throwing a bearskin rug in with a man that had been mauled to death by a grizzly, just in case the afterlife was a tad on the nippy side."

Claudia leaned against the credenza, looking as if the wind had been knocked from her. "You're insane."

"I knew you killed him, but I couldn't piece it all together until I walked into this room," Effigy admitted.

"It was an accident," Claudia snapped. "David lost his footing and we both fell."

Effigy slowly pulled out a row of knitting. "Last week you couldn't remember who fell first. You know what I remember? I remember the house smelled of fresh paint and burning wood that day. It was a balmy seventy-four degrees and yet that fireplace was blazing."

"We both fell."

"I hope you don't mind that I used your phone to call your handyman, Ned Farr. Ned said he painted this room that day. He thought he'd done a wonderful job. You thought otherwise. You tore into Ned like a rabid dog. You wanted red, but David was the one paying him. David wanted green."

"David lost his footing," Claudia persisted. "He flailed, pushing me forward as he fell backward. It happened so fast I don't even remember screaming."

Effigy shook her head and pulled out another row of pink. "Ned made a hasty retreat out the front door just as David pulled into the garage around one. I imagine you were still in here steaming when David came inside. There was a heated exchange, David turned his back, and you clobbered him with that club."

"You have no idea what you're talking about."

Effigy ripped out the rest of her knitting. "Lucky for you Ned left without gathering up his drop cloths from the floor and furniture. You used one to drag David's body to the stairs. You burned that cloth and any others that were bloodstained in the fireplace. Then you waited for me and the Ladies League to show up for your grand finale."

"It was an accident. A horrible, horrible accident."

"For a B-list actress you've got spunk, tucking that golf club in next to David for everyone to see. It was a showstopper all right. But here's the rub, Claudia, it doesn't matter how much Bon Ami you scrubbed it with, traces of David's blood will still turn up."

Claudia picked up the phone on David's desk and dialed the police. "Someone's in my house," she whispered into the mouthpiece.

"You call that acting? Put some emotion into it."

17

"Claudia Carlisle. 28 Cobbles Lane. I'm alone," she sobbed, pulling a revolver from the desk and pointing it at Effigy. "My husband owns a gun, but I've never used it."

"She prefers five irons," Effigy clarified.

"What are you doing here? No! Please don't!" Claudia let out a shrill scream and ripped the phone cord from the wall.

"Bravo," Effigy applauded. "Now what?"

"I fatally shoot the intruder. Would it really surprise anyone that it was that psychopath Effigy Price? She was obsessed with David. She broke into our house while I was at his funeral service. For whatever reason, she blamed me for his death."

"Probably because you killed him."

"She was going to kill me."

"I was not. I came for a confession."

"Do you have any idea what it's like to be an actress turning forty? It's hard enough landing a two-minute radio spot let alone a movie when you're living in the middle of nowhere. This was supposed to be our summerhouse. Summer stretched out through the end of October so David could take in the goddamn fall leaves while he golfed. That was two years ago. Do you have any idea how many ham-and-bean church suppers, potluck dinners, and pancake breakfasts with the local loons I endured for him? Or how many of your mind-numbing Ladies League luncheons?"

"You have the penthouse."

"David's penthouse? He was selling it. He sprung that one on me right after he told me to get over the paint color. I'd been reduced to a bit player in my own marriage."

"You could have divorced him."

"I could have done a lot of things, but it's a little too late for any of them now. I don't even remember picking up the golf club, just swinging it as hard as I could. You want a confession? I know how to use a gun. The only problem is I can't claim self-defense if you're sitting in that chair when I pull the trigger."

"Self-defense?"

"I threw myself down a flight of stairs to cover up David's murder. I'll be more than happy to stab myself with a knitting needle if it means getting rid of you. Get out of the chair and walk toward me."

"I'd love to, but my lumbago is killing me," Effigy declined, hunkering down in the wingback. "Be a dear and fetch me a hot water bottle."

"You miserable witch," Claudia screeched, charging at her. "I'll pull you out of that chair by the hair if I have to."

Effigy kicked over the knitting bag, spilling tightly wound balls of yarn into Claudia's path. Claudia's right foot stepped on a ball, throwing her off balance. Her arms flailed, her free hand grasped at air. Her left foot found another ball and flew out from under her. With a sickening thud, the back of her head slammed to the floor. Her shoulders, hips, and legs followed in succession as the gun skittered across the hardwood.

"It happened so fast," Effigy mocked, turning her attention to the den's entrance. "How long have you been standing there?"

"Long enough hear Claudia's confession and to know you can't knit," Coffey said, removing a pair of handcuffs from his duty belt.

"I can't jar preserves worth a damn either. Picking locks, on the other hand, is a hobby I've taken pleasure in for years."

Sharon Daynard has been offered the services of a professional hit-man, crossed paths with a serial killer, testified before grand juries, and taken lie detector tests. Her short stories have appeared in magazines and anthologies in the US and Canada. Her 51-word short story "Widow's Peak" received a Derringer nomination for Best Flash of 2004. She is member of the New England chapter of Sisters in Crime and a SinC Guppy. www.sadaynard.com

SENSITIVITY TRAINING

Albert Tucher

Jenny Freitas wanted the darkness back.

She usually loved the drive home to Honoka'a. The hypnotic simplicity of the dividing line in her headlights soothed her for the night's sleep to come.

But now the blue flasher overwhelmed the night. The pulsating light bounced off her rear view mirror and filled the car.

On the job she had lit up many a vehicle, but this was her first time on the other end of the transaction. Maybe a police officer should experience the civilian perspective, but that didn't mean she had to like it.

The cop pulling her over couldn't have picked a more isolated location. Jenny had just passed the few lights of Laupāhoehoe. Ahead lay a huge curve in the highway, one of the concessions that the works of man made to the deep gulches and the mountain slopes of the Big Island.

As she steered to the shoulder, she replayed the last few minutes in her mind. Okay, she had been going over the limit, but who didn't? When roles were reversed, she always gave the driver at least an extra five miles per hour.

Jenny stopped and sent her window down. With her right hand she unclasped her bag and pulled her shield out. She set it on the passenger seat and watched her side mirror.

The cone went dark. That was wrong.

She put the car in gear and floored the accelerator. The flashers came back on in her mirror, but she wasn't falling for it twice.

She steered with her left hand and took the radio handset from the dashboard.

"Who do we have on 19, around the twenty-four mile marker?"

"Shouldn't be anybody," said the dispatcher.

"That's what I figured. We've got an impersonator. I need backup."

"ASAP, Officer, but everybody's at an accident down toward Hilo. It'll take them a while to get to you."

"Okay. Heading north."

She leaned into the curve. It forced her to slow down, but it also made the headlights and flashing cone behind her disappear for a moment. That meant the pursuer couldn't see her, either. Instinct took over again. Jenny braked and turned left even harder. The car skidded to a stop at an angle, blocking the northbound lane. She put the transmission in park, and unlocked her door. For once her hand didn't fumble with the power switch, or with the seat belt release. She made a mental note to congratulate herself when she had more time.

Jenny snatched her shield off the passenger seat and pushed her door open. She threw herself out of the car and ran across the highway to the other shoulder. As she went, she drew her off-duty weapon from her belt holster.

She spared a tenth of a second on wondering about the other driver. The Hawaii County Police weren't currently on the lookout for a phony cop preying on women. Had this one been doing it elsewhere, or was he a virgin? She planned to make his first time his last.

The other car appeared. The driver had just an instant to register Jenny's car blocking the lane. Jenny would have steered around the obstacle, but the driver lacked cop reflexes. The tires shrieked, as the car stopped inches from Jenny's rear bumper. Jenny ran back across the highway and aimed her weapon at the driver.

A woman glared at her through the open window. Surprise made Jenny's hand waver for an instant, but she recovered and looked again.

She wasn't crazy. The driver was still female. What the hell?

First things first. The woman's right hand was out of sight. Jenny held her shield up.

"Both hands on the wheel," she ordered.

The woman glared for a moment, as if considering her options.

"Do it."

The woman complied. Her right hand was empty. So far, so good.

Jenny considered her next move. In uniform she would have had her handcuffs, flashlight, and radio on her belt. In her t-shirt and khakis she would have to improvise.

She tried the door handle. It was unlocked. She pulled it open and backed up.

"Out."

Again the woman obeyed. Jenny kept her momentum going.

"Turn around. Grab the car."

She stooped and pulled the woman's left foot back six inches to unbalance her. Jenny did the same with the right foot. She holstered her gun and frisked the woman. She found nothing. If the woman had ID, it must be in the car, which was another Camry and obviously a rental.

Was the woman from another island? Or the mainland?

"Now what?" said the woman.

"We wait."

"Tough cop. Can't handle a woman."

"Tough is good. Smart is better. Any weapons in the car?"

"Yeah. A gun. You want me to get it?"

"Don't move."

For a moment Jenny watched the rotating cone on the roof. Police items like this weren't supposed to be available to civilians, but they could always be had for a price. The Internet only made the transaction easier.

And the cone was all that the woman needed to pull off her impersonation. Visitors to the Big Island sometimes wondered aloud where the

21

cops were, until they saw a Camry or Impala with a flasher on the roof. Some officers drove their own vehicles and got reimbursed for mileage.

Jenny had stored her cone in her trunk, but as long as the bogus blue light kept flashing, she wouldn't need her own. Her backup would find her.

"So you were just cruising and looking to pull over a woman driving solo?"

"No, I wanted you, Officer Freitas."

The name shocked Jenny like a taser.

"Do I know you?"

"You killed my son."

"I what?"

Jenny had three years on the job, and this was the first time she had drawn a gun off the range. Grappling matches with suspects had never sent anyone to the hospital with more than cuts, bruises or sprains.

"Let's back up," she said. "Who are you?"

"Margery Rektor."

"From?"

"Seattle."

"Okay, who is your son?"

"Was. Donald Rektor."

"I'm not coming up with it."

"I knew it. You're like every other cop. Killing is all in a day's work."

"How did I kill him?"

"Don't play dumb with me."

Jenny saw that more blue light was bleeding around the bend in the highway. Seconds later a marked Hawaii County SUV appeared. As the vehicle came near, Jenny raised both hands, with her shield in her left and her off-duty weapon dangling from her index finger by the trigger guard. The approaching officer had a confusing scene to sort out, and Jenny planned to help as much as she could.

The car stopped behind Margery Rektor's rented Camry, and Officer Patsy Inaba climbed out. Jenny relaxed.

"Where's the blue light bandit?"

Jenny pointed at Margery Rektor.

"No shit," said Patsy. "What's that about?"

"I'm hoping to find out."

"Now what?" said Margery over her shoulder. "You work me over like my son?"

"I don't remember your son," said Jenny. "You want to tell me what happened?"

"He was here for the summer. Working. He should be back at school right now."

"What was he doing?"

"Crewing on one of the snorkel cruises. Kealakekua Bay."

22

That narrowed it down. Hilo Division had lent Jenny and Patsy to Kona Division on the dry side of the island for four months. The period did take place during the previous summer.

"How did I meet him?"

"You gave the boat a ticket."

Okay. It was coming back. Jenny remembered a small craft committing a basket of infractions, including cruising too close to protected reefs and lacking enough life jackets.

Jenny remembered having a hard time keeping a straight face, making a traffic stop on the high seas.

"And that killed him?"

"Not the ticket. You."

"I'm not following you."

"He gave you some lip. Everybody says so. I don't dispute it."

"Okay, I remember him. The name didn't stick. But I definitely sent him on his way, and there are witnesses."

"You tracked him down later."

"You're not making sense. If I tried to get even with every guy who mouthed off, I'd have no life."

"Well, my son has no life now."

"Where did I supposedly track him to?"

"Up the mountain in Kona."

"He lived up there?"

"Yes. For three weeks I didn't hear from him. The cops gave me the run-around. He'll turn up, he's with some girl, he's in Puna buying, what do you call it here?"

"Pakalolo," said Jenny. "Did he smoke it?"

"Don't you dare. I've learned how you cops do things. If he smoked marijuana, he deserved whatever happened to him."

"So what did happen to him?"

"A dog found him, down the hill from their house. You hear what I'm saying? He had to be found by a dog. The cops said he fell off the lanai and was killed."

Jenny hadn't heard, but by then she was back in Hilo.

"Where did you get the idea that I had anything to do with it?"

"Because somebody saw you at the house."

"Who?"

"So you can kill them too? My investigator found a witness. I'm not telling you his name."

"A local investigator?"

Margery said nothing, but Jenny took that as a yes. The woman probably didn't realize that she had already narrowed it down enough. This island with the land area of Connecticut, and a population not much bigger than Bridgeport's, didn't support many private investigators.

Jenny looked at Patsy, who had been standing motionless, as if she wanted to be invisible.

"You want to secure her gun?"

For a moment Jenny wondered whether Patsy had heard, but then the officer reached into the rented Camry. She came out holding a semi-automatic. She didn't seem to know what to do with it.

"Let me have your cuffs," said Jenny

She handcuffed the woman and stowed her in the back of the Ford. Patsy opened her mouth to say something, but then she turned away and got into the vehicle. She drove off toward Hilo. Jenny watched the tail lights disappear around the curve and wondered why something felt off.

Lanny Soares didn't put up much of a front. He shared an office with an insurance broker on the second floor of a two-story wooden building from the 1930s on Kilauea Avenue.

"To what to I owe the pleasure, Officer?"

"A client of yours. Margery Rektor."

His mouth became a thin, stubborn line.

"Lanny, I'm giving you a chance to do your client some good. And maybe yourself, depending on how deep you are in this."

"How does that work?"

"She tried to kill me last night."

"Now I'm definitely not talking."

"We got her. No wiggle room. If there are any mitigating circumstances, I figure you're the one who would know."

She watched him consider his options and come to a conclusion. An average citizen could shut up, but he had to coexist with the cops to stay in business.

"Did she say why she made a run at you?"

"Supposedly you did some work for her. You found somebody who put me near her son's place of residence around the time of his death."

"Whoa. She took the ball and ran right out of bounds with it."

"Meaning?"

"I found a witness who saw a young woman in a police uniform. I never said it was you."

Jenny knew that the information narrowed it down in the same way that had enabled her to find Lanny. Four hundred officers policed the entire island. Women were a minority. Fewer were young, and fewer still had been in Kona on the relevant date.

And only two of them had been involved in stopping the boat with Donald Rektor on it. Jenny knew she had an awkward conversation ahead of her.

The next day she sidled up to Patsy Inaba in the locker room. The space was tiny, and obviously had been converted from some other use.

"Thanks for the backup the other night."

Patsy glanced at her. Backup was part of the job.

"I've been wondering how to show my appreciation, and the best I can come up with is to interrogate you."

Jenny gave Patsy a steady look. Patsy returned it.

"What was Donald Rektor to you?"

Patsy stared for a long moment and then turned back to her locker. She put her uniform shirt on and started buttoning it.

"I dated him for a few weeks. That was a pretty awkward trip with his mother in the back seat."

Jenny wasn't surprised. This was another effect of the small population on the island. The personal and the professional could be hard to separate. Now that she thought about it, she remembered Patsy hanging back and leaving her to deal with the young man.

"You should have mentioned it."

"It was over. I dumped him the week before."

"It probably affected the way he acted that day. You should have given me a heads up."

"If I had known he was going to die, I probably would have."

"How involved were you?"

"Less than he was. You know the kind of guy who thinks he's in love on the second date? It got old fast. I wasn't that into him."

"Did you ever go up to his place?"

"Sure. But not after I broke it off."

Jenny studied Patsy. The other woman had the Japanese features that her name suggested, while Jenny was a classic Portuguese type. Their coloring was similar. A witness could have made a mistake at a distance.

Patsy returned the look, but cops knew how to do that.

"I assume he had roommates?"

"About a dozen."

No surprise there, either. Hawaii was expensive. Young people with menial jobs in tourism crowded together to make the rent.

"They'll back me up."

"I'm sure they would."

Patsy caught the implication.

"Most of them were college kids," she said, "They're gone, but the guy with the lease is kama'aina."

A permanent resident.

Patsy was looking more and more resentful.

"Are you Internal Affairs all of a sudden?" she asked.

"No," said Jenny. "Sorry. I'm not IAD, and now I know I don't want to be. Ever."

Patsy gave her a stony look that Jenny probably deserved, and then shrugged.

"Glad I could help you with that."

Jenny tried to put the whole thing out of her mind as she worked her middle shift, but back at the station she went to an office that she knew well. The door stood open, and she knocked on the frame. Detective Coutinho looked up. Not for the first time she wondered whether he ever went home. Probably not, since his divorce.

"Officer."

"Borrow your computer for a minute?"

"Sure."

No hesitation. Jenny wasn't sure how, but she had earned this man's trust. She would hate to lose it.

She searched for Donald Rektor. She had no date of birth for him, but the name yielded only one hit. She made a note of the DOB for next time, if there was one.

August 18, 1992.

She stared at the date for a moment and started another search. Up came the summons she had written for the boat offenses. It was dated August 18.

Happy birthday, she thought.

Coutinho was watching her.

"What's up?"

"That woman who was gunning for me?"

"Rektor?"

"I hope there aren't two."

Jenny explained her suspicions.

"Right now I don't have anything but a hunch."

Coutinho nodded."But you want to follow up. Let me make a call. Detective Kim is with Kona for a few months."

"Thought I hadn't seen him."

Coutinho pressed buttons and talked for a while.

"When are you off next?" he asked her.

"Tuesday."

"Get over to Kona. Kim will take you along while he questions the roommate."

Jenny left at five on Tuesday morning. She told herself that it was too early to eat anything, but she knew she just wanted donuts from the Punalu'u Bake Shop in Na'alehu near the southern tip of the island.

The penance for her indulgence took the form of the rush hour traffic in Kona. Hilo and Kona were starting to emulate the mainland in some of the worst ways, even if much of the island was almost deserted.

She found Detective Kim in Kona Division headquarters south of town.

"Coutinho thinks you have the chops to make detective," said Kim, whose own shield was pretty new. "Me, I'm reserving judgment."

She thought she discerned teasing behind his deadpan expression, but it didn't seem condescending.

"Your guy is a bartender. We should catch him at home at this hour."

They went back to the parking lot. Kim drove a Wrangler that was useful in the mud on the Hilo side of the island. It could also be good on the arid moonscape of the Kona side.

By now the sun was high enough to start feeling like a physical weight.

"My hair is too hot to touch," said Jenny. "Whenever I come here, I can't wait to get back to Hilo."

"You can't wait? I haven't seen rain in two months."

Kim took Highway 190 up the side of the mountain. The road climbed relentlessly. After a series of zigs and zags he turned onto a short dead end street with six houses on each side. All of them were typical whitewashed island boxes with glass slats on the windows. The slats were cranked open for the breeze that usually blew at this altitude. The house they wanted was on the downhill side of the road.

"Let's wake him up," said Kim.

Jenny pounded on the door, waited a few seconds, and pounded again.

"Okay, okay," said a young male voice. It was thick with sleep or hangover, or both.

The young man was in no hurry. Jenny pounded again. The door opened with an angry swish. A dark-haired man in his twenties stood in the doorway. Jenny's first thought was, *Damn, he's cute.*

It was true in spite of his petulant expression, which vanished when he saw her. He held his wrists out in front of him

"I'll come quietly, Officer."

He probably thought he was the first to come up with that line. Annoying men always did.

So much for cute.

Jenny waited for Kim to speak, but after a moment she realized that he was leaving it to her.

"Officer Freitas, Detective Kim," she said. "You're Sean Carver?"

"Yeah."

"We're following up about Donald Rektor."

"Still?"

"We have questions. Can we come in?"

"Jeez. I was up until three last night."

That, she knew, was a personal choice. This was known as the daylight island for a reason. Even the bars closed early by mainland standards.

27

"Mr. Rektor is dead. I think he's worse off."

Carver turned and went back inside. He left the door open for Jenny to catch, which she recognized as all the invitation she was going to get. She and Kim followed.

The place was a sty. Dirty clothes draped over every piece of broken-down furniture, and the air smelled like too many male bodies. Another bleary young man in nothing but boxers shuffled into view for a moment. He seemed unimpressed by either a woman or a cop.

Carver swept a pile of clothes off a dusty sofa onto the floor. Jenny had sat on worse. She and Kim took their seats.

"When was the last time you saw him?"

"I'm still not sure. He was just, like, not there."

"You didn't wonder where he had gone?"

"Maybe a little, but that's how things work here. I let guys crash, and some of them help me out. Maybe a guy loses his job and has to go back to the mainland. Or he finds someplace else to sleep."

"Does that violate your lease?"

"Having guests?"

"Guests. Right. How much do they give you?"

"Depends. Most of them sleep three to a bedroom. They contribute a couple of hundred. Once in a while a guy shows up flashing cash and wants his own room. If I have one, that's five hundred."

"How many guests do you have at any one time?"

"Might be two, might be a dozen."

"Which was Donald? Two hundred or five?"

"Two."

"Did his girlfriend come here?"

"The cop? Yeah, sometimes. Girlfriends don't usually like it here."

I wonder why, Jenny thought but didn't say.

"When was the last time you saw her?"

"Why? You think she did something to him?"

The young man looked eager for confirmation.

"Nothing like that. Did you know they broke up?"

Jenny caught the slightest pause.

"No," said Carver.

He hesitated again. "She didn't do anything to him," he said. "He just fell."

That was an interesting about-face, considering that the young man had just claimed no knowledge of what had happened to Donald Rektor.

Jenny glanced at Kim, but he wasn't giving her any kind of signal. She hoped she hadn't missed anything crucial. She stood.

"Thanks for your time."

Outside Jenny found the breeze refreshing compared to sea level, but the sun was even stronger.

"Let's see if the witness is around," she said. "The one who saw a cop."

28

She hoped the witness was mistaken, and Patsy wasn't lying about when she had last been here.

"Right across the street," she said after checking the number on the mailbox. "Kendra Pryor, age sixty-three."

Patsy knocked, and the door opened as if someone had been waiting for her. The woman confronting her looked like most white people who have spent many years in the subtropical sun. Her skin resembled a Gucci suitcase, and there was no way to guess what color nature had originally given her bleached white hair. Her brown eyes pierced Jenny, who realized that she could forget about challenging the woman's vision.

"Come in, Officers."

She led them to a living room that couldn't have been more different from the chaos across the street. Pryor pointed them to an immaculate sofa and took a wicker chair across from them.

"You're here about the young man. Terrible what happened to him, but something had to give over there. Young men without adult supervision."

"You're retired, Ms. Pryor?"

"Meaning, am I the neighborhood busybody? Yes, I'm retired. No, I'm not here all the time, but if I feel like staying in, I stay in. And I believe in live and let live, but that's the problem. They get loud over there, especially at night."

"Can you give us any idea of when the young man fell?"

"No. I heard he fell off the lanai in the rear. I can't see through the house, can I?"

"I guess not."

"It's not like there was any more commotion than usual."

"Tell us about the police officer who visited the house."

"Why? Don't you keep track of your own?"

"We're just trying to make a complete timeline."

The nonsense seemed to deflect the woman's suspicions.

"Well, I didn't call the police that time. It was daylight, and I tolerate more when I'm not trying to sleep."

"What did you see?"

"Young woman. Sexy little thing. Like you."

Pryor didn't seem to approve of sexy little things. Her eyes moved downward.

"Although you seem to have more practical taste in footwear."

"Practical?"

"Well, how was she going to run in high heels?"

What a difference a few hours made.

The sun was beginning the spectacular disappearing act that was one of the Kona side's most reliable attractions, when Jenny and Kim returned to the house where Donald Rektor had lived. Jenny would have liked to take the time to watch, but she couldn't.

"Sean," she said, "why don't you tell us what really happened?"

"I did tell you," said Sean Carver.

But his voice had thickened with panic.

"No, you didn't. You thought you were the only one left on the island for us to talk to. All the guys who were on the premises then are back on the mainland, and you didn't think we'd track them down."

She bored into Carver with her eyes.

"But we just talked with Elizabeth Carvalho. That name probably doesn't mean anything to you, but how about Amanda?"

Carver blinked several times.

"I think you were just being a pal," said Jenny. "It was Donald's birthday. You and the guys were going to do something for the occasion. What's wrong with that?"

She waited, but he still held out.

"How were you supposed to know what a bad day he had just had? You didn't know I had just written him a ticket that might have lost him his job. And his girlfriend had just dumped him. Did you know about that part?"

He looked down at his feet and nodded.

"So you hired a stripper. What young guy doesn't love a stripper? Was the cop idea yours?"

Another nod. That confirmed what Elizabeth had said, and Jenny's own experiences with young men supported it. Young men often needed some sensitivity training. Life itself often took care of that, if they lived long enough.

Donald Rektor didn't.

It had been easy to track down Elizabeth Carvalho. The small population of the Big Island didn't support a huge population of anything, including strippers. Fewer looked like Jenny herself. She and Elizabeth both traced their ancestry to the Portuguese laborers imported from the Madeira Islands and the Azores in the nineteenth century. The two of them might even be related.

"You thought he'd like it. But instead …well, you tell me."

"He flipped," said Carver. "Started screaming at us for being a bunch of assholes."

"What then?"

"He shoved Amanda away. She fell. He looked like he was going to go after her some more. A few of us rushed him to, you know, stop him. He was fighting us like a crazy man."

Carver breathed hard, as if the fight had just happened.

"I don't know how. He just went over the railing."

"And you left him?"

"Take a look. No way we could have gotten down there. And no way was he alive. We'd just get blamed for everything."

30

Jenny focused on him. She had seen it before, but it still mystified her. Some people could get used to anything, even knowing there was a dead body right down the hill.

"What about the other guys?"

"They were all leaving in the next couple of days. School was starting."

"I'm going to need names."

Maybe he could even remember some.

"You're under arrest," she said. "Failure to render aid, for starters."

She and Kim led the young man outside and stowed him in the car.

"I'd hate to be Donald's mother when she finds out it wasn't you," said Kim. "Of course, she might not believe it."

"I don't know which would be worse for her," said Jenny. "If she doesn't believe it, or if she does."

Albert Tucher is the creator of prostitute Diana Andrews, who has appeared in more than seventy hardboiled short stories in venues including THE BEST AMERICAN MYSTERY STORIES 2010, edited by Lee Child. Diana's first longer case, the novella THE SAME MISTAKE TWICE, was published in 2013. The characters in SENSITIVITY TRAINING are part of Diana's world. They also appear in the novella THE PLACE OF REFUGE. Albert Tucher works at the Newark Public Library.

GET ALONG LITTLE DOGIE

C. C. Guthrie

The battered blackboard on the shelf behind the cash register in Velma's diner showed meatloaf was on the dinner menu. My mouth watered at the thought of a meal with meat. I never thought I'd miss Navy chow, not that I was complaining. Everyone was in the same boat, sacrificing for the war. While I waited for my breakfast, I finished the last of my chicory with a splash of watered-down coffee and tried not to shudder.

"Dadgum rationing." The County District Attorney on the stool to my right shook his head in sympathy. "That stuff is terrible, but it's better than drinking plain hot water in the morning. Other than not getting any coffee, how are you settling in, Ranger Billy?"

Velma slid a plate of eggs and fried potatoes in front of me. Before I could respond to the D.A., Roy Carter's voice slammed across the diner.

"Maybe Ranger Billy should stop settling in and actually do his job."

Conversation in the diner stopped; heads snapped around at the comment.

"I heard another calf went missing the other day," Carter said. "Doesn't seem like the Ranger is doing much to stop cattle theft in the county."

Out of the corner of my eye, I saw Velma turn away from the kitchen pass-through where she waited for the next order and cross her arms.

I felt the itch start.

It wasn't the first time Carter had questioned my ability as a Special Ranger for the Great Plains Cattle Raisers Cooperative. His son had also tossed his hat in the ring for the job. Without the protection of a law enforcement position, the Carter boy was headed to the war in the Pacific. I hoped he'd have better luck than I did. But, at least I made it back.

I continued eating, but the D.A. wasn't one to ignore a fight. He swiveled his stool around to face Carter and stood up like he was addressing the jury. "Have some respect. You are talking about a commissioned Oklahoma law enforcement officer. The state doesn't give that authority to just anyone."

I didn't want to listen to people talk about me, but I wasn't about to walk out with my breakfast half finished. Besides, I'd heard it all before.

"He's only got one arm," Carter called across the room. "How's he going to do a job with only one arm? Answer me that. How's he going to do it?"

The café went silent. The cook poked his head out of the pass-through. Velma narrowed her eyes.

"He's a decorated Marine sharpshooter," the D.A. said. "He's a better shot than you are with two arms and he survived the USS Lexington going down in the Coral Sea. He can do the job."

Carter flushed a deep red.

The D.A.'s voice filled the diner. "Special Ranger Ben Billy's got the support of the Great Plains Cattle Raisers Cooperative, the State of Oklahoma, and me." Having said his piece, he sat down and finished his eggs.

Every time someone left the diner, they passed by and clapped a hand on my shoulder, always the right, and told me what a fine job I was doing, which added more color to Carter's face.

Velma cleared my plate from the counter and handed me a note. The town operator had called. There were multiple reports from the north end of the county about two old boys arguing over a steer and pointing shotguns at each other. Happy to leave Carter scowling from his corner table, I retrieved my hat from the peg by the door, left the diner, and headed out of town as the sun started to glow behind the mountains.

When I left California after the Navy let me out of the hospital, I saw the Rockies for the first time. Now it's hard to think of the highest points in Sugarloaf County as mountains. But everyone in eastern Oklahoma calls the Ouachita National Forest the mountains, so I do, too.

When I got to the section line road past the Primitive Baptist Church north of Izard, I found two old coots. Dressed in faded Big Smith-brand overalls and dark winter felt hats, they looked like every other farmer-stockman in the county. Pete Dobart had pulled a shotgun when he found Garvis Bascomb trespassing, about to slip a rope around a steer's neck. With an impressive barrel of steel pointed at his chest, Bascomb removed the rope and climbed back through the barbed wire fence. But instead of driving away, he pulled out his shotgun and aimed it back at Dobart.

"Ranger," Bascomb called when I got out of my truck, "you can see where that lying thief altered my brand." He waved a liver-spotted hand at a white-faced Hereford steer next to the fence, oblivious to the standoff.

The brand on the steer was not new.

Seeing his accusation hadn't impressed me, Bascomb pointed an arthritic index finger at Dobart. "He's got my steer that was stole last summer."

After I persuaded the two old boys to put down their shotguns, I got to the nub of the matter. They told remarkably similar stories, stories that smelled like a chicken house on a hundred-degree day. J.T. Rogers, who managed Roy Carter's Sugarloaf County Sale Barn, sold the two farmers steers, Bascomb, six months ago, and Dobart, three months back. J.T. told each farmer that a youngster headed for basic training wanted to sell his steer. But when the kid arrived late and missed the auction. J.T., big hearted that he was, said he bought the animal to help out. J.T. then sold the steers to Bascomb and Dobart at the price he paid, or so he said. Both farmers had a bill of sale, complete with details about the brands. Which, everybody knew, didn't prove a thing.

33

The same situation happening twice in six months? If I could, I'd have slapped a charge of greed against the two old farmers. You couldn't tell me they didn't know there was something sketchy about the sales. Unfortunately, the Oklahoma Criminal Code didn't address greed. As for J.T., I had him in my sight.

I walked back into Velma's for dinner and saw meatloaf was crossed out on the blackboard. Just my luck. I put my hat on a peg and went to what I'd started to think of as my stool. Velma poured tea and took my order for what was left: macaroni and cheese, fried okra, and black-eyed peas, my all-time least favorite vegetable.

By the time she brought my food, I was the only customer left, so she let her indignation rip, an anger that had been building all morning. "That Roy Carter is about as sorry a person can be," she said as she rubbed at a stain on the counter that was invisible to me. "He thinks he's the only one that's suffered in this war."

She never referred to her sorrows, a son killed at Guadalcanal and another captured by the Italians in Tunisia, who might still be alive in a German POW camp. Another thing she never, ever mentioned was my missing arm. Without talking about it, we had an understanding.

I left Velma getting ready for her supper customers and spent the afternoon thinking about the uselessness of a one-letter cattle brand.

The next morning the diner looked like it had the day before. The same customers were there, with one exception. As I had requested, Sam Gray sat in the back.

On my way to the counter, I detoured to the corner table where Roy Carter and J.T. Rogers sat. "J.T., you going to be in your office this afternoon? Like to talk to you about a couple of steers."

Carter looked up, mean expression on his face, cigarette dangling from his lower lip. "You got questions about my business, you talk to me."

I knew Carter would take the bait. He never passed up an opportunity to say he owned the Sugarloaf County Sale Barn and J.T. was just an employee.

The itch started, so I crossed my right arm over my chest. "Alrighty, tell me about the steers J.T. sold to Garvis Bascomb and Pete Dobart a while back."

Carter looked at J.T., who leaned back and stretched out his legs.

The diner grew quiet and I'm sure Velma's ears twitched with interest.

"Not sure I remember those steers." J.T. grinned. "Lots of cattle go through the Barn."

"Well, actually, that's my point. Bascomb and Dobart told me yesterday the sales didn't go through the Barn, that you bought and sold the steers personally. Mighty nice of you, buying steers so two young fellas didn't have to pay commissions or fees."

Carter frowned. He never liked to miss out on money.

34

J.T. shrugged. "Oh, I remember. I did it to keep the Barn out of trouble. By the time those kids arrived, the auction was over and we'd hit our purchase limit. I felt sorry for them, going to war and all. If the Barn bought the steers, the War Board would have fined us. Since private sales aren't subject to the regulations, I bought the animals." He smirked. "I sold the steers to Bascomb and Dobart for what I paid. Didn't make penny on the transactions."

On the face of it, J.T.'s explanation seemed reasonable. Only to an idiot.

I shuffled a little to the side so I could see the D.A.'s reaction without being too obvious. He cocked his head. I took that to mean he wasn't sure where I was headed, but would go along for the ride. "J.T., do you remember the brands on those steers you sold to Bascomb and Dobart?"

Carter barked out a deep smoker's laugh. "We see hundreds of brands a month."

J.T. smirked.

"That's ok, I've got the bills of sale you gave for the steers." I pulled the papers out of my breast pocket and looked over at Velma. "Can I use your blackboard? I'd like to show J.T. something."

Carter hooted. "Looks like our Special—" he put an emphasis on the word, "—Ranger is going to teach us a special lesson."

Carter wasn't nervous, but J.T. didn't seem as calm as before, but maybe that was just hope on my part.

The D.A. held the blackboard steady while I erased the day's menu with my handkerchief. I drew a circle and inside I added a G and an 8 lying on its side with a line extending length-wise through it.

"Velma," I invited, "how would you read that brand?"

"Well, going by the rules, outside to inside, left to right, top to bottom, I'd say it's Circle G Bar Lazy 8." She pursed her lips. "Pretty fancy. Who owns it?"

"Don't know, but that's the brand on Pete Dobart's steer right now." I turned to J.T. and clarified, "the steer you sold him three months ago."

"If you say so," J.T. said.

I erased the top of the circle, and turned the sideways 8 into a B by erasing the loops below the centerline. "Velma, what about this one?"

"With the half circle on the bottom, I'd say it's Rocking G Lazy B."

"That's Garvis Bascomb's brand. He took the brand on the steer J.T. sold him and changed it to that."

"I wouldn't know," J.T. said.

Carter lit another cigarette. His plate was a nasty looking mess of butts, ash, and egg yolk smears.

"What's your point, Special Ranger?" Carter asked. Again, the emphasis.

"Find it interesting the way the brand might have changed. If I erase the right loop on the B, that makes it a lazy P. If I erase the half circle at the bottom, I'm left with G lazy P, the brand on the steer when J.T. sold it to Bascomb."

With no comment from J.T., I added back all the parts I had erased. "See how that works? Start with a G Lazy P, the brand when Bascomb bought the steer. He changed the lazy P to a B and added a half circle on the bottom to get a Rocking G Lazy B, Bascomb's brand. Then if I complete the circle and add two loops on the bottom of the B, you get Circle G Bar Lazy 8."

J.T. held both hands in front of him. A "so what" gesture tells a lot. I miss making that gesture.

I took my handkerchief and erased everything on the blackboard except the G. In the far corner, Sam Gray stirred. "You use a G as your brand, don't you, Sam? Lost any steers lately?"

He leaned back in his chair and light reflected off his nearly bald head. "Lost a bull calf last spring. Finest animal I've seen in a long time. Planned to keep him intact and build up my herd."

Heads nodded. Everyone has had a calf like that, one they'd pinned big hopes on.

"What happened to it?"

"Last spring, Trudy, my wife, and I went to her sister's after they got the telegram about my nephew Carl being killed at Monte Cassino. We got home late, both of us still tore up about Carl, and I plumb forgot to pen up my cow and her calf. The next morning the calf was gone."

"Did you find a carcass?" the D.A. asked.

"I didn't find anything in my pasture, but my place backs up to the mountains," Gray said.

J.T. sat up straight. "What are you doing, Ben Billy? Trying to say I took Sam's bull calf? You heard him. Something got it. Could have been a coyote, a wolf, maybe even a bear."

Sam worried a toothpick around his mouth a few times. "Well, that's what I thought at the time. But if I saw my animal again, I'd know it."

Carter coughed, a deep, painful sound. "You think you can identify your bull after this long?"

Sam nodded. "I can."

Even the D.A. looked skeptical. "That's a bold claim."

Sam drew his lips into a thin line. "I'd know my white-faced Hereford anywhere."

Carter and J.T. stood up. "This is ridiculous. If you want to accuse J.T. of something, you know where to find him," Carter said.

The two men walked out of the diner and I turned back to Sam. "What makes your white-faced Hereford different?"

A deep flush crept up Sam's neck. "I'd rather not say."

"I've never seen the animal, and I could pick him out," Velma said.

Sam turned to face her. "Trudy told you."

She grinned and nodded.

Sam looked stubborn. "I'd rather write it down."

It only took him a few seconds. I gave Velma a piece of paper and she did the same.

36

The D.A. compared the two descriptions. "Where do we go from here, Ranger Billy?"

"I'll head out to Pete Dobart's place. Might need to take his steer into protective custody while I sort this out. Hate for evidence to disappear."

A crowd gathered at the edge of town around the holding pen behind Wilson's meat processing business where a white-faced Hereford steer looked unconcerned. Roy Carter and J.T. Rogers stood defiantly on one side of the pen. Bascomb, Dobart, Gray, and a self-appointed crowd of public opinion rallied by Velma stood on the other side. I climbed into the pen.

"J.T., Dobart says this is the steer you sold him." I walked the steer around so the brand faced the crowd. "This brand matches the description on the bill of sale you gave him."

J.T. did the "so what" gesture.

"I already showed you how the G brand on Sam Gray's bull calf could have been altered to get to the brand on this steer." I was careful not to accuse J.T. of anything.

J.T. crossed his arms. "Doesn't prove anything."

I addressed the crowd. "Every time an animal is sold, it makes money for the seller. If one person can sell the same animal two, maybe three different times..." I left the sentence unfinished.

"Prove it," J.T. challenged.

I pulled out my revolver and pointed it at the steer's head. A series of gasps from the crowd sounded like a steam engine chugging over the mountains. Everyone knew the steer wasn't close to full weight and would be worth more in a few years. "What do you say, J.T., how 'bout we test that old Judge Roy Bean story? After I shoot the steer, I pull back the hide and see what part of the brand is the oldest." I looked around at the crowd. "I think the G will have healed the most."

Sam Gray stepped forward. "No need to do it. This was my animal, my bull before someone," he shot a glare at J.T., "turned him into a steer. I know he's mine. I put my brand in the center of that red patch there, the exact shape of a heart. The G, my brand, is for Gray. But on this bull, well, now steer, the G stands for my wife Trudy."

Velma spoke up. "It stands for Gertrude, the center of my heart. Trudy was tickled pink about it when she told me one Sunday at church."

In the end, there wasn't enough evidence to charge J.T. with theft or selling stolen goods, but he didn't get off scot-free. He faced the justice of his neighbors, which may have been the harsher sentence. Word spread about Dobart's steer that might have started life as Gray's bull calf, about a steer that might have been stolen from Bascomb, about a brand that might have been changed multiple times. Ultimately, everyone turned their back on J.T. because they believed he did it first.

People in Sugarloaf County continue to slap me on the shoulder, always the right, and tell me I'm doing a fine job, even if I am a one-armed lawman.

C.C. Guthrie was born in Oklahoma where her family has farmed and ranched since Indian and Oklahoma Territory days. She now lives near Fort Worth, Texas. Her short story, *Step Away From The Cow*, appears in Fish Out of Water. No animals were harmed in the writing of *Get Along Little Dogie*.

THICKER THAN WATER

Micki Browning

The beach disappeared from her rearview mirror as she steered her patrol car into the lower west side of Santa Marietta. It was a little past midnight on a Tuesday and nothing moved that required her immediate attention. Sergeant Isabel de la Guerra stifled a yawn. Before becoming a cop, she would have covered her mouth, but considering all the things she touched during her shift, she didn't want her hand anywhere near her face—unless it was holding coffee.

A stack of paperwork awaited her attention back at the station. Twelve years of hard work to make sergeant, and yet some nights she was little more than a paper-pusher with a gun. Hardly seemed fair, but she welcomed the bump the promotion gave her paycheck. She could finally cut back on the overtime shifts she worked to make ends meet, spend more time with her son.

The luck of the draw had given her an all-male shift to supervise. They called her Mom when they thought she was out of earshot. At thirty-six, she was younger than half of the officers, but they'd become her boys.

Her gaze searched the shadows between the rundown apartment buildings. This was not the famed American Riviera tourists and A-listers knew. Here, hardworking immigrant families mingled with drug dealers, parolees, and mothers who sold themselves in front of their children. She knew these streets. They hadn't changed much in the years since she ran wild here as a child. Before she got pregnant. Before her mother's warning: "I brought you into this world, and I'll damn well take you back out if you don't straighten up."

She slowed, reluctant to return to the station and the mind-numbing paperwork without a caffeine boost. The lights of the mini-mart welcomed her as she turned on her blinker and entered the convenience store parking lot. A young man wearing a Raiders jersey and long dark shorts darted in front of her car. Isabel stomped on the brakes. They stared into each other's eyes for a nanosecond before the encounter registered with them both. Maybe it was the mask, perhaps it was the cash clutched in his fist. Either way, he had her undivided attention.

The robber darted into the shadows of a side street. Isabel slammed her patrol car into reverse and mashed the accelerator. The transmission strained. She activated her emergency lights, and alerted dispatch.

Braintrust must have realized he couldn't outrun a police car by staying in the street. With a final look over his shoulder, he pitched his mask toward a bougainvillea bush and bolted across the front lawn of a dilapidated Victorian.

Circle the block or follow on foot? One was definitely safer. She jammed the car into park and bailed out the door.

Isabel gauged the distance to the wooden fence and leapt, planting her left foot against the wood and grabbing the top of the slats with her bare hands. Momentum propelled her over, and she landed with a knee-numbing thud in the Victorian's backyard. It used to be easier, then again, she used to be younger.

A dark shape hurtled the far fence and she updated her position with dispatch as she ran forward. A dog in the neighboring yard barked and lights flashed on in some of the nearby houses.

Through her radio, she heard officers racing to help, calling out their locations. Isabel calculated the containment perimeter being erected around her, a buffer of safety created by teammates she trusted with her life. Another backyard, one more fence and the suspect should pop out onto the parallel street.

Adrenaline and exertion combined and pulsed past her ears, shutting out everything but her rasping breath and the radio. She cleared another fence and landed in the apocalypse. She tripped on a roll of chicken-wire. Her hands splayed into a patch of weeds, narrowly missing a pan of used motor oil. She raised her head. The glow from a porch light bathed the robber in jaundiced yellow. He pounded on the door of a ramshackle house and shouted to someone inside.

She lurched forward, and stumbled through a collection of aluminum cans. Closing the distance, she grabbed onto the back of his t-shirt and pushed him against the door. Too late, a warning tingled at the base of her neck. The door opened from within. The suspect lost his balance. Together they crashed to the floor.

Hip-hop music assaulted her ears. A thousand images imprinted on her brain. None good.

Isabel scrabbled upright. Drew her gun. "Police department. Stay back!" She aimed center mass of the closest threat. A gang member she'd arrested before. He stopped and raised his hands. Others moved closer.

She swung her arm in an arc. Muttered slurs buzzed around the room, all directed at her. The teen beneath her struggled to get out from under her weight and she grabbed the back of his head and thumped his face into the floor with her left hand. "Keep still, you're under arrest."

Her pronouncement provoked another round of resentment, louder than the music. The television lit the room with constantly changing intensity. She counted four members of a splinter gang and five girls. Empty beer bottles littered every surface, each one a potential weapon to use against her. She had to get out. The guys in the group moved toward her, fanning out in a semi-circle like wolves preparing to attack.

Options. She needed options. She tried to quell the fear that stormed through her body like a tornado. *Think.*

Someone killed the stereo, and in the sudden silence Isabel promised herself that she'd survive this night.

Her arrestee shifted. She had to move before he knocked her off balance. She placed the barrel against the back of his head. "Get up."

Isabel stood and yanked her prisoner to his feet. She clicked into negotiator mode and addressed the room. "My problem isn't with anyone here. I've got what I came for. We're leaving." She backed up, trying to watch everyone at once.

"Not with him."

That voice. She knew that voice—better than she knew her own. What the hell was he doing here?

A lanky teen stepped out of the kitchen.

For a moment, she couldn't speak. She had no breath. The television flickered, casting unfamiliar angles across his face.

"Go home, Ruben." She kept her voice low.

One of the girls struggled to her feet, clutching a red Solo cup. "Who you think you are?" she slurred. "Dumb bitch. Don't even know who she's talking to. Does she, Angel?"

Oh, God. They don't know. A rock settled in her stomach. Of course they didn't know. He'd be dead if they did.

Isabel gritted her teeth. "Don't do anything stupid."

"You can't tell me what to do." He dipped his hand to the small of his back and drew a gun. Pointed it at her.

For a moment, all she saw was the barrel.

She tightened the wrist lock she had on the youth in front of her. The pressure raised him to his tiptoes and she used him as a shield. Not the noblest thing she'd ever done, but she hoped that honor among thieves included not shooting one of their own.

"You don't want to do that," she said to the gunman. Her voice quavered and she hoped he didn't hear it.

"Let him go," he said.

She eyed his grip. Strong. No movement of the barrel to indicate nervousness. "You know I can't do that." In twelve years of policing, she'd only been on the receiving end of a gun on two occasions. Both times she'd been behind something far more substantial than a skinny gangbanger.

"No one messes with *mi familia*," he said.

His family. She willed herself not to blink. Everything could change in a blink.

"Put down the gun," she said.

His face had aged. Or maybe it was just his expression. When had she really looked at him last?

He took a step closer. "I got nothing to lose. What about you?"

He was trying to make this about her. About the two of them. Get inside her head.

The radio crackled close to her ear. The dispatcher repeated Isabel's call sign.

"They're calling you," Ruben said. "They want to know you're okay. Are you okay?"

She had a gun in one hand, a prisoner in the other and no way to answer

41

dispatch. "I've got it all under control."

A shorter kid stepped forward. "Come on, bro." His pants hung around his waist. The only thing stopping them from hitting the floor was a belt with the number 13 cut into the buckle. "Cops will be crawling all over this place in a couple minutes."

"Don't matter." Ruben looked straight at her.

"You haven't done anything we can't fix," Isabel said.

"Really?" He laughed. The ugly sound ricocheted around the room.

When had things changed? "It's never too late." She tried to convey more with her eyes. "Angel."

In the distance an officer yelled her name.

An unsettled grumbling crept around the edges of the room. Nerves stretched. She could taste the tension. "I can protect you from everyone but yourself. Let's go. We can still go. Start over."

She dared not blink, not even when her eyes became so dry they started to tear. She imagined his finger, tense against the trigger. "Why are you doing this?"

"I finally have your attention."

She focused on Ruben, as if seeing him for the first time. The images she recalled seemed shrouded in shadow, blurred. Gone was the child who'd needed her to open his closet and check under the bed before she left for work at night. Gone was the boy who said he understood when her shift fell on his birthday. And Christmas. When she missed his soccer matches.

The person in front of her was no longer a boy. His chest had filled out, his shoulders broadened. Ruben Angel de la Guerra. He had his father's dark looks, the same cowlick that sent a rogue lock across his forehead.

Isabel hadn't seen Ruben's father since the day she announced she was pregnant, two days after turning sixteen. He told her to get rid of it. Kill their unborn child. She'd renounced him and the gang that same day.

Ruben had asked about him once, but by then his father was dead, killed in a turf war. Instead of grief, she'd experienced relief; relief that her son was safe from his father's influence.

The gnawing in her stomach returned. She hadn't escaped her past at all.

"Izzy! Where are you?" Officer Kaplan shouted. Closer now.

Her tongue felt glued to the roof of her mouth.

Ruben shrugged. "You have to choose."

Isabel shook her head. "You won't shoot me."

He laughed. "Bet your life on it?"

The words flashed her back to the academy. Drill sergeants filled her vision, spitting challenges. *Can you handle the consequences of your actions? Are you willing to bet your life on it? Yes? Wrong answer*, they'd yelled. *Nothing's worth dying for.*

But they were wrong.

The others had stepped back, watching with the intensity of jackals that

42

recognized that some fights belonged to others.

As a cop, Isabel had learned how to use her fear, acknowledge it, manage it. But this was different. Primal. Fear infused her every cell and her body hummed with it. And it was for her son. Her family.

This was the life he'd chosen in the moments she wasn't around. When she worked extra shifts, desperately trying to prove to herself that Ruben didn't need a father. Not when he had her.

Another emotion flickered in her breast, too weak at first to recognize, but then in a gasp, it flamed, undeniable. She was proud of her son. Proud that others deferred to him. Ruben led this group, commanding respect in a world where his word meant everything.

Resolve straightened her spine. She'd gamble her own life, but she'd sworn an oath to protect everyone else.

Sweat dampened the t-shirt under her ballistic vest and slicked her hands. Each second brought her officers closer to finding her with a gun pointed at her heart. She couldn't let her worlds collide.

"There are officers surrounding this block. The only way out is with me. You want to fix this? Come down to the station. We'll sort this out. Together."

He shook his head.

"Then I'm leaving."

She stepped backward, pulling her prisoner with her free hand. Mid-step, she felt her sweaty grip weaken. Skin slid against skin. She couldn't readjust, and she felt her control slip away.

The teen spun, and broke the wrist lock that held him captive. He shoved away from her and stumbled into the center of the room, leaving her exposed. Vulnerable. Alone.

She held her free hand palm up toward Ruben. "You are everything to me," Isabel said.

Heavy footsteps crashed across the porch.

His face lost all expression. "We both know that's a lie."

The jangle and creak of gun belts announced the arrival of two officers. Isabel gripped her gun with both hands, the fingers of one settling between the knuckles of the other.

Was anything thicker than blood?

Her elbow dropped into a shooting stance.

Ruben's eyes shifted, targeting one of her officers and his gun followed.

Isabel squeezed the slack from the trigger. The gun bucked. Shattered her heart.

She holstered her weapon. A crimson flower bloomed across Ruben's shoulder.

He swung the gun back toward her.

She closed her eyes. Waited.

Two shots rang out in near synchronicity. She opened her eyes. Two more splotches of red. Surprise etched his face. His legs crumpled.

Isabel caught him, but he was too heavy. She cushioned his fall as best she could. Pulled him onto her lap. Cradled him.

Blood seeped through her fingers, soaked her uniform. She burrowed her face in her son's hair and inhaled deeply, desperate to drown the guilt that smelled like smoke, but puddled like water.

FBI National Academy graduate **Micki Browning** worked in municipal law enforcement for more than two decades and retired as a division commander. Her award-winning novel, *Adrift*, was published in January 2017 by Alibi and is set in the Florida Keys. Her short stories have also garnered awards and appeared in *Mystery Weekly* and other anthologies. Micki resides in Florida with her partner in crime and a vast array of scuba equipment. Learn more at MickiBrowning.com.

AFTERNOON DELIGHT

Steve Liskow

The woman on the bed had a strawberries-and-cream complexion and chestnut brown hair that spread across the pillow. A few hours ago, she would have been beautiful, but now her brown eyes exploded from a face the color of a cloudy sky. Trash Hendrix watched the techs taking evidence shots.

"Accident, you think?" Jimmy Byrne, Hendrix's partner, sifted through the woman's purse. "The guy got too rough, she choked, and he took off?"

"Could be." The ME aimed his light into the woman's mouth, empty now that he'd removed a crimson thong from her throat with forceps. "Rigor's just starting. Only dead a couple of hours."

"Will you look at this." Byrne held up the woman's wallet. "The driver's license looks like our girl in better days. This is Elayna Shaeffer."

Hendrix felt his stomach tighten. "Like in TV stud anchorman Kenneth Shaeffer?"

"Yeah," Byrne said. "Just like that."

The motel clerk who found the body disagreed. He had licorice hair, olive skin, and the inflection of a tape loop.

"No." His eyes rolled toward the TV on a wall bracket. "The man had not blonde hair like the television announcer." The last two words came out with seven equally-stressed syllables. "This man had dark hair and a moustache, and he was very thin. His shirt of flannel did hang loose on him."

Hendrix and Byrne looked at each other.

Under TV lights, Kenneth Shaeffer, the highest-paid newscaster in Connecticut, looked tall, buff, and assured. Under fluorescents, he still looked tall, but his skin tone resembled Mountain Dew and his blue eyes watered heavily. Vomiting for ten minutes after identifying his wife's body didn't help.

"Christ." His body language was so scattered he could have been triplets. "What the hell was Elayna doing at that dump?"

The Turnpike Lodge was one of over thirty No-tell motels on the Berlin Turnpike south of Hartford. Elayna Shaeffer died in room 114.

"Your name is on the register." Hendrix tried to keep the anchorman's attention. Everyone already called him "Trash," and when Lt. Savickas teamed him with Jimmy Byrne in Major Crimes, they became "Trash and Byrne."

"I already told you that's nothing like my handwriting."

"Mr. Shaeffer, where were you around noon?"

45

"Health club. I was there from about eleven until...I don't know, probably one or so. Then to the studio."

"Where's your health club?"

"Rocky Hill."

Elayna Shaeffer's cell phone showed an incoming call at ten-fifteen that morning from a blocked number.

"No idea she might be seeing someone else?"

Shaeffer watched his fists clenching and opening. "I thought everything was...perfect."

Byrne circled The Body Shoppe twice to find a parking space. Beyond the parking lot, a nameless mall squatted like a discount Stonehenge, the featured attraction apparently the Plexiglas bus shelter on the Silas Deane Highway where two women in jeans and a man in khakis smoked under the July sun. Behind the stores, Hendrix saw an alley with five Dumpsters and three light poles.

The woman behind The Body Shoppe's check-in counter had a bubbly happiness that made Hendrix understand why restrooms have silhouettes on the doors. When she breathed, the "B" logo on her t-shirt became three-dimensional and her name tag, which called her "Amanda," shimmied like Jell-O.

"Kenneth Shaeffer?" Her Listerine blue eyes had to be contacts. "You mean, like the news guy?" Those eyes never left Byrne.

"Just like that," he said.

"He was here earlier. I said hello when he checked in." Amanda's voice rose at the end of every sentence.

"Do you remember when?" Hendrix asked.

"Um, noonish?" Amanda inhaled again and Hendrix decided her contacts weren't her only artificial ingredients. "Our members swipe their ID so we can keep track of how often they come in. And we need them to check in for our liability coverage, too." She said the word "liability" as if she'd practiced.

She led them through a labyrinth of malevolent-looking machines. Two of the six HD TVs on the wall flashed Elayna Shaeffer's picture. Hendrix ignored the misspelled closed-captioning while Amanda tapped five numbers on a touch screen. Kenneth Shaeffer's name appeared.

"Do you assign the ID numbers?" Byrne asked. Four wall fans whirred from various pillars, just loud enough so their conversation stayed private.

"Most people use their date of birth," Amanda said. Trash and Byrne peered over her shoulder at the screen. Shaeffer logged an hour on an elliptical trainer, half an hour on a bicycle, and another half hour on a Stairmaster. No wonder the guy looked cut.

"How often is he here?" Hendrix asked.

Amanda led them back to the main computer. Her sweats showed no panty line. Mr. Shaeffer hadn't missed a Monday, Wednesday, or Friday in six months and alternated between Saturday and Sunday for a fourth day.

46

"What else do the machines tell you?" Byrne looked at them as though they were old friends. Hendrix felt flabby.

"Well, the Nautilus equipment is tied into the system so you don't have to remember a whole bunch of different weights and settings." Amanda's voice slowed down as though she still needed to practice that part. "The cardio machines, the bikes and stuff, you enter manually. How many minutes you work out, level, calories, stuff like that."

"Pretty complete information," Byrne remarked.

When Amanda blinked at him, Hendrix thought he heard wind chimes. "Is there anything else I can show you, Officer?"

Thursday morning, Shaeffer, who aged ten years overnight, ushered Trash and Byrne into the house in Wethersfield. The living room carpet was neutral beige and the furniture subtle mahogany that whispered "taste." The sofa had five sections, each big enough for tennis.

Teresita Vargas, the maid, sat on the section near the window. She wore a Huskies t-shirt above sprayed-on jeans, her brown eyes swimming in tears. In happier times, Hendrix suspected those eyes would be devastating.

"Ms. Vargas," he asked. "Do you remember what time Ms. Shaeffer left the house yesterday?"

"No." The woman's voice felt like taffy ready to melt in his mouth. "Wednesday is my day off."

"How long have you worked here?"

"Two years. But I do—did—very little. Ms. Shaeffer liked to clean and iron. She said it helped her think."

"How did she act on Tuesday?"

"Happy. Like always. I remember she went shopping in the morning."

Shaeffer disappeared into the kitchen. Teresita folded his newspaper and put it next to his coffee without seeming to realize she was doing it.

"She would come home excited about helping the library, or the children, and now she is..."

In the kitchen, Hendrix found Shaeffer staring into the open refrigerator.

"Mr. Shaeffer," he said. "Could you make a list of anyone who might have a grudge against your wife?"

"You didn't know Elayna," Shaeffer said. "There's no freaking way anyone could stay mad at her."

"Make a list anyway, OK?"

Hendrix returned to the living room where the maid's voice shook slightly.

"When Mr. Shaeffer went to the West Coast, they called each other many times each day."

"How long was he away?" Byrne asked.

"Three days. I usually have little work here, but when he's gone, there is nothing at all."

Byrne's eyes flickered toward Hendrix. "Do you know if there were any other men in Ms. Shaeffer's life?"

"She would not even look at another man. Never. Not for a second."

"Did she have any special friends? You know, ladies she shopped with, or maybe at the health club? Maybe Twitter or e-mail?"

Teresita played with her charm bracelet. "She often got requests about raising money. She helped out for many causes."

Hendrix nodded at the stairs. "Could we please see the bedroom?"

The master suite was as impressive as the downstairs. The king-sized bed had sliding doors in the headboard and matching drawers in the frame. The maid ran her fingers slowly over the pillow on the right side of the bed.

"Ms. Shaeffer sleeps…" She swallowed and corrected herself. "Slept on this side."

Hendrix inspected the nightstand. The clock radio was set to WNPR. The top drawer held tissues, two romance paperbacks with dog-eared pages, an emery board, birth control pills, and a flashlight. When he pushed the books aside, a gleam caught his eye.

"Handcuffs?"

Teresita's face turned crimson. He opened the next drawer and found several other accessories that June and Ward Cleaver never mentioned.

"Hey, Trash?"

Byrne stood at the bureau, where angled mirrors reflected three of him holding up sets of lingerie, all in bright colors, none designed for winter. A box in the back of the bottom drawer held an array of latex, leather, and plastic in more colors than the lingerie.

Hendrix saw the maid look toward the stairs, where Shaeffer was still struggling to avoid bumping into furniture.

"Ms. Vargas, is this stuff hidden because Mr. Shaeffer doesn't know that his wife is bi-sexual?"

Teresita started crying again.

According to the DMV, the Nissan that "Kenneth Shaeffer" drove to the motel belonged to Ace Auto Rental in Hartford. The woman behind the counter had short hair the color of chewed gum and wore a blouse crisp enough to shatter. When Byrne smiled at her, she scrolled through the computer files. Five minutes later, the printer hummed out a pixilated five by seven print of the man who'd rented the car and a photocopy of his driver's license. He had returned the car at 1:05 the afternoon Elayna Shaeffer died, even before her body was found.

"People always look awful in their license shots, don't they?" Byrne said.

"The Triple-A pictures are better," the woman replied. "They take a little more time, so occasionally they get the people with their eyes open."

Byrne held up the picture. "Trash, the guy's wearing the same shirt in both pictures."

Hendrix turned to the woman again. "Do you remember anything else about this man? His posture, maybe? Or his voice?"

He watched the woman's eyes turn thoughtful. Amanda's from the gym had simply glazed over.

"Well, he was coughing a lot," she said. "And his voice was hoarse, like he had a really bad cold."

"Jesus." Fred DeNino, producer of Breaking News in Hartford, had shoulders that belonged on a coat hanger. His tie hung loosely below his open collar and his eyes crinkled to pinpricks. His energy level suggested he munched coffee grounds straight from the can.

"Freakin' tragedy. We're all just blown away."

"Did Shaeffer get along with everyone here?" Hendrix asked.

"Well, Howie—Howard Larkin—dated Elayna before she dumped him for Ken." DeNino's office smelled like a dirty ash tray.

He frowned at his monitor. "Howie's got his résumé out a few places, I think. He was really hoping Ken would take that LA job they offered him a few months ago. That way Howie could move up to evenings."

"Is he around so we could talk to him, too?" Hendrix asked.

Larkin appeared a few minutes later. He was several inches taller than either Hendrix or Byrne, with dark hair and a moustache, a lot like the picture from Ace Auto Rental.

"Howie," DeNino said. "Can you cover for Ken again tonight?"

"Sure." Larkin's eyes flickered to Trash and Byrne. DeNino left them in his office, already pulling his cigarettes from his shirt pocket.

"God." Larkin's fingers adjusted his tie, then his tie tack, then his collar. "Whoever did this must be crazy."

"That's one possibility." Watching Larkin's hands, Hendrix decided he'd never play cards with the guy. "We were wondering how you felt when Shaeffer didn't take that job in LA."

Larkin straddled a folding chair across from the desk. "Bummed. I know he was interested, but he said Elayna wanted to stay in Connecticut."

"We understand you dated her before Shaeffer."

"Yeah." Larkin glanced toward the door. "She was with me until they met at the Christmas party a few years back. They clicked on the spot and she said good-bye to me that night."

"How did you feel about that?"

"Like I was gut-shot."

"Something special, was she?"

Larkin's eyes drifted toward the window. "Every time we were together was like brand new. She kept things…fresh."

49

"Did she ever suggest having someone join you?" Hendrix asked.

"Christ, no way I'd want to share her with another guy."

"Or another woman?"

"Oh, man." Larkin's hands tightened on the back of the chair. "Don't do that."

"So you never went out with her again after she met Shaeffer?"

"Uh-uh. They invited me to their wedding, and I've talked to her at a couple of the station's lame parties, but that's it."

Byrne cleared his throat. "Mr. Larkin, where were you around noon yesterday?"

"Here. I usually am from seven until three." Larkin picked up a roll of breath mints from DeNino's desk. "After you guys were here yesterday, Fred asked me to cover for Ken, too."

Trash and Byrne rejoined DeNino in the hall.

"I guess the funeral's gonna be Saturday." DeNino stared through the door to Shaeffer's office. A framed picture of Elayna stood next to the monitor on his desk. She wore a man's unbuttoned white shirt that fell to mid-thigh, and Hendrix couldn't see anything else under it. Her smile looked like it could cure cancer.

Hendrix thought the coffee at Josie's Diner tasted like they roasted their beans with a blowtorch.

"That phone call," Byrne said. "Maybe the guy imitated Shaeffer and suggested they get together for a nooner. Sleazy place, maybe she'd think it was sexy."

"Well, we know she liked to play games." Hendrix watched steam rise from his cup. "But why couldn't she tell it wasn't her husband?"

"The woman at the rental place said he was real hoarse. He was disguising his voice. And he used a burner so she wouldn't recognize the number."

Byrne built walls with the containers of sweetener.

"You think that maid's been with Elayna? Getting off, as opposed to being off?"

Hendrix tapped the blueberry muffin on his dish. "Could be, but I don't know where to go with it. Even with a wig and moustache, she couldn't be the guy who rented the motel room."

He tried to force the pieces to fit. "Why did the guy kill her at the motel?"

"What do you mean?" Byrne rearranged the sugar packets and used a salt shaker as a turret.

"Well, he made a fake driver's license, so he knows where the Shaeffers live. And he knows Larkin enough to look like him in the picture and for the motel clerk. That can't be a coincidence."

50

"But the whole disguise thing's a joke, Trash. Larkin's got an alibi thick as cement. And Shaeffer's always at the club on Wednesdays, so the guy's not framing anybody. Not so it'll stick."

"But that's what I mean." Hendrix's muffin felt solid enough to drive nails. "Wednesday was the maid's day off. He could have killed Elayna at the house and nobody would have found her for hours. Hot day, too. If he cranked up the AC, we wouldn't be able to determine the time of death, and Shaeffer wouldn't have an alibi anymore."

Byrne dunked his own muffin in the coffee, but it didn't seem to get any softer.

"So where does that leave us?"

Google and the *Hartford Courant*'s site turned up even more hits for Elayna Shaeffer than for her husband. She was active in so many causes that Hendrix wondered if she had a clone.

"No traffic accidents." Byrne drummed his fingers on his desk. "No gambling, no DUIs, no nothing. How about you?"

Hendrix's wrist throbbed from clicking the mouse on his PC. "None of the dating or sex sites have her picture or a user name, and the swinger sites don't have her registered. If she was cheating, she was discreet about it."

"You think we should check all the other No-tells and see if she and Shaeffer did any day trips before?"

The yellow pages listed two hundred fifty-three hotels and motels in the Hartford area. Hendrix printed out the list and the pair started calling places alphabetically.

When Shaeffer appeared with his enemies list an hour later, he'd aged another five years.

"Teresita," he said. "All she does is cry. I sent her home. Then I couldn't stay there alone, so I went over to the gym, tried to work out. But people kept coming up to me…"

His list only had three names. Hendrix watched him stare at the wall as though it were a video monitor.

"Mr. Shaeffer?" Byrne asked. "We're wondering if this man lured your wife away from home by pretending to be you. Did the two of you ever go to motels during the day for sex, just to spice things up?"

"No." Shaeffer fought his lower lip back under control. "Actually, if we'd thought of it, we probably would have."

"Did you ever tape yourselves?" Byrne asked. Hendrix knew he was listening to the voice of experience.

Shaeffer still watched that invisible monitor. "She suggested it a couple of times, but I worried about…I didn't want to." His face reddened.

Byrne rattled Shaeffer's list. "But she liked role-playing, right?"

"Yeah. Dressing up and...stuff like that really turned her on. Sometimes, we'd go out somewhere, she'd bend over so I could see that she was wearing sexy underwear. Or maybe nothing..."

His cheekbones seemed to have buckled so his perfect profile looked merely human.

After he left, Hendrix called thirty more motels, which put him at the letter G.

"This case has got more loose screws than Stanley Hardware, but how do we put them together?"

"You kidding?" Byrne was building a chain of paper clips. "We don't even know which screws are loose."

Back at the Turnpike Lodge, the clerk's eyes appeared so oily that Hendrix expected to wipe streaks off the Ace Auto Rental picture when he handed it back.

"Yes. This is the same man." The words came out with equal inflection and stress. "I remember the shirt. It was too big. I think he lost much weight."

The shirt. Hendrix felt one of the pieces slide into place.

"Jimmy, I've got an idea."

The fourth discount clothing store on the Silas Deane Highway featured green, black, and white plaid flannel shirts like the one the killer wore in the photographs. A size XXXL was marked down from $21.95 to $16.95.

"Beautiful." Hendrix felt the soggy summer air clog his chest.

"So the guy bought the shirt here," Byrne said. "Maybe. So what?"

"There's more," Hendrix said.

When they revisited the mall near The Body Shoppe, he smiled. They were four miles from the Turnpike Lodge.

"I think I've got it," he said.

Byrne stared at the Plexiglas bus shelter and listened until Hendrix finished. "OK. But now how do we prove it?"

Hendrix turned to face The Body Shoppe. "We need to consult an expert."

"Amanda, right?"

"I think she likes you," Hendrix said.

Byrne smiled like Santa Claus on Viagra. "She can't help it."

The next morning, they found Kenneth Shaeffer battling a Nautilus machine. Sweat soaked his t-shirt, but he seemed to be winning.

"Ms. Vargas told us you were here," Hendrix said.

"I'm going to let her go." Shaeffer was lifting 230 pounds. Hendrix guessed that his wife weighed half that. "I may even sell the house. The memories…"

"I'm a little surprised you came back here," Byrne said. "Pretty ugly associations now, I'd think."

"I push myself with the weights, I can turn off my brain." Shaeffer finished his set and wiped his face. He moved to another machine and punched his ID on the keypad.

"That's connected to the server, isn't it?" Hendrix watched numbers appear: the target weight, the proper seat height, the number of repetitions.

"Yeah. It keeps track so I don't have to."

"The funeral is tomorrow, isn't it?" Hendrix saw Amanda leaning over the counter to smile at Byrne.

"Calling hours tonight," Shaeffer said. "I don't know how I'm going to get through it. Looking at Elayna's mother and sister…" His voice faded.

"Have you thought about seeing someone?" Hendrix asked. "A grief counselor?"

"Not yet. Maybe…" Shaeffer finished adjusting the weights. "I still don't know why Elayna was at that motel."

"We think you told her to meet you there, have a little fling in the afternoon."

Shaeffer's eyes flickered. "You mean the killer pretended to be me. You said that yesterday."

"No. You." Hendrix looked down at Shaeffer on the seat.

"Excuse me?" Shaeffer's hands looked strong enough to bend the machine's steel bars.

"Right." Byrne crowded Shaeffer from the other side. "You used a throwaway phone so her log wouldn't show your number."

"You guys are saying dangerous things." Shaeffer's voice turned raspy. "Don't forget that I was here."

"Sure," Hendrix said. "Byrne here, he joined up yesterday. Amanda— the girl at the front desk?—showed him how to use the machines. Would you believe it? He's already done over a hundred hours on the treadmill."

Shaeffer's eyes narrowed. "If you only joined yesterday…"

"It's easy," Byrne said. "The same way you did it Wednesday. The cardio machines aren't connected to the front desk."

"Yeah." Hendrix watched Shaeffer's eyes flick toward the door. "You swipe your card to log the time when you check in, but the system that logs your workouts only puts the date, not the time. And the cardio machines aren't on that system, so you can enter anything you want."

Shaeffer's knuckles turned white.

"You parked that rental car behind the mall Tuesday night and left your own car near the Ace Auto Rental in Hartford Wednesday morning." Hendrix felt his voice picking up speed. "You took the bus from there to that mall next

53

door, checked in here, logged in two hours of exercise, and slipped out the back door and across the parking lot to the rental."

"That's so—" Shaeffer's eyes flickered toward the exit.

"Don't interrupt," Hendrix told him. "You changed into the wig, moustache, and extra-large shirt that made you look skinny, killed your wife at the motel, and dropped off the rental in Hartford. Then you changed clothes again in your own car and drove to the studio."

"You should have killed her in your own bed," Byrne said. "But you were so careful to make it look like you had an alibi that we had to ask ourselves why."

Shaeffer's sneakers danced on the floor. "I loved her. Don't you understand that?"

"But you found out about her affairs."

"Affairs, my ass. My wife loved me and I loved her. She wouldn't even look at another man."

"No," Hendrix agreed. "Not another man."

Shaeffer's feet stopped moving.

"What happened?" Byrne's voice softened. "Did she forget to put something away, or you find an e-mail, or what?"

"No. You have to understand…"

"Big TV personality." Hendrix picked it up. "You wanted that LA job, but you were afraid that if you went out there, Elayna would go wild, and that would destroy your reputation. You were stuck either way. If someone found out around here, smaller pond, it would be even worse."

"I don't have to listen to this crap." Shaeffer stood, his face blotchy. "I'm calling my attorney."

Hendrix saw two college types in Body Shoppe shirts approaching and reached for his badge. Byrne drew a folded paper from his pocket.

"Mr. Shaeffer, this search warrant authorizes us to inspect both your home and the TV station. We're looking for a digital camera with the pictures you took of yourself in the wig and moustache to put over your real driver's license picture. And we'll inspect the PCs for the Photoshopped images."

Shaeffer's face melted to the same greenish-gray hue he'd had at the morgue.

Behind the check-in counter, Amanda smiled at Byrne.

Steve Liskow's stories have earned a nomination for the Edgar Award from MWA and won the Black Orchid Novella Award (twice) and Honorable Mention for the Al Blanchard Crime Fiction Award (three times). He has also published eleven novels, and *The Kids Are All Right*, the fourth in the Zach Barnes series, was nominated for the Shamus Award. A freelance editor, he is a member of both MWA and SinC. Visit his website www.steveliskow.com

JUSTICE DUE

Jack Bates

Momma brings our wagon to a stop outside The Dusty Door Saloon. On her lap is my daddy's six-shooter. She checks the chamber. Snaps it shut. Takes a deep breath. Fills her spirit with determination. Lets out the air but keeps the confidence.

"All right, Josie," she says to me. "You stay here. Anyone but me comes out of The Dusty Door, you snap the reins and you get your sister to Auntie Clara's house down in Abilene."

"I wish you wouldn't do this, Momma. Leave it to the law."

"The law here ain't gonna do nothing, Josie. Someone has to make Lloyd Stockwell pay."

"He's the richest man in Texas. Rich men never pay."

"This one will. With interest."

"At least let me do it, Momma. Daddy taught me to shoot, not you."

"Do you think you can kill a man any easier than me?"

I can't immediately say. "We should have just sold him our land. Then Daddy would be alive."

"He'd be dead inside, Josie. Men like your father need land. They need to work otherwise they die a slow, empty death."

Momma climbs down from the bench. She walks around in front of our horses.

"Momma?"

She stops. Looks at me over her shoulder. "Remember what I told you."

I nod. Pull tighter on the reins. I watch Momma go up the steps to the plank porch outside The Dusty Door. Sour notes from an out-of-tune piano float over the ornamental scrolls of the batwing doors. The braggadocio inside blows louder and harder than the wind in the streets. It all goes silent as soon as Momma pushes her way through the swinging gates.

At first I can see her head over the scroll work.

"Lloyd Stockwell!" Momma shouts. "I'm calling you out." She steps away from where I can see her.

There's some laughter. Some prodding. Some nasty things said about my momma. I can't see Lloyd Stockwell but I can hear him.

"Gentlemen. Please."

The room quiets.

"Mrs. Butler," Stockwell says. "I'm going to suggest you put down that gun."

"Not until I put a bullet in you."

Another man speaks. "Mrs. Butler. Please. You have your daughters to—"

I count one shot. Silence. Then a second shot.

I wait.

It's not Momma I see coming out to the porch. A man steps out of The Dusty Door like he's looking for someone. There's a tin star on his chest but he isn't the law. He sees me. Other men push past him. A couple of them carry Lloyd Stockwell out of The Dusty Door.

"There's a wagon," one man says. "Put him in the back."

The men carrying Lloyd Stockwell load him next to my younger sister. She kicks a shovel as she moves out of the way. Momma planned on making Stockwell dig his own grave like he did my daddy after Stockwell accused Daddy of stealing some of his cattle. I guess she thought going into the saloon with Daddy's gun in her hand was all she was going to need to get a man like Stockwell to do what she wanted. I guess she thought wrong. Men like Stockwell know the hand before it's dealt.

I know my daddy. Knew my daddy. He'd never steal another man's cows no matter how hungry his own family might be. Momma believed Stockwell had his men put Stockwell branded steers on our spread and just said my daddy stole them. The man with the tin star just stood there and watched as Stockwell hanged my daddy for something he didn't do. Stockwell wanted our land but Daddy wouldn't sell. Only way to get us off our land was to kill us.

The man who told the others to put Stockwell in the back comes down from the porch. "Give me the reins, girl. We've got to get Mr. Stockwell to Doc Bailey's."

The reins slip from my hands. I slide over and climb off the wagon. The man snaps the reins. Our horses respond. My sister Raelene screams for me. She's still in the wagon. I want to run for her but I remember my momma didn't come out of the saloon. I go up the porch steps to the doors. The man with the tin star tries to stop me.

"My momma is in there," I say.

The man says, "She's dead, Josie."

And I say, "I know." It makes me cry.

The man holds me. The edge of the tin star pinned to his vest presses against my breast. He lets me cry. I take a breath like Momma did. Summon up my courage. Go inside.

Momma lies belly down on the floor. Her head points at the exit. There's a dark stain in the middle of her back. Size of my fist. Daddy's revolver rests next to her right hand.

The man with the tin star comes in. He looks at the bartender. The two women who wait tables. The piano player. They're all at the bar.

"This how she fell?" I ask.

"We didn't move her, hon," one of the women says.

I look up at the man with the tin star. "He shot my momma in the back."

"It all happened so fast," the man says. "She shot him and—"

I hold my daddy's revolver. A bullet has been fired.

"Show me how she shot him."

The tin star man stops. "How's that again?"

"Show me how it happened. Where was Stockwell sitting?"

The other woman at the bar pulls a chair from a table in the center of the room. "Right here, hon."

I carry my daddy's gun to the table. Sit down. "Momma was standing right there."

Sheriff Tin Star wipes a hand over his face. "Don't you think we ought to call the undertaker?"

"It can wait, Sheriff. My momma isn't going anywhere. Stand where her feet are."

The sheriff moves to the spot. "I don't know what you think this will prove."

"Use your hand as her gun. Show me how she shot Stockwell."

He makes a sideways L with his thumb and finger of his right hand. He bends his knees to make himself more my momma's size. It's plausible. Single shot. Hits Stockwell in the shoulder.

"You sure that's how she shot him?" I ask.

"Just like this." He does it again.

I stand. I don't use my daddy's gun. My L comes up on my right hand. "This how Stockwell did it?"

"I'd say so."

"My Momma turned to run or something?"

The sheriff doesn't say anything.

"Sheriff?"

"Stockwell stood and fired."

"He was shot in the right shoulder."

"Yeah."

"But he fired with his right hand?"

The sheriff looks uneasily around the room.

"The man's shot. He needs two men to carry him out. But he manages to shoot my momma in the back?"

The sheriff wipes a hand over his face again. "Your momma fired first."

"My momma didn't fire at all."

"I showed you." He raises his finger gun again. "Just like this."

"My momma was left-handed, sheriff. Three times you showed me she shot with her right hand. Momma knew she couldn't shoot Stockwell. She was leaving when he shot her in the back. Someone else picked up my daddy's gun and shot Stockwell with it to make it look like she'd shot him."

57

"I got witnesses—"

"So do I." I look at the saloon staff. "Someone's going to lie to a judge."

The sheriff wipes his face with his hand. "Josie. You don't know who you're dealing with."

"Yes I do, Sheriff. I'm dealing with a coward."

I march out of The Dusty Door Saloon. My daddy's gun hangs like an extension of my hand. With a raise of my arm I can point my metal finger and watch the coward cringe and cower. Anyone tries to stop me, I'll point my finger of death at him, too.

"Josie." The sheriff follows me out into the street. "Don't do this."

"You going to shoot me in the back like Stockwell did my momma?"

"He's got men. Judges."

"I'm supposed to have the law on my side, but all I've got is my dead daddy's gun."

"Let me go talk to him."

"Stockwell doesn't talk, Sheriff. And he sure as heck doesn't listen."

"He'll kill you and that'll leave your sister Raelene all alone."

I stop. Raelene is only twelve. I've seen the way men of this town look at her. I'm older by six years but the men hardly notice me. It's almost as if they're thinking 'That Josie is a fair woman but Lord, when that Raelene comes of age, give me strength.' Without me there to protect her, what kind of life will she have?

"Give me your gun," the sheriff says.

"Sheriff. That just isn't going to happen."

Some of the men who sat in The Dusty Door Saloon when my Momma went in, who saw what happened to her, who ran instead of helped, now stand along the boardwalks on both sides of the street watching me.

"You men know what happened to my momma. Now you stand there like ghosts of yourselves. Go hide under your beds. Lock yourselves in your cellars. Drown your fears in the rotgut you drink at The Dusty Door. You're worthless to me. You did nothing when Stockwell killed my daddy. You ran when Stockwell killed my momma."

I hear my daddy's voice in my head. 'The only person you can count on, Josephine, is yourself. You got a problem, you handle it. Somebody offers to help, well, that's fine. But don't go asking for assistance.'

I am in this alone.

By the time I reach Doc Bailey's, I feel as spent as the one chamber in my daddy's gun.

Raelene sits in the back of our wagon. Stockwell leans on the sideboard. I don't like the way he strokes my sister's hair with his free hand. The other dangles from the end of a sling.

"Take your hands off my sister."

58

Stockwell turns his head. "And if I don't?"

I raise my metal finger. He jumps back, reaches for his own gun with his good hand because his shooting hand is in a sling. He no sooner grabs the grip of his revolver when Raelene grabs the shovel handle. She swings the tool like Paul Bunyan clearing a path through the trees. The backside of the spade wallops Stockwell in the face. His gun falls. The blow only stuns him. Makes his nose bleed a trickle. Raelene may be a Butler but she's got more of our momma in her than she does our daddy.

Raelene jumps down. She runs to me.

The cocking of a gun hammer haunts me.

"Drop it, Lloyd."

I don't need to turn to know the sheriff is behind me. He's finally stepping up to his responsibility as the law. Lloyd Stockwell's laugh knocks him back a step.

"You think that star on your chest means something, Davey? You forget who give it to you?"

"Lloyd. I'm going to ask you one more time."

Stockwell sniffs. Drags his sleeve over his bloody nose. Winces. "Then what?"

"Just do it, Lloyd."

Some of the men who'd watched me march down the street now stand in line on either side of me. Some of the men have pistols. Some of the men have rifles. Some of the men have fists. Stockwell eyes the lot of them.

"That the hand you're all playing now?" Stockwell asks. "Doubling down on a pair of pocket queens?"

"Come on, Mr. Stockwell," one of the men says. "You can't shoot us all."

"I ain't aiming to shoot you all, Ty. I only need to shoot one."

Stockwell means me. I'm not folding on his bluff. "Only problem is, sir, I'm not turning my back to you. I'm not walking away like my momma did."

"Your mother came gunning for me," Stockwell says. It's pretty close to being a plea.

"Because you murdered my daddy."

"He stole my cows."

"It isn't stealing if someone gives it to you."

"I didn't give him any cows."

I look him square in the eye. "How else they wind up on our spread?"

"He stole them."

"No, he didn't," the man named Ty says. "You had us cut his wire. You had us drive six steer onto his land. You had us re-string the fence where we cut it."

"I don't know what you're getting at, Ty." Stockwell speaks to everyone. "He's lying, I tell you."

59

"Most of us was there to see it happen," Ty says. "I had to ask myself, 'If a man is willing to behave as such to my neighbor, how might he behave to me?' "

"This is nonsense, I tell you. None of it is true."

A man about to fire on another man always gives himself away. In this case Stockwell sniffs. I see his elbow stiffen. He moves his thumb over the hammer. Even though he does all of this in the tic of a second, he takes too long.

But I take longer. My daddy's gun no longer feels like an extension of my anger. It's heavy. An encumbrance. As heavy as the millstone hung around the Ancient Mariner's neck. Momma knew this. It's why she decided to leave The Dusty Door. Why daddy walked away when Stockwell accused him of rustling. Why I let my daddy's gun fall to the dirt. Truth and justice are supposed to be the measures of a society. Not violence.

Stockwell has me. He sees my gun in the dirt. His gun is coming up from his side. It didn't matter Momma's back was turned or that Daddy walked away or that I dropped Daddy's gun. Evil lives in men like Lloyd Stockwell.

Stockwell is going to kill me.

The shot that makes me jump comes from behind me. Stockwell contorts. His gun fires into the wagon ruts. He falls forward on crossed feet. Dust flies up when his face hits the dirt. Lloyd Stockwell is dead.

Sheriff Davey holsters his revolver.

"Thank you, Sheriff."

"For what?"

"Justice due my family."

He thinks about it and says, "I was just—I was—just…justice?"

He takes off his tin star. Tosses it onto Stockwell's back. Walks off down the road.

He and I have two different views of justice.

Jack Bates is an award winning writer of short fiction, stage and screenplays, and one children's book. He writes in a cramped room in a creaky old house north of the Motor City.

CHAINS

Claire A Murray

I didn't set out to be a hero. No one does. Burning building, child running into traffic, someone swipes the purse off a little old lady crossing the street—you react. Suddenly, you're a hero.

Today began like so many others. Up early. Coffee at the computer. Dress and leave for work. Make a mental note of the groceries to pick up on the way home. Traffic is light this early in the morning.

I report in to roll call, one of only two women on our small police force, and listen to the cases night shift cleared. What's left open and important? Teen in a dark hoodie who's preying on senior citizens. Little thug waits until they're halfway across the street, then streaks across and knocks them over. Takes a purse, wallet, watch—whatever he can grab in a few seconds. Beats feet so fast the victims don't even realize they've been robbed.

Another domestic violence call last night at 133 Second Avenue, third floor. We've been there a lot, mostly at night. Husband's in jail now but he'll be out by mid-afternoon, wait and see. Wife never files charges. The report says the kids, ages three and five, look like they haven't eaten in days. No money from him for food but there's always some for bail and booze. Child Protective Services will visit today. We'll go with CPS to make sure they're safe while doing their job.

The recital goes on, then we're free to hit the streets. I'm alone today. My partner Roddy—Eddie Rodriguez—is home with the kids while his wife is in the hospital having baby number three. There was some problem with the birth but he says mom and infant will be okay.

He lives in the neighborhood I've sworn to serve and protect, been encouraging me to move here. Maybe I will. He's taught me a lot since I joined the force a few years ago. Unlike some, he's never disparaged me for being a woman in a man's world. He never makes me feel that I'm not up to the challenge of keeping his back covered in a situation—all one hundred and thirty pounds of me. Neither of us is suited to be chained to a desk, at least not now in our lives, but he's taught me to think ahead.

A beat cop has to be part cop, part social worker. Well, that's probably true of being a cop in general. But it seems more important when you're walking a neighborhood all day. As Roddy says, "Earn the respect of the people. Otherwise, you can't help them because they won't trust you."

I cut my route short this morning and head back to the station to wolf down a sandwich while changing into a clean uniform shirt. I'm due in court to testify this afternoon. After court, I return to the station and learn that last night's domestic berserker on Second Avenue is out. CPS is on the way to get the kids. A patrol unit is already there. I take a car to back them up, wishing Roddy were here to be my backup. Since I'll be a third on scene, it should be all right.

The trip to Second Avenue isn't long but I wonder the whole way—does the father ever go after the kids, hit them like he does the mother? Will CPS remove them from the home? What'll that do to the mother? My parents were poor, just barely scraping by on Dad's janitor's wages. They argued, but they didn't hit each other. Oh, I got spanked when I misbehaved, but I never saw or heard him hit Mom, never saw bruises and welts like I've seen on this mother. We've tried to get her to leave—take the kids and go to a safe house where she can start over. Will she do it this time?

I arrive at the scene, one of several apartment buildings on the block. The rest is a mix of three-family houses and commercial buildings. Next to 133 is a three-story abandoned warehouse. Everything on the bottom floor was boarded up after evicting vandals who'd set the building on fire last year, but the broken upper windows remain untouched. Their second floor windows are almost up to the height of the third floor at 133, so no one can get in from ground level.

Everything looks quiet as I park on the street. Then I hear shouting and breaking glass—see a chair landing in the narrow driveway between the apartment building and warehouse. Looking up, I see the mother jump from a third floor window toward the warehouse. She makes it—almost—hanging by her fingers off the ledge of an open window.

She's gotta weigh over two hundred and fifty pounds. I pray she's got a strong grip. Seconds count and I'll never get the boards off the warehouse door in time. I run up the three flights in her building. The living room is first on my right and I smash out a window with a child-size chair, clearing the glass with my baton. Hearing shouts and scuffling in the next room, I shout to the patrol unit that I'm on scene and helping the mother.

I take a running leap out the window, across the gap, and crash through a closed window, shielding my face with my arms. Most of the window panes were already cracked or broken, but I'm covered in glass as I tuck and roll. I stop at the edge of a gaping hole in the floor left from the fire. My radio slips from its holster and falls through—not good. I pull a large shard of glass from my thigh.

The mother's cries for help snap me back to the moment. I rush to the other window and grab her wrists. "Hang on," I shout as we lock arms. Her fright-filled eyes tell me she thinks she's going to die. I see the patrol unit across the gap, facing away from me as the husband struggles while being cuffed. Officer Donovan turns back and picks up an axe off the bed. No wonder she jumped.

Do they know where I am? My shout to them comes out as a weak croak. I'm out of breath from hauling the woman up so she could get her hands

62

over the inside sill to hang on better. She's strong and athletic, despite her size, and uses her feet to gain leverage against the outside wall. Once her shoulders are past the window sill, I give a big yank to get her upper body inside, ignoring the creaks and groans of the floor beneath me. She's in far enough to make the rest of the way herself, which is good 'cause I'm on my butt on the floor.

As soon as she's safely inside, she turns on me, fear turned to anger. "You arrested Dickie last night. Now he's blaming me—why couldn't you leave us alone?"

Yada, yada, yada. Her tirade is familiar. Cops are good when they stop the victim from being hit, shot, knifed—whatever. Then we're evil because we arrest the abuser. I hear Roddy's voice in my head. "Abuse is a chain that tightens around the victim and drains all reason—leaving only fear, low self-esteem, and raw emotion."

She gets up from the floor and advances on me, the spittle coming faster than her words. "You took my babies—ruined my life. What do I have without them?"

Good, CPS had whisked the kids away before I'd arrived. I wouldn't want them to witness what's going on now. They've suffered enough, even if no one has hit them. Their scars will be emotional—the sudden intake of breath at the sound of a raised voice, the clenched stomach when they see a curled fist, that sudden drop in confidence when called upon by an adult and they don't have the right answer. Worse yet, they may grow up to become abusers—repeating the vicious emotional and physical pattern they learned from their father.

I stand and fend off her blows without retaliating, backing up each time she pushes me. We've made many calls to her apartment. Already, she's in the familiar pattern of pain and crisis, emotionally chained to the man who abuses her. I keep my voice low, soothing. "We're not your enemy. We're trying to keep you and the kids safe." Nothing I say makes any difference. I let her get it out of her system while looking for a way out of here.

Most of the floor is gone or so charred it won't hold much weight. She pushes me again and I step back, hearing too late the groan of the uneven floor. As it gives way beneath us, I grab her arm and pull her close, trying to shield her from the long fall. I land on my back, on a mezzanine-type landing I didn't know was between the two floors. This, too, creaks and groans. She rolls off me. I can breathe again. Pushing against the landing floor, I tempt fate and stand, motioning her to remain still. What's left of the floor is its own island, disconnected from everything except the support beam beneath us—and no way off. About twenty feet from where we landed, the exposed beam is cracked, almost split.

This isn't my day to die, I tell myself. I have too much life left to live. Roddy's face flashes across my mind. He's a good partner who's ignited my desire to go back to school, rise in the ranks of the department, and do more with my life outside of work. I want to become a detective and solve crimes, not die in a burned-out warehouse because some wife is too shell-shocked to realize we've saved her and her kids' lives, not ruined them.

My radio is gone—no way to call for help. Do we have time to wait for a rescue? Did the patrol unit hear me say I was helping the mother? Can I get back to a window and call out for help? My bleeding leg throbs. The floor sags and groans. Gotta get outta here.

The beams above us, almost at roof level, still hold chains and pulleys from the warehouse's days of hauling heavy items between floors. Can I use those to lower her, then me, to safety? I turn to the mother. "Wait here. I'm going to grab a chain and see if I can use it to lower you to the bottom."

She nods and stands up, no longer acting as if I'm the enemy. She looks more scared than anything. I crawl onto the thick beam on my hands and knees until I can reach a double strand of chain that runs through a pulley attached to a beam near the roof. Good, it has some leeway. I crawl backwards, dragging the strands of heavy chain with me, palms and fingers splintered and bleeding from the rough beam. When I reach the landing, she helps me stand. I have no idea how safe that upper support beam is, so I pull with all my strength. It holds. We pull on it together. The beam and pulley hold against our combined weight, with some creaks and groans that make us both shudder.

We've said little since our fall, but she is compliant when I explain what I want her to do next. "I'll lower you to the bottom," I tell her as I slide my baton through one of the links. "Hold my baton tight. Use your feet to grip the chain." She grabs each end of the baton and I see her knuckles whiten.

"Good. Now wrap your leg around the chain, like this." I show her how. She looks at me askance but says, "Okay." Despite the quiver in her voice, she obeys.

"When I say ready, place your other foot on top of the first. It'll take some strain off your arms." She hesitates and I have to coax her. "Look, you did great on the window ledge. You can do this, too. I'll be holding this other strand to slow your descent."

Her face whitens more as she bites her lower lip. Can't she feel the floor sagging beneath us with each passing second? She takes a deep breath and hoists her full weight onto the chain, clamping one foot over the other with the chain between them. I push her over the opening, slowly to prevent any sudden jerks on the chain. It seemed like a good plan in my head. But the strand I'm holding suddenly rushes through my hands, burning through layers of skin. She's falling too fast. She'll break her legs when she hits bottom. Ignoring my tears and painful, bloody hands, I grip tighter and sag my rear end to let my weight help slow the chain's movement.

I hear splitting noises and more groans from the beam above. Where's the patrol unit? They should have the husband in the car by now. This floor's falling apart. If I jump onto my strand of the chain, I'll go up but it should slow her down.

Heavy banging noises from below distract me. I look down and see movement against the boarded up doors. They'll be too late to catch her. I yell down. "Jump off when you're near the bottom. Roll away, so the chain doesn't fall on you."

Passing seconds feel like eons. Can't wait. I swing out over the open area, all my weight on the chain to slow its momentum—just as the landing gives way. My one hundred and thirty pounds aren't enough to slow her descent for more than a few seconds. She continues down at a fast clip as I rush upward.

What's that? Is the upper beam cracking more? I daren't look. But I do. The beam gives way. The sudden break changes my direction and my rising body shifts to downward free fall.

"Jump!" I yell.

I look down as the front door smashes open and the patrol unit pushes through. I see their upturned faces, following her gaze as she points at me. My body rushes toward the beam I leapt from oh so recently. I sigh with relief and pray she'll take this as a sign to move on with her life. I'm glad Roddy isn't here to see this.

I didn't set out to be a hero today. No one does. It just happens. Today, it happened to me. Today, I died so someone else could live.

Claire A. Murray is a member of Sisters in Crime, its Guppy and New England chapters, and the Salem Writers Group. She has a half dozen short stories published and has an amateur sleuth series on hold while she works on a fantasy novel set in a medieval society on another world. She is the regional manager for a return-to-work program for mature job seekers and is a dog enthusiast.

DEADLY DISCOVERY IN DALLAS

Sanford Emerson

It was obvious to anyone who cared to look—and there were some folks doing just that on a crispy Maine afternoon in mid-September—that Mrs. Grania "Granny" Liberty was a very fine looking woman indeed for her age. That she was a natural redhead was also evident, as she was standing bollocky bare-ass naked in the middle of Jack Frost Hill Road holding a rope attached to a sad-eyed Brown Swiss milk cow. Apparently completely unfazed by the state of her increasingly public appearance, she was, also obviously, mighty pissed off.

"Martin," she shouted at the top of her rather prodigious lungs as I pulled up next to her. "Maaahtin, you lazy bahstid! I've told you and told you to check Molly's tether before you come inside. Martin? Get your sorry ass out here and help me!"

About ten minutes earlier, Snort Benson had come running into Sally's Motel and Bar and Live Bait and Convenience Store all aflutter, interrupting the consumption of my second Shipyard Pumpkinhead Ale. Breathless as usual, Snort announced to all three people present that the Animal Control Officer (that would be me) was needed at once for an all-fired big cow-related emergency up on Jack Frost Hill.

Well, hell!

You see a few years ago, I agreed to be the constable up here in Dallas Plantation, which is a usually quiet community of about three hundred people in the northern part of Franklin County in the beautiful western mountains of the grand State of Maine. Since I retired from the Coast Guard I've lived in an old hunting camp on the side of Saddleback Mountain that I inherited from a former Coastie cook after helping him through his final days in a nursing home by losing cribbage games, swapping stories and sneaking him late night screwdrivers.

Being the constable isn't really that big a deal, as the Board of Assessors, the three folks we elect at the yearly town meeting to run the plantation's official affairs, made no bones about telling me when they came around to talk to me after they found out I had some law enforcement experience in the service. They were quite adamant that although I would have the ancient and honorable titles of Constable, Fence Viewer, Deputy Fire Warden and Animal Control Officer, I was not, under any circumstance, to carry a gun or a badge and "for God's sake, don't arrest anybody!" To authorize that, they explained, the plantation would have to pay for me to go to the police academy down in Vasselboro, which is some expensive. Since I can always use a few extra bucks to cover my tab at Sally's, I said no problem. So basically they pay me minimum wage and mileage to spend a couple of hours a week taking care of the odd "stuff" that needs doing around the plantation.

66

"Stuff" like Granny Liberty's cow standing in the middle of a public thoroughfare, where she, and now Granny, could easily be hit by traffic, if there had been any traffic, which, to be truthful, there seldom is.

Actually traffic did look like it was beginning to pick up as word got around about all the goings on. As I pulled up I counted three pickup trucks, a shiny new green Subaru with New Hampshire plates and a pulp truck with half a hastily tied down load—all of them lined up next to the driveway into the Libertys' landscaped, well-tended gentleman's farm.

Bailing out of The Beast, my new pickup, I grabbed my old army blanket out of the space behind the front seat and tried to drape it around Granny's shoulders as she shouted louder and increasingly profanely after this Martin fellow. Since I know her husband's name is Wilbur and that he was probably at his office on Yawkey Way in Boston, I began to wonder just who Martin was.

Granny, God love her, suddenly looked at me as if I'd just stepped off a flying saucer. Her hair was damp and I could smell jasmine and bourbon. She looked at the cow, the blanket over her shoulders and the gathering crowd and began to scream. Then she laughed. Then she screamed some more.

"He's dead, the bahstid," she said in between shrieks. "He's finally dead! I finally did it!"

Well, hell!

Out of the corner of my eye I saw the canary yellow Jeep Wrangler belonging to our rural mail carrier, town gossip, and fire chief, Marti Wallace, pull in behind The Beast.

"Granny," I said, trying to keep the blanket covering her critical parts. "Grania! It's Bobby. Bobby Wing. Listen to me. We've got to get the cow out of the road before she gets hit."

Surprisingly, that's all it took. Granny looked around again, stopped screeching and let me lead her and the cow over toward Marti's Jeep on the shoulder of the road. Marti put her arms around Granny's shoulders, pulled her around to the rear door of the Jeep, and sat her inside amidst the mail and turnout gear. I spied Bear McGillicuddy, the owner of the pulp truck, in the crowd and handed him the cow's tether. Bear's on our one-truck volunteer fire department with me and Marti and fifteen or so other good citizens. He's also the biggest man in the plantation by a good fifty pounds. Luckily for all of us his disposition pretty much matches that of the cow I now entrusted him to secure back on Granny's property.

"Off her meds again, I'd say," he said, shaking his head as he walked up the driveway with Molly in tow. A few in the crowd nodded in agreement. Just about then I heard a siren from the direction of Rangeley, the next town over where Northstar Ambulance has its regional base.

"Franklin County Dispatch got a 911 call on her a few minutes ago," Marti said from beside her Jeep where she was kneeling, holding Granny's hand. "I heard it on the fire channel and came right over. Looks like Bear's right about the meds, though. Too bad."

Granny's usually a very nice, refined lady. She's about my age—"fiftyish"—and most everyone in the plantation likes her and her mister, even though they're from away. Her gardens are pretty famous locally and she's even started giving free lessons since the state extension named her a Master Gardener.

He's Will Liberty—"Wave'm in Will"—the third base coach for the Boston Red Sox. They have an apartment down in the city where Will usually stays during the season. If the Sox don't make the post-season, which doesn't look real likely, he should be arriving in a few weeks to settle into his off-season role of rugged outdoorsman, gentleman farmer and ski instructor. He's a good guy to have a beer or two with—full of baseball stories.

Anyway, somewhere along the line Granny got bit by a demon. Shortly after the two of them bought their place here about five years ago, she started having wicked temper tantrums in public for no particular reason. She'd also do strange stuff and say some pretty weird things. I heard that once, at a Board of Assessors meeting, she made a proposal to require all the cats in the plantation to wear bells to warn away the chickadees. Finally Will threw out the liquor and took her down to Boston to some doctor the team uses. He gave her some meds and, after a couple of noisy relapses a while back, she slowly got better. Now she goes to Alcoholics Anonymous meetings in Rangeley once a week, sees a traveling counselor at the Rural Health Center and generally seems to be pretty normal by plantation standards—or at least she did up until about fifteen minutes ago.

Just about as the ambulance pulled up, Bear came booking it back down the driveway just feather white.

"Bobby," he said, gasping for air. "You gotta come look. There's a dead guy in the hay barn!"

Well, hell!

After twenty-five years in the Coast Guard as a machinist and a chief gunner's mate on fast cutters, I've seen more than my share of death, in more forms than I can count, but, mister man, this turned out to be a new one. After briefing the paramedics, I walked up the long, curving, flower-lined driveway toward the impressive, colonnaded house. Bear didn't come back up with me because he was busy being sick in the ditch behind the ambulance. It didn't take me long to find out why.

The sliding door on the front of the hay barn behind the house was only part way open and I could hear the deep bellowing roar of a good sized diesel engine at full throttle. Stepping into the dimly lit space I saw Will's big Kubota tractor nestled up tightly to the front row of big round hay bales which filled about three quarters of the place. Stepping over a puddle of Bear vomit, I spied a man's head with a mess of dried blood around his nose and mouth and open goggle eyes staring down at the six-foot-long steel bale spear which had the rest of him skewered between the loader frame on the front of the tractor and the center of the bale behind him.

The barn was full of exhaust fumes and I coughed and retched just a bit myself as I reached up and shut off the engine. About then Mark Blake, one of the paramedics from the ambulance, appeared next to me with a jump pack of emergency medical equipment in each hand. Seeing what I was looking at, he set them down as they were obviously going to be useless in this situation.

"How's Granny?" I asked him as we stood there.

"She'll be fine. We'll take her down to Franklin Memorial Hospital for an evaluation, but I don't think it's anything more than acute ETOH."

"Huh?" I said.

"She's blind drunk," he said, with a cough.

"Not off her meds?"

"She says she's not but the hospital will check. My partner stayed with her and called in for a police response based on what Bear said. The sheriff's sending a deputy. Do you know this guy?" Mark asked as he climbed up onto the loader mechanism of the tractor.

"I'm guessing he's the Libertys' hired hand, but I've never met him, so I'm not sure," I said.

Mark pulled on a blue rubber glove and felt the guy's throat. "No pulse, cool to the touch, stake through his heart. I don't think this boy's riding with us today." Hopping back to the ground he coughed again and said, "This place is probably full of carbon monoxide. Come on. We'd better go outside and let it air out."

"Sounds good to me."

We shoved the door all the way open and headed back down the driveway.

"I almost forgot," Mark said. "Granny wants you to call her husband. She says her cell phone is on the kitchen counter and he's number one on her speed dial."

Will answered on the third ring. "Hi, hon. Bad timing. I'm in the pregame staff meeting. Can I call you back?" He sounded stressed. The season was petering out and, sadly, so were the Sox.

"Will, it's Bobby Wing from up in Dallas Plantation. It's important."

"Bobby? How'd you get Granny's phone? Is she OK? Just a minute." I heard him making his excuses to the manager and then heard a door close. "Hello?" he said as he came back on the line.

"She's OK, Will. Physically anyway."

"The middle of the road?" "Naked?" "Drunk?" The pitch of his voice rose a little with each question as I told the sad tale. Finally he sighed. "I guess I don't know what to say, Bobby. Thank you. I'll be up there as soon as I can. Tell Martin to make sure everything is locked up and the animals are tended to before he goes home tonight."

"That's another thing, Will…"

"OK, you people," Deputy Douglas Elvin Berry—as proclaimed by the extra-large shiny brass name tag pinned to his rather tight uniform shirt—said as he hoisted himself out of his cruiser. "I'm in charge now. What's going on here?" Pulling up on his gun belt and down on his campaign hat, he peered at the bunch of us with something, I thought, bordering on contempt.

"Oh, God!" I heard Mark say softly to the other paramedic, who looked like she was still in high school. "Deputy Dog. How'd we get so lucky?"

Thankfully Marti took the lead. I tried to keep a straight face.

69

"Hi, Dog," she said. "It sounds like we've got an unattended death in Mrs. Liberty's barn. It's full of diesel fumes right now and we're letting it air out so it's safe to enter. The medical examiner's been called, too."

"Who's the stiff?" Dog asked, chomping down on his gum, which popped loudly.

At that point I just lost it.

"Who the hell are you and what the hell are you laughing at?"

"Sorry, Deputy," I choked out. "I'm Bobby Wing, the plantation constable. I got the original call and sort of found the body. It's been tough." I shrugged and tried to look contrite.

"Constable, huh?" he said, glaring at me with a pretty good *Heat of the Night* Rod Steiger impersonation. "I heard about you. You never got any training, did you? I'd be real careful about what I called myself if I was you. Impersonating a Law Enforcement Officer is a serious offense!"

"I'll be careful, Deputy," I said.

Somebody behind him snickered and Dog jerked his head around, actually sneering at the crowd.

"We're not absolutely sure yet who the deceased is," Marti said, pointedly interrupting. "Bobby, Bear McGillicuddy, and the paramedic here are the only ones who've seen the body and they don't recognize him. He might be a guy named Martin. We don't know his last name. He's Mrs. Liberty's hired hand."

"Martin? Martin's deceased? Martin's dead?" Granny started shrieking again from the back of the ambulance where Mark and his partner had, thankfully, just gotten her strapped in for transport.

"Oh, crap!" Marti said. "That's Mrs. Liberty. Let me go talk to her."

"You do that," Dog said, raising his voice as she walked away. "And tell her if she doesn't quiet down I'll take her to jail for Disorderly Conduct!"

"Jail!"

Marti hurried to the back of the ambulance.

"His last name is Stevens," I said. "Martin Stevens. I just talked to Granny's husband on the phone. He's driving up from Boston and should be here later tonight."

Dog extracted a notebook from his back pocket and pulled a stubby pencil out of the wire spiral that held it together. Squinting a bit he checked his watch. "Right. 14:33 on scene. Deceased ID'd as a Martin Stevens. Got a date of birth, Constable?" he said, drawing out the last word a bit longer than I thought necessary.

"No, and I'm not sure that's who it is, either." I managed to register only a slight, hopefully innocuous, smile. "Will says he lives up at the Chicken House."

"Oh, for the love of Pete!" Dog threw up his hands, dropped his pencil and then had to grab for his hat, which threatened to tumble off his head. "Not another one of them frickin' hippie commie cult chicken freaks? Just great! I can't ever get a straight answer out of any of them crazy canucks."

I held my tongue as he squared away his hat and retrieved his pencil. The pacifist Community of Satin down on the Saddleback Lake Road has always struck me as a pretty nice, steady bunch of chicken farmers with a funny name and a good collective ability to judge character. Someday I'll tell you all about them, when we've got time.

"Carbon monoxide poisoning, you said. Farming accident, right?" Dog sounded eager but the light in his eye was fading a little. It also started to sound like he was looking for an easy out. I guessed his forte was writing traffic tickets.

"Sorry," I said. "The place was full of exhaust smoke from the tractor, but I'm betting the ME's going to say that the cause of death was a two inch diameter steel stake through his heart."

His face fell. "The hell you say? Oh, this is just frickin' great! I'll never get home for supper at this rate!"

About then a handsome old white Mercedes sedan pulled into the line on the shoulder behind the New Hampshire Subaru. I watched with a twinge of envy as the single occupant slowly unfolded himself from this very fine Teutonic masterpiece of diesel-powered engineering.

"ME's here," shouted Mark from the back of the ambulance.

Eimon Jeffries, MD, stepped up onto the ambulance's high tailgate. He had to duck his large, shaggy white head to look inside.

"Hey, guys," he said to the paramedics. "Hey, Grania. How you feeling, my girl?"

Granny, strapped to the gurney and incapable of rising, looked back at the doctor with unabashed affection, and attraction, as did the female paramedic. Doc Jeffries, you see, put himself through med school as a male stripper.

"I'm much better, Doc, but they're taking me to jail!" A touch of panic crept back into her voice. The doctor looked at Mark, who shook his head.

"ETOH, Doc. We're running her down to FMH for an eval."

"It's OK, Grania." Doc's voice rumbled from deep in his barrel chest. "You're not going to jail. I'll come down to the hospital in the morning and check on you, OK? You'll be fine. You'll be safe. Don't worry."

"Good," Granny said, breaking a smile. "That's good. I'd like that."

Even I felt better.

"Hey, Dog," Doc said as he walked over to us. "What you guys got this time?"

"I don't know yet," Dog said nervously as the ambulance rolled away. "I thought we had a farming accident. Maybe carbon monoxide. But the constable here just said different."

"Hey, Bobby. How's The Beast running?"

Doc and I both like big diesel engines and the solid steel that tends to surround them. I filled him in on the events of my afternoon so far as the three of us walked up the driveway.

We all stopped at the barn threshold and looked around. The door was now fully open in the afternoon sun and most of the diesel smoke was gone, so the visibility was a lot better. I pointed at the drying puke pool on the pole barn's hard-packed clay floor.

71

"I stepped over that and walked straight to the tractor and shut it off. Mark came in the same way and we both left as straight as we could after he checked the body."

"Well, from here he looks pretty dead to me," Doc said. "Does it look like anything has changed since you left?"

Without moving, I looked around carefully. The field treads of the tractor had dug themselves into the surface of the floor about six inches and sprayed loose dirt against the wall behind it, which I hadn't been able to see through the diesel smoke earlier.

"Looks to me like the guy jumped off the tractor while it was still in gear and it shishkabobed him," Dog said before I could answer Doc's question. His face was going a little pale.

"No, I don't think so," I said. "I tinkered this tractor for Will last spring. Thanks to federal safety regs it has an electric interlock that kills the engine if the driver gets out of the seat with the transmission in gear. Since it was running full blast when I shut it off, it had to have been in neutral."

"Which means," Doc said slowly, "that our new friend here did not meet his demise as the result of some terrible, tragic farming-related accident."

"Nope," I agreed. "Somebody had to have been driving."

"Well, lah dee frickin' da!" Dog said with a happy grin. "It's a suspicious death and that's a case for the staties! I won't have to talk to them commie frickin' chicken farmers after all!"

Doc called the Chief Medical Examiner's Office in Augusta from his Mercedes while Dog happily wrapped everything he could see in yellow "Sheriff's Line—Do Not Cross" tape and then parked his cruiser directly in front of the driveway with all the emergency lights going. Marti left to finish her mail route, the rest of the rubber-neckers got bored and drifted away, and Bear drove his pulp truck back to his woodlot.

Strangely the New Hampshire Subaru didn't move. I brought this to Dog's attention. He was sitting in his cruiser reading an old Nick Fury comic book.

"Probably nothing at all. Somebody will be back for it. Don't worry about it."

It was well after dark by the time I got to the Chicken House, more properly known as the Mother House of the Community of Satin. I'd been interviewed twice by two different state police detectives, been fingerprinted and had my shoe treads photographed. I'd also submitted a hand written statement about the events of my afternoon. They warned me to be quiet about what I'd seen for now and told me to go home. I didn't.

Happily, the first person I ran into was Tangerine Gilchrist. Angie runs the home school for the Community kids and is the single mom of two teenagers, a boy and a girl. She graduated from McGill University up in Canada with a Master's Degree in Education, and she likes beer and baseball—except she's a Blue Jays fan. I still like her anyways. And she's a wicked looker.

"You're here about Martin Stevens?" she asked. "Why?"

I told her. She laughed.

"That's impossible. Your victim can't be Martin Stevens. I just had supper with him in the dining hall."

I asked her if she was sure. Oddly she paused and said, "Things are seldom what they seem."

"Yeah," I said. "And skim milk masquerades as cream." My late dad was a Gilbert and Sullivan fan and *H.M.S. Pinafore* was always one of his favorites.

Her eyes widened and she smiled. Somehow I felt a change in the air.

My phone started ringing pretty much as soon as I got to sleep. First the state police detective sergeant in charge wanted to know why I'd gone up to the Chicken House without his permission. I told him that it was wicked dark out, I was half asleep and I wasn't aware he was my boss. Then he wanted to know why I hadn't called him about Martin Stevens being alive. I reminded him that it was late, I was tired and I still wasn't aware he was my boss. He told me about the Obstructing Government Administration law. I don't think he likes me.

Next Will Liberty woke me up to tell me that the hospital had put a deputy sheriff on guard outside Granny's room and wouldn't let him in to see her or tell him why. I told him to call Woody Hanstein, a lawyer friend of mine down in Farmington.

Finally Doc called to tell me, in confidence of course, that he was watching when they rolled the tractor away from the barn wall before de-spearing the guy by now known to not be Martin Stevens. Under the left front wheel they found a loaded and cocked Colt M1911 .45 caliber semi-automatic pistol, which turned out to be stolen. Oh, and that New Hampshire Subaru also turned out to be stolen.

I knew they were feds as soon as they pulled into my dooryard. I was sitting on my screen porch in the morning sun with my old Maine Coon cat, Lummox, enjoying the view of the early fall foliage down in the valley, drinking my second cup of coffee, and reading the *Daily Bulldog* on my iPad. Our local on-line newspaper had a picture of the Liberty house surrounded by "State Police Line—Do Not Cross" tape, which had apparently replaced Dog's at some point, and a four line story which basically said that state police detectives were investigating an "incident" at the home of Red Sox coach Will Liberty and the story would be updated as more information became available.

Two guys in gray windbreakers got out of their gray car and walked up to the porch door. Lummox raised his head, peered stonily at them from his perch on the porch railing and yawned.

"Bobby Wing?" asked the older looking one.

"Yup."

"Can we come in?"

73

"Do I need a lawyer?" I asked, mindful of the numerous legal warnings I had received in the past few hours.

"Do you think you do?" the younger one asked.

"I sure as hell hope not," I said. Lummox sighed and rolled his eyes. I swear to God.

They looked beat. I offered coffee and Country Kitchen donuts from the Rangeley IGA.

They looked at each other and the older one shrugged, "Yeah. That would be good. We've been up all night."

Lummox, two Deputy US Marshals and I sat on my porch for the next hour drinking coffee and discussing the situation. They told me a bunch of wicked confidential stuff, so forget this next bit.

It turns out that "Martin Stevens" was living at the Community of Satin as his cover identity with the Witness Protection Program. It seems that the Community, since they moved to the US from Newfoundland six years ago, has provided the most secure and problem free placement of this type in the whole, entire country. The marshals wouldn't admit it, but I got the distinct impression that they had other "clients" in residence besides "Martin." I was amazed that this was possible given the extensive plantation grapevine and its primary driver, Marti, and I told them so.

Without missing a beat the older one said, "Martha Wallace has been a great asset to us over the years. We hope you will be, too."

Well, hell!

Turns out Martin had called in as soon as he got back to the Chicken House yesterday afternoon. The dead guy was a known professional shooter who had somehow tracked Martin down and tried to collect on the substantial contract bounty out on him. Having developed a few professional skills of his own over the years, Martin successfully used the only weapon available to him to defend himself, the bale spear on his tractor. I was impressed by his guts, and his ingenuity.

Finally the marshals told me about the challenge and countersign to use if I ever needed to talk to a Community member about their little "sideline" in future. Whoever thought that one up must have been a G & S fan too, which explained Angie's sudden change in attitude.

Despite her self-incriminating public rant, Granny was cleared as a suspect when Will told the detectives that she was afraid of his tractor and wouldn't go near it. Also there were no prints on it except Martin's.

The state police detectives at the scene had all been briefed on a "need to know" basis and agreed to close the case as self-defense. Dog Berry, who didn't pass muster, I guess, was told to forget everything he'd seen that day because if he ever talked about it to anyone, he'd wind up just another piece of ass sitting in a federal Super-Max cell somewhere in Colorado for the next twenty years. Later the sheriff gave him a week off without pay for missing the stolen car, especially after it had been pointed out to him. I admit I chuckled a bit when I heard about that. We haven't seen much of him since.

A new recruit was introduced at the October Firemen's meeting at Sally's—one Martin Stevens from the Community of Satin. He told us that, although he was a city boy, he'd really become very fond of life in Dallas Plantation and everybody he'd met there so far. Seems like a nice guy.

After CPR and First Responder re-qualifications were finished and the bar was reopened, Marti asked to talk to me outside.

It seems Granny told her weekly AA meeting that, after sixteen months of sobriety, she had a slip. She'd been trying all summer to fend off a groundhog that was chowing down on her beloved gardens, even trying one of those humane cage traps to no avail. She finally resorted to an old fashioned leg hold trap, which had worked on the day in question. When she saw that the poor thing was rolling in pain and trying to gnaw off its paw to escape, she panicked, grabbed one of Will's souvenir baseball bats and beat it out of its misery. Turns out that's what she was screaming about. Covered with blood and gore she ran into her laundry room and threw all her clothes in the washer. She also dug out her security stash, a pint of Jim Beam she had hidden inside the motor compartment of the drier, and jumped into the shower with it. After sixteen months her tolerance for alcohol was pretty non-existent and she quickly blacked out, coming to in the back of Marti's Jeep. She exchanged her sobriety chip for a beginner's model and started all over. The group gave her a standing ovation.

A month later the Board of Assessors paid me thirty-four dollars and fifty cents, less withholding, for my efforts on this case. They cut my mileage request in half, though. They reasoned that my initial response to the loose cow report was indeed something they should pay for but getting home after everything was over with was my own responsibility.

Well, HELL!

Retired after a thirty-five year career in law enforcement and corrections in Maine, **Sanford Emerson** runs a woodworking shop. He meets with Bobby Wing on a semi-regular basis at Sally's. He writes down what Bobby tells him and edits the result for language and hyperbole – Bobby tends to exaggerate! Previous yarns have appeared in *Red Dawn* and *Windward*, Level Best Books' New England crime anthologies for 2015 and 2016. Sanford could write a book but since it appears nearly every retired cop in Maine does that eventually, he probably won't.

ANNIE GET YOUR GOAT

LD Masterson

"I was out back, in the yard, giving Gertrude a bath."

Oh, come on. I know this guy just got bashed in the head but the ER doctor said he was totally lucid.

"Excuse me?" I asked.

"Gertrude. That's Duke's prize Nubian."

Yeah, that was a *lot* clearer. "Nubian?"

"Goat. Dairy goat. Gertrude is—"

"A goat. Got it. Okay, you were in the back yard bathing a goat."

Sean Tate reached up and fingered the white bandage wrapped around his head. His longish hair was pushed up and hung over the top of the gauze like some sort of blond mushroom. I'd noticed him around town. Nice looking, early twenties like me...never quite pictured him bathing a goat.

"Then something hit me," he went on. "Wham. And next thing I know, I'm downstairs on a gurney and some doctor's yelling at me to wake up."

"And you didn't see or hear anyone approach you before you were hit?"

He started to shake his head then winced as though the movement was painful. "No, ma'am. Nothing. Neither did Gertie. She's real skittish that way. If someone had been trying to sneak up on us, I would have known it."

My turn to wince, at least mentally. *Ma'am.* Ouch. I knew it was the uniform. Hard for the guy in the johnnie-gown to use "Miss" when addressing a woman with fifteen pounds of police gear—including a semi-automatic—strapped around her waist, no matter what her age.

"Not much of a watch-goat," I smiled, trying to put him at ease. "Okay, was that your usual routine? I mean, if someone wanted to attack you, would he expect you to be in the yard today...bathing the goat, around that time?"

"No." He shook his head again, gently this time. "We don't usually bathe Gertie unless she's really filthy or we're getting ready for a show. This was more of a medical thing. She's been losing her fur. Some kind of skin problem."

"Ah, so that's why you were wearing surgical gloves. The doctor mentioned you were wearing gloves when they brought you in. You didn't want to touch her skin."

"Not exactly, it was the shampoo—"

Duke Stamper blustered into the room like the high wind before a summer thunderstorm. Six foot four, two-eighty, full head of white hair

76

accenting his white summer suit—he made the room smaller. He wore a not unpleasant mixture of bay rum and pipe tobacco, just strong enough to overpower the smell of antiseptic. And his attention was all on the patient. I'm not sure he even saw me.

I get that a lot.

"Sean. Good God. Are you okay? Mrs. Miller called my office, said you'd been attacked."

Mrs. Miller. Now *that* name I knew. Ran the bakery in town. Great donuts.

"Mrs. Miller? How did she…?" Sean scrunched up his features like he was trying to remember.

"She's the one who found you, boy. When she was delivering my bread. Called for the ambulance."

Sean straightened in his bed, I think in response to Duke's use of the term "boy," and seemed to gather his thoughts. "I'll have to thank her. I'm okay, Mr. Stamper. Just a whack on the head. Took some stitches and they want to keep me overnight for observation, but I'll be back to work tomorrow."

"No hurry, boy. No hurry."

It was odd to hear Sean address Duke as Mr. Stamper. I'd never heard him called anything but Duke. It was more like a title than a name. Of course, I'd never had occasion to address him as anything. I took a quick intake of breath, ready to break in, when Sean asked, "Is Gertrude okay?"

Duke stiffened like he'd been struck. "Gertrude? What about her? Why wouldn't she be okay?"

"That's what I was doing…when I got hit. I was bathing Gert. Didn't Mrs. Miller see her?"

"No, she didn't say…" His voice trailed off and he turned away from Sean and me, the very picture of a man trying to work something out in his mind. This was my chance.

"Mr. Stamper—"

"McCullough!" Duke's voice exploded in the quiet of the hospital. "That bastard stole my goat."

Now he rounded on me.

"You. You're one of Sheriff Block's, right? Why are you just standing around here? That son of a bitch Chet McCullough stole my Gertrude."

I pulled myself up to my full five foot two and tried to look official, if not formidable. "Deputy Anna Lopez, Mr. Stamper. I was questioning Mr. Tate when you arrived. Trying to find out what happened."

"I just told you what happened. Chet McCullough attacked Sean so he could steal Gertrude. Oh God…unless he killed her. I wouldn't put it past the son of a bitch." He did a quick pivot toward the door then turned back to me. "I'm going home to search for Gertrude. You tell Sheriff Block I want him at my place. Himself. Not some little…deputy."

I was lucky that Duke stormed out of the room before I could answer. My quick tongue has gotten me into trouble before. I finished questioning Sean—not that there was much left to ask—and headed to the Stamper place.

Sheriff Block was already there. I wasn't surprised. The good old boy club was pretty strong in these parts and I knew Duke Stamper was a member, as was Sheriff Walter Block.

The Sheriff and Duke were arguing nose to nose in the doorway of a small barn. My boss didn't have Duke's bulk but he was every bit as tall. Didn't seem like backup was required so I took a look around.

The well-kept lawn around the house was a deep green but in this area it was just dirt, dry and dusty in the summer heat. The air was ripe with an assortment of smells, mostly animal but with the scent of honeysuckle mixed in. I wandered over to a pen occupied by three goats—none of which, I guessed, was the prize-winning Gertrude. They were all girls, as witnessed by their generous udders, and Nubian—based on my quick Google search. Each had long drooping ears like a lop-eared rabbit, and a generous Roman nose. Their coats were short and smooth with no missing fur that I could see.

As I approached, all three moved to greet me. I assumed they were looking for a snack but they seemed just as happy to nuzzle my empty hand or let me scratch the tops of their heads. I could see why Duke was so worried about Gertrude. It would be easy to get attached to one of these girls.

My goat bonding ended when the sheriff left Duke in the barn and motioned for me to join him at what appeared to be our crime scene. A large metal tub was still filled with water—not soapy, like I expected, but with an oily sheen floating on the surface. Odd, I hadn't found their coats to be oily.

"You interviewed Sean Tate?" he asked me.

"Yes sir." I pulled out my notepad. "Mr. Tate said he was here washing Mr. Stamper's goat, Gertrude, when something struck him in the head and he lost consciousness. He doesn't remember anything after that until he woke up at the hospital."

Block pointed at a small dark stain in the trampled dirt. "That's where Carol Miller found him. I imagine most of these footprints belong to the rescue boys that came and got him."

"Mr. Tate said he didn't see or hear anyone approaching. He didn't think the goat did either." The words sounded foolish as I said them but the sheriff just nodded.

We circled the area, searching for any sign of prints that didn't fit the general pattern but came up empty.

"Walt." Duke was coming across the yard toward us. I guess he'd gotten tired of waiting. "I'm going over to Chet McCullough's and find out what he's done with my Gertrude. You coming with me or what?"

The sheriff moved to intercept him. I stood by the tub, scanning the area in all directions. The nearest cover was twenty-five to thirty yards away. Hard for someone to have crossed that distance without being noticed. How had Sean Tate not seen his attacker?

Finally, Sheriff Block left Duke and headed, not for his own car, but for my unit—motioning me to follow. He moved to the driver's side and held out his hand for the keys. It rankled, having my ride taken over that way, but I bit my tongue and got in on the passenger side.

"I'm leaving my car here so Duke will know I'm coming straight back," he explained, then went through the process of adjusting the seat and mirrors. "Damn, Lopez. How short are you?"

"You could have saved yourself the trouble and let me drive." I was pushing it a little but he let it go. We pulled out of Duke's driveway and headed west, away from town.

"We're going out to Chet McCullough's place. See what he has to say about all this."

"Why does Duke think McCullough took his goat?"

The sheriff snorted. "Because the Fair's a month away."

My expression must have told him I was clueless.

"Duke Stamper and Chet McCullough have been competing with each other since they were boys. Who had the fastest car. Prettiest girl. Best hunting dog. They got into shooting contests—rifles, slingshots, hell, even crossbows. And every hunting season it was who got the biggest buck. Then they got into livestock, showing 'em at the Fair. Whatever one of them did, the other one had to top him. Last few years it's been dairy goats, Nubians...and Duke's Gertrude took the blue ribbon the last three years running. Didn't go down well with Chet."

I sat there, digesting what he'd told me. One word kept echoing in my head. "Sheriff, you said they were good with slingshots."

"Yeah, slingshots, rifles—"

"Couldn't a slingshot deliver enough of a blow to knock a man out and leave a wound that would need to be stitched? There was plenty of cover near the house, close enough to where Sean Tate was hit. A man with a slingshot...if he was good enough..."

Block cast me a sideways look as he drove. He was quiet long enough for me to wonder if I'd put my foot in it.

"Yeah. Chet McCullough would have had no trouble taking Sean out with a slingshot from that distance. Good thinking, Lopez."

I admit it. I puffed up some at his words. I knew I wasn't the sheriff's first choice for my position. I wasn't local—and that was big with him—plus I was short, with more curves than this uniform was designed for, and I had a two-year degree in law enforcement from a community college, but no experience. That put me at the bottom of the candidate list. But the town council was under pressure to hire some minorities and I was female *and* Hispanic. Two boxes checked for the price of one. So my minority status got me in. Now I had to prove I belonged.

Chet McCullough was the mirror opposite of Stamper. Five nine and rangy. Reddish hair going thin in front. His voice was low and slow and probably a pleasure to listen to when he wasn't mad. Right now, he was mad.

"That's a crock of bull, Walt, and you know it. I didn't touch Duke Stamper's goat. And I sure as hell didn't whack that hired hand of his. Didn't need to. My Frances is come into her own this year and I'm gonna beat Duke Stamper fair and square. You watch and see."

"I hear you, Chet, but someone put Sean Tate in the hospital and run off with Gertrude, and Duke's right sure it was you. It'd help if you let us look around some."

McCullough had met us at the gravel drive in front of his house but I could see the usual outbuildings and a couple pens in the back.

"What the hell. Knock yourselves out. You ain't finding no missing goat here."

I believed him. About finding Gertrude, that is. He wasn't stupid enough to have a stolen goat someplace where we'd come across it. He walked us through the barn, opened a shed that held various farm equipment, and stopped by a pen that held a pair of goats. As with Duke, they were both female and looked like Nubians to me.

"This is Frances." McCullough gestured toward the larger of the two girls, beaming with fatherly pride. "See? Why would I be messing with Duke Stamper's stock? My girl's the sure winner this year.

She looked pretty much like all the others to me.

"Yeah, she's a fine looking goat," the sheriff agreed. "We'll be going now. Thank you for letting us look around."

We cut across the yard, passing close to the back of the house. There was a large covered porch with a pair of high back rockers. Under one, lying on the wood floor, was a really nice slingshot. I caught the sheriff's eye and nodded toward it. He gave me a short nod back but didn't say anything. I guess there was no point in letting Chet McCullough know we'd seen it. Wasn't like we could take it in for a ballistics test or check McCullough for slingshot residue.

"What do you think?" Block asked me as we left the McCullough place behind.

What *did* I think? "Well, I don't think not finding Gertrude there means anything."

He grunted what sounded like agreement.

"I think if McCullough really believes he's got a winning goat, he'd want Gertrude at the Fair…so he could beat Duke outright. But that could have been all smoke. If he's not sure, he gets Gertrude out of the way, his goat wins, and he can still claim he would have beaten her." I went over the rest of it in my mind. "There was the slingshot. But if he used it on Sean Tate, it seems a little careless to leave it sitting in plain sight like that."

"Or cocky."

I waited for more, but the sheriff just pursed his lips in silence. The A/C was almost too cold as it dried the sweaty dampness of my shirt. I crossed my arms over my breasts then quickly lowered them for fear the gesture might be misinterpreted as defiance.

The sheriff drove back to Duke's and left me to re-adjust my seat and mirrors while he went inside. I sat there a couple minutes, debating what to do next, then headed back to County General. The doctor that had treated Sean Tate was still on duty. I managed to pull him aside for a couple quick questions and got the confirmation I was looking for. Yes, Sean's injury could have been caused by a projectile from a slingshot, even from thirty yards away.

I went upstairs and found Sean watching football in his room. He was gentleman enough to mute the sound when I came in.

"Any sign of Gertie?"

I got the feeling Sean, unlike Duke, was genuinely concerned about the goat and not just the upcoming competition. "Not yet. You know your boss thinks Chet McCullough took her. How about you?"

"No. Not if he got a good look at her."

"What do you mean?"

"Well, I'm not saying he wouldn't have whacked me on the head, but if he'd seen Gertrude, he would have left her and laughed himself back to his place."

"I don't follow."

"I told you. Gertie got into something, I'm not sure what, and she was having a bad reaction to it. Her skin was all inflamed and her coat was coming off in patches. No way Duke could have taken her to the Fair that way."

Oh crap. I'd missed that. "But I thought the judging was based on milk production or butter fat or something like that."

"Well, that's part of it, but a lot of the judging is based on appearance, and the condition of her coat counts."

Yeah, I should have figured. It's never enough for a woman to do the work, she has to look good while she's doing it. "So if Chet McCullough had seen Gertrude up close, he would have known she couldn't beat his goat this year, so there'd be no reason to take her."

"Well, that's what he would have thought."

"But…?"

Sean lifted himself up and leaned forward, his eyes dancing. "I'm taking night classes, training to be a vet tech. I took some pictures of Gertie's rash into my teacher and we came up with a medicine bath, you know, to treat her. And it was working. By Fair time, she would have been right as rain."

A light bulb went on. "The gloves. You started to tell me before…it was the medicine you didn't want to touch? Is it dangerous?"

"No. Not at all. But it's hard to wash off. Especially the B12 compound."

I remembered the water in Gertrude's bath. "It's oily."

This time he laughed. Dang, he *was* cute. "Not just that. It can be really spooky later on."

I lifted one eyebrow.

"It will glow in the dark. Or at least under black light. I remember the first time I washed her with it…" With the mention of Gertrude, a shadow fell

81

across his face and he dropped back against the pillows. "I was really looking forward to telling Mr. Stamper. Now I'm not sure if I should."

"He didn't know? That she was getting better?"

Sean sighed. "I wanted to surprise him."

I returned to the station in time to see Sheriff Block striding across the small parking lot heading for the street. He waved at me to join him.

"Come on, Lopez. You might as well be in on this."

I had to break into a light jog to keep up. "Where are we going?"

"Just got a call. Duke and Chet are getting into it outside Dewey's Pub."

One block over. That explained why we were walking.

The crowd that had gathered spilled off the sidewalk and into the street, with cars trying to wind their way slowly around. At Block's signal we went to deal with the traffic first.

"Okay, all you people out of the street. Back on the sidewalk. Back on the sidewalk." The sheriff never needed a bullhorn. I worked the outer edge of the crowd, one person at a time, and herded them out of the street while he unsnarled the evening traffic. Then Block moved into the crowd which parted for him like the Red Sea and I followed in his wake.

"I knew it would come to this," Duke was yelling. "That you'd resort to cheating instead of taking another loss. But I never thought you'd stoop so low as to steal my Gertrude."

"I didn't steal your damn goat," Chet fired back. "I didn't have to. My Frances is going to take that blue ribbon this year."

Some of the crowd were supporting Duke, some were for Chet, but I think most were just enjoying the show. A little entertainment at the end of a long, hot day.

Duke appealed to his supporters. "You all hear this? You hear what he's done? Come Fair time, Chet McCullough needs to be disqualified. He's a cheater."

"Duke Stamper, you s-o-b, I'm about to knock those crazy lies of yours back down your damn throat."

They were circling each other, fists clenched, about ready to go at it. Duke had the size but my money was on Chet. Or maybe I just liked rooting for the little guy. It became a moot point when the sheriff shoved his way between them.

"All right, knock it off. *Now.*"

The two separated but continued to make threatening gestures around Block.

"I'm not letting him get away with this," Duke blustered.

"And I ain't taking any more of his wild accusations."

"If you don't settle down, I'm going to run you in for disturbing the peace, the both of you."

They stopped yelling for a moment and I saw my opening.

"Sheriff, if it's okay with you, I think I can settle this."

Block gave me a curious look. "Okay, Lopez. What have you got?"

Everything quieted and all eyes were on me. I said a quick prayer that this was going to work.

"You know that Sean Tate was giving Gertrude a bath at the time of the…goat-napping." There was a general murmur of agreement. "In fact, when he arrived at the hospital, he was wearing gloves, like surgical gloves. I asked him about it and he told me he was using a special shampoo on Gertrude that he'd made up himself. He didn't want to get it on his hands because it was really hard to wash off, especially a couple ingredients that would glow under a black light. He said his hands would glow for a day or two, no matter how much he washed them."

"Fine." Chet McCullough pushed forward. "Get a damn black light. Check my hands."

"That wouldn't prove anything," Duke countered. "He could have been wearing gloves. Like Sean."

I turned to Duke. "I wasn't going to test his hands, Mr. Stamper. I want to test yours."

Everything went still and Block narrowed his eyes at me. "Lopez."

"Sheriff, I have reason to believe it was Duke Stamper who assaulted Sean Tate and took Gertrude. Plus, just now when I mentioned Sean's shampoo staining his hands, Duke slid his into his pockets."

"This is bullshit. Why would I steal my own goat?"

"Because you didn't want her to lose at the Fair. Gertrude has a skin condition," I explained to the others. "She was losing her fur. She wasn't…showable. And he didn't have another goat to go up against Mr. McCullough's Frances."

"Well, I'll be damned," McCullough said quietly.

All the bluster went out of Duke Stamper. He slumped and gestured helplessly. "It wasn't that. I just didn't want to put Gertrude through the humiliation of losing. The girl's always been a champion."

"She might have been this year, too" I told him. "That medicine Sean's been using on her? It's working. He thinks she'll be ready to show by Fair time."

Duke opened his mouth as if to answer me then just shook his head.

"Where's Gertrude?" the sheriff asked Duke.

"At my cousin's. Over in Wyan County."

"Hey, Sheriff," Chet McCullough broke in quietly. "I'm okay with just letting this whole thing go."

The sheriff shook his head. "Not your call, Chet. Duke put Sean Tate in the hospital, and he's got to answer for that." He gave me a rueful smile. "Deputy Lopez, you broke this one. It's your collar."

"Yes sir." I pulled out my cuffs and stepped behind Duke. "Duke Stamper, you're under arrest for assault…"

LD Masterson lived on both coasts before becoming landlocked in Ohio. After twenty years managing computers for the American Red Cross, she now divides her time between writing and enjoying her grandchildren. Her short stories have been published in numerous anthologies and magazines and she's currently working on her second novel. LD is a member of Mystery Writers of America, Sisters in Crime, and the Western Ohio Writers' Association. ldmasterson.author.blogspot.com OR ldmasterson.com

NO SAFE PLACE

Harriette Sackler

Trench huddled in the recessed doorway of a dilapidated store front. It was an area of town filled with businesses that had seen better days and abandoned buildings deserted by bankrupt merchants. Logan, his black lab and only friend in the world, lay beside him and their shared body heat kept them warm. They slept, but their rest was tempered by the need for hypervigilance. They were never safe.

Trench was awakened by Logan's low, throaty growl. He gently touched the dog's soft muzzle to signal silence. They waited.

It was only a moment before they heard the *thwack* of an object hitting another. Then moans and cries of pain. Trench knew what the sounds meant. Another street person had been victimized. Nothing unusual. It happened all the time. After dark, predators stalked the streets, beating the hell out of poor souls who had nowhere to go and very little to live for. These wretched people owned nothing but the clothes they wore and the refuse of others that they salvaged from trash bins. And yet, there were some who targeted them for vicious attacks just for the fun of it.

When all he heard was soft whimpering from down the block, Trench rose and, with Logan at his side, quietly walked toward the sound. Damn, it was Pops, a harmless old drunk who'd been on the street for the better part of his life. Blood seeped from a cut on his head.

"Hey, Pops, can you hear me?" Trench lightly shook the old man, trying to determine the extent of his wounds.

"I hurt so bad, dammit," Pops mumbled. "Wasn't doin' nothing. Just sleepin'." Pops' voice faded as he lost consciousness.

"Hold on, buddy. I'll get help." Trench rose to his feet.

Phone booths were a thing of the past, and even if they weren't, they'd be vandalized in this part of town. Trench, didn't have a cell. He usually didn't have anyone to call. But he knew where he could go and find someone to get Pops to a hospital.

Trench and Logan quickly walked the three blocks to Blessed Sacrament, the Catholic Church that provided food and emergency shelter for the area's homeless. Father Pat, a kind and understanding cleric, lived in the rectory and let it be known that he was always available, no matter when. Trench had reluctantly formed a bond with the priest, who listened to him and never judged. Father Pat had served as an army chaplain during Desert Storm, and Trench was able to talk to him about Afghanistan, the nightmares, guilt, and inability to settle back into the life he'd left back home. Call it what you wanted. It didn't matter. War could ruin a guy's life and leave him adrift in a world where he no longer fit in.

Trench rang the rectory's doorbell. In short order, Father Pat stood before him, tying the belt of his robe and then running fingers through his unruly gray hair.

"Trench, come in. Come in. You, too, Logan." Father Pat stepped aside and let the man and his dog enter. "Is something wrong? It's not like you to pay a visit in the middle of the night. Not that I mind, you know."

"It's Pops, Father. That poor old guy had the shit beat out of him. He needs a hospital fast."

Father Pat's face registered his concern and anger. "Not another one! When will it stop? Go into my office and call 9-1-1 while I get dressed. Leave Logan here in the den. Then we'll head out."

Trench and Father Pat arrived at Municipal Hospital's emergency department just minutes after Pops had been brought in by the EMTs. A critical care team had already begun the process of assessing his condition and attempting to stabilize him. There was no one who could give Trench and Father Pat any information until there was something definitive to report, so they left their names at the front desk and took seats in the waiting room, anticipating a long night ahead.

"Trench, since you've been on the street, how many guys have been assaulted? Ten? Twenty? More?" Father Pat asked.

"Jeez, I haven't been counting, but I can tell you that it happens way too often. They sure as hell don't have much to steal. They keep to themselves. They can't defend themselves. But someone has it out for them."

After six months on the street, Trench still didn't count himself among the street people. For him, it was temporary, not a way of life. When he returned home from deployment, he just couldn't settle in to the life he'd lived before. He was different. He couldn't pretend he wasn't. Trench had tried to adjust to being back home, but he no longer related to the predictable and ordinary days that loomed ahead. He didn't sleep, and he wasn't able to talk about his feelings. And Trench needed to handle it his own way. With Logan, his best friend and partner, he headed for the anonymity of the big city streets.

Two hours passed before a haggard and rumpled doctor came into the waiting room, looking for the family or friends of Charles Evans. When no one responded to his inquiry, he elaborated by adding, "brought in from Vine near Fifth."

Father Pat and Trench both rose from their seats and joined the doctor.

"How is he, Doctor?" the cleric asked.

"Well, your friend took quite a beating. He's elderly, frail, and not in the best of health. Past hospital records indicate that Mr. Evans is homeless and has lived on the street for many years. Is that correct?"

"Yes, it is," Father Pat said. "We know him as Pops. He's lived downtown for as long as I can remember."

"Well, it's apparent that Mr. Evans was beaten with an object, most likely a heavy stick or club. His clavicle is broken, as well as several ribs and his left shoulder. Most worrisome are the blows to his head, which resulted in a fracture to his posterior skull. We're monitoring him for intracranial swelling or bleeds. We should know more in about twelve hours. For now, his breaks have been tended to, and he's resting ."

"Have the police been here yet?" Father Pat asked.

"Not that I know of. But, in any instance of assault, they come in at some point. In the meantime, feel free to call me with questions and to check when you'll be able to see Mr. Evans. Just ask for Dr. Staples. Oh, by the way, do you know if he has any family we can contact?"

"I'm sorry, Doctor, I don't. All too often the homeless lose touch with families and are pretty much on their own." Father Pat knew of many instances where the homeless in his parish had faced crises and death with no one to care about them.

Trench and Father Pat left the hospital and walked toward Blessed Sacrament.

"I'm going to visit with the police precinct commander in the morning," Father Pat said. "I want to know what's being done to find out who's assaulting these men. Why don't you stay at the rectory tonight, Trench? You can shower, shave and have a comfortable night's sleep and then go with me to the station tomorrow."

"Thanks, Father. Sounds good. I know Logan would enjoy a night indoors." This wouldn't be the first time Trench and Logan stayed at the rectory. None of the shelters would permit pets on the premises, so on bitter cold nights, they camped out with Father Pat.

The following morning, after a hearty breakfast prepared by Mrs. Taylor, the rectory's housekeeper, Trench and Father Pat headed out. Logan was sprawled on the sofa in the den, as content as he could be and basking in the welcome attention from the priest and Mrs. Taylor. Trench knew that his best buddy deserved to be part of a family.

When Trench and Father Pat arrived at precinct headquarters, it was only a five-minute wait before they were ushered into Captain Edward Miller's office. They were offered seats which they accepted and coffee which they declined.

Captain Miller rose from his chair to shake hands with each of his visitors. He was a large man with a strong presence that reflected his authority, tempered by a warm smile.

"Father, it's good to see you again. I hope all is well."

"Likewise, Captain. Thank you for taking the time to meet with us on such short notice."

"My pleasure. My pleasure. I'm always happy to see old friends. And who might this be?" The Captain looked toward Trench.

"This is another friend of mine," said the priest. May I introduce David Trench, a decorated veteran who served three tours in Afghanistan. We've had the opportunity to get to know each other over the past six months, and I can say he is truly a fine young man."

"Mr. Trench, it's a pleasure to meet you. Welcome home, and thank you for your service.
Now, how can I be of help to you?"

Father Pat glanced at Trench, then began to talk.

"Captain, last night an elderly homeless man was viciously attacked while he lay sleeping in front of a building on Vine Street. Luckily Trench was nearby and able to quickly get to the rectory to alert me. We called 9-1-1, and the poor man was taken to the hospital where he has been admitted in critical condition. For the hours that we sat in the emergency room, no officers came by to take a report. And, as you know, this is not a solitary case. There have been numerous other assaults on the homeless in the past months. I wanted to inquire about the steps that are being taken to apprehend the person or persons who are responsible for these attacks. They have all taken place in my parish, and I'm extremely concerned for the safety of potential victims."

The captain was silent for a moment. When he spoke, he looked at Trench.

"Mr. Trench, may I ask why you were in the vicinity last night? That area of town is generally deserted after businesses shut their doors, except for the homeless who visit the shelters in the area or sleep on the streets."

Trench deliberated furnishing the captain with information about his personal situation, but then decided it was necessary for the precinct commander to know.

"Captain, I'm one of the homeless that spend their nights on the street. My best friend and companion is my military working dog who I adopted after we both ended our last tour of duty. Shelters don't allow dogs in their buildings, and I won't leave Logan under any condition.
So we stay together on the street."

"I see," said the captain. "If you don't mind my asking, don't you have family that can help you out?"

"I do," Trench answered. "But when I came home, I didn't fit in anymore. I wasn't the same person. I needed to go off alone until I could work things out. From what I hear, a lot of guys do the same thing. Like a wounded animal, you could say."

"Mr. Trench, I truly wish you well. We have any number of officers who have come home in much the same way. I'm happy to say that they've been able to recover and move on. I hope that will be the case with you. Now, Father, let me answer your question."

The captain rose from his seat and turned to gaze out the window behind his desk. He clasped his hands behind his back and began to speak.

"Assaults on the homeless are difficult cases to crack. First of all, they tend to be sporadic so we never know when they'll occur. For that reason, it doesn't make sense to place an undercover officer out there. It would be poor use of manpower and resources with the likelihood of negative results. Second, the homeless community is very insular. They keep to themselves and, more frustrating, they avoid interaction with law enforcement. They don't always trust us, and with good reason, I might add. We roust them from their campsites, arrest them for vagrancy, public intoxication, and panhandling in front of businesses and on crowded streets. Too many officers view the homeless as nuisances and useless. Overall, it's a bad situation."

The captain returned to his seat. "We know there are those who prey on the homeless. Kids come into the city with the intent of beating up a bum, just because they can. There are others who, homeless themselves, will attack one of their own for small change, a warm blanket, or a bottle of cheap wine. Believe me, I want to help, but just haven't figured out how to do it."

After a short silence, Father Pat spoke. "Ed, you're a good man. We've known each other for twenty-five years, and I've never doubted your honesty and integrity. Is there anything we can do to help?"

The captain leaned back in his chair, clasped his hands over his middle, and looked up toward the ceiling. When his gaze returned to the two men, he spoke. "Yes. As a matter of fact, I think there is. But, mind you, it's your decision. Trench, you could act as a Neighborhood Watch in the area where most of the assaults have taken place. Your dog is also military and would have your back. I'd provide you with a cell, so that you can report suspicious activity right away. I'd instruct my officers to respond immediately to your alert. Father, if you would let Trench come by the rectory each day to charge the phone and keep you apprised of events that would be a good thing. You can also reach out to the homeless with the message that the police are working to keep them safe. I think they'll listen to you."

Trench hesitated before answering. This wasn't at all what he had in mind when he took to the streets. He sought solitude and anonymity as a way to heal, not police work. But how could he say no? It wasn't in him.

"I'm on board, Captain," he said.

After leaving the precinct, armed with a police issued cell phone, Father Pat and Trench walked the short distance to the hospital to check on Pops. They were informed that the patient had been transferred to the critical care unit, so they rode the elevator to the fourth floor and inquired at the nurses' station about Pops. One of the nurses seated at the desk looked up from her computer and smiled .

"Let me page Dr. Staples for you. He'll be able to give you an update."

Within minutes, the doctor appeared and directed them to a small lounge only a few feet away.

"Mr. Evans is in very serious condition. The trauma to his head has resulted in damage, hopefully temporary, which has left him disoriented and unaware of his surroundings. Because of his generally poor physical condition, it is likely that the various bone fractures he suffered will be slow to heal, and even then, he will always have difficulty with ambulation. He cannot go back to the streets. Our social worker is attempting to locate any relatives Mr. Evans may have. If she's unsuccessful, it's likely he'll be placed in a state facility or nursing home."

"Has he said anything at all about the assault?" Father Pat asked.

"The nurses say Mr. Evans has uttered the same word over and over again: 'Blue. Blue.' Nothing else."

Both Trench and Father Pat looked puzzled. *Blue.* Was that a person's name? The color of a car or a piece of clothing? Or maybe nothing at all to do with the attack. Neither knew the answer.

"Can we visit with Pops?" asked Trench.

"I'm afraid not," Dr. Staples responded. He's been heavily sedated so he can rest and heal. It will be days, if not longer before he'll be out of the woods. Why don't you check in with me in a few days? I'll be able to speak more definitively then. And if there's any change in his condition, I'll give you a call."

When they arrived at the rectory, they found Logan in front of the fireplace in the den chewing on an enormous bone. His tail wagged at the sight of the two men, but he continued chomping on his wonderful new possession.

Mrs. Taylor was sitting in a rocking chair not far from Logan. "I hope you don't mind, Mr. Trench. When I went food shopping this morning, I got a bone from the butcher. Logan seems to be enjoying himself so."

"Not at all, Mrs. Taylor. It's good to see him so content. He certainly deserves it."

Mrs. Taylor had a delicious lunch of soup and sandwiches prepared for them. Chocolate chip cookies still warm from the oven and steaming hot coffee completed the meal.

"Trench, why don't you get some sleep before heading out tonight?" Father Pat asked.

"Sounds good. I want to be alert while I'm on duty."

More than a week went by without incident. Trench and Logan periodically patrolled the downtown area that served as the night refuge for so many of the area's homeless. No strangers walked the streets, and its inhabitants slept undisturbed. While Trench hoped that the area had seen the last of the violence, deep inside he knew it was unrealistic to expect such an abrupt end to the attacks. Logan also remained vigilant. His unshakeable bond with Trench made him an extraordinary partner. More times than Trench could count, Logan had alerted him to the presence of enemy snipers, hidden explosives, and other life-threatening danger.

On the eighth night of patrol, Trench heard a scuffle from a doorway about half a block away. Logan tensed, and emitted a low, barely audible growl. Trench held his lead firmly, and they both walked forward. The figure bent over the pile of rags on the ground was so engaged in what he was doing, that he didn't hear them approaching.

"Get the hell away from him," shouted Trench. "Back up now, and I mean now!"

When the figure turned toward the man and his dog, Trench gasped. The assailant was dressed all in blue. But not just any blue clothing. A police uniform. He held a nightstick in his hand, and the smirk on his face reflected pure hatred.

"Move along, you worthless piece of trash, or you'll be next." As he spoke, he withdrew a revolver from his gun belt and pointed it at Trench.

"I'd have no problem blowing you away, along with your mangy dog. A cop resisting an attack and taking out one more piece of useless garbage littering our streets."

Trench reacted as he did in combat.

"Logan, attack!" he yelled, dropping the dog's lead. Logan immediately flew through the air, landing on the cop and taking him down. He sank his teeth into the arm that had been holding the gun. The officer screamed at the top of his lungs, but Logan didn't let go.

Trench pulled out the phone he'd been given and dialed 9-1-1, reciting the special instructions he'd been told to use. In a matter of minutes, the sound of sirens filled the air.

The rogue cop was arrested and later charged with multiple counts of felony assault. . The police released information about his work history that revealed he'd been cited for the use of excessive force on numerous occasions. He had no friends on the force. The disgraced officer showed no remorse for his actions, but rather ranted about the human detritus littering the streets. His words were met with disgust. Captain Miller, as well as the police commissioner and mayor, denounced him and vowed that justice would be done. The poor soul who was saved from the final beating had so many blankets wrapped around him, he suffered only minor injuries.

Shortly thereafter, Pops finally began to improve and was transferred to a rehabilitation center.

The story of the veteran and his military working dog went viral. They were hailed as true heroes, both on and off the battlefield. And a public cry demanded better post-deployment services for both human and canine warriors.

Every day, the media congregated in front of the rectory, hoping for an interview with Trench. They weren't even rewarded with a glimpse of him or of Logan.

On the fourth day of the vigil, Father Pat appeared before the men and women of the media and gave a statement.

"Ladies and gentlemen, David Trench thanks you for your interest. But he is not a man who seeks recognition or accolades for doing the right thing. He just wishes to live his life quietly and in private. He asks that instead on focusing on him and his partner Logan, you focus on the plight of this country's soldiers, both human and canine, as they return home from life-changing experiences overseas. He also asks that you spread the word about the growing number of people who are homeless in this country, many of them returning soldiers. For these reasons, he will not be delivering a statement himself."

Father Pat spent quite a bit of time answering questions, but did not divulge the one piece of information he would release in several days.

David Trench and Logan were no longer at the rectory. They had gone home.

Harriette Sackler serves as Grants Chair of the Malice Domestic Board of Directors. She is a multi-published, two-time Agatha Award nominee for Best Short Story. As principal of the Dames of Detection, Harriette is co-publisher and editor at Level Best Books. She is a member of Mystery Writers of America, Sisters in Crime, Sisters in Crime-Chesapeake Chapter, the Guppies, and the Crime Writers' Association. Harriette is the proud mom of two fabulous daughters and Nana to four grandbabies. She lives with her husband in the D.C. suburbs. Visit Harriette at www.harriettesackler.com

LAST CALL FOR BUFFALO

Randall DeWitt

Standing on the sidewalk in front of the latest sports bar to open in downtown Buffalo, I wondered what asshole thought this was a good idea. I walked up to the entrance, decorated by artwork depicting a cartoonish yellow field goal post with a football sailing by on the right, and drew a deep breath. More than twenty-five years had passed since that horrible night. With a shove of my hands on the heavy wood doors, the gates of hell swung open revealing what promised to be the most difficult reporting assignment of my life.

Everyone knows that O. J. Simpson played for the Buffalo Bills. What's not widely known is that he was their all-time leading scorer until the team's field goal kicker came along and surpassed him. Yet, it's the kicker's name, Scott Norwood, not the alleged killer's that invokes a visceral reaction in Bills fans. Strange as it seems, missing a game-winning field goal by only a foot or so wide right against the Giants in Super Bowl XXV, with only four seconds remaining, is more notorious in these parts than anything O. J. was ever accused of doing off the field. Why anyone *ever* would open a bar in downtown Buffalo dedicated to that precise moment in time was completely incomprehensible. Every place I looked, a picture or piece of memorabilia from that game stared back. Of that field goal try. Of Scott Norwood. Of the jubilant Giants. Behind the bar. Over the bar. Everywhere. God only knows what the men's and ladies' rooms were like.

What was the owner of this place thinking?

Remembering to breathe, I walked over to the deserted bar and wedged myself in between a couple of stools, confident that I wouldn't need either of them. I wouldn't be there long enough. All I needed was to find out what mental hospital had recently discharged this purveyor of pigskin perversion and I could go back to the office and write my piece. I called out back with a hello that echoed throughout the bar with loneliness and despair.

I looked at my watch just to confirm that it was still lunchtime. Every other pub or restaurant in this prime area of downtown would be crowded with patrons, finishing up their burgers or wings, as still others waited for the next available table or seat. The sounds of plates and glasses being cleared from tables would be punctuating the constant drone of dozens of conversations. But in this place, get rid of all the obnoxious material on the walls, stack the tables and chairs up at one end of the bar, and it would be easy to confuse it with a storage facility for unwanted "bartifacts."

"Can I help you?"

93

The voice startled me. I'd been so engrossed in the vast emptiness of this place, so devoid of any customers, I'd somehow let someone sneak up on me. I looked at the stocky man behind the voice. He was a tough looking guy, neatly dressed.

"Are you the owner?" I asked.

The man nodded.

"I'm Tim Hannigan. My editor called about an interview."

"Great. What would you like to know?"

Somehow I resisted asking him outright if he was out of his mind. "Maybe a little background information about yourself and—"

"Why a Super Bowl XXV themed bar in downtown Buffalo?"

"Exactly," I replied.

"Take a seat. Would you like a beer?" he offered.

"No thanks," I said, refusing to sit down. "I won't be here long."

"Suit yourself."

The corner of the man's mouth curled so subtly it was almost undetectable, unlike his accent. I'd earned my journalism degree at Northeastern, so I was more than familiar with the nuances of the Boston accent, even one as minimal as his. He wasn't fooling anyone just because he made an effort to pronounce his Rs. Sure enough, he introduced himself as Frank Shaunnessy, an ex-cop from Lowell—a city north of Beantown that I'd been to more than a few times.

"So, what possesses someone like yourself to come all the way out here to Buffalo and open a bar like this?" I asked. "I mean, you do realize that the people around here still aren't over the game you've got plastered all over your walls, don't you?"

"I do," he replied. "But that game changed my life."

This ought to be good. He won a million dollars betting on the Giants, or was in Tampa to watch the game and met his wife from Buffalo there, or the ghost of a dead relative made Norwood miss that field goal, or—

"That game nearly killed me," he said lifting his shirt, displaying scars I can only describe as an impressive game of connect the dots. His finger pointed from one spot to the next three times. "These four were where the bullets went in."

I pulled out the bar stool to my right and sat down. For the first time since entering the place, I realized there was more to this bar than just a gloating Giants fan's attempt to hook up Buffalo's collective testicles to a car battery. The curl that had only teased at the corner of Frank's mouth seconds ago was now somewhere in between a suppressed smirk and an all-out shit-eating grin. He'd known all along that I wasn't going anywhere until I'd heard the whole story.

"There's coffee on if you'd rather," he said, "or did you change your mind about that beer?"

"Anything on tap will do," I replied.

As Frank poured my beer, I tried to find the journalistic side of me that I'd obviously left outside on the sidewalk tied up to a fire hydrant. I retrieved a small notepad and pen from my back pocket and scribbled to catch up on the comments I'd already missed. In the time it had taken to fill a glass of beer and place it in front of me, Frank was already taking me on a virtual tour of Lowell and raising points of interest along the way.

One moment he was at Cawley Stadium, talking about how the stub-footed kicker Tom Dempsey used to play semi-pro ball there before making it to the big leagues with the Saints and kicking the NFL's first 63-yard field goal. The next, he was at a sports bar on Market Street. Having made many road trips to the bars in Lowell during my college days, I was more than familiar with the places he was talking about.

At the time, my attention would've been focused on the girls from UMass-Lowell that came out to drink on Friday nights. But I could picture the place, summed up by red brick walls with Red Sox, Bruins, and Patriots memorabilia displayed everywhere, pretty standard stuff for a Boston area sports bar. The bristle dartboards were in one corner, well lit, much like most of us college students—a mix of both legal and underage drinkers with fake ID's, and a handful of large, cathode ray tube televisions supported in heavy-duty brackets hung from the ceiling in various strategic locations.

"Of course, I spent a lot of time there because I owned the place," he was saying.

Wait. What?

"I thought you said you were a Lowell cop?"

"I did," he replied. "I didn't say I was a good one."

Caught off guard a second time, I tried to conceal my surprise with a sip of beer. So far, I was looking more like a preschooler spellbound at the library listening to story time than a reporter with nearly two decades of experience. I tried to formulate a question and get it out, but Frank made certain I didn't get the chance.

"Oh yeah, you're looking at a dirty cop. Not because I owned a bar while I was on the Lowell Police Department. And it wasn't because I took bribes, fixed tickets, or anything like that either."

"So what was it then?" I managed to jump in and ask, my timing feeling off. Again, I attempted to cover my presumed awkwardness—this time, however, by downing half the glass in front of me.

"I'm getting to that," Frank said, turning and walking back over to the taps to pour another beer.

I could tell he really enjoyed leaving me in suspense. I started to wonder whether his timing was natural or if he was following a script for a one-man act he was developing. Either way, the dramatic pause worked. He literally had me on the edge of the bar stool I once thought unnecessary.

Frank grabbed a fresh glass, tilted it under the spigot and pulled the lever back. When he was done, he came back and placed the beer down on a fresh coaster in front of me. I chugged down the last mouthfuls of the first beer and then waited as Frank snatched up the empty glass, placing it into a gray plastic bus tub.

"Hey, you hungry?" he asked. "I could fire up the kitchen and whip something up for you."

"No, thanks," I said, wondering what surprise he'd have in store for me back there. Gourmet grilled cheese...black and blue burgers...crab cakes...pan roasted squab?

"Anyway, I was telling you about being a cop. Any cops in your family, Tim?"

I shook my head.

"In the Police Academy, everything is pretty black and white. But when you graduate and go out on your first patrol, you quickly learn the job doesn't always work that way."

If I was writing a piece on how my taxpayer dollars don't always seem to afford me with the proper respect I deserved from the police, I would've had a whole slew of questions for him. Like, how come *I'm* the idiot when they were the ones who just waved me through an accident scene at the same time a fire fighter is yelling at me to stop? Or, why do I get pulled over in a supermarket parking lot because it's almost dusk and my lights aren't on, yet they watch but don't stop a car that passes me on a stretch of road with a double solid yellow? Or, how come when someone steals a bag of Skittles from Walmart, it requires an all out response complete with flashing lights and sirens, but when someone runs over my hand-carved novelty squirrel mailbox, no one shows up for over an hour?

My attention reverted back to Frank and the decline of his once idyllic police values. As I listened to one of Lowell's ex-finest expound on his lost virtues, I didn't give another thought to my many frustrations with the Buffalo Police Department. I've often been accused of not letting things go. In my defense, the cops could've at least acted interested in catching the culprit who'd made road kill of the wooden rodent that collected my mail at the end of the driveway. I swear a three-legged bloodhound blinded by cataracts, with olfactory senses so stopped-up it couldn't smell extra-strength Mentholatum would've been more useful.

"In my case," Frank was saying, "I crawled into a bottle whenever I wasn't working a shift. Until, that is, this hot, little badge bunny hooked me and I straightened myself out long enough to get married. But it didn't last. It wasn't long before I was drinking all night again and divorced."

Finally, something I could relate to. But my marriage didn't end because I drank too much. It was because I drank too little. There were too many times I'd faced down my ex, sober, after she'd gone on a shopping spree, or had broken the vacuum cleaner for the tenth time by running over its cord. There was a reason I didn't let her trim our shrubs with the electric hedge clippers. If I did, my 100-foot extension cord could probably be measured with a couple turns of a yardstick.

"Any kids?" I asked.

"No."

So much for my theory he'd moved from the allure of Nor'easters to the charm of lake effect snow to be near a son or a daughter.

"After the divorce, I decided to parlay my talent for drinking into buying the bar on Market Street. It was a natural fit."

"So what went wrong?" I asked.

"Nicky Gats."

"Who?"

"Nicky Gats," Frank repeated. "One of the area's biggest bookies. Someone introduced him to me, the next thing you know, he was in the bar all the time."

I'd never had a substance abuse problem, but I'd had my share of friends who did. In almost every case, there's a guy, always there with that next gram, eight-ball, or whatever. The kind of guy who's supposedly a good buddy but is really just a selfish bastard looking out for himself. Unfortunately, I knew the type all too well. My brother was "that guy" for years and, although he had most people fooled these days, he's still the same piece of shit he always was. I pitied Frank if Nicky Gats was anything like my brother. From what I was hearing, Nicky was my brother's doppelganger.

"Every Saturday, Nicky was in the bar taking my bets on college football, then on Sundays, the pros. I'd go up a thousand on him, then down a thousand and on and on like that through most of that fall. Then I hit a real cold streak."

"Something tells me Nicky didn't mind extending you credit so you could try to get even."

"Right up until the Super Bowl." He nodded, as the start of another one of his subtle grins formed. "By then I was into him for a hundred large and Nicky decided it was time to call in my debt."

"Giants versus the Bills," I blurted out as if somehow Frank had forgotten.

"I was so far in the hole with Nicky Gats, he owned me, Lowell cop or not. He'd set up shop in my bar and there wasn't a thing I could do about it. I'd gambled myself all the way to a role in racketeering."

"So what did you do?" I asked.

Frank smiled. He had no intention of giving up the answer without first dragging out the tension some more.

"The bar closed down at four o'clock to have a private party for the hundred people who'd bought into our Super Bowl pool at five hundred dollars a square. We put on a nice dinner for them. I mean, for that kind of money, they should at least get prime rib with a baked potato. Hey, you sure you're not hungry?"

Before I could answer, Frank told me to bring my beer out back to where he'd whip us up a couple of turkey clubs. By the time I'd come around the bar and met him in the kitchen area, he'd already started toasting the bread

97

and was taking out containers of fresh turkey, pre-cooked bacon, lettuce, and tomato from the refrigerator.

"When things begin to pick up around here, I'll have staff manning the kitchen full-time. In the meanwhile, I'm it. Anyway, where was I? The Super Bowl party had started and about an hour later Nicky strolled in like he already owned the place."

"What did you do? Bet your bar on the game?"

"I didn't have a hundred grand just sitting around to pay Nicky off with, and he wanted my bar so—"

"So you took the Giants... all or nothing for your bar?"

The toast popped up and Frank pulled six perfectly browned slices out, dropping them onto a cutting board. Then he started to pile on the turkey.

"Not exactly. I didn't want to just get even. I wanted Nicky to regret screwing with me. So I decided to parlay picking the winner with the over-under for a five to two payout. If I won, it'd pay off a quarter mil with the first hundred thou going to Nicky to square my debt."

I'd never been one to gamble much, wasting a buck or two every other week on lottery tickets was about all the money I'd ever put at risk. But even I knew that by parlaying his bet, keeping his bar was a lot less likely. The chances of picking the winning team in any football game is basically a coin flip. By saying he'd pick the over-under as well, Frank was betting he could call *two* coin tosses in a row, reducing his odds of winning to one in four.

Frank finished spreading the mayonnaise on the last of the toast, secured the pieces in place using those frilly-looking tooth picks with the ruffled plastic ends and then cut each turkey club into triangles. After shoveling the sandwiches and some chips onto two plates he'd taken down from a stainless steel storage shelf, he motioned for me to go back out to the bar with a nod toward the door.

"In case you don't remember," he reminded, "the over-under was forty and a half."

"And with eight seconds left in the game, and the score Giants 20, Bills 19," I confirmed, "everything came down to Norwood's field goal attempt. If the kick had been good, the Bills would've won with the over but, instead, the Giants won with the under."

"Now don't lose your appetite," Frank warned as he placed a plate and a folded cloth napkin in front of my spot at the bar.

"You picked the Giants and the under," I begrudged.

"I couldn't believe Norwood missed that field goal," he said. "It was practically a chip shot. Because he choked, I was getting my bar back and a big payout."

"I don't get it."

"What don't you get?"

"If you won the bet, then where's the problem?" I asked, still waiting to hear how the shooting figured in. If it turned out Frank was nothing more than a Giants fan who'd just duped me into listening to what it was like to be on the winning side of that kick, I would've considered shooting him myself. Granted, up until now it had been an okay story. But it wasn't the one I'd been sold on. If the ending to Frank's tale went something like—three weeks later he got drunk in Cancun and a Mariachi band member shot him because he wouldn't shut up about his winning bet—it was going to be a real disappointment. Unless, of course, I wanted to track down the pistola-packing musician and rewrite the piece from his point of view.

"Would you like another beer?"

I shook my head. I wanted to hear his answer without waiting for him to make another trip to the taps and back.

"It didn't take long for the bar to clear out once the game was over," he continued. "It'd been a hell of a party. The pool paid out for score changes, end of quarter scores and double for the final score. Everyone enjoyed themselves. I'm sure you won't find this hard to believe, but many of them were over-served."

"Were you drunk?" I asked.

"Not so bad that I couldn't throw my badge onto the dashboard and make it home all right. I let the bar staff go home as soon as the tables and counters were cleared. The rest of the cleanup could wait until the next morning. Nicky was still there, sitting with one of his goons at his usual booth in the back. I told him it was time to leave. That's when I found out Scott Norwood's kick wasn't the only thing that had missed wide right that night."

"I don't understand—"

"With all the noise in the bar, Nicky didn't hear my bet right. He insisted I'd picked the Giants and *the over*. He said I was going to sign my bar over to him or he'd put a bullet in my head."

What followed can only be described as a shootout reenactment every bit as good as the daily shows they put on at the O.K. Corral in Tombstone, Arizona.

The way Frank recounted the story, Nicky's threat escalated from colorful language to guns in seconds. Frank said he pulled out a gun he kept by the cash register, or in this case, a finger gun for demonstration purposes, and began popping up and down behind the bar, dodging imaginary bullets. His index finger returned fire once at Nicky and Nicky's cohort but missed. Frank spun and simulated being wounded twice but fought valiantly on. He jerked his thumb down at his finger and said that the fake shot found the center of the goon's chest, dropping him to the floor for good. Just then, Frank recoiled from another gunshot wound, but claimed to somehow exchange one more volley with Nicky. During the simultaneous shots, Frank took one to his chest. He pretended to stumble a few steps, then said he collapsed in a puddle of stale beer and blood.

"What happened to Nicky?" I asked, desperate to know the ending.

"The last I saw him before losing consciousness, he had a strange expression on his face. It must've been the bullet hole in the middle of his forehead." Frank wiped at the counter with a bar rag. "How's that club sandwich?"

How's my sandwich? I nodded as if a waitress had just asked me the same question while I had a mouthful of food.

"I nearly died from all the blood I lost," Frank continued after a brief pause. "It took me months to recover at a hospital in Boston."

"You were really lucky," I remarked, regretting it almost as soon as I said it.

"Was I? After a state police investigation, I was tried and convicted for my part in Nicky's bookmaking operation and spent three years in medium security at the Mass Correctional Institution in Concord, followed by one more in MCI Shirley. Oh yeah, and I lost my pension when I was fired from the police department."

"I guess that missed field goal really did change your life."

"It did," Frank replied. "But enough witnesses at the bar heard me pick the Giants with the under and no one could really blame me for killing Nicky in self-defense. And off the record, I knew enough about Nicky's business that my bet got paid off. How do you think I could afford this place?"

"You still haven't explained why you opened a Super Bowl XXV themed sports bar out here, in the middle of Buffalo," I pointed out.

"Well, the reason's this. Super Bowl XXV was a great game worth every bit of entertainment value, but it was only a game. There's more important things in life than whether a kicked football went between two uprights twenty-five years ago or not. Take it from someone who knows. It's time for Bills fans to let it go."

I finished up my beer and asked for my tab. Frank, of course, said it was on the house. I thanked him, then told him I'd be back.

"Make sure you tell your friends," he said with his now familiar, wry smile.

As I walked out those same wooden doors that had taunted me only an hour or so before, maybe it was the free beer and food, maybe it was the bright sunlight warming my face, but I felt optimistic for Buffalo, for the Bills, for Frank Shaunnessy and his downtown sports bar, *Wide Right*. Maybe we do all need to appreciate life a little more and learn to let the small things go. And maybe that slip of paper under my windshield wiper wasn't a parking ticket. Seriously, the meter could've only been expired for a few minutes.

Son of a bitch!

How is it that cops have all the time in the world to wait for a parking meter to run out, but get impatient with me when I have trouble finding my car registration in the glove box?

Randall DeWitt is a past winner of the Derringer Award for flash fiction.

THE LETTERS OF PATRICK BUSHELL

Gavin Keenan

Chief Alcide Duprey strained to lift the heavy box of records from the floor of the musty jail cell. The basement lock-up had been used as storage since the construction of new cells by the WPA in 1936. Poised to retire after thirty-two years with the Ipswich Police Department, Duprey was looking to put things in proper order. This would be his final task.

He placed the box on a nearby table and withdrew a sturdy, expandable folder marked *June 1913*. He unwound the brittle cord securing the flap and peered inside. A nickel-plated Colt Police Positive .38 caliber revolver with a stenciled barrel rested atop a scuffed leather shoulder holster. Four .38 caliber rounds and two spent shell casings of like caliber were sealed in a manila envelope. Placing these items aside, he removed a thick portfolio bound in heavy string. These were the reports of the Essex County District Attorney, Medical Examiner and State Constables, as well as his own and those of former Chief Patrick Bushell.

His iron-grey moustache shadowing a frown, Duprey reached into his pocket and removed a packet of letters he had received two weeks before from Collum Bushell, a Catholic priest. Their contents evoked strong memories of both friendship and tragedy during a raucous era. He pulled up a chair and began to read.

March 21, 1937
Dear Chief Duprey,

My name is Collum Bushell and my father was former Ipswich Chief of Police Patrick Bushell. Following his death last year, I discovered among his papers these letters that he had written to my deceased great-uncle James Bushell, a captain with the Lawrence Police Department. They concern my father's time as chief in Ipswich and the troubles he experienced during the Great Mill Strike of 1913.

My father was born in Lawrence in 1875. When he was a young boy, his mother died of consumption and his father sent him off to live with relatives in County Leitrim, Ireland. He grew up on the family farm there and received a rigorous education at a school run by the Sisters of Mercy. He returned to Lawrence in 1891 and worked in the mills. In 1898, he joined the Lawrence Police Department and then married my mother, the former Carmella Serra. He was later promoted to lieutenant and during the Bread and Roses Strike of 1912, was seriously injured when struck by a bullet fired by a person unknown. He rarely spoke of this but once mentioned to me his suspicion that the shot was fired by a Pinkerton detective hired by the mill owners to incite violence.

At about this same time, my sister Gina had developed a respiratory condition exacerbated by the foul atmosphere of industrial Lawrence. Her doctor advised that Gina's survival would be more likely if she lived near the sea air. Father learned that the town of Ipswich was seeking a new police chief with experience in dealing with labor unrest. Through the intercessions of my great-uncle, Father received the appointment, and we all moved to Ipswich in the summer of 1912.

Although Father spoke of you often and with great fondness, he avoided talk of his experiences in Ipswich. When I would ask him he would reply cryptically, "They were bad times, best forgotten." As these letters reveal, you shared many of his experiences. Perhaps you share his opinion as well.

Blessings,
Fr. Collum Bushell, C.P.
5801 Palisade Avenue
Bronx, New York

Duprey set Collum Bushell's letter down and lit his pipe. He then turned his attention to those of his old friend.

August 2, 1912
8 Mount Pleasant Street
Ipswich

Dear Uncle,

I hope this letter finds you in good health despite this sweltering heat. Carmella, the children and I have been in Ipswich for three weeks now, and I am happy to report that all is going as well as can be expected. We have found a second floor flat near the downtown and live among the many French-Canadians here. Their church is nearby, and the parish priest, Father Vermette, has welcomed us.

The police force is small, just six men and myself. The town is expansive but sparsely populated away from the central area. The townspeople are a curious bunch, many native born of long lineage to which they are only too happy to boast. Some are wealthy and live on large estates that dot the countryside, but most are simple farmers and merchants, or shop foremen at the mills. The expanding immigrant population includes French, Poles and Greeks, with a smattering of Jews and Italians. These folks work in the mills from dawn to dusk and mostly keep to themselves.

My first week as chief was very trying to my spirit. I am resented by most if not all of the men. I suppose this is due to my being an outsider. One man in particular, Alcide Duprey, has been very unfriendly to the point of hostility. I am told by a member of the Selectmen that Duprey has aspirations to be chief and was crestfallen by my appointment. But I am familiar with the jealousy within police forces so I expect to weather the storm.

Our little Gina's health has shown marked improvement away from the city. After church last Sunday, we boarded one of the local naptha launches and cruised the Ipswich River into the bay. The children were enthralled by the ocean and Gina's breathing was noticeably eased by the salt air. We disembarked on a beach known as Crane's and enjoyed a picnic lunch on the white sand. Collum ventured to the water's edge but did not partake of my offer of swimming instruction. Gina and Michael remained with their mother, building castles and walking among the dunes. At days end, we steamed back to the town landing, thoroughly exhausted and burned by the sun. Oh, how wonderful it all was!

I close with my heartfelt thanks to you for all the assistance you provided in my gaining this position. I know that were it not for your influence with Mr. Lawrence and others, it would have come to nothing. We are all forever in your debt. Please give my love to Aunt Anna.

Your loyal nephew,
Patrick Bushell
September 7, 1912
Town Hall
Ipswich

Dear Uncle,

Your kind words of encouragement are much appreciated. The wisdom you so generously impart bolsters my resolve to succeed. However, I must convey to you the challenge that I face here. Regrettably, I find the majority of the force to be comprised of lazy and untrustworthy political appointees. Just last night I returned to the station at eight p.m., only to discover the officer on duty asleep at the desk in full public view. When he failed to awaken in my presence, I kicked the footstool out from under his legs and berated him as he gathered himself up from the floor. This morning I called a muster of all the men and read the riot act. I ordered that all officers remain on the beat during their respective tours and complete a full written report of their activities at shift's end. The recalcitrant sleeper had the temerity to question my order, stating that things were never done this way previously. I lashed out that they damn well would be from now on, and if he did not like it, he could return to work on his father's pig farm. To my surprise, I later overheard Patrolman Duprey comment to some of the others that in his opinion, my mandates were long overdue. In truth, Duprey is the most able and conscientious member of the force, and I am sure that he holds the lazy among us in the same contempt that I do. Perhaps I will reach the man yet.

My continued affection to you and Aunt Anna.

Fondly,
Patrick

November 1, 1912
Town Hall
Ipswich

Dear Uncle,Greetings to you both and best wishes on this Day of All Souls. We are all healthy and Carmella sends along her thanks for the gift of the knitted shawl for Gina. Collum attends school now with many young children from nearby. Most of the Polish and Greek children forgo formal schooling to work with their parents at the mills. A shame indeed, for even in the poverty of my youth in Leitrim I was afforded a decent education by the church.

I can report some progress with the disposition of the force. At my urging, one of the least capable officers resigned last week. I hope to recruit a more suitable replacement but fear local politics will dictate the result.

An interesting event involving Officer Duprey occurred on Saturday last. While on patrol he was summoned to a disturbance at the Saint Lawrence Literary Society for Polish immigrants. There, he was confronted by several brawling Poles who had been agitated by a member of the I.W.W. urging membership in the union. Unable to quell the brawlers, Duprey withdrew and sent word to me requesting assistance. I promptly joined him and as we went inside, I observed a full scale Donnybrook in progress. Keeping my short billy club concealed in the sleeve of my tunic, I ordered that all disperse immediately or face arrest. This enjoinder came to nothing, and as Duprey went to seize a particularly belligerent drunk, he suffered a punch to the face. I advanced on this man and dropped him with a thrust of the billy to his gut. Another Pole was given a flattened nose for good measure. This impressed the brawlers we meant business, and they soon dispersed. Duprey collared his attacker and we marched him outside and to the station. While locking him in the cell, he ardently apologized and begged forgiveness. This is a very pleasant aspect of the Polish. They are willing to own up to their transgressions and hold no grudges.

Duprey remarked that he appreciated my assistance and admired my use of the billy. I immediately urged it upon him and commended its use in the trade. He carries it now and I am compelled to ask if you could forward me a replacement from your supply locker. I will gladly reimburse the city for all costs related.

The days grow cool with the trees bare of leaves. Winter beckons for certain.

God Bless,
Patrick

January 1, 1913
8 Mount Pleasant
Ipswich

Dear Uncle,

Sad greetings to you and Aunt Anna on this first day of the New Year. I received your letter yesterday with the tragic news from Leitrim, and my heart is rendered numb with pain. Cousin Liam was as a brother to me, and to learn that the foreclosure of his farm had driven him to such despair that he hanged himself is maddening. What is to become of his family now? How will they keep from starvation? I rage at the evil landlords who so abuse our people and the vile crown that supports them. There will be no peace in Ireland until they are eradicated from the country.

My thoughts are morbid in light of my cousin's death, but recently I have reflected on our common adventures of only a year ago in Lawrence. The difficulties we encountered with the tens of thousands of striking mill workers remain as vivid as if they had been yesterday. Bread and Roses, indeed. Blood and Roses would be more fitting, and I have the scarred shoulder to prove it! Nonetheless, I do maintain a grudging admiration for the pluck shown by the strikers and give them just due for achieving their common objective.

I observe similar restiveness among the immigrants here and note an increased presence of agitators from the I.W.W. With the mills paying less than four dollars for a sixty hour work week, the climate is ripe for similar conflict. The worker demands justice and a decent wage, the mill owners, increased profit. As before, we are trapped between them.

I close with some good news. Recently, I recommended to the Selectmen that Alcide Duprey be promoted to sergeant. The Department requires a strong second in command, and Duprey's seniority and past military experience in the War with Spain make him the clear choice. Any resentment he once held toward me belongs to the past and I have come to trust his abilities and judgment. He will be promoted next week.
Your nephew,
Patrick

January 21, 1913
Town Hall
Ipswich

Dear Uncle,

I hope that both you and Aunt Anna remain warm in this frigid weather. I understand your remonstration that my duties concern the preservation of law and order, and not the assurance of justice and fair pay. You are correct, of course. Justice is the work of God and Judges. Yet there exists tremendous poverty among the people here. Our Poor Farm exceeds capacity, turning away destitute individuals and whole families seeking work, food and shelter. Sadly, the police can offer them nothing more than the threat of arrest for vagrancy and an admonition to move on to the next town.

Last week, Sergeant Duprey and I were called to a tenement house to apprehend a deranged Greek man with a knife. In his squalid third floor apartment we found him threatening his wife and children with a bloodstained stiletto. On the floor lay a man in a pool of blood, clutching his gut and crying in pain. We ordered the Greek to surrender the knife, and when he failed to do so, Duprey drew his revolver and shot him in the leg. The noise was deafening in the small room and the children wailed in terror.

I initially suspected marital infidelity as the cause but learned that the man had recently been dismissed at the mill for his membership in the I.W.W. Thus enraged, he swore to return to the mill to attack the foreman when his cousin intervened and got stabbed for his trouble. Now both remain in dire condition, their survival doubtful. The tenement is owned by the mill, so what the future holds for the woman and her children is unknown.

Yesterday, I received a visitor who identified himself as Robert C. Applegate. A sawed-off dandy of a man, he claimed to be monitoring the I.W.W. and other union activism at behest of the mill owners. I immediately disliked him for his unctuous manner and suspect he is either a Burns or Pinkerton detective. I observed he carried a nickel-plated revolver in a shoulder rig and asked him his reason for going about so armed. He retorted that his work involved security and payroll transport, making a firearm necessary. I cautioned him that I would countenance no violence or gunplay in town, and that he would be wise to leave the weapon with me for safe-keeping. He sneered at my offer, and I then showed him the door. He and his kind are nothing but trouble, and I bitterly remember the havoc they created in Lawrence.

God Help us,
Patrick

February 5, 1913
Town Hall
Ipswich

Dear Uncle,

Carmella and I extend our very happy wishes to you on your birthday. Here at the seacoast, the damp breeze carries a penetrating chill, and life continues apace. Carmella enjoys the company of the few Italian women in town, and together they attend church, visit each other's kitchens and encourage the children in play. The majority of my waking hours are spent at work with little time for recreation of any sort.

You will recall the Greek lady and her children whom I mentioned in an earlier letter. I have since learned that her name is Nicolena Markopoulos, and on Monday morning I was again called to assist an officer with a disturbance at her address. A small crowd had gathered, agitated and protesting vociferously as Applegate and another man were discarding the family's modest belongings onto the street. Upon my inquiry, Applegate claimed that their rent was in arrears. A Greek man then approached me and said in broken English that the rent had been paid by his fraternal organization. I asked for proof of this, but the man could produce none. Still, I implored Applegate to forestall the eviction until I could investigate further. He refused, and remarked that I could take them to live in my home if I was so concerned for their well-being. As I was about to reply to his impudence, the Markopoulos woman approached me holding a babe in her arms and without a word spat in my face. Mortification rendered me speechless, and I turned on my heel and left the other officer to witness the injustice. Even now, anger wells within me.

Your nephew,
Patrick

March 15, 1913
8 Mount Pleasant Street
Ipswich

Dear Uncle James,

Thank you for the visit last Sunday. It was wonderful to see both you and Aunt Anna in such robust health. As you observed, our little Gina has been recovering from a late-winter cold, but the doctor now assures us she is out of any danger of respiratory distress, thank God.

The labor unrest here grows more volatile by the day. The mill workers increasingly resent management and view the police as mere agents of the owners, thus treating us with suspicion and hostility. Many workers are taking membership in the I.W.W. and talk of picketing and strikes are heard daily. These union sentiments are held mostly by the Greek and Italian workers who occupy the bottom of the labor hierarchy. The Yankees, Poles and French-Canadians keep the better jobs and give wide berth to the dissatisfied others. The owners respond by employing Mr. Applegate and his thugs to carry out escalating acts of retaliation: firings, evictions, and assaults, thus making the task of keeping the peace here all but impossible. The Selectmen heed the wishes of the owners and have expressed their increased alarm toward what they call the growing anarchist threat. They expect that in light of my experiences in Lawrence, I will respond with appropriate force to suppress any uprising. How this is to be done with six men is beyond me.

I must end on a sad note. You will recall the Markopoulos woman I have mentioned before. Following the eviction of her family, some sympathetic members of the Greek community took charge of her children, providing each with a warm home. Mrs. Markopoulos herself took shelter in a squatter's shack behind Lathrop's Ice House, awaiting the fate of her husband who remains confined pending trial on the death of his cousin.

By reason of melancholy or some other measure of insanity, the poor woman was discovered yesterday to have hanged herself from the branch of a tree. The scene was more sad than gruesome, her pathetic form dressed in black and suspended from a simple leather belt as she knelt in the fading snow. I cannot comprehend a hopelessness so profound that would cause a mother to orphan her children. God rest her troubled soul.

My continued thanks and blessings to you and Aunt Anna.

Patrick

April 27, 1913
Town Hall
Ipswich

Dear Uncle James,

Yesterday, over seven hundred Greek and Italian workers went on strike at the Ipswich Mills, seeking wage parity with their Yankee counterparts. The strike was called by the I.W.W. organizers after the owners refused to make any wage adjustments. The strikers then set about forming picket lines which the Yanks and others who continue to work must traverse daily.

The mill owners immediately urged the Selectmen to deputize a number of their loyal employees as Special Police to maintain order and protect their property. I opposed this, however the Selectmen overrode my objection. Sergeant Duprey and I are now saddled with thirty untrained, mercenary, strike

108

police. That supposedly intelligent people fail to see the inherent danger of arming the anointed to suppress the benighted is beyond my comprehension.

Please give my love to Aunt Anna.
Patrick

May 15, 1913
Town Hall
Ipswich

Dear Uncle James,

I send a brief note to apprise you of recent events. The I.W.W. leadership seems determined to repeat their Bread and Roses success here in Ipswich. They encourage the strikers to act in a most disorderly and confrontational manner. Twice daily, there is jostling and fighting along the picket lines as three hundred workers enter and exit the mills. They are denounced as "scabs" with an occasional brick thrown in their direction for good measure. The police stand between the pickets and workers and have confiscated a number of knives and clubs carried by those on both sides. The Special Police are hostile toward the strikers, and I constantly must prod them to remain neutral in their actions.

There are a number of nocturnal conflicts, and assaults, vandalism and the like. Last night, a small gathering of strikers leaving the Greek Coffee House were accosted and severely beaten by a group of unknowns, leaving one with a broken arm and fractured skull. I suspect Applegate and his associates, but have no proof. A barn belonging to a Yankee foreman was later burned to the ground, probably in retaliation.
Your nephew,
Patrick

June 12, 1913
8 Mount Pleasant Street
Ipswich

Dear Uncle,

By now word has reached you concerning the tragedy here of June 10th. I was in command of the mill strike detail, and late in the afternoon we were positioned near the main gate to prevent an expected violent confrontation there. As the workers exited the mill, they were met by hundreds of strikers and a heavy barrage of bricks and bottles thrown from the picket line. I ordered the men to force the strikers to the opposite side of the street, and in so doing, many of the officers sustained injury from the thrown objects. It was then that shots rang out from a window on the second floor of a nearby tenement. I turned and observed a man I recognized as Applegate firing his nickel-plated revolver toward the crowd. I drew my Colt and fired twice, striking the window frame near his head and forcing him back. These reports compelled the already anxious officers to draw their weapons and fire into the crowd. To my horror I witnessed a young Greek girl crumble to the ground as she was struck by a bullet. I rushed to where she lay and observed what was surely a fatal wound to her head. I called two nearby officers to assist me in moving her from further danger.

Duprey and I then moved along the line of officers ordering them to holster their revolvers, eventually bringing some control to the ranks. The panicked strikers moved away from the mill and up the small rise of Union Street. We then pushed toward the tenement. We found the room from where the shots were fired vacant but observed specs of blood on the wall adjacent to the splintered window. We then heard the approach of the 6:15 Boston and Maine and rushed to the depot. There we saw Applegate holding a bloody kerchief to his face as he crossed the platform to board the train. We stopped him at gunpoint, and I threw him to the ground. I reached beneath his jacket but found no weapon. He protested his innocence, claiming he had been injured trying to escape the angry mob. Duprey manacled his hands, and we commandeered a livery to take him in. I told Duprey to secure him in my office and then relay a signal requesting additional help at the mill.

I immediately returned to the mill and the carnage there. A dozen policemen and twice that number of civilians were injured by bricks and bottles. Several strikers suffered gunshot wounds, and the poor Greek girl, Nikephorous Popoulakos, lay dead beneath a blanket, a bullet through her head and her blood trailing into the gutter. I remained at the mill throughout the evening until sufficient officers from Haverhill, Lawrence, and Salem arrived to maintain order. In all, twenty-three strikers were in custody and charged with rioting.

When I returned to the police station, I found Applegate chained to a steam pipe in my office. The downstairs cell block was filled beyond capacity, and the Keeper of the Lock Up, a kindly man named Eustace, was overwhelmed by the tumult. Applegate complained that I had no reason to hold him in custody. I informed him that he was to be charged with firing his pistol in public and inciting a riot resulting in death. He smirked at me and said, "You are mistaken. I had no weapon. I wasn't even near the mill." I then seized his swollen jaw and ripped a splinter from his skin, telling him that if my shots had not gone wide, he would be laying on a slab next to the poor girl. He hissed that I couldn't prove anything, and I slapped his face, knowing that he was probably right.

I remained at the station ruminating over the day's tragic events and my failure to maintain peace and safety. By 2:00 a.m., the prisoners had settled into sleep and I relieved Mr. Eustace, telling him to return at 9:00 a.m. for court duty. After he departed, I unchained Applegate and led him downstairs. As we stood before a cell filled with incarcerated strikers, Applegate stiffened and gasped, "You can't put me in there." In response I unlocked the cell door and forced him behind the bars. The other prisoners stirred from the commotion, and Applegate reached out toward me and begged me not to leave him alone with those people. Unmoved by his plight, I returned upstairs.

Shortly thereafter, I heard the sounds of a brief struggle and perhaps a muffled groan, soon followed by an eerie quiet. At 6:00 a.m. I checked the lock-up and found Applegate hanging from the neck by a belt drawn around the bars of the cell window. The others prisoners were asleep or feigning to be so until I rapped on the cell bars. When Sergeant Duprey reported for duty we cut down Applegate's lifeless form and removed him from the cell. The District Attorney interrogated the other prisoners who all claimed to have slept through the night and witnessed nothing of Applegate's end. I gave a detailed statement indicating that Applegate had been in custody for incitement and assault and that I had locked him up pending arraignment.

Both the District Attorney and the Selectmen were incredulous of my statement, stating that I had no evidence justifying Applegate's arrest. They held a kangaroo court in Town Hall, where the mill owners and Applegate's employer demanded the Selectmen dismiss me, claiming I had sacrificed an innocent man. The chairman, playing the part of Pilate, urged me to resign. Seeing no avenue of support, I tossed my badge on the table and left in disgust. To hell with them all.

Your nephew,
Patrick

Duprey put the letters aside and leaned back in the chair, letting the memories wash over him. After the Selectmen fired Bushell, they had urged the appointment upon him, but surprisingly, he refused. He wasn't one to be disloyal to his friend. That afternoon, he went to see Bushell who told him, "Don't be a fool, Duprey. Taking the job would be good for you and no skin off my arse, believe me." After a sleepless night, Duprey relented and since then had served as chief of police.

In late July of that year, the labor trouble at Ipswich Mills ended when the owners fired the striking workers and immediately set about evicting them from their homes. Duprey recalled with sadness the sight of over one hundred families wandering the streets, carrying what few possessions they had salvaged from the curbside.

He remembered the excitement of the station agent as he showed Duprey the nickel-plated revolver and shoulder holster found secreted behind a livery crate at the depot. The letters R.C.A. – P.D.A. were stenciled on the barrel, and when Duprey examined the cylinder, he counted four live rounds and two spent shell casings. Finding Bushell later that day, he expected him to be relieved by the proof of Applegate's treachery. "Cast it down a well for all I care," Bushell had commented sourly. "The District Attorney has already determined I acted wrongly. This changes nothing."

111

Duprey presented this evidence to the District Attorney and cursed his cowardice when he remained steadfast in charging that an I.W.W. agitator had fired those first shots from the window. In early August, Duprey said goodbye to his friend as Bushell boarded a Portland-bound train with his family. Bushell wished him well, and promised to contact him once they were settled and he began his new job with the railroad. Duprey told him that his firing had been all balls, but Bushell cut him off. "Things work out for the best, Alcide. Applegate got what he deserved. My conscience is clear." Bushell never returned to Ipswich.

Duprey gathered the file and Bushell's letters. The mill had long been closed, the owners following the lure of cheaper labor down south. Now many of the workers who had survived those perilous times were struggling again in the Great Depression. Duprey opened a steel door leading into the furnace room and stood before the coal-fired boiler. *Let the dead bury the dead,* he mused as he fed the papers into the fire box.

That evening on his final walk home, Duprey paused on the Choate Bridge and slipped the cursed revolver over the railing. He nodded in satisfaction as it sank below the roiling waters to settle in the mud of the Ipswich River. He judged that his old friend would have wanted it this way.

Gavin Keenan is a retired Ipswich Massachusetts Police Chief. His award winning writing has appeared in *True Blue*, by St. Martin's Press, *Felons, Flames and Ambulance Rides* by Oak Tree Press, *Rogue Wave* (2014) by Level Best Books and *Mystery Readers Journal* (2016). His story, "We Take Care of Our Own," was short listed for the 2014 Al Blanchard Award.

CHRISTMAS SHIFT

Dale T Phillips

Delacourt scowled at the clock on the wall. Four minutes to midnight. His gaze ran over the decorations hung about the station house, and he sighed. Christmas was so depressing, the worst of the holidays, because it reminded him he didn't have a life. No wife, no kids, no relatives to spend the holidays with, which was why he'd volunteered to work the Christmas shift, letting the other members of the small police force go home to their families.

It was a quiet time, as even the bad guys had taken the night off for Christmas. Not that there were a lot of bad guys in this sleepy little coastal Maine town. They didn't get a lot of violence or major calls. He'd turned off the happy holiday music on the station radio; he couldn't stand to hear any more of it. Radio stations started playing jolly Noel songs as soon as the Thanksgiving turkey had been cleared away, and it was too much to bear. So all was silent, and not a creature was stirring.

Delacourt wanted a drink more than anything, but knew it was a terrible idea, as he wouldn't stop once he began. It would be too easy to slide into uselessness, and he was conscientious enough to wait to get plastered until he got home. Another merry goddamn Christmas. He'd be here on New Year's Eve, too, another depressing time.

The only other person in the station was old Clarence, the dispatcher. He'd been sitting on the other side of the room, viewing something on his laptop, but now he closed it, stood up and stretched, and came over.

Delacourt roused himself into cordiality and spoke. "Whatcha watching?"

"*It's a Wonderful Life,*" the older man said. "I put it on every Christmas Eve. Did you know an angel named Clarence is the hero?"

Delacourt smiled. "That so?"

"Yup. George Bailey is the protagonist, but it's Clarence that saves him. Shows George that he matters because he's an important part of the community. Has friends and family, so he's actually the richest man in town, not old Potter."

Delacourt was no longer smiling. "Guess I must be broke, then."

"Yeah, I was gonna ask you. Nobody ever volunteers for this shift. Even though you're the new guy, you wouldn't have automatically got stuck with it."

"No reason not to."

Clarence shook his head. "Me, it's understandable. I'm old, and everyone I ever loved is dead. But you're a young guy. You must have someone."

"No family, and haven't made any friends since I moved here."

"Geez, that's too bad."

Delacourt shrugged.

Clarence went on. "Heard you were in the service. Iraq, wasn't it?"

"Yeah. Why I moved here. I didn't want anything that reminded me of sand or the desert. The beaches are all rock."

Clarence stuck out his lower lip. "You know we got a real desert, not far away from here?"

"In Maine? You're pulling my leg."

"Nope, a genuine classified desert. Not super big, you unnerstand, but enough to qualify."

"Think I'll skip. I had enough of sand to last me a lifetime."

"Why'd you join up?"

"Thought we could do some good over there. Turns out we couldn't. Hitch was over, and I left, went back for some criminal justice credits at a local college. Got into law enforcement, and saw you needed someone here. Thought it would be nice and quiet."

Clarence spread his arms. "Yup. That it is. Usually, nights this slow, I play cribbage with whoever's on, after my movie's over."

"Cribbage? What's that?"

"Ah, can tell you ain't from New England. It's a card game with a board you peg points with. Wanna learn?"

"Why not? It's not like there's much else to do."

"Ayuh."

Clarence came back with a deck of cards and a short board with tiny holes drilled in it. He sat down across the desk, and Delacourt took the cards and began shuffling. He looked up at the clock. Twelve minutes after midnight. Officially Christmas Day.

"Merry Christmas, Clarence."

The older man looked up, glanced at the clock, and smiled. "Ayuh. Guess it is. Merry Christmas to you. Maybe Santa will bring you somethin' nice this year."

He hasn't done too good lately, thought Delacourt.

A crackling sound interrupted their game. Both men looked over at Clarence's console. Someone was calling in, their words sounding panicked. Clarence moved quickly and thumbed the mike, speaking crisply. He turned back to Delacourt, who had put the cards down and stood up, waiting to hear. "Somebody just shot Santa."

114

As the ambulance settled the strapped-in, red-and-white-clad shooting victim and closed the doors, Delacourt looked from the four men gawping by the front of the bar across the street to the man standing before him.

"Okay, tell me again," Delacourt prompted.

"Well, we was all inside drinkin' and Billy, that's Santa, gets up and says he's going home. We made a few jokes about him deliverin' toys and all, and he waved us off and went out. 'Bout a minute goes by, and we heard a shot. I was closest to the door, so I went out. Saw him layin' here, and had Ray call you."

"So this Billy, what was he doing in a Santa outfit, drinking in a bar so late on Christmas Eve?"

"Said he'd come from a party."

"Did he say where?"

"Nope. Wasn't at the Elks or the V.A., they're both closed tonight. Musta been someone's house."

Delacourt did not relish the idea of knocking on doors at this time of night. "Did you see anything when you came out?"

"Just Billy lyin' there."

"No one nearby, no car pulling away? No other sounds?"

"Nope. And I was first, so no one over there woulda seen anything either."

"I'll be asking anyway. Thank you. You can go back over now. Please don't say anything until I talk with them all. I'll be over in a minute."

Delacourt gave the ground another close scan, but he saw nothing. There was no snow yet, and no clues on the bare street he could discern, such as discarded cigarette butts or a spent shell casing. One dark blotch showed where the victim had bled, but it looked like he had just fallen where shot and hadn't moved. This wasn't television, so there would be no crime lab rushing in to scoop up every hair and fiber on the street. No crime scene tape around the area, no teams of investigators, no official photographers, just him. Delacourt took out his cell phone and snapped a few shots of his own.

He looked down the street. If the witness had been truthful about going out right after the shot and not seeing or hearing a car pull away, the shooter hadn't been in a vehicle. Delacourt eyed the dark, empty windows of the main street. He'd find out the angle of the wound, and maybe have some idea of trajectory, see if the shot had come from one of those windows. Be a pretty good one, if so. Meant the shooter was very skilled, to be sure of hitting a target so well at thirty feet or better. Otherwise, it seemed like the shooter had been on foot, maybe close to the victim.

And the victim was still alive, so maybe he'd seen his shooter. Delacourt would go to the hospital as soon as he was done here. He'd talk to the denizens of the bar, but doubted anyone had seen or heard anything, and it didn't look like there would be any other witnesses. Could be a tough case. He'd find out the caliber of the gun, see who in town had one of that type that people knew of. Might get lucky.

He'd checked, and the guy still had his wallet on him, so robbery wasn't the likely cause of the crime. Maybe something from the party the man had come from? Delacourt didn't relish having to question a roomful of people. Then he *would* have to call more people in, ruin somebody else's Christmas. Wouldn't make him very popular in town, either. As an outsider, he was automatically suspect. Ah, well, it wasn't like he had any friends anyway.

Might as well start with the witnesses at hand. Delacourt walked over to the bar and went in, enjoying the warmth after the chill of outdoors. He gazed longingly at the bottles cheerfully standing with pert invitation on the racks behind the bar, and wished he could partake, forget all this.

All eyes were on him. "You all know why I'm here," he said. "I need to find out if anyone saw anything or knows anything about the shooting. I'll talk to you one at a time in the back there. Anybody want to go first, get it over with?" Delacourt said this to gauge their mood.

No one spoke or volunteered, they just looked at each other, as if waiting for someone else to make the first move. Delacourt pointed at a red-faced, bald man in a plaid hunting shirt. "How about you, sir?"

The man grinned at his companions, and wobbled a bit as he got off the stool.

"You okay?" Delacourt took the man's elbow to steady him.

"Sure. Just had a few pops, that's all." The man slurred a bit when he spoke.

"First of all, is everyone here who was here when you heard the shot?"

The man squinted and looked around. "Yeah, all still here."

"Good. Let's have a seat." Delacourt took out a notebook and clicked his pen. He took down the man's name and address and phone number before getting down to the rest.

"You live alone?"

"Last two years, ever since Gladys died," said the man.

"How long were you here tonight?"

The man squinted again, as if calling up a hard-to-reach memory. "I got here after nine."

"So just over three hours. Tell me what went down."

"We were just drinking, shooting the shit. Billy was in that suit, so we were needling him a little. I feel bad about it now. Is he gonna be alright?"

"He's getting medical care now. What was his mood like?"

"Seemed pretty happy, you know. Like all was good."

"When did he get here?"

"About eleven."

"So about how many drinks did he have?"

"I don't know. Three? Four?"

"Did he say why he was wearing a Santa suit?"

"Said he'd been to a party."

The man burped, and Delacourt was assailed by a whiskey and garlic smell. He kept his face impassive. "Did he say what kind of party or where?"

116

"Nah. But he acted real sly about it, like it was something cool he'd done, like if we knew we'd be impressed."

Delacourt wrinkled his brow. "Did he say anything else about it?"

"We asked, but he said it was a secret."

"A secret Christmas party?"

The man shrugged. "Hell if I know. I wasn't invited."

Delacourt asked more questions, but got no further useful information. He let the man go back to his drinking, and had another of the men come over. This one was at about the same level of inebriation, and the story was much the same. By the time Delacourt had gotten through everyone, including the bartender, the only sober one, he'd found nothing more. He came to the realization, though, that he wasn't the only lonely man in town.

Stumped for an answer, a motive, or a suspect, Delacourt decided to go to the hospital and see about the victim. He checked in with the nurse at the desk.

"Hey," he said, showing his police badge. "I'm Delacourt. The shooting victim that was brought in, how's he doing?"

The nurse looked up, and he was startled to see how attractive she was, even though she looked tired. Her voice was mellow, pleasant. "He came through surgery okay. Bullet didn't hit anything vital."

He'd had a quick peek at her name tag. "Thank you, uh, Rachel. Any chance I'll be able to talk to him tonight?"

"That's up to the doctor. Shouldn't be a problem, though."

"Good. Did you run a tox screen on him?"

"Of course. Didn't need one to know he'd been drinking, though."

"He'd been at a bar before he was shot."

"That'll make you smell like whiskey, sure enough." She yawned.

"Long night?"

"Shows, huh?"

"You're working the Christmas shift, too, I see."

"Might as well, let the family folks have it off."

"Same here." He wanted to linger, and since he had no other witnesses to question, and no leads, he thought he could tarry. "You wouldn't have any coffee around, would you?"

She smiled. "Might be some left in the break room."

"I'll be eternally in your debt."

"It'll be my Christmas present to you."

They went to a small room and the nurse filled a paper cup with coffee and handed it to Delacourt, pointing out the sugar. "There's milk in the fridge."

"Black's fine, thanks. You're a lifesaver."

She smiled. "Comes with the job description."

They walked back to the desk. She spoke again. "I *heard* there was somebody new in town. You like it here?"

"Seems like a nice little place. Good people. Except for one, it seems. Who'd shoot Santa on Christmas?"

117

She smiled. "Have to tell you, this is not an ordinary occurrence. I worked the night shift at an ER in Boston, and we'd see a lot of bad stuff, but here…"

"I saw your crime stats. Hasn't been a shooting here for years. And that was a hunting accident."

"It's a good place to settle down."

Delacourt took a sip of coffee, and decided to go for it. "You come back for family?"

"None left, now," she said. "Boston was nice, but this is still home. What made *you* move here?"

"A quiet place was something I needed after I got out of the service. I got tired of getting shot at."

"I can see where you might need a change of pace."

"Hasn't been any danger here yet. Of course, there's no one at home to worry if there was."

She smiled again. "Nice subtle way of letting me know you're single, Detective. Of course, I already noticed you didn't have a wedding ring on. Me either." She held up a hand. "With these crazy hours, it's hard to meet anyone and have a serious relationship. So I guess we're a couple of loners."

Before Delacourt could reply, a doctor walked by, frowning at a clipboard he held. He glanced at them.

Nurse Rachel spoke. "Doctor Lajois, this is Officer Delacourt. He wanted to know if he could talk with our patient."

"Not now, he can't. The patient is still under sedation."

Delacourt spoke. "When do you think I'd be able to question him? He might give me an idea of who shot him, so of course earlier is better."

Lajois frowned again. "Give it another hour, he should be awake enough by then."

Delacourt checked his watch. "Okay. Can you tell from the wound what angle the bullet hit him?"

"Straight on."

"So it was somebody on his level. Anything you noticed about him, other than the Santa suit and the smell of booze?"

"Evidence-wise you mean? Can't help you there," the doctor said.

"Wait," said Rachel. "There was another smell. I'm trying to place it. Perfume. Somebody else wears that brand."

She put her hand to her brow as both men watched her. "Evelyn Walsh. She was in here two days ago. I remember."

Delacourt felt his pulse increase. "That's terrific. You know where she lives?"

"In this town? Of course." She gave him the address. He turned to go.

"One more thing," she said. "It's *Mrs.* Evelyn Walsh. Be careful."

Delacourt nodded. Interesting news indeed. He called Clarence and told him where he was headed.

118

In the driveway of the Walsh residence, Delacourt saw that the lights were on. He got out and opened the trunk of his cruiser. He stared at the bulletproof vest. Silly to think he'd need it, but then again there *was* a shooter on the loose. He let discretion be the better part of valor and shrugged it on. He drew his weapon and checked it.

Delacourt stood on the front step and rang the bell, pistol by his side. He heard someone approach behind the door. They paused. He called out. "Mrs. Walsh? I'm Officer Delacourt, and I'd like to talk to you. Please open the door."

There was no answer. "Mrs. Walsh?"

Bullets punched through the door and into Delacourt. He staggered back, and heard a muffled curse from just inside the door. Furious, he snapped a powerful front kick at the lock, and another. The door burst inward, Delacourt following. He saw a man with a gun looking rather shocked as Delacourt hit him in a solid tackle, taking him down to the floor in a hard slam. The man grunted as Delacourt flipped and handcuffed him. Only when Delacourt sat up did he realize he was bleeding.

An hour later, Delacourt was looking into the concerned face of Nurse Rachel.

"Does it hurt much?"

"Doesn't feel very good. I've never been shot before, and I was in a war zone."

"They said you had a vest on, and it saved your life."

"Well, you *did* tell me to be careful."

"I didn't tell you to get *shot*. I feel bad, because I told you where she lived."

"Yeah, but you didn't know her husband was home. He'd found out she was partying with Santa before he came back, smacked her around, and went after Santa. He was packing a suitcase when I got there, and we would have had a fugitive on the run. You stopped that."

"What are you saying? That we make a pretty good team?"

"Could be," he replied. "Maybe we should try it again sometime."

"As long as it doesn't result in you getting shot again."

"One's enough for me."

She bent and kissed his forehead. "Merry Christmas, Officer Delacourt."

"Merry Christmas, Nurse Rachel."

Dale T Phillips has published novels, story collections, non-fiction, poetry, and over 60 short stories. Stephen King was Dale's college writing teacher, and since that time, Dale has found time to appear on stage, television, in an independent feature film, and compete on *Jeopardy* (losing in a spectacular fashion). He co-wrote and acted in *The Nine*, a short political satire film. He's traveled to all 50 states, Mexico, Canada, and through Europe.

THE RUNNER

Steve Roy

Vincent Schitelli stared at his half-empty glass of bourbon and contemplated killing himself for perhaps the thousandth time. It was an utterly useless thought, of course, for that train had long since left the station. Still he savored it like fine wine.

Perched at the end of a time-worn mahogany bar, he dropped the last shreds of a Chesterfield to the floor and stubbed it out with his toe. The dark perfume of stale booze and fresh despair permeated the place, and from a small stage in the corner, Frankie Lymon, young once again and so pretty for a man, sang about fools falling in love.

A neon Budweiser sign shared its pale ruby glow from behind the bar. It sparkled through the amber liquid in his glass and brought to mind summer sunsets, which may never have happened, but which he still remembered.

"Ten years in a fucking oak barrel, it smells the same, it tastes the same, it burns the same goin' down," he muttered. "But the shit might as well be mother's milk."

When he'd first arrived it seemed like heaven; all the booze he could drink, all the time to drink it and no one bitching at him to pay his tab. Pretty sweet deal, or so he'd thought. But the booze had no pop and when he realized he couldn't get drunk anymore, that's when he knew it was really Hell.

No one had ever accused Vincent Schitelli of being either a subtle or deep thinker, but even he couldn't miss the blatant paradox of fate. His career as a drunk had mirrored his career as a cop and both ended badly in '72, with a bullet instead of a payoff envelope. Still the idea of getting his own personalized, permanently sober Hell, well that was irony, wasn't it?

He opened his eyes without realizing he'd closed them. Maybe he'd nodded off. He couldn't always tell anymore. Frankie Lymon had finished and Ricky Nelson was now strumming through some solo guitar work.

During a break in the set, a short burst of voices floated across the air. Most mornings Schitelli had the place to himself but others would drift in as the day aged. Despite the crappy liquor, it was a popular spot because they booked such bitchin' acts. Even Hell had some good points.

He felt the vibration from his pocket first then waited patiently for the sound to follow. In time, it did, the first seventeen notes of "Gilligan's Island."

120

"Fucking mutt," he growled, then grabbed the pager and held it up to the dim light.

Schitelli worked for a company called the Abaddon Group and his pager was company issued. For some reason, management took perverse pleasure in making his life unpleasant in ways both great and small. His boss, Raymond Gillespie, held the title of 'Executive Vice President - Reclamations Unit.' Among his other duties, the bastard controlled pager messaging and ring tones from his office on the fifteenth floor of the Legion Building. Sometimes he'd use "Gilligan's Island," sometimes "The Brady Bunch," sometimes "Bewitched," but it was always some lame-ass sitcom jingle. The guy was a damn laugh riot, all right.

The page meant another job assignment and at this late stage of existence, he couldn't believe he still had to punch a clock, but there it was. Christ, it had been nearly thirty-six years since he'd tasted the lead from three bullets. You'd think they'd have structured some kind of retirement package for him after all that time.

"Fucking mutt," he muttered again, looking down at the pager's illuminated text message. Just one word: Runner.

The Abaddon Group liked their fancy titles almost as much as they liked their TV jingles. Vincent Schitelli's business card labeled him a 'Senior Regulator - Reclamations Unit,' but he had no illusions. He was a cop all over again, only this time with no protection envelopes from the local store owners, and no late night rolls in the back of his car with rousted hookers, and certainly no donuts. No, what he mostly did was collect the trash, or more accurately, find and return the runners, the ones who tried to escape.

The traffic along Bayshore Drive moved like cold oatmeal and it took him nearly thirty minutes to make the four miles to the Legion Building. The Charles River shimmered along the way like a cold, gray ribbon. It was always cold and gray on this side of the river, even when the other side lay bathed in bright sun. It made him long for the days when sunlight was not so dearly bought.

Schitelli pushed through the revolving door of the Legion and immediately winced at the harsh glitter of fluorescents reflecting off a limitless expanse of chrome and glass.

"How's it hanging, Carlos," he said to the pock-marked security guard working a crossword puzzle behind the desk. Schitelli couldn't recall a time when Carlos hadn't been on duty behind that desk, or a time when he hadn't been working a crossword.

"Low and easy, my man. Say, you know a three letter word for land of endless wandering.

"You writing my bio, son?"

121

"Huh?" Carlos said, looking up from his desk.

"Never mind. The word you're looking for is 'Nod'."

"Nod? Yeah, that's it, thanks."

"Gillespie waiting?" Schitelli asked.

"Sure, go on up," the security guard said and returned to his puzzle.

Schitelli entered Gillespie's cramped office without knocking. It smelled of Vitalis and ham sandwiches, not a pleasing combination even in the best of circumstances. Gillespie was at his desk, a grey steel number topped with black laminate and surrounded by matching grey file cabinets, which were jammed into every available space. There might have been a hundred of them there. There must have been a thousand.

Pushing a small pair of rimless glasses up the bridge of his nose, Gillespie pondered a manila folder as he popped the last of his sandwich into his mouth. A dab of Gulden's Spicy Brown had fallen near the edge of his desk and waited patiently for an opportunity to stain the man's tie, which it surely would do in short order.

"What is it now?" Schitelli asked.

Gillespie continued to read as if he hadn't a care in the world. Still it was obvious he'd been waiting.

"We've got another Runner," his boss said as he looked up with an acidic glare, which described his personal feelings for Schitelli much more accurately than mere words. "Why else would I call you?"

"I don't know. Maybe you were just jonesing for my snappy personality."

"Have you been drinking, again?" Gillespie said as he sniffed the air theatrically. "Tell me, why is it whenever I need you, you're in a bar?"

"Probably whenever I'm off duty and at a bar, you find a reason to need me. Must be a yin and yang kind of thing. Besides, you meet a better class of people in bars."

"You're never off duty," Gillespie said as he pushed the folder across the desk. "We've made that clear to you, repeatedly."

The name Donovan Halpern had been neatly embossed on the folder's tab. Schitelli grimaced at the pictures inside and whistled through his teeth at the young thug's accomplishments. It was a prodigious record, achieved in a remarkably short time.

"Looks like a real hard case," he muttered. "I like 'em that way."

In Schitelli's world, there were just two types of people, hard cases and spooks. Now hard cases, they were destined for this little slice of life from their first breath. They walked through life wearing their jaded accomplishments like a badge of honor and he'd never once regretted bringing one back.

But spooks were a different story. They weren't bad people. Mostly, they were just guys, sometimes girls, who got caught up in one of the world's

122

three tragic wrongs, you know, wrong place or wrong time or wrong company. But the politics of punishment being what they were, a lot of them ended up on this side of the river, as well. Schitelli found it more difficult to bring them back.

"Halpern's as hard as they come. Killed eleven people before we got hold of him the first time. The regular authorities only had him listed for three, but of course, we have better data."

No question, the data was better on this side. For some reason, efficiency flourished away from the sunlight.

"Tell me something, Gillespie. How is it folks at the top let mutts like this stroll away so easily?"

"First of all, our area of responsibility is retrieval, not incarceration. That's a completely separate department and how they attend to their duties is none of our affair," he said. "But as you already know, there is a method to their actions. After all, perception is critical to our goals."

"I know, I know. You like our residents to see what they're missing."

"Of course. It would be easy enough to lock them away," he said with the tight little smirk that Schitelli found so grating. "But a taste of what they gave up makes the matter more gratifying, more meaningful."

"Fucking mutts," Schitelli muttered. "I've dealt with some heartless bastards in my time but you guys win the prize."

"We all have our roles and I can't say I like your choice of pronouns. There is no us and them at Abaddon. We're all part of the same team here."

Schitelli extended his middle finger.

"My team has one member, Gillespie." he said. "Just one."

"That's one crappy attitude, Mr. Schitelli. "It will inhibit your career growth. But then again, you've never cared too much for advancement, have you? Now make the damn pick-up and keep your opinions to yourself. And please try to bring this one back in one piece."

"Out of my hands, Boss," Schitelli said as he headed out the door. "Easy or hard, the shape these guys come back in is up to them, not me."

The file said Halpern had been gone less than twenty-four hours. It was a fresh trail and if he hurried, he'd be back on his barstool by sunrise.

Moments later, Schitelli emerged into the sunlight at the Wilshire Building on Devonshire Avenue. He'd walked through the building's gleaming glass wall as if it were nothing more than a patch of fog. That's how people from his side traveled, windows and mirrors, chrome and stretches of water, any reflective surface would do. If people in the real world understood how his side moved about, they'd never look at a reflection again.

Schitelli paused for a moment and savored the air. It always felt cleaner on this side. As the sun kissed his face he was tempted to find a food stand and knock back a couple of chili dogs, but he knew the results would be as unsatisfying as the bourbon.

According to the file, there'd been a blood bath on G street the night before, so that was his first destination. A guy named Fergus had been found hacked to death with a machete in his third floor walk-up, his girlfriend and their six-year-old daughter lay in pieces close by. A Jamaican gang had apparently laid claim to the neighborhood's burgeoning Meth traffic and since both parents had lengthy arrest records and a well-known affinity for crank, the cops assumed nothing more than a territorial dispute.

Schitelli knew better. Donovan Halpern had entered this side close to the G Street location and he'd left behind a calling card for those who could see it. His trail would be visible even now, a subtle, glittery back trail. All Runners left it in their wake but it was impossible to see if you didn't have the gift. That's how Schitelli had gotten his job in reclamations, because he could see that trail.

He'd once asked Gillespie about it, why the Runners left that trail behind and why he and precious few others could see what most others couldn't. Gillespie had responded with his usual tact. "How the Hell should I know? Just be glad you got that sight of yours, otherwise with your record, you'd be shoveling coal."

Gillespie had laughed as he said it, so Schitelli had never been sure if there really were furnaces somewhere down there and mounds of shoveled coal to keep them glowing. He'd quickly decided he didn't want to know, so he never asked again.

Still, he had his own theory on the trails, one developed over endless glasses of impotent bourbon, waiting for a buzz that would never come. Schitelli figured the trails were nothing more than happiness. The mutts who ran were so damned happy to get away, that their joy literally dripped off like beads of sweat.

When Schitelli arrived it was obvious that Halpern had landed in Southie. First of all, that damn glittery stuff was everywhere, like confetti after a parade. Starting at some rundown bodega, the trail followed straight and true through the guy's old haunts. The stuff had begun to fade, like it always did in time, but it still sparkled in small drops and pools.

But the violence was the real giveaway. Being free again, most Runners invariably left a mess in their wake, either through a deep seated inattention to social niceties or just pure meanness. They couldn't help themselves. After all, most hadn't gotten there because of their stellar self-control.

As he followed, he thought he saw a second trail emerge from the first here and there, as if one followed in the steps of the other. If he didn't know better, he'd have sworn he was following two instead of one, but that was impossible. Abaddon's data was always flawless.

The path soon left the main thoroughfares, winding a circuitous route along back streets and dark alleys. It was all familiar to Schitelli, the places to score, the places to prey, the places to hide. He knew such places, knew them in every city and town, knew them like he had some "Twilight Zone" Zagat Guide embedded in his skull.

Ninety minutes before midnight and ten minutes past a liquor store hold-up where he'd smoked a Korean shop owner, Donovan Halpern stepped into his ten-dollar flop-house room on Hatch Street. He'd scored almost two hundred dollars from the Korean and had shot the confused store owner beneath his left eye for no more reason than that he didn't like the way he talked and if truth be told, because he didn't like the idea of a slant owning a store in his old neighborhood either.

Halpern paused without turning on the light, feeling a presence in the darkened room. His mind didn't always follow in the smoothest progressions but his instincts remained true. Before turning to run however, he hesitated and in that moment a bullet tore through his knee, taking with it the kneecap, along with substantial chunks of gristle and bone.

Halpern hit the floor just behind the gunshot's echo, grasping the remains of his shattered knee with his left hand. He winced in pain but refused to make a sound.

Vincent Schitelli walked over, flipped on the single light switch, and watched Halpern struggle with something on his belt clip. The knee shot had to hurt like Hell, yet the guy was groping for his gun.

"Still trying to win, eh, Donovan? You have an overdeveloped sense of self-preservation. I find that annoying."

Another round from Schitelli's Ruger sounded in the empty apartment. It plowed through the bony socket of Halpern's elbow, forcing him to drop the Smith & Wesson he'd just pulled from his belt. He screamed at last but since screams were as common as gunshots in the neighborhood, the risk of interruption was minimal.

"Enough," Halpern grimaced, holding up his left hand to ward off another round. "I'm done." Pain at last overcame his lifelong bout of bad-ass.

"Oh you're done alright," Schitelli said, then placed a bullet in the guy's other knee just for kicks. He kicked Halpern's Smithie across the floor and leaned down to cuff him, and that's when he heard it, two words from across the room that said things might have suddenly gotten genuinely fucked up.

"No, please."

Schitelli whirled around, his gun coming level with his eyes as his finger started to squeeze. What he saw there was the face of a frightened bird painted on the body of a boy. Perhaps seventeen years old, the boy's eyes held no deep thought or dark motive, just fear.

125

"Don't shoot him anymore, mister," the boy pleaded. "For God's sake, don't shoot him."

"What's goin' on Halpern? Who's this mook?"

"Aw, fuck," the hard case said as he wiped something warm and unaccustomed from his right eye. "He's my kid brother, Nicky. He never should've been on the other side in the first place. He was with me when I got greased and he only fired his gun because he was so damned scared. Can't you see, he's not right? That's why I took him with me when I bolted this time."

"Fuckin' Gillespie," Schitelli whispered to himself. His growing anger began to coat his throat like battery acid. "That bastard never said nothin' about no kid."

Schitelli stared at Nicky Halpern, a boy with a distant stare and a thin line of drool escaping from the corner of his mouth. He watched as the boy trembled like a rabbit waiting on a hawk's talons. He'd almost made up his mind to leave the kid behind when his pager went off.

Da da. Da da da da da da. Da da. Da da da da da da. The theme from *Bewitched*.

"Fuck," he muttered again. With greater effort than he could have imagined, he pulled his eyes away from the nearly catatonic kid and glared down at his pager.

Bring them both it said.

Schitelli hadn't shed a tear in as long as he could remember and he didn't shed one in that run-down tenement room either, but it was a close thing.

With a sigh dredged from the pit of his soul, Schitelli hefted Halpern over his left shoulder, oblivious to the flow of blood staining his shirt (it wasn't the first he'd ruined or the hundredth). He guided the hard case's terrified, half-bright kid brother into the bathroom and looked at his own reflection in the cracked mirror there. What he saw was a face that couldn't remember what joy felt like.

"Come on, man," Halpern pleaded. "Leave him behind. Ain't you got no heart at all?"

"No," Schitelli lied. "It would appear not."

With that, the three of them climbed through the mirror and back to the other side.

"Nice work Mr. Schitelli," Gillespie said as he watched the sad little trio walk though his door. "Record time. Though I specifically asked you to be more careful."

"Don't sweat it," Schitelli replied, dropping the torn up Runner to the office floor. "They'll put him back together. They always do."

126

Schitelli guided Nicky Halpern into one of the office's side chairs. His hand brushed the kid's shoulder for a moment and he winced at the way the kid's breathing caught in his chest.

"What about him?"

Gillespie stared up at the old cop but said nothing, for no words were required.

"Fuckin' mutts," he muttered and turned away.

He was indeed back at the end of the bar before sunup. Jim Croce was banging out a couple of tunes on an old Gibson as Schitelli again watched the red neon sparkle through his glass.

He took a sip and thought of Nicky Halpern: wrong place, wrong time and wrong brother.

A couple of little changes and things might have been different for the kid and even as that damnable thought formed in his mind, Schitelli cursed its birth. The sharpened life of a cynic was the only one he'd ever known or wanted. But lately, he found it increasingly difficult to maintain his edge, to not hope for something more. Schitelli thought that of everything they'd done to him over here, that was perhaps the cruelest. After all, what power did Hell possess without the hope of something better?

In time, Croce gave way to Lynyrd Skynyrd, and they in turn passed the baton to Sam Cooke. And through it all Schitelli drank and he drank and he drank some more and at the end, he still had nothing to show for his efforts.

As morning fell into day which dissolved into an interminable night, Schitelli absently fingered the timeworn gold shield from his wallet, number 2930, and he wondered when his pager would summon him again, and more importantly, how. Who could tell? Maybe the whistling introduction from the *Andy Griffith Show* next time. He'd always liked that little tune.

Steve Roy lives in Atlanta, Georgia. He is an attorney by training, a business owner of necessity but a writer by choice because he believes we find ourselves in the tales we tell. He has had short stories published in various periodical and anthology formats, including *Read by Dawn, Shadow Regions, Futures Mystery Magazine, Deathlehem Revisited* and *Crooked Holster*. He is currently seeking an outlet for his second novel, *Wednesday's Child*.

THE CATTLE RAID OF ADAMS

Keenan Powell

One Summer Day, 1890
Adams, Massachusetts

"You're not my father, Liam!" Kevin shouted as he pushed away from the table, rattling dishes.

Kate, still on her feet, held a ladleful of porridge mid-air. "You're not excused."

"And you're not my mother!" Kevin spit out just before he banged the door closed.

Kate wheeled back as if she'd been slapped.

Liam held up a hand. "I'll go after him in a moment." He nodded toward the table. "Take a seat. Go on, finish your breakfast."

Twelve-year old Clare sat motionless in her chair, her sky-blue eyes bright. She set her spoon down neatly. "May I be excused?"

"Oh, now, don't you want a little bit more?" Kate's tone softened. "You've hardly eaten."

"No, thank you."

"Then you may be excused."

Clare glided from the kitchen, head bowed, fine yellow hair billowing like a nun's veil.

Kate set the pot back on the cooker. "She's off to pray again."

"It's no harm to anyone," Liam said.

Kate collected the abandoned bowls and carried them to the sink. "But it doesn't get the chores done." She wiped her brow with a wrist, pulled back the tangled mass of auburn hair, adjusted her hairpins, and rolled up her sleeves.

Liam sipped his tea. Better to let the moment pass. Kate, his twenty-five-year old sister, had worked hard keeping the house and caring for their younger brother and sister since the time when their mother could no longer.

It was no way for a young woman to spend her life. She should be going to parties, finding a husband, preparing for a family of her own. At times, she brandished the grief of her lost future like a knife. At other times, it fell from her in great globs like a tree oozing sap. If she didn't find joy in her life soon, she would petrify into something hopelessly bitter.

128

Liam's porridge had grown cold and congealed, but he ate it anyway. Food was not wasted in the Barrett home.

"It's a fine breakfast you made for us yet again, Kate Barrett," Liam said. "Thank you."

Liam found Kevin huddled in the shed, arms wrapped around his skinny frame, head bent as if heavy from thought. Chickens pecked nearby and the cow dipped into a trough of fresh hay.

Liam ducked as he went inside to join Kevin. "Have you fed them already?"

Kevin grunted.

Liam reached for the pitchfork to clean the cow's stall.

"Done," Kevin said.

"Good lad." Liam replaced the pitchfork and took position beside Kevin, shoulder-to-shoulder, overlooking their home, a little plot of rocky land, and the valley beyond. Sweet morning air carried the scent of green things growing. Birds twittered from afar. A wall of sunlight sailed across the land as grass whispered in the breeze. In the distance, the mist that skirted Mount Greylock glowed.

Kevin drew circles in the dust with his boot. "Why can't I get a job? All my friends go to work at the mill as soon as they turn fourteen. I could make money. We could have things. I could buy Ma a new dress."

Kevin's face was turned away but Liam could imagine how it looked. His keen gray eyes would be clenched to fight back tears. He had long ago given up his curls, insisting Kate shear his hair like a working man's. Just the other day, Liam had noticed fine hairs growing on Kevin's upper lip, where all the Irishmen of Adams, Massachusetts, wore thick mustaches.

Liam hadn't allowed his mustache to grow, still thinking himself as not quite the man his father was despite the resemblance. And in a few years, Kevin, like Liam, would be the image of their father. Taller than most, broad-shouldered, with a strong jaw and thick, wavy golden hair.

But for now, Kevin was still a head shorter than Liam. Growing up would be fraught with challenges: learning how to be a man, who your friends were and weren't, talking to girls, making responsible choices. It would be especially hard for Kevin, fatherless as he was. Liam did the best he could for Kevin, recalling his own lessons at that age.

Liam had been fortunate. Their father, a good man, guided him until he was seventeen years old but Kevin was barely six when he had died. Kevin was old enough to remember their Da. And so he resisted the authority of his older brother and sister. He dreamed things would have been different had Da lived. If life were fair.

129

And so, things should have been different. Their father would have come home every night after a quick stop at the pub, whistling a fiddle-tune as he strolled up the lane, the faint scent of beer about him when he kissed and hugged his children. Liam would have been practicing law instead of keeping peace as an Adams town constable. Kate would have had a family of her own. Their mother would have been happy.

"Kevin," Liam said, "you're a smart lad. Da always wanted you to go to college. You could do so much more with your life than breaking your back." Liam gave Kevin a nudge. "Besides, that pretty Mary Ellen Cooley will like you better if you're a doctor or a lawyer."

Kevin, and everyone in Adams, knew that Liam had given up love when he took his father's place. Liam already had a family to support, he dared not create another one. And now his lost love was married to a storekeeper with a child on the way—as it should be. Liam was happy for her.

Kevin blushed. The air was heavy with his distress.

He jabbed his toe into the dirt. "Da's gone. You quit school to go to work."

"I had to," Liam said. "You don't."

As they surveyed the valley in silence, a man came walking up the road, his image dark in the shade of sycamore trees. A large and muscled man, he had the straight back of one who worked hard for his living.

As he drew closer, Liam could see the heavy dark mustache and the peaked cap he knew covered the balding head of Fergus Cooley.

"Good morning, Mr. Cooley," Liam called. "The bull again?"

"Good morning, Constable," Cooley answered as he stepped into the light. Fergus Cooley had known Liam all his life, a friend of his father's, but when Liam had joined the Adams Police Department, Mr. Cooley insisted on addressing him formally. He was his own man now, Mr. Cooley had said, and deserved a show of respect.

"It must be Madigan who's letting him out at night," Cooley said, "to cover his own cows. Now Old Sampson's spent and wandering down the road and I can't get near him. Sure, I'd hate to see him get into somebody's crops. Good thing Kevin here has a way with that old bull or I'd never get him home."

"Can I go?" Kevin's voice cracked.

The Cooley farm was larger than the Barrett's, with more land, more cows, and even a few pigs. For children, Cooley had been graced with six daughters, all beautiful and intelligent, with voices like songbirds, hard-working as well, but none of them was as strong as a lad. And no one could sweet-talk Old Sampson the way Kevin did—he had the knack.

But it wasn't the company of cattle Kevin sought. When he helped around the Cooley farm, he was frequently invited in for a meal at the same table where their oldest daughter, the pretty Mary Ellen sat.

130

"Run in and kiss Ma good-bye," Liam said.

Kevin gave Liam a frown, the one he wore when he said, "She doesn't even know I'm there." But Kevin would never say such a thing in front of someone who wasn't family. Ever since their father had drowned during a rainstorm on his way home from the pub one night, their mother hadn't been the same. Most of her days were spent sitting in front of a window, waiting for him, an old rag doll cradled in her arms.

Liam ruffled Kevin's hair. The embarrassment was enough to drive Kevin into the house.

During Liam's first walk of his beat, he fell into the flow of children meandering towards school. A couple of redheaded boys ahead of him dragged their feet as they looked furtively from side to side. Liam resolved to make sure the stragglers found their way lest hooliganism was on their minds.

It was two of the O'Flaherty boys, those renegades, from a family with too many children for one mother to keep track of while their father worked long days in the mill. Mr. O'Flaherty came home often enough, Kate had observed last Sunday after Mass, when she saw Mrs. O'Flaherty with child again, a babe in her arms, another tugging at her skirt and a constellation of redheads swirling about her.

Just as Liam lengthened his steps to catch up with the boys, a woman called, "Liam! Liam!" and then louder "Constable Barrett!"

Sadie Monaghan, short and round, rolled with a sailor's gait toward him from the direction of her boarding house, a young woman in tow. Sadie still wore her kitchen apron, stained with the morning's chores, having no doubt spotted Liam from her window and taken quick action to catch him. The girl's face was twisted and wet with tears.

"Good morning, Mrs. Monaghan. What can I do for you?"

"This is Maime O'Brien." Sadie held up the girl's arm. "She's been unjustly dismissed from her position. Tell him, Maime."

The girl took a deep breath and shuddered.

"It's like this, Liam," Sadie continued. "Maime is, was, a maid up at the Stewart house. A little gold box has gone missing and the master of the house, Mr. Reginald Stewart himself, is after accusing Maime. Nothing but a box, if you please! Look at her, will you? Does she look like a thief to you?"

Maime looked thin, young and frightened, hardly thief material in Liam's mind.

"How is she to get another position, thrown away as she was under a cloud? It's dreadful, simply dreadful. She didn't do it, I tell you. I just know. And I know you're the one who can help her. You will must find the culprit and restore Maime's good name. I know you will."

131

Mrs. Sadie Monaghan was said to have the second sight. Having not been so blessed and having never witnessed a particularly miraculous prediction by her, Liam was not sure if it was true or if she liked people thinking it was true so as better to impose her will. Yet, she was a friend of his mother's and his mother had been a believer. And the people of Adams gave deference to the authority of Sadie Monaghan…just in case.

"Tell me about this box."

"It's made of solid gold, sir," Maime whispered, out of breath from sobbing. "They kept it on a table in the parlor, a gift from the governor himself to the missus, it was, in thanks, when he last stayed with them last fall. The mister would point it out to all his visitors. 'This is the box that the governor presented to my wife,' he'd say."

"When did this box go missing? And please don't call me sir. Liam will do. Or Constable. "

"Yes, sir, Constable. I mean Liam, sir." Maime blushed. Although it wasn't difficult for men to talk to him, when women tried, especially young women or girls, they'd trip over their words and then fall silent. One night while doing dishes, Liam had asked Kate about it, what he could do differently. She laughed, called him an "eejit," and punched him in the arm. He didn't ask again.

It was just as well, Liam had no need for talking to girls except for police work.

Maime wiped her eyes with her sleeve. "The box was there yesterday morning when I did the dusting. And it was gone today. When I asked the housekeeper about it, she went to Mrs. Stewart who was having her breakfast with Mr. Stewart and they called me in and that's when…" Her next words were lost in sobbing.

Sadie patted Maime's back. "Shush, shush, *macushla*," she crooned. "Liam will fix it. I'm certain of it."

To Liam, Sadie said, "We'll leave you to it then." And with that, she spun Maime around and led her down the street.

There was no defying the second sight of Sadie Monaghan.

When Liam turned back the direction from which he came, the O'Flaherty boys were long gone. To school, Liam hoped.

Mrs. Crawford, the Stewart's housekeeper, answered Liam's knock. Her bird-like stature seemed to swell, filling the doorway and blocking his entry. Small dark round eyes stared at him like those of a crow, prepared to defend its sparse dinner. Her graying hair was pulled back severely into a bun. Her black high-collared dress with tight bodice would have been comely if worn by a friendlier woman.

After she stated that Mr. and Mrs. Stewart were unavailable, Liam said, "Perhaps you can help me, then."

"I do not think so, young man." This woman would not be tongue-tied in Liam's presence.

"I understand that a gold box went missing."

"The culprit has been identified and sacked, as well she should be."

"And I'd be happy to listen to your observations. But this is a police matter now as a theft is a crime, so I will need to investigate to the satisfaction of the law."

"As I said, we have identified the culprit." Mrs. Crawford's thin lips pressed into a line.

"Let's not jump to conclusions, Mrs. Crawford. After all, if the thief goes undetected, the Stewart family may lose more valuable possessions."

And that would not go well for Mrs. Crawford, she was sure to see that.

Liam rested his eyes on her in a kindly, but earnest way. He wasn't leaving without more information.

"Very well, young man. Follow me, if you please."

Liam followed the housekeeper to the kitchen and sat at the table she pointed him to. A lone young woman with bright unruly red hair under her cap scrubbed potatoes in the sink.

"Teresa, make this young man some tea."

Teresa curtsied. When she recognized Liam, her blue eyes went wide, and scarlet rose from her collar splotching her pretty, freckled face.

It was Teresa O'Flaherty, sister to the boys Liam had followed that morning. She was too young to be a friend of Kate's and too old to be a friend of Clare's but he knew her in passing, having seen her with her clan at Mass. Who could miss all that red hair?

"Now, Mrs. Crawford, please tell me about this missing gold box."

"It was there yesterday morning and now it's gone. Or so I've been told."

With shaky hands, Teresa set a cup of tea in front of Liam and then a cup in front of Mrs. Crawford. Liam thanked her, looking her full in the face. Teresa chewed her bottom lip.

"Stop that, girl," Mrs. Crawford said. "Get back to your work."

Teresa curtsied again and returned to her task.

"When was the last time you saw the box, Mrs. Crawford?"

Teresa dropped a bowl of potatoes, shattering the bowl and sending potatoes rolling across the wooden floor in all directions.

Liam reached down to catch a potato. As he raised himself out of his chair to help Teresa, Mrs. Crawford waved him back down.

"Ach! Another broken dish!" Mrs. Crawford hissed. "Clean that mess up, girl. When you're done with that, go down to the store for sugar. I'd expected a delivery yesterday and I could have sworn I heard someone coming to the servant's door. But when I checked the larder this morning, still there was no sugar."

As Teresa cleaned, Liam said, "I know your time is valuable, Mrs. Crawford, and I don't want to take up any more than is necessary. The box, do you remember when you last saw it?"

The housekeeper looked thoughtful for a moment. "I'm rarely in that part of the house. You know how it is, you don't notice things when they are in place and when they go missing, you can't remember the last time you saw them. I'd have to say my last clear recollection of the box was several days ago."

Teresa stood by the servant's door, waiting to be dismissed.

"Off with you, now, and don't forget the sugar," Mrs. Crawford said.

"I'll head on as well, Mrs. Crawford. Thank you for your time."

Teresa darted out with Liam behind her.

"Hold up there, Teresa. I'll walk you."

Teresa slowed as Liam caught up in a few long strides. "Why would Mrs. Crawford think the sugar had been delivered yesterday?"

"I couldn't say, Constable."

"Did someone come to the servant's door?"

"Perhaps."

"Do you know who it was?"

"What time would that be, Constable?"

Liam caught Teresa's elbow, made her stop and look up at him.

"Let's not obstruct justice, Teresa. You know what time I'm talking about. Yesterday afternoon when Mrs. Crawford thought she heard someone at the servant's door."

Teresa had hardened her face when she first looked up at Liam but within a few seconds, her features dissolved into panic.

"Please don't get me in trouble, Constable. I need this job, for my family. The boys aren't old enough to work yet and Da is the only one with a job just now."

"I'll do my best to protect you, Teresa, but you understand Maime O'Brien lost her job over this matter. Do you think that's fair?"

"She doesn't have anyone to support. She can get another job."

"Not with the reputation of a thief." Liam allowed the consequences to soak into Teresa's mind. With a bad reputation, Maime was unlikely to get a job that didn't cater to the foulest whims of men.

"They didn't mean no harm, I'm sure of it."

"Your brothers?"

"They come for tea every afternoon. I give them some biscuits, that's all. It's not like we're stealing. I'm allowed to eat while I'm there and I save my

134

portion for the boys. I'd left them alone in the kitchen with Maime while I brought up potatoes from the cellar. When I came back, the boys had left. The next morning, we noticed the box was missing. It must have been them. Maime knows who took the box, but she didn't say anything lest I lose my job."

"She's a good friend to you," Liam said. "I'll see about getting this box back. And, Teresa…

"Yes, Constable?"

"The less said, the better."

On his way back to the station house, Liam walked past the Cooley farm. Old Sampson was back in the field, contentedly sunning himself. Cooley was inspecting the fence when he spotted Liam. He hollered and beckoned, then strode down to the house.

When Liam was halfway up the lane, a fierce little terrier intercepted him with a mad dash from the barn, yapping to sound the alarm. Liam stopped, afraid the terrier would shred his pants should he try to approach further.

Cooley strode out of the house, something in his fist. When he met Liam, he shooed the dog away and opened his hand.

In his palm, Cooley held a little gold box.

"The mother found this with Mary Ellen's things this morning," Cooley said as he offered the box. "Sure, but look at it! How would she come into possession of such a fine thing?"

Liam took the box and flipped open the hinged lid. Inside, it was inscribed "To Mrs. Stewart, with fond thanks, the Honorable John Q. A. Brackett" in delicate script.

"I'll return it to the rightful owner, Mr. Cooley."

"There will be no problems, then?"

"None for you, sir."

As they talked, the raised voices of boys drifted to them from down the road. Mary Ellen Cooley, who already promised to grow into a dark-haired beauty one day, walked with quiet dignity, studying the uneven road in front of her while to one side of her, the two red-headed O'Flaherty boys bounced into each other like a couple of goat kids, trying to get her attention. To her other side, Kevin shuffled, hands stuffed in his pockets.

Liam slipped the box into his own pocket and went down to meet them. The terrier trotted forward and Mary Ellen scooped him up in her arms.

"Kevin, will you be helping Mr. Cooley this afternoon?" Liam asked.

"Just for a bit, then I'll be home."

"Off with you now. And I'll bid you a good afternoon, Mary Ellen."

Kevin and Mary Ellen circled around Liam as he continued to hold the O'Flaherty boys in his gaze. When they were well out of earshot, Liam pulled out the box and held it up for them to see.

The boys began to step from one foot to another, as if they were infested with fleas.

"This is a serious matter, lads. Maime O'Brien lost her job over this missing box."

Color drained from the face of one. "I told you so," he said as he elbowed his brother.

"Shut up!" the other said with the same defiant face his sister Teresa had shown.

"But we can make everything alright," Liam said, "if you go along with my plan."

Liam escorted the boys to Sadie Monaghan's boarding house where they met with Sadie and Maime. The boys apologized for stealing the box and causing trouble. Maime smiled kindly at them when they explained it was to impress a girl.

"That's all well and good, isn't it?" Sadie asked. "But Maime's reputation is in tatters still. How is she to get her job back?"

Liam gave Sadie a wink.

At the Stewart mansion, Liam explained his plan to Teresa and she agreed. Teresa retrieved Mrs. Crawford from elsewhere in the house and brought her back into the kitchen.

"You again?" Mrs. Crawford asked when she saw Liam.

"Has the gold box turned up yet?"

"We told you. Weren't you listening? It's been stolen."

"How well did you search the premises, madam?" Liam asked as he eased around Mrs. Crawford.

Liam drifted out of the kitchen into the dining room, opening the sideboard doors, peeking into corners with Mrs. Crawford peering over his shoulder. He slowed his pace as he stepped into the parlor.

"See! It's not there," Mrs. Crawford pointed to a bare spot on the mantle.

"I'll have a look around, just the same."

"I haven't time for this nonsense. Have Teresa show you out."

"Certainly, madam."

Liam waited as the clack of Mrs. Crawford's wooden heels receded down a hallway, then he wandered back into the butler's pantry. "Teresa, please fetch Mrs. Crawford."

136

When the housekeeper strutted in, Liam pulled open a cupboard. "I believe I've solved your mystery."

Liam reached to a shelf far too high for Mrs. Crawford to see, picked something up, took it out and put it on the countertop. It was the little gold box.

Mrs. Crawford drew breath sharply. "How did that get there?"

She looked at Teresa accusingly.

"I couldn't say, ma'am," Teresa said, her eyes downcast.

"An innocent mistake, I'm sure," Liam said. "May I give the good word to Maime?"

"I'll need to speak with the Stewarts, of course, but they are fair people," Mrs. Crawford said. "Have her back tomorrow morning, ready for work."

Liam's last call on his beat was always the pub. Not that he drank, having taken the oath when his father died, but it was the hub of Irish male society and, so, the second-best source of information in Adams, Massachusetts, the first being the ladies auxiliary. It was late afternoon and men would be coming in for a drink before going home to their dinners.

After his eyes adjusted to the dark, he saw Cooley and Madigan, nose to nose, necks and shoulders bulging with anger, their faces florid.

"You're wasting Sampson!" Cooley yelled.

"Can I help it he likes my cows better?" Madigan, a bearded, short, barrel-chested man, shouted back. "You should fence him!"

"It's not my fences! There's nothing wrong with my fences! Someone opens the gate and lets him out. If it isn't you, who is it then? Who benefits? That's what I want to know! Who benefits? You!" Cooley gave Madigan a hard push.

"You're a liar!" Madigan pulled one arm back just as Liam took position beside them.

"Enough of that now!"

Madigan blinked and dropped his arm. Cooley stepped back.

"If a punch is thrown, both of you will spend the night in jail and there'll be no one to do your chores in the morning. Does that make sense to you?"

"I didn't steal his bull," Madigan sputtered.

"Ah, but you didn't return him, did you, Mr. Madigan?" Liam said. "And for the time being, you must admit that you benefitted when Sampson visited your cows."

Madigan jerked his head in agreement.

"Would it not be fair, then, that you pay for the service?"

"I've no money," Madigan scoffed.

"No, but you will have calves. Mr. Cooley, would you be satisfied with a calf?"

"Just one?"

"Mr. Cooley," Liam urged, nudging the man toward reason.

"Just one, then, but my pick."

"Done," Madigan said, extending his hand.

Cooley considered for only a moment before reaching out his own hand. They shook.

That night, Kate served lamb stew for dinner. As Liam said grace, Kevin fidgeted and Clare stabbed him into place with a judgmental stare. The stew was eaten, but there would be more tomorrow as Fergus Cooley had brought them lamb meat, of which he said he had too much and it would only spoil if not put to use. Kate had been inclined to refuse charity but Cooley told her it was payment for all the work young Kevin had done on his farm.

When dinner was finished, Liam invited Kevin to take an after-dinner walk, as had been their father's habit. Each took comfort in his own thoughts as they strolled in the sun's long evening rays.

"I solved a mystery today, Kevin," Liam said with a lowered voice. "And I'm telling you this in the strictest of confidence."

Kevin leaned in as Liam had intended him to.

"The O'Flaherty boys caused a bit of a ruckus."

"When don't they?"

"True, true enough. But this was all to please a fair maiden."

"Mary Ellen."

"She's the one, right you are. It seems they ran across a little gold box that didn't belong to them and presented it to her as a gift, causing all kinds of trouble for the people who lost the box and the person accused of stealing it."

"That's just like them."

"Thoughtless, it was. It was thoughtless indeed to create such turmoil for mere folly. After all, the heart of a girl is not won by trinkets."

"If trinkets don't win the heart of a girl, what does?"

"Being a solid man. A responsible man. A man who does the right thing by his family and his friends. A man who owns up to his mistakes. Like our father."

The valley was cast into shadow and the temperature cooled as the sun set behind Mount Greylock.

"Shouldn't we be getting back?" Kevin asked.

"Not just yet, brother. I have another story to tell you. Mr. Cooley and Mr. Madigan nearly came to blows over Sampson today. Cooley suspected Madigan of taking Sampson to cover his cows without payment. Madigan

138

accused Cooley of lying. If they'd fought, they would have both ended up in jail."

Kevin went quiet.

He was still silent as he and Liam rounded up the road to the Cooley farm.

When Fergus Cooley stepped out of his house, Liam and Kevin stopped some distance away, signaling they wanted to speak privately. The little terrier trotted ahead of his master to greet them and sniffed at Kevin's hand. Kevin scratched its ear as Cooley strode down to them.

"Good evening, Constable, Kevin," Cooley looked at each curiously.

Liam rested a hand on his brother's shoulder and Kevin cleared his throat.

"I have a confession, Mr. Cooley. It was me who let Sampson out."

Cooley frowned. "And why would you do that, young Kevin?"

"So I could bring him back."

On the porch, Mary Ellen stood with her five younger sisters behind her. Liam looked over Cooley's shoulder in their direction. Cooley turned around, took in the view and turned back.

"Ah, I see. With my daughters reaching courting age, I should expect more of this?"

"I'm afraid so, sir," said Liam.

"Will you tell Mary Ellen?" Kevin asked Cooley.

"Will my bull wander off again?"

"No, sir. Never. And I promise to work your farm every afternoon after school."

"And would you walk Mary Ellen home every afternoon after school since you'd be coming in the same direction?" Cooley laughed.

"If that's alright." Kevin's voice broke as he spoke.

Cooley extended his hand, still laughing. Kevin hesitated, staring at the great paw before him. With the awkwardness of a fourteen-year-old not quite knowing how long his limbs were, Kevin reached out his hand.

And they shook.

Keenan Powell illustrated the original *Dungeons and Dragons*, then ditched art for law school. The day after graduating, she moved to Alaska where she continues to practice. Her article, "Criminal Law 101," was published in *The Writer* magazine. Currently she writes the column *Ipso Facto* for the Guppies' newsletter. She has two short stories publishing in 2017: "The Velvet Slippers" in *Malice Domestic 12: Murder Most Historical* and "The Cattle Raid of Adams" in *Busted! Arresting Stories from the Beat* published by Level Best Books.

THE PROGRAM

Cyndy Edwards Lively

Emmitt Speaks stooped to duck under the black and yellow plastic tape strung between the oaks at the edge of the playground. Knee-high grass made for slow progress. By the time he reached the steep bank overlooking the creek, his shirt stuck to his back, and he felt like he was gargling rather than breathing the August air.

Phoebe Sorenson shaded her eyes with a hand as she looked up from the creek bed. Tendrils of hair that had escaped from her ponytail curled around her sweat-soaked face. The homicide detective greeted Emmitt with a sympathetic look and a nod in the direction of the body lying face-up in the shallow stream. "Rierson said he was another one of yours."

Emmitt had more than twenty-five years on the job, most of them in the Winston-Salem Police Department's Juvenile Section. He liked the young homicide detective; she was sharp, meticulous, and a team player. He couldn't say the same for Rierson. The man was arrogant, abrasive and in Emmitt's experience—generally uncooperative. It was a good thing Phoebe was primary on the case. Rierson wouldn't have bothered to notify him.

"I appreciate the call," Emmitt said. He stared down at the body of a young black male, barely into his teens. "Deshawn Reeves. What can you tell me, Phoebe?"

"Not much, so far. A Reynolds High School student spotted the body around eight when he was cutting through the park on his way to school. Ran up to the school to get help. The principal and the resource officer," she consulted her notebook, "John Tate, came down to have a look. Tate called it in."

"Who ID'd him?"

"Tate did. Said the boy was a CCS kid. Trouble with a capital T."

Emmitt worked with the Center for Community Safety, a group that had been organized to help turn around repeat juvenile offenders. Most of the kids referred to the center had spent time in Forsyth County Youth Services, some in state detention.

"How did he die?"

"Gunshot to the back of the head. Still waiting on the ME. I'm keeping the area clear for the crime scene techs. Tate and the principal already tracked up the stream bed pretty good when they went to check on him. I don't want anyone else down here."

"What's taking so long? I thought you said he was found around eight."

140

"Big wreck on 52. Three or four cars and more than one DOA. ME's got her hands full this morning." Phoebe shifted her gaze to the body. "What can you tell me about the kid?"

"The last I heard," Emmitt said, "Deshawn was accepted into a program run by a church out in the county and was doing well. Off drugs, attending school, staying out of trouble. Guess the report was overly optimistic."

"Any connection you know of to Juan Ramirez?"

Emmitt shook his head. "Other than both having contact with CCS, I can't think of any. I doubt they ran in the same circles."

Juan had been two years older and barely spoke English when he entered the system. The first time he was arrested for breaking and entering, he had only been in the country a few weeks. His third arrest earned him six months in the Stonewall Jackson Youth Development Center in Concord. Three months after his release, his body had been dumped in a shopping center parking lot on the east side of town. Cause of death, a bullet to the back of the head. Rierson was the primary on Juan's homicide investigation. It had been five or six weeks, and Emmitt hadn't heard of any progress on the case.

"Rierson said Juan was dealing cocaine," Phoebe said. "What about Deshawn?"

"He was using marijuana and cocaine and doing neighborhood B & E's to buy drugs when he was arrested," Emmitt said. "We never had any evidence he was selling. Like I said, the last I heard, he was off drugs and doing well. Rierson thinks Juan's death was drug-related?"

"That's the current theory."

Emmitt stared down at the dead boy. Drugs and violence often went hand-in-hand, but these kids were younger than the usual victims. It was hard to imagine them as a threat to anyone. "If you want help with the notification, I'll go with you. I know Deshawn's grandmother. She's going to take this hard." The woman was a member of Emmitt's church, and he'd known her for more than twenty years. She'd asked Emmitt for help when the boy had been arrested.

Phoebe gave him a grateful look. "Thanks, Emmitt. I really appreciate it. I'll give you a call when I finish here."

On a Saturday afternoon a couple of months later, Phoebe called again. Emmitt was mowing the grass. The weather was unseasonably warm, and recent rains had encouraged a growth spurt that had the lawn looking scraggly. He took the phone from his wife in one hand and the glass of iced tea she held out to him in the other and smiled his thanks.

"What can I do for you, Phoebe?"

"Emmitt, I hate to bother you on your weekend off, but there's been another shooting."

"Another kid?"

"Yeah, I'm afraid so. He was dumped in the Coliseum lot last night or early this morning, over near the Education Building. A worker coming in to set up fair exhibits spotted the body. No ID. I was hoping you could have a look, see if you recognize him."

"You think it's tied in with the other two?"

"Too soon to say. But he's about the same age, and the MO looks similar."

Emmitt drank down the last of the tea in two long swallows and set the glass in the sink. "What's going on here, Phoebe?"

"I don't know, and I could use some help. We haven't made any progress on the other two kids. Working a possible drug connection hasn't produced any leads. Everywhere we've looked has been a dead end."

"I'll be there as soon as I can," he said.

"Another boy's been shot?" his wife asked when he hung up the phone.

Emmitt looked into eyes that mirrored his distress. "Phoebe wants me to have a look. See if I know him."

He showered and dressed in record time and gave his wife a brief hug on the way out the door. "I don't know how long I'll be, but I'll give you a call if it looks like I'll be late for dinner."

"Someone's out there killing kids," she said, her eyes on their two youngest sons who were shooting baskets in the driveway. "Dinner can wait."

When Emmitt pulled into the parking lot, he didn't have to guess where to go. A fire truck, an EMS van, and a half dozen police cruisers blocked access to the area near the Education Building. He added his car to the mix and threaded his way to the tape. Phoebe spotted him and waved him in.

"Thanks for coming, Emmitt." Her welcoming glance almost made up for the scowl Rierson gave him when he stepped closer to the body.

"What're you doing here?" Rierson asked.

"I called him," Phoebe said. Her expression told Emmitt she was embarrassed by her partner's surliness. "I thought Emmitt might help us make an ID."

Emmitt was struck by the similarity to the scene in the park two months earlier. The kid was in his early teens, sprawled face-up on the damp, oily surface of the lot. This time it was a white boy, and Emmitt knew him. "Bryan Mabe."

"Another juvenile delinquent." Rierson shook his head in disgust.

"He's only thirteen or fourteen," Emmitt said, glaring at Rierson. "He's been in trouble but nothing to earn him something like this."

"I didn't say he had. Just that none of these kids were angels. They ran in rough circles, and it got them killed." Rierson stalked off before Emmitt had a chance to reply.

"Sorry, Emmitt," Phoebe said. "He's frustrated and taking it out on everyone in reach. What do you know about Bryan?"

"His mother contacted CCS for help about a year ago when he was arrested with a bunch of kids who were vandalizing cars in West End. He'd been skipping school and hanging with gang members. She wanted to get him into a program, get him turned around before something more serious happened. The

142

last I heard, he was doing better." Emmitt turned to Phoebe. "If I remember right, he was referred to the same church group as Deshawn Reeves."

"Then they might have known one another," Phoebe said. "We were never able to find any connection between Ramirez and Reeves. The Ramirez family left town as soon as the ME released the boy's body. We couldn't locate them after Reeves was shot."

"Did you talk to anybody at the church about Deshawn?"

"Rierson did. The pastor told him Deshawn quit the program a couple of months before his death. Just stopped coming."

Emmitt thought back to the conversations he'd had with Deshawn's grandmother after the boy's death. She'd been distraught and insistent that Deshawn was doing well, staying out of trouble. At the time he'd suspected it was wishful thinking on her part. This news pretty much confirmed it.

"It'd be worth checking to see if Bryan ever attended the program," Emmitt said. "We might get a lead that links these kids." The first two deaths had been connected by police suspicions and, apparently, not much else. This third shooting made it clear someone was out there killing kids. "I want to be in on this, Phoebe."

"There's going to be a taskforce. We can use all the help we can get."

A month passed, and they were no closer to catching the person who'd shot three teenage boys and dumped their bodies in public places around a city that had never imagined itself the home of a serial killer. The SBI and FBI consultants were stumped. There was no sign of a sexual angle, no common thread the profilers could identify. Emmitt had interviewed family members and friends of the victims to no avail. No one was able to provide a clue as to why the boys had been killed or who was responsible.

Working for weeks through contacts in the Hispanic community, Emmitt finally spoke with the Ramirez family by telephone. In the country illegally, they'd returned to Mexico after their son's death and were reluctant to talk to the police. From them, he heard the same refrain as he had from the other families: their son was off drugs, going to school, on the right track. Those people at the church were miracle workers. The family had no idea who'd wanted Juan dead or why.

Emmitt finished the call and thanked the young woman who'd graciously agreed to translate for her help. When he returned from escorting her out of the maze of cubicles occupied by the Criminal Investigation Division, he sank into his chair with a sigh. To hear the families and friends tell it, the boys—while not exactly model citizens—were living the straight and narrow at the time of their deaths. For weeks, he'd chalked it up to no one wanting to speak ill of the dead. Now he was beginning to wonder.

He paged Phoebe. It'd been a few days since they'd spoken, neither wanting to discuss the lack of progress. When his phone rang, he was still trying to decide how to convince her to see things his way. The whole investigation had proceeded on the premise that the boys were involved in something that had gotten them killed. That they'd seen something or known something that made them a danger to the drug or gang community. So far, nobody had been able to come up with anything that linked the boys to illegal activity at the time of their deaths. Or to each other.

Emmitt picked up on the second ring. "Phoebe, just wanted to let you know I finally got through to the Ramirez family. They insist they don't have a clue who killed their son or why, but the parents are convinced that Juan was getting his act together. Claim he was off drugs and going to school when he was killed. And apparently, he was part of the same church youth group as Deshawn and Bryan."

"Well, they were right about the school attendance and the drugs. The school records confirm that all three boys attended regularly, only a few excused absences among them during the months prior to their deaths. Their drug screens were all negative, too."

In spite of being a member of the taskforce, Emmitt wasn't privy to all of the information Homicide had accumulated on the cases. He cursed himself for not asking sooner. "So, it looks like the drug angle is off base. If they were dealing, they most likely would've been using."

"Rierson still thinks it's a possibility."

"You know that's unlikely. And there were no stashes of cash found at any of their homes."

"I know," Phoebe said. "But at this point, we don't have much else to go on."

Emmitt could hear the frustration in her voice. "All of the families said the boys were attending that church program when they were killed."

"Rierson talked to the pastor about Bryan. The guy told him the same story he had about Deshawn. Both boys quit the program a couple of months before their deaths. We didn't know about Juan."

"Well, that doesn't fit with what the families are saying. They insist the boys were off drugs, in school, and participating in the church program. Now you're telling me that you have conformation of the first two. We need to look at the church. It's the only link we've come up with so far. Has anyone talked with the other kids in the program?"

"Rierson took care of that angle," Phoebe said. "I'm sure he must have interviewed everyone who had contact with the boys." Her words were belied by the hint of doubt in her tone.

"We need to do it again, push harder," Emmitt said. "The kids may be afraid they'll get into trouble if they talk to the police. They may know something they're too scared to admit."

Before he hung up, Emmitt had Phoebe's agreement they would re-interview the kids in the church youth group. Phoebe would find out when the next meeting was and get back with him. He was relieved he hadn't had to suggest leaving Rierson out of it. She hadn't mentioned bringing her partner along.

There was a chill in the air and not a cloud in sight. The hardwoods sported a brilliant display of color that made Emmitt glad he'd escaped from his cramped cubicle that passed for an office. He drove while Phoebe navigated, calling out the turns as they wound their way deeper into the countryside. The final turn led them down a dirt road with still no sign of the church.

"This place is out in the middle of nowhere," Emmitt said. "I didn't know we had spots this remote in the county."

"You need to get out of town more often." Phoebe smiled at him. "This area near the river is still pretty undeveloped, and I hope it stays that way."

"Is a deputy meeting us out here?" Emmitt asked. They were well outside Winston-Salem city limits. Technically, the sheriff's office had jurisdiction.

Phoebe shook her head. "They're leaving it to us. They're part of the taskforce, but I get the feeling they're happy to let us take the heat for the lack of progress on the case."

Emmitt was pleased they were on their own. His experience with teens had taught him it was usually better to talk to kids without a show of force. Phoebe's petite size and youthful appearance made her naturally less threatening than him. Over the years, he'd learned how to put young people at ease in spite of his line-backer bulk.

They rounded the next curve and got their first view of the church. It looked like hundreds of others scattered throughout the South: a white clapboard rectangle with double front doors, a small steeple rising from the roof in front, and rows of windows down the side. No stained glass. A gray, one-story cinder-block building met the back end of the church at a right angle but didn't appear to be connected to the older, wooden structure. The gravel parking lot held a battered pickup, a late-model sedan, and an old school bus that'd been painted blue and emblazoned down the side with HOLY CHURCH OF REDEMPTION in tall black letters.

Emmitt pulled into the lot and parked their unmarked car beside the bus. When he and Phoebe climbed from the car, a man emerged from a door at the end of the cinder-block building and walked briskly across the gravel toward them. Slim, medium height, light-brown hair cut short, he had the look and carriage of a former military man.

"Detective Sorenson, I'm Reverend Michaels," he said as he extended his hand to Phoebe. "We're glad to have you come out, but I'm sorry it's under such sad circumstances."

Phoebe shook his hand and tilted her head toward Emmitt. "Reverend Michaels, this is Detective Speaks. He works in the Juvenile Section. As I told you on the phone, we're here to talk to the kids in the CCS program. All of the parents have given their permission for us to speak with them."

"Nice to meet you, Detective Speaks."

145

Michaels's handshake was firm and dry. His hand felt small in Emmitt's larger one. Before Emmitt could respond, the man turned and started back across the lot toward the door he'd exited. Emmitt and Phoebe stepped quickly to follow in the pastor's wake.

"The boys are in the Education Hall. I told them we were having visitors this afternoon but didn't mention who was coming. I thought it would be better if you explained what you're here about. As I'm sure you know, these boys haven't always had the best relations with the police."

When Michaels reached the door, he opened it wide and waved them in. "First door on your right."

"Just boys?" Emmitt said. "There aren't any girls in the program?"

Michaels shook his head. "We don't approve of mixing the sexes. All of our school classrooms are segregated, and we don't have enough staff to offer a girls' program at this time. Maybe in the future, if we prove successful with the boys."

"You have a school out here?" Emmitt asked.

"Holy Redemption has a small school for our members' children, elementary through high school. We're accredited with the state and offer a Christian-based curriculum."

Michaels opened the door and gestured for Phoebe and Emmitt to precede him into the room. "Boys, this is Detective Sorenson and Detective Speaks. They're here to talk with you this afternoon. When you're finished, come to the chapel for closing prayers." He gave Emmitt and Phoebe a slight nod, backed out the door, and pulled it closed.

There were half a dozen teenage boys occupying metal folding chairs around a Formica-topped table. A Bible lay open on the table in front of each boy. Expressions ranged from guarded to apprehensive as Emmitt and Phoebe took seats at the table.

Emmitt took the lead as they'd agreed on the ride out. "Detective Sorenson and I are here to talk about Juan, Deshawn, and Bryan. We're hoping you boys can help us out."

"Just how you figure we can do that?" The question came from a lanky kid whose corn-rowed head bowed over his Bible, his eyes fixed firmly on the pages.

As if on cue, the rest of the boys returned their gaze to the books in front of them. Emmitt wouldn't have picked the kid as the leader; he wasn't the largest by a long shot and didn't appear to be the oldest. But it was clear the others were following his lead.

"We know Juan, Deshawn, and Bryan were part of the youth program out here, so you must have known them. Anything you can remember about them might help us find out who killed them." Emmitt addressed his remarks to the whole table, searching faces to gauge the response. No one looked up.

"They quit the program." Again, the lanky kid. This time he met Emmitt's gaze with a cool, appraising look. "We don't know nothing about what they into. We already told that other detective."

146

"That's part of what we'd like to find out," Emmitt said, "when and why they quit."

His statement was met with silence. Eyes stayed firmly glued to the Bibles, but the boys' anxiety was palpable. Fingers gripped pages too tightly. Several of the kids were sweating in spite of the cool breeze blowing through a partially opened window. Emmitt made a mental note which of the boys appeared the most frightened. He would start the interviews with them.

Two hours later, Emmitt and Phoebe went in search of Reverend Michaels. They found him in a small office at the opposite end of the Education Hall from the classroom where the boys were sitting. He looked up when they stopped at the open doorway.

"Finished with the boys? I hope you got what you needed."

Emmitt smiled, pretending an optimism he didn't feel. "Thanks for letting us come out to talk to them. Easier to have them all in one place."

The detectives said their goodbyes and returned to their car. The sun had dipped almost to the horizon, and the bite in the breeze rattling the leaves of the trees surrounding the parking lot had Emmitt wishing he'd brought a heavier coat. He switched on the heater as they pulled onto the dirt road.

"They all said the same thing," Phoebe said. "Practically the same words."

"I thought we were going to get something out of a couple of them once we had them alone," Emmitt said, "but they stuck to the party line. Those kids know something they're not telling, and they're scared. They're in over their heads and don't know how to climb out."

The voice kept fading in and out, making it difficult for Emmitt to hear all the words, but the fear came through loud and clear. "You gotta help me. I'm gonna be next." Young, probably African American, and most likely male, although terror raised the voice's pitch to a near squeak.

Cradling the receiver against his shoulder, Emmitt reached for a pad on his desk. "Where are you, son?"

"In the woods down by the river. He got a dog with him."

Emmitt had given his card to each of the boys after he and Phoebe questioned them at the church. It listed his direct office line and his cell phone. He'd figured the kids had discarded them as soon as he was out of sight. "How close to the church?"

"I don't know." The kid cleared a gurgle from his throat. "I been running a while."

The Yadkin River ran north-south about a mile west of the church property. "You heading north or south?" His question was met with silence.

"Are you moving with the river on your right or left?"

"Right." The voice sounded slightly stronger.

"What's your number?" Emmitt wrote it down. "You have my card?"

"Yeah."

147

"Call me back on my cell. Keep moving in the same direction and keep the river in sight. We're on the way."

Emmitt fretted through the time it took to get patrol on the road and notify the sheriff's office, hoping they had someone closer to the area than the WSPD. He sprinted to his car after catching Phoebe at her desk. She slid into the passenger seat as he turned the key in the ignition. Emmitt handed Phoebe his cell phone. "Keep him on the line."

They rode in silence except for the occasional word of encouragement Phoebe spoke into the phone. She told the kid to keep quiet, that she would do the talking. Emmitt cursed himself for blindness. He'd known the kids were scared, but not the source of their fear.

Two cruisers from the sheriff's office and a WSPD patrol car were already parked in the church lot when Emmitt's car skidded to a stop, spitting gravel from beneath the wheels. One of the sheriff's deputies stood beside his cruiser, microphone in hand. Emmitt jogged over. "Have they located Michaels?"

The man gave a brusque headshake. "There's a lot of woods to search. Dogs are on the way. We've got a team working its way up the river from the south. Hope to catch him in-between."

"The kid says the reverend has a dog of his own."

This information was relayed to the officers and deputies in the woods. Emmitt took his cell phone from Phoebe. "Find a place you can hide and stay put," he told the kid. "Sheriff's deputies are on the way up the river toward you, and a team's coming from the direction of the church."

Time crept past. Emmitt stared into the woods, as if by concentrating very hard he could manage to see what was happening a mile away. The sharp crack of gunfire broke the tense silence. Two shots followed, echoed through the still, afternoon air. Emmitt gripped the phone, his words coming close to a shout. "Are you OK? Talk to me, kid."

"What was that?" The young voice was a shaky whisper, but the boy sounded unharmed.

Emmitt listened to the garbled words from the car radio. "They've got Michaels. Just stay where you are until you see the deputies coming up the river. They'll bring you in."

The three of them sat in Emmitt's car, Emmitt and the kid in back and Phoebe up front in the passenger seat. The kid was wrapped in a gray thermal blanket one of the deputies had provided and was sipping on a cup of hot chocolate Phoebe had scrounged from the church kitchen. The boy had refused to set foot in the building.

"I wanted to tell you when you was here the other day, but Lamont wouldn't let me." Emmitt's suspicion that the lanky kid was the group's leader was confirmed. "He said we'd all be OK if we just kept our heads down and our mouths shut."

"Juan, Deshawn, and Bryan were still part of the group when they died?" Emmitt said.

The kid stared into the cup clinched in his hands. "At first, we just thought it was some kind of strange happening. Reverend Michaels said Juan been backsliding, doing drugs on the sly, dissing the Lord. But Juan hadn't let on to any of us, and we was pretty close."

The boy took a big swallow from the cup, leaving an ellipse of chocolate on his upper lip. "When Deshawn died, Reverend Michaels said the police was coming out to talk to us. We better tell them we hadn't seen Deshawn in over a month. That he dropped out of the program. He said if we didn't, they'd shut the program down, and we'd all be going to Youth Development on account of how the program was part of our probation. We was scared. None of us wanted to go back inside. We did what he said."

"And after Bryan was killed?" Emmitt prompted.

"Reverend Michaels said the police told him Bryan was into bad stuff that got him killed. Staying in the program and keeping to the ways of the Lord was the best way to stay safe." The kid stared out the car window toward the church. "We should've told what we knew. Maybe Bryan still be alive." He glanced back at Emmitt as if for confirmation.

"Any idea why Michaels did it?" Emmitt spoke softly, holding the kid's gaze.

"He say the Lord pull out bad weeds so good crops can grow." For the first time, Emmitt could see a glint of tears in the boy's eyes. "Guess he figured some of us just too bad to grow."

Cyndy Edwards Lively is a retired pediatrician living in Winston Salem, NC. Her story "Family Business" appeared in *Windward: Best New England Crime Stories 2016*. In 2015, *Mission Mars: Building Red* featured "First Wave" a murder mystery set in the near future. "Negotiate in Good Faith" was published in *Mystery Times Ten* (2013) and "Day Hike" in *Mystery in the Wind* (2009).

IDA MAE BUYS A CROWN VIC

Kate Clark Flora

Some women just got kind of funny acting when they went through the change. That was how Roy explained it to the guys down at the VFW when he told them about Ida Mae taking that self-defense course over to the police department. Mort said no wife of his was gonna rush out after dinner night after night so she could learn how to beat up men and Tooley said it made him glad he didn't have no wife.

Roy said he didn't mind. It sure beat havin' Ida Mae run around with some younger guy, like Pat's wife had done, or dye her hair red or gain fifty pounds, and so far, she hadn't forgot how to cook. Besides, them damned hot flashes made her so cranky he guessed he didn't mind having her go out. Better'n having her out in the yard in a tank top in January, wavin' her arms about like she'd been doing. People drivin' by could see that.

Few weeks later, though, Roy stormed in loaded for bear. Had to belt down a beer and a chaser before he was calm enough to talk. Mort and Tooley were all agog, waitin' on what he was gonna say, and when he finally spat it out, it was a pisser. "Left me a note on the table." Roy slammed his big fist down on the polyurethane. "Said dinner was in the oven and to help myself 'cuz she was going on a ride around with one of the police. Man works all day to put food on the table and keep a roof overhead and this is what he gets. First she's learnin' to kick guys in the balls, then she's riding around with cops. Next the woman'll want a police scanner and a gun."

"Which one?" Tooley asked, probably trying to recall whether any of the Dorsmont cops were old enough to be attracted to Ida Mae, who wasn't a bad looking woman if you didn't mind 'em sort of skinny and full of pep. Tooley liked his women soft and generous and horizontal. Liked 'em married, too, so they wouldn't try and stake a claim on him.

"Which gun or which police scanner?" Mort asked.

"Which cop, dummy," Tooley said. "Who's she ridin' with?"

"One of them woman cops," Roy growled. "Ask me, women got no place bein' cops. They ain't big enough. Can't handle themselves. Look at what them hormones do. Look at Ida Mae. Sensible woman all her life, now she's gone flat out nuts."

"Sheesh." Tooley sounded worried. "You don't suppose, now that she can't have kids, Ida Mae's getting interested in women?"

150

"Hold on there!" Roy smacked the bar. "This is my wife you're talking about." He finger-combed his thinning ginger hair, scowling. "All I said was she was riding in a cop car. Besides, they wouldn't hire no lesbos to be on the police in Dormont. Chief Rathbone wouldn't wanna be around no dykes. Wouldn't want his cops around 'em, neither."

He signaled the bartender for another, and hunkered down on his stool, staring glumly at the TV. In the back, where his goddamned shirt wouldn't stay tucked in, he felt a draft whenever the door opened on what Ida Mae, who had a high falutin' fondness for words, called his callipygian cleft. "Butt crack," he'd told her. "No need to get fancy." But Ida Mae liked fancy. Always trying to tart him up, like a man who'd given her a nice house, a nice yard and a nice life wasn't good enough.

"She say which cop?" Mort persisted.

"That new black one," Roy said. "Sorta short and stocky?"

"Then you got no worries," Tooley said. "Ida Mae'd never be interested in her."

Like that batshit Tooley thought Ida Mae might be attracted to some other woman? Like her own husband wasn't man enough for her? He still performed nice and regular and Ida Mae never gave no sign she wasn't satisfied. He wished he'd never brought it up. Mort and Tooley were such dumb buggers.

A few minutes later, Al Lamoreau came in and started bitching about his boss, and about that fat bitch Louene down to the town offices who busted his balls every time he went for a permit. Everyone got talking about Louene and how wide her ass was and they forgot about Ida Mae.

Next morning at breakfast, Ida Mae was buzzing like a wasp in autumn, talking at him about her ride along like she thought he gave a damn. "We had us a domestic," she said, "over at those new houses they built up where the pig farm used to be. And LaTonya let me come in with her and watch, just like I was one of the police. Good thing I did, too. There's this poor woman, prettiest little thing you ever saw, all banged up and crying. She's holding this little baby and it's crying, too. I told her why didn't she let me hold it while she put some ice on her face, and she just passed that baby over like it was a sack of groceries. That poor thing was soaked right through. I had to change everything, right down to the skin."

He's trying to eat eggs and sausage and she's talkin' wet diapers? Woman really was losing it. Three kids and she'd completely forgot he didn't like to hear about stuff like diapers. He'd never changed a kid in his life. Some of the men now were so pussy whipped they'd stay home with the kids and let their wives go out to work. Roy was grateful he'd been born and raised when men and women knew their places. These days, you even saw women driving trucks and delivering mail. He didn't mind if Ida Mae wanted to do something womanly, like her nursing, but no wife of his was taking a job away from some man.

151

But she goes right on talking, doesn't notice that he isn't interested. "So the husband comes in from another part of the house, sees the police officer is a woman, and starts saying these awful things about how women are wrecking the world and castrating all the men. He says she...he means Officer Jones...has got no right to be in his house unless he says she can come in. His wife can't let her in because she don't have her name on anything. LaTonya doesn't let him rattle her at all."

Ida Mae poured him more coffee but didn't stop the story.

"Then another cops shows up, a great big guy. He doesn't try to take over or anything." Ida Mae's eyes were shining. "He just waits for LaTonya to tell him what she wants him to do, which is take the husband in the other room so she can interview the wife. Anyway, after I've cleaned up the baby, he starts fussing. I ask should I fix him a bottle and the woman just sighs and shrugs and says she can't think about that, can't I see she's busy talking to the police? Like I was hired help or something."

She raised an eyebrow. "You done?"

He nodded. She swept his dirty dishes into the sink and held up the coffee pot. He shook his head. "You want more toast or anything, Roy? Or I baked some rolls. Cinnamon, the kind you like."

"Couple rolls would be good," he said, reaching for the paper.

"Can you imagine any mother, even one's been beaten up, that doesn't think of her child first?"

"Dunno." He turned to the sports page.

Ida Mae put two rolls on a plate and stuck them in the microwave. "Tommy's bringing his girlfriend tomorrow for dinner and you've got to be home. Clay and Annie Lee are coming. So don't go hanging around down there at the VFW, drinking all afternoon, and forget about it, okay?"

He slapped the paper down on the table. "Since when did I ever—"

Then he remembered. The last time Ida Mae'd planned dinner with the kids, he'd been watching that new football league with the guys and he had forgot. Maybe because dinner with the kids mostly gave him heartburn. Tommy was okay, but his lazy other son, Clay, had some mouth on him, and he never could get used to the way Annie Lee tried to dress like one of them women on TV—tits hanging out and her skirts up to God knew where. He'd talked to her about it once, about what men thought when they saw women dressed like that. She'd just patted his arm and called him a dinosaur. Like he didn't know how men's minds worked.

He was out back in his workshop, soldering the handle back onto a favorite tool, when Ida Mae came in. She just stood there, waiting to get his attention. She knew he hated to be bothered when he was workin'. Man's workshop was supposed to be a place where he could be alone. He finished and turned on her. "What's so all-fired important you gotta bother me here?"

"I was just wondering, Roy. You know what I was saying this morning about that man at the domestic? How she didn't own a damned thing and it was his house and he could throw her out in the street if he wanted?" He just grunted. "Well, so I want to know. Do you own this house, Roy, or do we?"

"Sheesh, Ida Mae. You innerup me when I'm workin' with a dumb question like that?" He started putting things away. He liked things orderly. Liked to know everything was in its place. "It's both of our names on the house, doncha remember, so if anything happened to me when the kids were little, the house would be yours without us spending a lot of money on lawyers?"

She smiled timidly and backed toward the door. "Thanks, Roy. I was just wondering about it and all."

"Hey!" he called after her. "What we eatin' tonight?"

"Fried chicken. Tomorrow I got roast beef," she said, "mashed potatoes and gravy. I wonder if Tommy's girl likes gravy? He's never said what she eats. Only that she's pretty and sort of shy. If she's shy, Roy, you'd better not tell any of your jokes."

"I ain't making no promises." He wiped his hands on a rag. "Maybe you oughta lay off that cop stuff, you know? It's giving you ideas about things you don't gotta worry about." He looked at his watch. "Got to pick up some stuff down to the hardware store and then I'm heading over to the VFW. And doncha worry. I'll be home for dinner. Tonight and tomorrow. Biscuits," he added. "Gotta have biscuits with my chicken."

The next morning, he was heading for the door when Ida Mae put a hand on his arm. She was wearing that pants suit she wore for special meetings, and lipstick, but she hadn't mentioned anything. "Family dinner," she said. "Sober."

He pulled his arm away. "I think you're gettin too big for your britches."

She squared off nervously. "Sober," she repeated, looking so small and timid she made him feel like that guy who beat up on his pretty little wife.

Roy'd never raised a hand to Ida Mae. Raised his voice, sure. She could be damned irritating. A man had to keep a woman in her place or all hell broke loose. Look what had happened with Pat's wife. Claiming he was cruel and abusive and had drove her to having affairs. Shirley had always been goin' on about something. If Pat had only told her to button her lip once in a while, acted like a man instead of a wimp, she might not have run wild like that.

But Pat said that Shirley was going through the change and it took her pretty hard. Usta cry all the time and got weird in her head and couldn't remember stuff and all. So maybe Shirley havin' that affair was just craziness. Sheesh. He didn't know why women had to go all crazy and all. He woulda thought if they didn't get their periods anymore they'd be happy. Didn't make sense to him. Spend all those years bitchin' because you gotta have a period, then stop havin' it and bitch about that.

153

He ducked through the back door, grabbed his coat and hat, and got in the truck. Tryin' to understand women made his head hurt. He'd feel a whole lot better once he'd got through work and could go down the VFW and have himself a beer.

During family dinner, Ida Mae gave the funny little duck of her head she did when she was gonna say something he might not like. "Going to be out Thursday night. Renewing my CPR. They're giving a course at the hospital."

"That's cool, Mrs. Bean," Tommy's girlfriend Erin said. "You're a nurse, aren't you?"

"LPN," Ida Mae said. "Never did get to finish my RN on account of Tommy coming along. Then we had Clay and Annie Lee, and by then, I was so busy I couldn't even think about any more school."

"You could go back now," the girl said. "You got no kids at home. You must get pretty bored, keeping this big house up with no one but you and Mr. Bean."

"Oh, I keep myself busy, dear. Seems like there's always lots to do."

"Pass the taters," Roy said.

"You make real good mashed potatoes," Erin said, passing the bowl to Roy. "My momma's are always lumpy and she doesn't put in near enough salt and butter. Trying to look after my dad's blood pressure and cholesterol. I guess you don't have those problems, huh, Mr. Bean?"

Roy didn't like discussing medical things. Wasn't real comfortable talking with strange young girls, either, especially pretty ones like this. Ida Mae'd never have dared speak to his father this way. This girl was more like Annie Lee, who didn't have no limits. He grunted and speared another piece of meat. Then said, "Tommy, how're things going at work these days?"

"Oh, Tommy's been made assistant manager," the girl said.

Tommy blushed and grabbed another roll. "Yeah," he said. "And with my promotion, me and Erin have been thinking we'd get married."

"Sheesh," Clay said, "you're already living together. What's the rush?"

Annie Lee bounced in her chair, making them loose boobs jump around in her shirt like Jell-O. "Oh, jeez, can I be a bridesmaid? I mean, like, are you going to have a real wedding and all?"

And Ida Mae said, "Oh, gee, Erin. I think it's real sweet of you and Tommy to come to dinner like this and tell us your good news."

Good news? Roy wanted to drag Tommy out to the workshop, ask if he'd knocked the girl up. Offer some money for an abortion, if that's what they needed. Didn't the kid know how hard it was to get anywhere with a wife and a kid? Roy loved Ida Mae, sure, but he'd never got over wishing he'd waited until he'd saved a little more, could of bought his own place earlier, instead of waiting for the old man to die before taking over the shop. Fretting over money all those years had been no picnic. Not that Ida Mae'd been pushy about getting married. Only that she wouldn't sleep with him until they were. Tommy didn't have that problem, so why the rush?

But he couldn't bring that up during family dinner, so he said to Ida Mae, "Why can't you do your CPR during the day?"

"Because that's when they're offering the course, Roy. So working people can take it. It's just the one night."

"What you need it for anyways?"

Ida Mae pushed a piece of meat around her plate. "I was thinking I might go back to work. Like Erin said, it doesn't take all my energy to keep up this house. I could start saving toward our retirement. Maybe we could even spend a few weeks in Florida or something. A lot of people do."

"Long as there's dinner on the table."

"Jeez, Daddy," Annie Lee said, "anybody'd think you didn't care about anything but food. And here mom's finally thinking about doing something with her life."

"It ain't the first time she's worked at nursing," he said. "And food's important, girlie. Ask any hard workin' man."

"Dinosaur." Annie Lee rolled her eyes. "Admit it," she said. "You just don't want her to have any life except waiting on you."

"Annie Lee, don't sass your dad," Ida Mae said. "We're trying to have a nice family meal here."

Annie Lee shrugged. "So, Erin, you going to have a big wedding or what?"

The girl looked down at her plate. "Guess we haven't gotten that far yet," she said. "We only just decided about getting married." Roy wondered if her folks were balking at paying for a wedding when the kids were already living together. "Are you going back to nursing, Mrs. Bean?"

"Call me Ida Mae, honey, would you please? Mrs. Bean makes me feel old."

"Yes, ma'am," the girl said.

Roy looked around at the empty plates. "We got any dessert?"

"Strawberry-rhubarb pie." Ida Mae jumped up and started clearing. Erin got up to help. Annie Lee didn't move.

"We got ice cream?" Clay asked. "Cuz it's no good without ice cream."

"Of course we do." Ida Mae smiled. "Out in the freezer. You want to get it?"

She'd always been sweet on Clay. Clay had been sickly when he was little. Roy thought Ida Mae was still surprised he'd grown up into such a strapping boy. But Clay'd come out lazy and spoiled, because Ida Mae'd never let him be spanked.

When Clay didn't move, Roy said, "You heard your mother. Go get the ice cream." Kid shot him a dirty look, got the ice cream, and dropped it on the table with a thump.

"Happy?" he said.

"Take more than a lazy bum bringing in ice cream to make me happy."

155

"Oh, fuck you, old man."

"Clayton Bean!" Ida Mae's voice was louder than usual and had more snap. "I won't have that language in my house."

"Oh jeez, Mom. Give it a rest. You know me and Dad don't get along. I don't know why you insist on pretending we're a normal, happy family."

Roy watched, astonished, as Ida Mae rushed up to her son and grabbed his chin in one small hand, turning the boy's face to hers. "We *are* a normal, happy family, Clay, compared to what's out there. You're just too darned selfish to notice." Roy thought he was gonna fall off his chair. "You ought to look around you some. See how bad families can be." She went all red in the face and turned away, like she was as surprised by what she'd done as the rest of them.

Next day, down to the VFW, Mort dropped beside him with a thump and ordered a beer. "Hear your son's gonna marry one of the Davis girls, that skinny little dark-haired one that's got a boy's name. Aaron, is it?"

"It's Erin. E.R.I.N. Irish, I think. Where'd you hear that?"

"Her old man was over to Agway, pickin' up some lawn patch. Said he'd gotta get the yard in shape if they were gonna have a wedding. Clerk, you know, Old Hal Burrows, he asks which kid is it? Guy says his older daughter's marryin' Tommy." Mort leaned back on his stool. "So what? You didn't know?"

"They was over to dinner and told us."

"You don't sound too pleased."

"Boy's just getting started. They get married and then she'll be wantin' babies and they'll never get ahead. You know how it is."

Mort looked like he was gonna give a speech, but then Tooley heaved himself up on the next stool and ordered a double bourbon. "Whew!" he said, mopping his face. "Damned near got caught coming out of Tiny Parker's house today."

"What you doin' at Tiny's?" Mort asked, though they both knew.

Tooley barked a laugh. "Givin' his wife what Tiny don't bother to do no more."

"You're a damned fool, Tooley," Roy told him. "Tiny's the best shot in town and he's always got a loaded gun on the rack. Why you want to mess with him?"

"Ain't messing with him. Messing with his wife. Speaking of wives, I hear yours has got herself a job."

News to Roy, but he wasn't about to let on. He leaned back on the stool and tucked his shirt in. With Tooley's big mouth, he'd know soon enough.

"Hear she's gonna work for the police department. I'm surprised you're letting her. Kind of a rough place for a proper lady like Ida Mae."

Keep calm, Roy told himself. Tooley was an asshole.

"What kinda job?" Mort asked. "She's too old to be an officer."

"Dispatcher." Tooley waggled his caterpillar brows. Mort was bald as an egg, but Tooley's hair was like a pelt. "From now on, you call 911, you're

156

gonna be telling your personal business to Ida Mae. She'll bring home great stories. Like the time fat Louene went to the toilet in the dark and her husband had left the seat up? She gets stuck and when he's trying to haul her up, his back goes out? They hadda holler for their kid to call 911."

Tooley drank off half his bourbon, staring at Roy. "Ain't you upset about your wife workin' nights with all those men?"

Roy made a show of checking his watch. "Oh, hell, I'm late," he said. "Promised to go by and help Tommy move some furniture." He slapped a bill down on the bar.

He was at the door when Tooley called, "She'll look real cute in a uniform."

She was wrapped in a faded apron, stirring a pot on the stove, clouds of steam rising up around her. She looked around when he came in, smiling like she was glad to see him. "You're early. Everything okay?"

"You're fuckin' jokin', right?"

She snapped off the burner. "Is something wrong? Did something happen at the shop?" She came toward him, arms out, to comfort him.

"Stay the fuck away from me," he said.

"Roy, your language..."

He knocked over a kitchen chair. Then a second. That got her attention. "Was I gonna be the last to know, Ida Mae? Your own husband's gonna be the last person to know about your new job?"

"I don't have a new job."

He threw a chair against the wall so hard it chipped the paint. "That asshole Tooley says you're going to be a police dispatcher."

Ida Mae edged toward the door, watching him like some nervous animal might. "Roy, you're gonna wreck those chairs. I worked real hard refinishing them."

"Hold it right there." He knocked the spoon from her hand, leaving a smear of tomato red on the counter and the wall.

She stopped. "You're scaring me, Roy, coming in here yelling and swearing and knocking things around."

"You're not doing it," he said, towering over her. "You're not taking an unwomanly job like that. Working around rough men and criminals."

"Police officers aren't all men and they aren't rough at all, Roy. Not around me. And there's nothing unfeminine about being a police dispatcher. Lots of women do it. Dispatchers help people, just like nurses do. They stay calm when everyone else is upset. Sometimes they even save lives right over the phone. Like when someone's choking or needs CPR."

Roy felt a tightness in his chest. Was he having a heart attack? "That's bullshit!" He slammed his fist on the table. "The things you'll hear, maybe see? That's no job for a lady."

157

"Chief Rathbone, Roy, he was the one who suggested it. I said I couldn't decide anything without discussing it with you." She stood straighter, but her voice was shaky. "It's a good job for me. Someone with medical training who's been a wife and mother. It's keeping cool and keeping track. Knowing where everybody is, what's going on and what needs to be done."

He kicked a fallen chair. When she reached out to stop him, he swung on her. "You're my wife. Your job is to be here keeping my house and taking care of me and the kids. Not being with cops and criminals and listening to strangers talkin' personal on the phone."

"The kids are grown, Roy. And I won't be any less of a wife to you because I've got a job. Most women have jobs."

"Womanly jobs," he said.

He wouldn't have minded if it was the lightbulb factory. Lots of the wives worked there. It was steady work and the money wasn't bad.

"I'll be happier if I have a job," she said. "You know how I've been lately."

"You're happy enough," he said, trying not to think of her standing in the yard in her tank top, tears running down her face. Trying not to think of the times he'd found her standing in the doorways of their kids' rooms like she was still checking up on them.

"Roy, I'm miserable. The kids are gone. All my friends have gone to work. You're down at the VFW with your friends."

"Don't you start up about that," he said. "It's not like I've haven't always gone to the VFW." She wasn't gonna flip this so he was in the wrong.

She bent to right the third chair just as he kicked it. His foot slammed her in the side and knocked her hard against the wall.

Slowly, looking as surprised as he felt, she pushed herself to her feet, rubbing an ugly bruise on her face. She moved so that the table was between them.

He didn't know what to do, so he said, "When's dinner, anyways? I'm starved."

Her voice was slow and cautious, like someone would speak to a menacing dog. "You said you weren't coming home for dinner, Roy. You're playing poker with the boys."

Christ. He'd let that batshit Tooley get him so upset he'd forgot about poker night. It was all Ida Mae's fault. Damned woman and her crazy ideas. And now she's acting like he's dangerous, when he'd never done anything to her. Not like some guys down to the VFW, bragging about beatin' their wives. All he'd done was kick a chair. Not his fault Ida Mae'd gotten in the way.

"Forget it," he said, "I was just stoppin' in to find a shirt that will stay tucked in. Too damned little material in 'em these days, you ask me."

She looked at his belly and then away, not sayin' anything. He wornt no different from any other man. Men in their fifties got bellies. They got tired and grew bellies and their wives went crazy.

I gotta go," he said, shoving his arm into his jacket sleeve. "Forget this police dispatcher nonsense. You oughta spend some time getting your head right."

"I think I am getting my head right." She drew her hands up to her hips, squaring her shoulders. "What you just did, Roy, kicking me and knocking me into the wall? That's an assault."

"It ain't no—"

"Look around," she said. "A cop comes in here, what's he gonna see?"

Roy looked at the knocked-over chairs, gouges in the plaster, tomato sauce splashed on the walls. The bruise on Ida Mae's cheek. "I didn't do nothin'," he said.

The steam from the pot had made the hair around her face curl. Other women got all fat and old-looking. She looked almost like she had at seventeen when they'd met. He checked his pockets for wallet and keys and grabbed the doorknob, forgetting what he'd said about the shirt.

"Hold on a minute," she said, touching the bruise. "I'm sorry you don't like the idea, but I am going to seriously consider this job. The kids think it's great. They say I'd be good at it."

He made his voice real loud, like he sometimes had to to get her back under control. "You heard what I said."

"I heard." She gave a little nod. "But did you hear me? I don't think this is nonsense. I think this is what they call a career move. The beginning of a brand new life. Now, you want nonsense?" She smiled as she picked up her spoon and rinsed it. "Next thing you know, I'm gonna be wanting a police scanner so I don't miss anything."

The smile grew. Impish. Playful. The way she'd looked when they were dating. Back before taking care of him and the house and three kids had taken that smile away. Before he'd understood a man had to keep a woman in her place or all hell broke loose.

"Then," she said, lightly tapping the bruise again, "maybe I'll want a gun of my own."

"Like hell you will."

Behind her, the pot snapped and hissed. Steam rose in a cloud around her head. Whatever she was cooking, it smelled great. His wife was a damned good cook.

Roy jingled the keys in his pocket and jerked the door open. Hadda get out of there before this turned into a real fight. Before he heard any more of her crazy notions. He'd set her straight tomorrow.

"I'm going," he said.

"Bye, Roy."

Ida Mae held the spoon like it was a magic wand, swinging it through the air in front of her. "Yup. First a scanner," she said. "Then a gun." She covered her mouth with her free hand, stifling a giggle. "And you know what, Roy? Once I make a little money, I might even buy me a nice Crown Vic."

Kate Clark Flora writes true crime, strong women, and police procedurals. Led Astray is her latest Joe Burgess police procedural. Her fascination with people's bad behavior began in the Maine attorney general's office chasing deadbeat dads and protecting battered children. In addition to her crime fiction, she's written two true crimes and a memoir with public safety personnel. 2017 will bring Shots Fired: The Myths, Misconceptions, and Misunderstandings About Police-Involved Shootings

THE DRIVE-BY

Alison McMahan

Little Seyha's face was about to become one of the most famous in L.A., but Seyha didn't know this; she was busy performing an Apsara dance move for her grandpa.

"Toe down, toe up, turn, toe down, toe up, turn," called out her mother. Seyha was barely three years old, but she could do the complicated move perfectly. Her father recorded the rotation of her stubby toes, the flexion of her pudgy knee, the smile on her sienna-colored face and the sparkle in her chestnut-colored eyes.

She finished with a flourish, her elbow up, her palm parallel to the floor, her fingers flexed backward. Her mother and grandfather and their friends applauded. Her father grinned from behind the camera as she called to her *Taa* and her grandpa lifted her up onto his lap, hugged her and kissed her. Together they counted her tiny toes in Cambodian: *moy, pee, bay...*

Outside the bungalow the night was quiet, the air humid and tangy with brine and cooling asphalt.

Mostly at night people stayed inside, doors locked. But Pranath Chea stood by her open door in the house across the street from Seyha's, trying to coax her aged dog back in. A Chevy Blazer fractured the stillness, engine gunned, windows open, a pop song blasting out of souped-up speakers, *you can't touch this, you can't touch this.* Pranath glanced at the driver, grabbed up her Chihuahua and shut her door.

The music seemed just as loud with the door closed. It was almost— almost—loud enough to cover up the shatter-splutter of the gunfire. Pranath peeked through her peephole. A shooter had emerged from the sunroof, and there must have been one or two more shooting out the passenger side windows.

The bullets, hundreds and hundreds and hundreds of them, sprayed into the windows of the house across the street.

Seyha's parents and their friends were hit dozens of times.

Only one bullet hit Seyha. It went through her and through her grandpa, killing both of them instantly.

The VHS camera was still recording when the police arrived.

When they knocked on her door, Pranath at first refused to open it. She refused many times, until a new police officer arrived, and spoke to her in Khmer.

A Cambodian Police Officer. This Pranath had to see. She unlocked the multiple locks and turned the multiple bolts on her door and opened it.

161

Thavary Keo stood in front of Mrs. Chea's house, holding a flashlight for the forensics officer collecting the shell casings. Her boss, Sergeant Adam Brown, came up to her, accompanied by another police officer she hadn't seen before.

"Officer Keo. Whatcha got?"

"Dark colored Chevy Blazer, maybe brown. She only saw the driver, sir. Says he was Mexican."

She glanced at the unknown officer. He looked Mexican, too. Her fingers tingled; there was a sour taste in her mouth.

The other officer didn't frown, he didn't smile, nor did he pretend he hadn't heard. He simply stood there.

She looked back at her sergeant, caught him squinting at her, his eyebrows raised.

"Oh, sorry." Her sergeant turned to the officer next to him. "This is Officer Carlos Urrieta. He'll be your partner."

"Sir?" Thavary had only been on the force a few weeks, and all that time she'd either done paperwork or shadowed the sergeant.

Sergeant Brown patted her on the shoulder. "Why don't you two get to know each other? And while you are at it, finish the canvass. Go together."

And he was gone.

Thavary craned her neck to get a good look at Officer *Uur-hee-et-ta.* Not that he was that tall. He had thick hair, but he'd cropped it close to his skull. She wondered if it would be curly if he let it grow out. He had curved, elegant eyebrows, his brown eyes were clear, his build was slim, athletic.

He had thin but expressive lips, and right now they were half-smiling at her while his eyes twinkled. Condescending.

She could be condescending too. "You're too pretty to be a cop."

The smile disappeared as his mouth pinched. His back went stiff. He started to cross his arms over his chest, then looked at her again and the smile returned.

"Better for me to be pretty than you. Do you even meet department height requirements?" His voice had the lightest trace of an accent.

"No. Department wanted Cambodians, so they waived the height requirement. Just like they overlooked your fake green card."

The forensics officer, who was now on his feet tagging evidence, snorted.

But Urrieta just smiled, a real smile this time, one that reached his eyes. "So, can you canvass, or did they overlook that too?"

Thavary felt the heaviness in her chest lighten a little. "Let's go see, shall we?"

They went up to the next house.

The bungalow was occupied by a Chicano family. Urrieta greeted the man in Spanish but the man's round face pursed into one giant wrinkle of disdain. "Speak English, man, you're in America."

He spoke without a trace of an accent. Thavary wondered if he could even speak Spanish.

The father talked to Urrieta while Thavary spoke to his wife, a grandmother, and his daughters, most of them teenagers, huddled in the kitchen. The women had all been at the Saturday night mass at a local church and had missed everything. Thavary noted the name and address of the church and went back to Urrieta, who was still talking to the head of the household.

"Lemme show you something." The man led them out to his front porch and pointed at the street light. "They shot that out. Only street light on our block. It made it safer for the children. Can you do something to get it fixed?"

Thavary studied the light. Sure enough, it had been blasted to bits, and there was a trail of broken glass below it.

"But this is a one-way street." She waved her hand back and forth, indicating the direction of travel from the corpse-filled house to here. "Did you see anything yourself, sir? Did you see them drive by?"

"I heard gunfire. Went to look. Saw the car just as they stopped shooting into that house. Then they drive down, stop right here, under the light," he lifted both hands as if he was holding a rifle and pointed one index finger straight up, "and the guy sticking out the sunroof blew it out, *paow.*"

Urrieta had his notebook out. "Could you describe him?"

The man looked Urrieta up and down. "Latin. Skinny. Close cropped hair. Like you."

Thavary smiled to herself. She walked down the porch steps and over to the street lamp, and turned her powerful flashlight beam onto the asphalt under it.

"Thanks for your help, sir." Urrieta joined Thavary under the street light.

"So they only shoot at one house." She pointed at the crime scene bungalow. "Shoot up the house first. Then come here, after everyone has seen them, *then* shoot out the light." She pointed her beam up at the shattered lamp. "Stupid."

Urrieta clapped her on the shoulder. "Come on. You're riding with me now."

Thavary followed him to his black-and-white, then raced ahead of him to the driver's side. She held out her hand for the keys. "I drive."

Urrieta pulled back his fist with the keys in it. "Not on our first date. Besides, can you even see over the steering wheel?"

"So where were you at seven p.m.?"

"What do you mean?"

"That Chicano witness said the sunroof shooter looked like you."

Urrieta turned and stared down at her. "Now you're trying to piss me off."

"So, where were you?"

"I'm a Long Beach police officer. Just like you."

163

"Yeah. And just like me you only have this job because the mayor's office thinks having more Khmer and Mexicans on the force will help them stop the gang violence. And just like me, the white cops don't want to work with you. And just like me, they're looking for a way to get rid of you. "

"You're accusing me of being a gang member. Me, a cop." He was in an aggressive stance now, ready to get violent.

Just like that.

Thavary stepped right up to him, which only emphasized that the top of her head barely made it to his chest.

"You accuse me of not being a good cop."

"I did not."

"You say I'm little. You say we onna date. You insult me."

"Well, you are little. That's just the truth. But you accused me of being a gangbanger. You want to make trouble for me."

"Only if you make trouble for me."

Urrieta paused and glanced back at the bungalow where they could see the silhouettes of the Chicano man and his entire family watching them through their living room window, the light from the TV pulsing behind them.

Urrieta lowered his voice. "Look, if we want to solve this case, if we want to make sure they don't fire us, we need help. We need a snitch."

Thavary felt a flutter in the void that was her stomach. "Why, you know snitches?"

"I don't." Urrieta unlocked the car door. "But I know people who know people. We can go find them. But I have to drive. Where we're going, they see a Cambo driving down the street, they'll shoot you." He slid into the driver's seat. "First, I gotta make a stop."

He drove them to a little house in back of Anaheim street. He parked the cruiser a few doors down and they walked up to the front door. There was loud music blasting in the back yard.

Urrieta went in without knocking and found a middle-aged woman rinsing roasted peppers in the sink.

"*Mami, el olor de esos chiles me dio   hambre desde el recinto.*"

Urrieta's mother, thin like her son but not so tall, hugged him. She glimpsed Thavary over his shoulder and her eyes went wide.

"*Por qué traes eso aquí?*" She pulled away from her son, her now-narrowed eyes never leaving Thavary's face.

"*Ella es mi* partner." He gestured for Thavary to step forward. "Officer Thavary Keo, this is my mother, *Mami*, Thavary and I just got assigned to work together."

"Mucho gusto, Senyorha Ur-hee-ieta."

Mrs. Urrieta looked from Thavary's face to her son's. "*Ay Dios mío.*" She dried her hands on a dishtowel and held one out for Thavary to shake.

Urrieta spotted someone in the backyard. "I'll be right back." He picked up a large bowl of potato salad from the kitchen counter and went out the back

164

door. Thavary started to follow him but Mrs. Urrieta pulled her back. "Por favor, help me, help me peel the *chiles*."

Thavary pulled a roasted pepper out of the sink and peeled it. Her duty belt kept her from getting too close to the counter, and some peel fell to the floor. Mrs. Urrieta bent down to pick it up.

Thavary watched Urrieta through the window. He set down the potato salad, greeted several young men who were hanging a string of colored lights, setting up chairs, pulling beers out of ice-filled coolers, or boxing with the helium-filled balloons tied to the fence.

After hugs and pats on the back, Urrieta approached a man who stood over the grill, swathed in smoke. An older, heavier, version of Urrieta himself.

"Is that your husband?" Thavary put the peeled chile on the plate with the others.

"No, no father. Father dead. *Es su tio*."

"His uncle."

The woman smiled and handed her another *chile* to peel.

"He good boy, my son."

"I hope so. I hope he's a good cop."

Mrs. Urrieta dropped the knife she was using and looked up at Thavary, her eyes wide, worry lines along them, her mouth slightly agape, worry lines there too.

"He is good cop. He want to. But best thing for you, for him, you never come here again."

Thavary handed her the knife she'd dropped. "Why not, Mrs. Urrieta? What are you afraid of?"

Mrs. Urrieta glanced through the window that looked over the yard, and then back at Thavary. "Just better. For you, for him. Don't come back."

Urrieta walked in. His mother handed Thavary a paper bag. "Make him eat."

Urrieta snatched the bag from Thavary, his caramel-colored cheeks now tinted pink. "*Mami*, she's my partner. Not my girlfriend."

Thavary took the bag back from him. "*No problema, Señora Urrieta.* I'll make sure he eats."

Urrieta looked from Thavary back to his mother. "Well, if it's going to be like that, *dale otra para ella, mami*."

His mother quickly rolled up two more *chile con quesos* in tinfoil and dropped them into another bag along with a container of potato salad.

"Okay, time to go."

Thavary bowed over her folded hands and then reached for the bag. Mrs. Urrietta gave her a hug. "*Ten cuidado*."

The video of little Seyha dancing her perfect Apsara dance in the last few minutes of her life played on all the news channels. Her picture was in every paper. By mid-week huge posters of her large chestnut eyes, her backward-flexed fingers just visible above her baby curls, appeared on seemingly every storefront in Long Beach and in many surrounding communities.

Casualties from the gang wars were nothing new, but somehow little Seyha and her golden ankle bracelets had captured the imagination of greater Los Angeles. In the few seconds it had taken her to die, Seyha had become the poster child for the cause of stopping gang violence.

The Cambodian community burst into action. There were twenty-four hour vigils in front of Seyha's house, which instantly became a morbid tourist attraction. There were nightly marches along Anaheim Street.

On the one hand, Thavary was glad little Seyha would not be forgotten, just another staring face in yet another newspaper article about the gang wars.

On the other hand, it made it difficult to find their snitch.

Thavary and Urrieta finally went off duty late Friday night. Thavary changed out of her uniform, walked out of the station and saw Urrieta, still in his uniform, getting into their cruiser.

"Need a ride?"

"Sure." Thavary got into the passenger seat.

It was slow going as the marchers still clogged the streets, partying now instead of protesting.

"It's impossible to find this guy with all this." Urrieta drummed on the steering wheel with both hands, a habit that made Thavary's neck and jaw stiffen.

"At least the Mexicans have gone quiet."

Urrieta turned and stared down at her. It was dark enough that his pupils were enlarged, making his eyes look black. "All the gangs have gone quiet. Not just the Mexicans. It's out of respect for the child."

"Or maybe they're being smart. For once. Because so many cops are out." She waved her arm in a gesture that took in themselves and the extra foot patrols watching the crowds.

"We're always out," Urrieta flicked on his turn signal. "That's what we do. We patrol."

"And look for snitches. What's this snitch called, anyway?"

Urrieta swiveled the car around in a U-turn. "Luis. He's really just a kid. Always wears white pants, a white jacket, and lots of bling. Thinks it makes him look fancy. But he knows things."

"Trail's going cold." Thavary studied every figure in every doorway, looking for Luis.

"I know, I know." Urrieta tapped out the rhythm on the steering wheel again.

"Hey wait, stop here."

Urrieta hit the brakes. "You see something?"

"No, no trouble. I just want to get some cakes. For you to take to your mother."

166

Urrieta opened his mouth, but Thavary got out of the car before he could object.

Thavary wove her way through the group of teen Khmer girls that always seemed to be hanging around the front of the bakery, eating their sweets and giggling.

Inside, she greeted the wizened Khmer baker and made a selection. As she waited for the old man to load her choices into a cake box, she watched the crowd of Khmer girls through the plate glass window.

A group of Chicano boys approached the girls, whistling, cat-calling and making lewd hand gestures.

Thavary couldn't hear exactly what they were saying, but it was clear which girl was the object of the boys' attention. While the other girls went silent and stepped back, she stepped forward and tossed her soda straw at the boy who had cat-called the loudest.

Thavary paid for her cakes, took the box, but stood by the door without going out. She nudged the door open and listened to the kids.

"You're too skinny for me, anyway. Why would I want you?" The girl dropped her half-filled soda into the garbage bin.

The skinny boy's buddies howled, slapped their thighs, egged him on to answer. Thavary could see his gang tattoos peeping up from his t-shirt collar.

"I'm skinny like my knife is skinny, *puta*." His hand went to his pocket.

Thavary walked out the door, holding the cake box in front of her with both hands. She assessed the frightened girls, the reckless girl, the boys egging on their leader.

She handed the box to the reckless girl.

"Oh! For me? Thank you!" The girl tried to open the lid, as if nothing were happening.

"Don't you dare." Thavary turned to the boys. It was unclear if her words were aimed at the girl or at them.

"You hurt a woman, that's a lotta bad Karma."

The guys were quiet for a moment, processing her words. Then they all burst into laughter, clutching their sides. One even rolled on the ground.

Thavary smiled, as if laughing with them.

"I'll show you bad Karma, you slanty-eyed Cambo!" The skinny gang member grabbed her by the arm.

Thavary twisted her wrist expertly and stepped behind him. She had her arm around his neck in a chokehold before he knew what had happened. Because he was taller than she was, she had to pull his head back by the hair until his ear was level with her lips.

"I'm Cambo, and I'm your bad Karma."

Now it was the girls' turn to crow and laugh.

"Now I let you go, you stand up, you go home."

Skinny's face was red from bending so far backwards. Thavary let go of him. He straightened up, slowly.

167

Thavary brushed herself off. She turned to the girl to reclaim her cake box.

Skinny lunged toward her, knife in hand.

Thavary turned. She blocked his knife arm, holding the badge in front of his eyes. "Long Beach PD."

A collective gasp.

"You?" The gang boy said. "You're a cop?"

"She's a cop, and so am I." At the sound of Urrieta's boots on the sidewalk the kids all stepped back.

Skinny flicked his knife shut.

Thavary took the knife from him, then got up into his face. "You remember this Cambo. This Cambo is your bad Karma. Really bad Karma for you." She put the knife in her pocket.

"Hey, that's mine." Skinny wailed theatrically.

Thavary pretended she hadn't heard him. She tucked the badge and chain back into her shirt. "What's your name?"

"We going, we going, no bad Karma man, no bad Karma." Skinny waved his hands around.

"His name is Luis," said the girl Skinny had harassed.

Belatedly, Thavary realized that Skinny was indeed dressed all in white, with several gold necklaces around his neck, unlike his buddies, who looked like they had robbed an Army Navy store.

"Ah. Luis." Urrieta stepped between them, his hand resting on the cuffs on his utility belt. "So nice to meet you. Please stay here. Rest of you, go home. Go home!"

The guys backed off the sidewalk. A couple stumbled right into the street. In a moment they were all gone.

Thavary turned to the lead girl and took back her cake box. "And you. Don't invite trouble."

The girl pouted, but swished off with her friends. They were all giggling again before they reached the end of the block.

"You gonna arrest me?" Luis asked Urrieta. "I didn't do nothin'. She assaulted me."

"We're not going to arrest you tonight." Urrieta opened the back door to the cruiser. "As long as you cooperate." Thavary stood behind him, leaving no way for him to go but into the cruiser.

Once they had him in the back of the squad car, and they were in their seats in the front, Urrieta took over. He had a long conversation with Luis in Spanish. Thavary pretended to be interested in her cakes. She did really well at hiding her ability to understand until she heard Luis say something about the fact that Seyha's grandfather—Luis called him *el Taa de Seyha*, as most people did who had seen the video—was the real target.

"The old man?"

Urrieta and Luis turned and stared at her.

"So you speak Spanish, too?"

Thavary shook her head. "But I understood that. Anyway, it makes sense. It was the only house they shot at. That means it was targeted." She pointed at a poster of Seyha in the now darkened bakery store window. "The pretty baby wasn't the target."

"Word is, Seyha's grandfather was the head of the Exotic Jewel Orchid Coterie. So the El-Els did you a favor, taking him out." Luis grinned. Like they were all buddies.

But Urrieta wasn't having it. "But why did you blow out the light afterward? Why make sure everyone could see you?"

Luis shrank back into the seat. "Not me. The gang, man. The El-Els. I wasn't there, man. I just gave you information. Now we done." He lifted one hand and rubbed the tips of two fingers against his thumb, signaling he wanted to be paid.

Urrieta got out of the car and yanked the back door open. "Hey, you told us something we didn't know, so we won't arrest you for assaulting a police officer."

Luis scrambled out of the back seat, then poked his head into Thavary's window.

"Don't I get my knife back?"

"Knife? What knife?" Thavary smiled at him sweetly.

Luis muttered some curses in Spanish but wasted no time getting away from them.

Thavary waited until Urrieta was nearly to her parents' house before speaking again. "So, is your uncle the head of the El-Els, or is he just middle management? Urrieta sucked in his breath. "How'd you know?"

Thavary didn't want to betray his mother. "I can't believe you took me right to an El-El gang member. Now I must have a price on my head."

"He's not. Just some of his friends. And I took you to protect you. They saw you with me, they know you're my partner, they know I stay out of their business, so they will stay out of ours."

Thavary felt like she'd been doused with ice water. "Stay out of their business… you're a cop."

"And you're a refugee from Pol Pot." Urrieta didn't take his eyes off the road. "The world is complicated."

Thavary wondered if he'd somehow gotten access to her file, or if he was just guessing.

Time would tell. "So…was everybody at that barbecue a gang-banger?"

"That's my family. Just cuz we Latin doesn't mean we all gang-bangers."

"Take off your shirt."

"I'm driving."

Thavary pulled out her gun and pointed it at him. "Take off your shirt."

"All right, all right, *chinga tu madre*." Urrieta pulled the car over.

169

"Leave my mother out of it." Thavary kept the gun trained on him while he went through the process of undoing various straps until finally he unbuttoned his shirt. Now he was down to his vest and t-shirt.

"Take off the vest."

"And let you shoot me? Forget it."

Thavary aimed her service weapon at the middle of his chest.

"Okay, Okay. If you want to see me naked, all you have to do is ask nicely."

He pulled off his t-shirt, slowly, humming an off-key strip-tease tune.

But the effect was ruined when his shirt snagged on the seat belt.

Chiseled abs, rounded pecks, no hair. Did any Mexicans have chest hair?

No tattoos. Thavary let out the breath she'd been holding.

"Turn around. Let me see your back."

He was fit and trim enough to turn his back to her without getting wedged between the steering wheel and the seat.

She had to admit, her new partner was way too easy on the eyes.

Thavary was doing paperwork in the precinct when she felt someone watching her and looked up.

Mrs. Urrieta.

Thavary jumped up and led her to the chair in front of her desk. "Officer Urrieta will be back soon." She sat back in her chair, still studying her visitor.

Mrs. Urrieta looked around, as if her son might appear at any moment. She seemed to be holding back tears.

"Actually, I came to see you." She leaned across the desk and put her hands over Thavary's. Thavary grasped her hands in return, trying to be comforting.

It took her a moment to realize that Mrs. Urrieta was sliding an envelope across the desk to her, under their clasped hands.

Thavary slid it off her desk into a drawer.

"My son's uncle, he give me that." Mrs. Urrieta unfolded a handwritten letter. "That envelope full of money."

Thavary slid the drawer open. "It's your money, Mrs. Urrieta."

Mrs. Urrieta shook her head. "He gave it to me, but it not my money. It's blood money. Says so here." She pounded the letter into the table with one fingertip.

"I can't read Spanish, Mrs. Urrieta."

"It says he hired to do drive by. He hired to kill *Taa Seyha*. They pay him good money. At first he happy. He didn't know about baby. Then he see Seyha's face everywhere, make him cry. Make him cry. So he give me all his money and he…he gone. Finished."

170

Mrs. Urrieta held a crumpled tissue to her face and rocked back and forth.

Thavary gave her a moment. She tried to read the letter.

She was going to have to learn Spanish.

"Mrs. Urrieta, does it say in here why he was hired to kill *Taa Seyha*? Or who hired him?"

Mrs. Urrieta shook her head. "He no snitch."

She blew her nose with a ferocity that made some of the other police officers look up from their paperwork. Thavary pushed a box of tissues closer to her.

"Please, read me the part where he says he's finished."

Mrs. Urrieta read it to her.

Even with the siren's flashing and blaring, by the time they got to Urrieta's uncle he had already collapsed on the kitchen floor. Urrieta dropped onto his knees next to him, searching his uncle's pockets. "What'd you take, Uncle? What'd you take?"

His uncle shook his head. He patted a piece of paper that was pinned to his chest. Thavary unfolded the paper. It was a picture of Seyha from a newspaper. Written across her face in red lipstick were the words "I killed Seyha. Seyha, I'm sorry."

"Where is that stupid ambulance?" Urrieta ran out the door. Thavary tried to unpin the piece of paper, but before she could undo the safety pin she realized Uncle Urrieta was trying to say something.

She leaned her ear close to his lips.

"The guy who paid me," he said, forcing the words out between long rattling breaths "he Cambo. Like you."

He let out one last long rattle and was still.

Thavary sat next to Urrieta on the porch. They watched the EMTs take his uncle's body away.

Thavary wondered if she should tell her partner about his last words.

But Urrieta had his head in his hands, sunk down like he was never going to be able to hold it up again.

She tried to respect his grief.

But she couldn't.

"You should have told me the truth. Your uncle was no middle-man."

Urrieta looked up at her, huge circles under his eyes, his cheeks sunken.

"You should have told me you spoke Spanish."

"You should let me drive."

"You should give us a little time to get used to each other."

"Your uncle said a Cambo hired him."

This brought Urrieta to attention. "A Cambo?"

171

"Yeah. At first I thought he was messing with me. But it makes sense. Some wannabe Cambo gangbanger tries to take over. But he has to kill the current Cambo gang leader. So, great idea: pay a Mexican gangbanger to take out his rival. Make it look like business as usual, drive-by as usual, but make sure everybody sees it's Mexicans. So they play the music real loud, they take their time with the MAC-10 shooting those .45s, then they stop under a light to make sure everyone sees them. Because that was part of the job: make sure everyone thinks it's gang war as usual."

"*As usual,*" Urrieta breathed out sarcastically.

"Almost worked, too." Thavary was pleased to see him back.

"So we got a new up-and-coming Cambo gang leader out there."

"Yeah."

"And we got Mexican gangbangers doing hits for money."

"Looks that way."

They watched the gurney go up the ramp into the back of the ambulance. The doors swung shut with a clang.

Urrieta shook his head. "Shit." His chin sank back onto his chest.

Thavary grabbed his arm and shook him. "We're gonna catch this Cambo gang. You and me. We're gonna catch them and put them away."

Urrieta looked at her in astonishment. "But —"

"We're wasting time. We got to catch this guy."

She held out her hand for the keys.

For once, Urrieta just handed them over. "That's your set."

He'd put them on a new keychain with a framed picture anchoring them all together.

A picture of Baby Seyha.

Alison McMahan writes for The Big Thrill and *Publisher's Weekly.* Her historical mystery, *The Saffron Crocus* (Black Opal Books, 2014), won the Rosemary for Best YA Historical and the Florida Writers Association's Royal Palm Literary Award. Short mysteries: "The New Score" (*Fish Out of Water Anthology*, Wildside Press, 2017) and "Kamikaze Iguanas" (*Scream and Scream Again*, MWA anthology for middle grade readers, edited by R.L. Stine, HarperCollins, 2018). www.AlisonMcMahan.com

THE OWL AND THE PUSSYCATS

Verena Rose

Two bright blue orbs and two brilliant yellow ones were all that could be seen in the pitch black darkness that night. Finding themselves in the same tree, the blue-eyed cat and yellow-eyed owl didn't quite know what to make of each other.

One hour earlier.

The Solstice in the Hills cat show was nearing its end, with the Saturday evening judging about to take place in the center ring. All exhibitors were making last minute checks of their cats in their cages so that they could rush off to see the Battle of the Breeds—Kitten Division. Lydia Morgan was no exception because, really, who doesn't love kittens? She checked her cage and then rushed along with the crowd to get a seat for the competition. Lydia was finding it difficult to contain her excitement. She was spending an entire weekend with like-minded people, and she was also getting to show her two beautiful Ragdolls for the very first time.

Lydia Morgan was what some would describe as a woman of a certain age. Divorced for many years, she had grown children and teenaged grandchildren, all with busy social lives. Six years ago she had decided to fill some of the void by bringing home two fluffy kittens. She originally thought about getting a puppy but eventually realized that a dog just didn't fit her lifestyle. Also being a lover of cats, she started researching different breeds. One day on the internet she found just what she was looking for—the Ragdoll. She learned that Ragdolls are very dog-like and love following their humans around devotedly. They have brilliant blue eyes and a floppy demeanor when being held—hence the Ragdoll name. Lydia knew she'd found her new companion so she contacted a local breeder, and before all was said and done, she brought home twelve-week-old brother and sister kittens. She had been happily owned by the two beauties ever since and she named them My Lord Grantham and My Lady Grantham, *aka* Mylo and Myla.

That would have been the end of the story if the cat show community had not changed their rules and created a House Pet category allowing cats that had been fixed to compete. Knowing that she had two beautiful examples of the breed, Lydia wanted to show them off, so she decided to start entering them into shows. Her first foray into the cat show world was going to be at the Tennessee Valley Cat Fanciers' Solstice in the Hills.

The conference room for housing the cats and their owners when they weren't competing was empty. A door at the back of the room hidden by draping and left carelessly unlocked slowly opened, allowing a hooded intruder to enter. He stealthily made his way to Row RD looking for RD018. The boss had told him the cage would have blue ribbons attached, and would house two cats, one male and one female. It was a good thing the cages had numbers because a lot of them had blue ribbons. He finally found the one he was looking for. Sure enough, there they were, two cats, a big male and a smaller female, and, yes, the blue ribbons. He'd just started working for the boss, and he didn't like the idea of snatching these cats, but he knew he had to follow orders or suffer the consequences. The boss had the goods on him, and it was either catnapping or jail. He took out a pair of bolt cutters and made quick work of the lock. It wasn't difficult as the combination lock wasn't intended to keep people out, only to keep the cats in the cage. He'd overheard some of the owners saying earlier that some cats were very good at escaping their luxury cages.

Just to be sure he had the correct cats, he checked the card on the front of the cage and confirmed that, yes, the cats were a male and a female. He opened the door and tried to coax them out. Even though the female was being difficult, he managed to get them both out of the cage and into a large duffel bag. Hurrying in case someone came into the room, he scurried back to the door and escaped unnoticed into the night. He thought the hard part was over, but he was about to find out how wrong he was. Struggling a bit, he managed to carry the heavy duffle bag to his van. He removed the male cat and put him into a cage in the back of the van. While wrestling with the big guy, he forgot to secure the top of the duffle bag. When he turned to get the female cat, he discovered she wasn't there. The little minx had escaped!

He knew he was in big trouble now.

Lydia Morgan came back to the conference room after watching the Battle of the Breeds—Kitten Division.

"Oh, no!" The cage was empty. "Mylo? Myla?" Lydia Morgan called anxiously. She only been gone for about an hour and she'd left the cats taking their evening nap. They'd done so well earlier in the day, each of them winning first place in their respective classes. And tomorrow they were to compete against each other for House Pet Best in Show.

But now Mylo and Myla were missing!

"What's the problem, Ms. Morgan?" asked Jeff Drury. The conference security supervisor came running when he heard her scream.

"Mylo and Myla are gone!" she said, trying to keep the hysteria out of her voice.

"How could they be gone?" he asked. "Are you sure they didn't escape their cage and are hiding somewhere? The only way into the show is through the main entrance. Everyone is checked in, the room is monitored, and only those with the proper badges are allowed in. "

"My cats are talented, but even they don't possess the where-with-all to employ bolt cutters. Can't you see the lock has been cut!" she said sarcastically.

"Mrs. Morgan, let's try to stay calm. There is no need for hysterics. We will get to the bottom of this." Jeff Drury had been hired by the event organizers from a security agency and obviously didn't know much about cats or their owners.

Shaking her head in exasperation, Lydia said, "Mr. Drury, I want my cats found. NOW!"

Myla, taking advantage of the duffle bag being left open, escaped and ran up the nearest tree.

As she ran up the tree, she yelled to Mylo, "Don't worry brother, I'll rescue you."

"Boy, what a doofus this guy is. He can't even manage to get us both into his van. And on top of that I wonder what master criminal sent him out to snatch two fixed cats from a show full of world class breeding cats. Something tells me that we were grabbed by mistake. Now I have to figure out a way to keep track of Mylo."

Using her powerful hind legs, she leaped from the tree onto the top of the van just as it pulled away. Inside she could hear her brother making plaintive noises. It wasn't a very long ride. Shortly they came to a small farm that was part of the Convention Center property. Before the man could get out of the van, Myla jumped down and again ran up the nearest tree.

She yelled to her brother. "Stay strong, Mylo. I'll get you out."

"You idiot! Where are the cats I told you to get? This can't possibly be them," said the boss as he held Mylo up by the scruff of his neck. "I only see one cat, and more importantly, this is not one of the cats you were supposed to snatch. You must realize this is a neutered male!"

Realizing how angry the boss was, Smitty started to shake. "Well, I was trying to be quiet. Everyone was just next door in the judging area. I didn't want to hang around too long," Smitty stammered.

"But can't you read? I told you to bring me the cats in cage RD016, the cage with all the blue ribbons. Look here, see this tag! It says this cat was in cage RD018," the boss said, losing his temper and throwing the cage tag at Smitty.

"But there were blue ribbons on this cat's cage! Like I said, I was trying to get in and out and not get caught!"

"Okay then, where is the other cat?" the boss asked. "I assume there *were* two cats in the cage."

By now Smitty was vibrating with fear. He knew the boss was not going to like his answer.

"Yes, Boss, there were, but the smaller one got away. When I got out to the van, I guess I left the flap of the duffle bag open. She must have wiggled free while I was putting this one in a cage. I hunted for a while, but I couldn't find her and it was getting late and people were starting to come back from the competition. I didn't want to get caught," Smitty said.

Doing a complete one-eighty, the boss said, "Well, what's done is done, but you'll have to get rid of this one and hope the other one stays lost. I doubt it will last long in these woods. I'm sure a coyote or bobcat will enjoy a tasty kitty meal. I guess now I'm going to have to take care of the plan myself. Considering what your father had you doing, I thought you'd be a better assistant."

Myla glared at the owl with her fiercest stare. Myla, being a sheltered house cat had no paws-on experience with the creatures she saw every day through the window at home. She wasn't sure whether this big bird was friend or foe. Since her greatest concern was figuring out how to get into the building where her brother was and helping him escape, she hoped the owl would get the message and not present a problem.

"Hey big bird, would you be willing to help me rescue my brother?" Myla said, not expecting an answer.

"Hoot, hoot!" said the owl.

"Well, I hope that means 'yes' because I'm going to need all the help I can get."

Back at the Convention Center, the Sheriff's Department had been called. While they waited, the staff performed a thorough search of the conference rooms and the arena to make sure the missing cats weren't hiding somewhere in the building. Unfortunately, evidence had been found outside that seemed to prove the cats had been taken from the building. Myla had had a purple ribbon attached to the tag around her neck, and a similar ribbon had been found on the ground right outside the door. It was proof that the security for the show was severely lacking.

"Ms. Morgan, I'm Sheriff Clarence Sharpe. I understand your cats are missing."

"Yes, my two Ragdoll cats Mylo and Myla were taken from their cage sometime this evening."

"How do you know they were taken, Ms. Morgan?" asked the sheriff.

"Because the combination lock on their cage was cut and removed."

"All right then, let me take a look and see what we can find."

176

"Sheriff, we have to find them as soon as possible. I just can't imagine why anyone would steal them. They're not breeding cats. And while they're very valuable and dear to me, they wouldn't be the cats most likely stolen from this room. Admittedly, they're both beautiful specimens of the breed but like I said . . ."

Just then Lydia remembered that the cat world had been very much in the news recently. An individual called the Cat Burglar had been stealing champion show cats and ransoming them back to their owners. So far he'd been quite successful at eluding the police.

"Sheriff Sharpe, what if somebody mistook them for another pair of cats? Their cage and the cage, or should I say kitty condo, of the reigning Grand Champions are right next to each other. Could it be the Cat Burglar has struck again? I know all of the stolen cats have been returned once the ransom was paid, but what if he doesn't try to ransom my cats? They aren't Grand Champions. Please, we've got to find them. They're very gentle and trusting, at least Mylo is, and I'm afraid they might get hurt once the thief discovers that they're not the correct cats."

"Boss, what do you want me to do with this cat?" asked Smitty, not wanting to hear the answer.

"I told you to get rid of it. What did you think I meant? Take it down to the pond and drown it. Then bury it so no one will find it."

"But Boss, he's such a beautiful cat and so sweet. Listen to him purring. Can't I keep him?"

"No. You. Can't. Keep. Him! Once they discover the theft we can't risk someone seeing him and recognizing him as one of the missing cats. And, for your sake, you better hope the other one doesn't show up either."

With tears in his eyes, Smitty said, "Okay, Boss."

He reluctantly picked up the cat, cradled him in his arms, and left the building.

Just as Myla was getting ready to climb down the tree and check out the building to find her brother, the door opened and the man came out with Mylo in his arms. Mylo didn't seem in any distress but knowing how trusting he was Myla couldn't be sure. She sensed something was wrong because the man was crying. He walked into the woods quickly, so she climbed out of the tree to follow, making sure she stayed in the shadows. She couldn't risk letting Mylo or the man know she was nearby. Stealthily she crept along behind them. All of the sudden she heard a loud MEOW!

Sheriff Sharpe was a veteran officer of the Swallow Forge Sheriff's Department, but this was a first for him. In his twenty-year career he'd never investigated a catnapping. If this was the work of the Cat Burglar, he'd eventually have to call in the help of the Tennessee Bureau of Investigation.

He was a dog lover and he certainly understood how devastating it was to lose a pet. But these circumstances were anything but normal.

He called in to the dispatcher. "Hi, Sarah, this is Sheriff Sharpe. I need you to put in a call to Agent Burke at the TBI. Tell him we have a situation here in Swallow Forge and that it might be a Cat Burglar case. Let him know I'll call as soon as I know more."

"I'll call immediately," said Sarah.

While he waited for Smitty to return, the boss paced the barn contemplating his next move. He needed to get back to the Convention Center soon or his absence might be noticed.

"MEOW, MEOW! Sissy, where are you?"

Myla heard her brother's plaintive cries and hurried through the woods as fast as her legs would carry her. When she came into the clearing, she saw a pond and the man trying to wrestle Mylo into the water. What was he trying to do? Then she knew. She saw him pushing Mylo's head under—and that wasn't good.

With fear pulsing through her body she screamed, "Mylo, fight! Use your claws! Scratch, Mylo, scratch!" She prayed he understood because she knew that Mylo thought his claws were for play. He had no idea they were also useful for protection.

Just as she was about to launch herself at the man she heard an almost undetectable flap of wings. She looked up just in time to see the owl diving straight at the man's head. When the owl hit, with talons extended, the man gave a blood-curdling scream and he dropped Mylo right into the pond. Myla ran to the edge just in time to see a bedraggled Mylo struggling out of the water. Myla didn't want the man to see her or to realize that Mylo hadn't drowned. Both cats ran as fast as they could back into the woods. As they were retreating, they could still hear the man screaming.

Sheriff Sharpe decided it was time to check with the uniformed deputies to see if they had been able to get a copy of the exhibitors list. He knew he needed to start the interviewing so he would have a better feel for the situation.

"Meade, do you have that list ready yet?"

Deputy Meade handed him several sheets of paper. "I have it right here, Sheriff. It lists all the exhibitors and the names and sexes of their cats."

"Thanks, Meade. Check with Mr. Drury to see if he has a room where we can conduct our interviews."

"Sure thing. I'll get right back to you on that."

While Deputy Meade was checking about the use of an interview room, Sheriff Sharpe went to speak with Ms. Morgan and give her an update on their progress.

"Boss! Boss!" cried Smitty as he came staggering breathlessly into the building. His face was streaming with blood and he had large talon marks all over his head, neck, and hands. "I was attacked! This huge bird swooped down and started clawing at me just as I was trying to drown that darn cat. I wish I'd never agreed to do this for you. Those cats are going to be the death of me."

"Well, Smitty, you don't have a choice now, do you? I know your secret, remember?" said the boss with a sneer.

"I dropped the cat in the water when the bird attacked me, and I don't know whether it drowned or not. I ended up diving in the pond for cover but before you ask, no, I didn't find the body. It still could be dead, though, that pond is murky, and the cat probably sank to the bottom. Cats don't swim, do they?"

"You better hope not, Smitty. I'm heading back to the Convention Center now, and I want you to stay here tonight. In the morning go back to the pond and search again. Dead or alive—find that cat!"

"Mylo you look awful, Are you okay?" asked Myla.

"I'm all wet and I don't like being wet! But thanks to that big bird, the man dropped me. He was trying to hold my head under the water. Why was he doing that, Sissy?"

Myla looked her brother over to be sure he was okay. He was a bit bedraggled, but as soon as she heard his purrs she knew he would be fine. So now, what? Myla knew it would be up to her to get them back to Momma. She also knew Momma must be scared for them, and would get help to find her and Mylo. In the meantime, the two of them needed to find somewhere safe to hide until morning. Just then Myla heard a hoot, hoot from up in a very tall tree. It was the yellow-eyed owl and it was trying to tell them something. It looked like there was plenty of room on the limb where the owl perched, so she nudged Mylo to start climbing. Once on the limb they curled up and fell into a fretful sleep while being watched over by the owl.

Sheriff Sharpe was ready to start interviewing. Based on what he'd seen and heard so far he wasn't looking forward to it. These cat people were intense when it came to the safety of their show cats. He'd already had several exhibitors accost him, frantic about not being able to leave and take their cats away from this "danger zone." It was late, and he knew everyone was tired and eager to get back to their hotels.

"Deputy Meade, would you please ask the first exhibitor to come in?"

"Sheriff Sharpe, this is Mrs. Fiske."

"Mrs. Fiske, please have a seat. There are just a few questions I need to ask you about this evening's events." The sheriff noted that Mrs. Fiske looked to be in her thirties and was very stylishly dressed.

"Of course, Sheriff. I'm happy to help any way I can," said Mrs. Fiske.

"Can you tell me where you were between the hours of eight and nine this evening?"

"Yes, I was at the kitten competition along with everyone else. I don't usually like to leave my precious darlings alone for too long, but with all the hype from the promoters about security, I assumed they would be safe for an hour or so."

"Were there still other exhibitors in the housing area when you left for the competition?"

"Honestly, Sheriff, I didn't notice. I was hurrying along to the arena to get a seat. The kitten competition is always standing room only."

"Thank you, Mrs. Fiske. That will be all for now. You can leave to go back to your hotel. On your way out, please give Deputy Meade a contact number where we can reach you."

Leaving Smitty at the barn, the boss took the van and headed back to the Convention Center. He hoped he could slip in without anyone realizing he hadn't been there all evening.

He drove past the Convention Center first to see what was going on. Spotting several police vehicles out front, he circled around to the back of the building only to find another police car back there. Now he was in a real pickle. How was he going to get in without being seen?

It was pre-dawn when Myla awoke to find that Mylo and the owl were both missing from the tree. She wasn't particularly worried about the owl—it knew how to take care of itself and had the weapons to do so. That had been proven by the events of yesterday evening. But Mylo was another story. He was a big softy and flopped over for anyone, hoping for a belly rub. He didn't realize they were out in the woods, where predators could eat him. Scrambling down from the tree, Myla caught her brother's scent and headed towards the smell. She only had to go a short distance before she found Mylo and the owl breakfasting on, of all things, filet of field mouse. Eeew! She couldn't believe her eyes. Mylo, the cat who wouldn't eat roast chicken when Momma offered it, was eating raw mouse. But the truly weird thing was, the owl was feeding it to him.

Lydia Morgan was trying to be patient and not bother Sheriff Sharpe but her cats were still missing. What would she do if they weren't found? Mylo and Myla were her four-legged family. And waiting for answers was making her imagine the worse.

"Lydia, are you okay? What happened?" asked her friend Betty Summers.

Betty lived near the Convention Center. In fact, that was one of the reasons Lydia had decided to enter this particular show, it gave her the opportunity to spend time with her old friend. She and Betty had grown up together but only got to see each other infrequently now that Betty lived in Tennessee.

"My cats are gone! The lock on their crate was cut, and they found Myla's ribbon on the loading dock. The police believe they were taken away in a truck or SUV."

"Oh, Lydia, I'm so sorry! You must be frantic not knowing where Mylo and Myla are. I know I would be and I'm only their auntie. All I can think of is their sweet faces and those soulful blue eyes. I can't imagine anyone being so cruel as to steal them. Didn't anyone see or hear anything? Wasn't there anyone in the room with them during the competition?" asked Betty.

"As far as I know there wasn't anyone staying with the cats during the kitten competition. I've been waiting for an update but it's so hard trying to sit still. My whole body is shaking with fear."

"Let's try to stay positive. I don't know him personally, but I've heard that Sheriff Sharpe is a top-notch investigator," Betty said, hoping to comfort her friend.

The boss wasn't happy about having to climb the fire escape to get into the Convention Center unseen. But it was better than blowing his cover and being arrested. If he played his cards right, he'd be able to throw the blame on his mortal enemy and no one would be the wiser.

Myla walked over to where Mylo and the owl were chowing down.

"Mylo, what are you doing?"

"Hey, Sissy. My friend has been feeding me this amazingly delicious meat."

"Don't you realize that your friend *killed that field mouse the two of you are eating? She could kill you, too, if she wanted to."*

"Myla, you're always so dramatic. She's not going to kill me. She likes me."

"Mylo, I am not being dramatic! I'm just being cautious. You always think the best of everyone and that can get you into big trouble. After you've finished your breakfast, we need to figure out how to get back to Momma. I know she's worried about us."

"Oh, by the way, Myla, since you're Miss Know-It-All, where is the litter box?"

181

Shaking her head, Myla walked away.

Bertram Smythe had had enough waiting. His cats were the stars of this show. Being treated like a common criminal wasn't acceptable. With impatience in his step he approached the door of the conference room and started to enter.

"May I help you, sir?" Deputy Meade asked.

"I want to speak to the sheriff," the portly gentleman said, attempting to enter the conference room. "I've been waiting here for hours while you conduct your interviews. I'm not accustomed to being treated in this manner."

"Sheriff Sharpe is interviewing everyone in the order they appear on the list of exhibitors. What is your name, sir?"

"What is my name? Well, young man, I am Bertram Smythe, world renowned breeder of Ragdoll cats. I breed nothing but champions."

"I'm sorry, Mr. Smythe, but I don't know anything about cats, cat shows, or cat breeders, so I've never heard of you."

"Well, take my word for it, I'm *very* important, and I demand that you tell the sheriff that I need to speak with him immediately."

"I'll let Sheriff Sharpe know as soon as he's finished with this interview. I was given orders not to interrupt him under any circumstances."

The boss's heart was pounding, but he was back in the building without anyone having noticed him entering. As he walked away from the fire exit door, someone called to him.

"Mr. Smythe, Mr. Smythe, there you are. I've been looking all over for you," Jeff Drury called as he ran up the hall.

"Jeffrey, what on earth is the matter? I just came down here to smoke," Benedict Smythe said, brandishing his Meerschaum pipe.

"Haven't you heard? Two cats have been stolen, and the police are here questioning everyone. Didn't your brother tell you? The cats were in the condo next to his. They are entered in the Household Pet category."

"REALLY! I bet Bertram didn't like that. He'd never want his cats mixing with the likes of household pets. It wouldn't surprise me if he had someone take them. He tells everyone that his cats are Ragdoll Royalty. And the fact is, they wouldn't be royal at all if it weren't for me," Benedict Smythe said with a sneer.

"You shouldn't say such a thing. Do you have proof?"

"My brother is a sneak and a thief, and he'd do anything to advance his cats." Changing subjects, he asked, "Where are we being interviewed? I think I have important information I should give the sheriff."

Smitty wasn't having a good evening. The wounds on his head and arms were stinging and throbbing, so he decided to take some aspirin and lie down for a while. At this point, he was beyond caring about the boss's threats. He closed his eyes, and it was only a matter of minutes before he was sound asleep.

Myla wasn't sure whether her brother was stupid or just trying to be funny, but she was not amused. She knew she was the Alpha but if they were going to get back to Momma, Mylo was going to have to bring his A-game. She couldn't believe that the owl and Mylo had bonded, but it certainly looked like the owl was being very protective of him.

"Mylo, do you think your new BFF can help us get back to Momma? I don't want to have to sleep in a tree too much longer."

"Of course she can. She's very strong. While you were asleep, she took me for a ride. She wrapped her talons around my middle, and we went way up in the sky. Maybe she can fly us back to Momma."

"That's not a half-bad idea, Mylo. Do you think she'd take me for a ride? By the way, how are you and the owl communicating?"

"I just talk to her the same as I do to you and she understands what I mean."

"Okay, then would you ask her to take me for a ride? Maybe while I'm up there, I can get an idea of where we are and how far away Momma is."

"Sure, I'll ask her. Her name is Octavia and she told me she's a Great Horned Owl. She also told me that she won't let anyone hurt us."

"All right then, let's get on with it. We need to get back to Momma as soon as we can," said Myla with more excitement than she'd felt during this whole mad misadventure.

The conference room door opened and Mrs. Fiske stepped out followed by Sheriff Sharpe.

"Meade, who's next for me to interview?" the sheriff asked wearily.

"A Mr. Smythe, sir."

"Present!" answered two voices in unison.

Both the sheriff and the deputy turned to see two gentlemen, identical in every way. Both were portly with graying brown hair and matching mustaches and goatees. Before the sheriff could respond one of the two said, "Benedict Smythe at your service. I think I have some very pertinent information for you."

Sputtering, the other gentlemen said, "I'm Bertram Smythe, and you can't believe a word my brother says. He's been jealous of me since I started beating him at all the cat shows."

"You wouldn't have beaten me if you hadn't stolen the most beautiful female kitten I'd ever bred. Then you had the audacity to lie and say she died. Eugenie didn't die, you still have her, you changed her name, re-registered her, and you never bring her to shows. But you show her offspring, and that's how

183

you're able to win all of the awards. And I know something else." Benedict raised his fist and shouted at his brother. "You're the Cat Burglar!"

"That's a lie! I am not—"

"Gentlemen, why don't you both join me in the conference room? It sounds like we have a lot to discuss."

Myla was very nervous. In fact, she was trembling all over. She watched as Octavia flew down out of the tree and landed right beside her. Mylo walked over to his sister and gave her a nudge and a sweet lick on the face.

"It's going to be okay, Sissy. Octavia won't drop you. Just don't wiggle or squirm too much."

"All right. I guess I'm as ready as I'll ever be. Please tell Octavia she can pick me up."

Then Myla heard meow, meow, *and an answering* hoot, hoot, *and the next thing she knew she was airborne. She closed her eyes but could feel the air rushing past as they made their ascent. Never one to be afraid for too long, she opened her eyes and caught her breath. The view was magnificent!*

They weren't in the air too long before she saw a very large building. Hoping that Octavia would understand her, too, she said, "Octavia, that's it! That's the Convention Center! Will you take me back to Mylo? We need to make plans to get back to Momma."

"HOOT, HOOT," answered Octavia.

Deputy Meade came into the waiting area and looked around until he spotted the person he was looking for.

"Mrs. Morgan, would you please come with me? Sheriff Sharpe would like to see you."

"Is there news?" asked Lydia Morgan.

Betty patted Lydia's shoulder and gave her a reassuring smile as she got up to follow Deputy Meade. He opened the conference room door and indicated she should take a seat.

"Sheriff, please tell me you have some good news for me."

"Mrs. Morgan, I can't tell you too much just yet because I haven't completely figured out what's going on. I know you're anxious for answers and as soon as I have more information I'll let you know."

"Do you know who did it?" she asked excitedly.

"I'm not at liberty to discuss our leads with you at this time. Why don't you head back to your hotel and I'll give you a call as soon as I know more."

"I can't leave here until I have them back. Or...well, I don't want to think about that," Lydia said as she started to tear up again.

"I think they have a lounge here. I'll tell security to let you in so you can at least be more comfortable. Do you have someone who can stay with you?"

"Thank you, Sheriff Sharpe. That is very kind of you. Yes, I have a friend here with me now."

Smitty woke up with a start. At first he couldn't understand why his face hurt. But then he remembered the altercation he'd had with the owl, and it all came back to him. He checked the barn, but the boss was not there. He knew he needed to check the pond again and hopefully he'd find the cat's body. Then he'd have to get back to the Convention Center. The boss would be waiting.

He got up, went into the bathroom, and looked in the mirror. He couldn't believe how much damage that dang bird had done to his face and neck. There was no way he could put bandages on everything. He just hoped no one asked too many questions.

He left the barn only to discover that the boss had taken the van. Now his only option was to walk back to the Convention Center.

Sheriff Sharpe returned to the conference room and said, "Mr. Smythe, I'd like to ask you a few more questions about the disappearance of Mrs. Morgan's cats."

"Certainly, Sheriff. I'm happy to help however I can. I am positive my brother took those cats. He thought he was stealing my cats and took hers by mistake," said Bertram Smythe.

"Please explain to me why your brother would want to steal your cats? He has award-winning cats of his own."

"Yes, but over the last year or so I've been beating him at every show."

"That still doesn't explain why he would take Mrs. Morgan's cats. He obviously would have known which cats were yours."

Bertram Smythe had no answer for that unless he wanted to start airing his family's dirty laundry.

Just as Myla and Octavia were returning to the tree where Mylo sat waiting patiently, they saw the barn door open. Out came the man who had tried to drown Mylo and he was heading their way. Keeping very quiet, they watched as he passed under their tree and walked down the path toward the pond. Fearing he might notice them if they moved, they all stayed very still. After a minute or two he returned shaking his head. When he had passed by, Myla noticed that he didn't go back into the barn. Instead he started walking down the road.

"We better get ourselves back to the Convention Center NOW," yelled Myla.

Octavia gave a "hoot, hoot" in agreement.

"Mylo, I think she should take me first. I'll hide in the big tree near the parking lot. As soon as she puts me down, she'll come back for you. Stay here in the tree and whatever you do, don't move. Wait for Octavia. Do you hear me?"

"Yes, Sissy, I hear you loud and clear. Don't leave the tree. Don't move. Stay here until Octavia comes back for me," Mylo said, rolling his eyes.

Octavia flew from the tree with Myla in her talons and headed for the Convention Center.

Smitty arrived back at the Convention Center just as Deputy Meade was coming out the door. Too late for him to hide, he figured he could brave it out and tell the officer he was just out smoking.

Since Sheriff Sharpe was interviewing the two Smythe brothers, Deputy Meade decided he could go outside for a few minutes to get some fresh air.

As he was leaving the building, he saw something very strange—a young man whose face and neck looked like they'd been through a meat grinder. Deputy Meade hadn't seen this man in the waiting room or at any time since they'd been at the Convention Center during the investigation. He found this curious because he thought he had accounted for everyone associated with the cat show.

Just as he was about to question the man, the deputy looked toward the skyline and saw a very large bird flying his way. And it looked like the bird had something in its talons. Before he knew what was happening, the young man had bolted and the bird was landing in a nearby tree. Not knowing what to do first, Deputy Mead called for help. As soon as he saw the other deputies in pursuit of the fleeing man, he walked over to the tree.

There, sitting on the ground, were two large cats. Before he could reach down to pick them up, they started running in the same direction as the man and the owl took flight in that direction, too.

Five minutes later, on the back side of the Convention Center, he and two other officers spotted a sight to behold. There on the ground, with his arms over his head, was the man who had bolted. The owl was perched on his head and two cats were sitting, pretty as you please, on his back.

Deputy Meade reached down and grabbed the man's arm and pulled him to his feet while the owl and the cats moved away, still watching.

"Who are you?" he asked the man.

"I'm Benjamin Smythe. Please don't let the owl hurt me anymore."

"Benjamin Smythe. Are you related to Bertram and Benedict Smythe?"

"Yes, Bertram is my father and Benedict is my uncle."

"Sheriff Sharpe, we have the cats and I think the catnapper too," yelled Deputy Meade. "Where are they?" asked the sheriff.

"The other deputies are bringing in the man, and I have the cats right here."

They looked down to see the two missing Ragdoll cats standing beside Deputy Meade. The cats looked very self-possessed considering their ordeal.

The sheriff looked at Deputy Meade and asked, "How would you like to return Mrs. Morgan's cats to her?"

"I'd be honored, Sheriff. Mrs. Morgan is going to be so relieved." Off they went down the hall, the big tall deputy and the two little Ragdolls.

Opening the door to the lounge, Deputy Meade looked in and saw Mrs. Morgan huddled in a chair crying. It made him feel so good that he was going to make this lady's day.

"Mrs. Morgan, I have a surprise for you." And before he could even say another word, the two cats rushed into the room and jumped into their momma's lap.

"Mr. Smythe, I think it's time for you to stop lying. We've got your son in custody, and he's told us how you've been stealing purebred cats to cut out your competition. He's told us that you are, in fact, the Cat Burglar."

Bertram Smythe didn't know what to do. He'd been stealing purebred cats ever since he'd gotten away with stealing Eugenie from his brother. Benedict had no proof that he had her, but seemed to know that his brother had lied to him when he told him that she was dead.

"I didn't steal those two cats that are missing. I swear I didn't."

"Bertram Smythe, we're placing you under arrest for the theft of two cats known as Mylo and Myla and belonging to Mrs. Lydia Morgan, We'll also be notifying the other jurisdictions where cat thefts have occurred."

Momma was so happy. She petted Mylo and Myla enough to satisfy herself that they were unhurt, then picked them up and along with her friend, Betty, they left the Convention Center to go to their hotel for the night.

As they were exiting the building, the cats both squirmed out of Momma's grasp and went running toward the tree. They had heard the hoot, hoot *of their friend Octavia. They ran up the tree and joined her for a final farewell. Mylo and Myla were very sad. They didn't have any friends at home so they didn't want to leave their new friend behind.*

"Myla, Octavia says to tell you that she'll be fine. We don't need to worry about her. She's just glad that she was able to help us get back to Momma."

"Please tell her that I'll never forget her," Myla asked Mylo as she was giving Octavia a purr and a lick.

"She says she'll never forget her 'not so feathered' friends either."

They came running back down the tree just in time to meet up with Momma. As they were leaving, they heard a final distant "Hoot, Hoot!"

As he was being led into the conference room, Benedict Smythe didn't know whether his plan had worked or not. He couldn't be sure that Smitty had stuck to the plan. But if he had, his Uncle Benny would see that he got the best lawyer money could buy.

"Mr. Smythe, please have a seat," Sheriff Sharpe said. "I've got evidence and eye witness testimony that your brother Bertram not only stole Mrs. Morgan's cats but that he's also the Cat Burglar. His son, Benjamin, has admitted that he has been helping his father and doing most of the dirty work. I'll need you to come in tomorrow and give a statement. For now you're free to leave."

"Thank you, Sheriff."

As he was leaving the conference room, Benedict Smythe had a very hard time keeping a straight face. His plan had worked perfectly, and now his hated brother's reputation in the cat world was ruined forever. Best of all, Bertram would be in jail for a long time, and he could finally get his beloved Eugenie back.

"Who says revenge isn't sweet?"

Benedict Smythe departed with a glint in his eye and a lightness to his step.

Verena Rose is the Agatha Award nominated co-editor of *Not Everyone's Cup of Tea, An Interesting and Entertaining History of Malice Domestic's First 25 Years* and the Managing Editor of the upcoming anthology *Malice Domestic 12: Mystery Most Historical*, due out in time for Malice Domestic 29 from Wildside Press, which includes her story "Death on the Dueling Grounds." Verena serves as the Chair of Malice Domestic, is one of the founding members of the Dames of Detection, and co-owner/editor/publisher at Level Best Books. When not indulging her passion for mysteries Verena works as a tax accountant. She lives in Olney, Maryland, with her four cats: Jasper, Alice, Matty & Missy.

MOST EVIL

Peter DiChellis

A maintenance gardener found the stout Russian gangster Dimitri Korov sprawled on dewy grass in a city park at sunrise, butt down in black gabardine slacks and a tan leather jacket, with a nine-inch ice pick slammed into his forehead and his eyes bugged open like a gargoyle's.

One look at the corpse and every cop called to the scene pondered the same questions. Who the hell could have stepped in close enough to kill a tough, streetwise thug like Korov face-to-face, hand-to-hand? How could anybody get that kind of drop on Dimitri Korov, catch him flatfooted for one clean stroke with long, shiny steel? Must have been somebody special, the cops figured. Somebody brutal and fearless.

Somebody exactly like rival mobster Goat Head Jimmy, the ferocious Haitian gang leader whose fingerprints crime scene techs found in congealed blood on the ice pick's wooden handle. But would a shrewd gangbanger like Goat Head really leave behind the murder weapon with his bloody prints on it?

A day later, Detective Janessa Ann Harley stood next to her desk at Robbery-Homicide Division, weighing the odd fingerprint evidence with her young partner, Detective Brennan Druckett. Harley, a fortyish woman, tall and solid with ebony hair and a caramel complexion, enjoyed riffing with Druckett, a freckled, red-headed man built as burly as a beer keg.

"Maybe the pick was left as a message or warning," Harley offered.

"Maybe Korov's goon buddies were nearby and gave chase," Druckett said.

Harley winked. "Maybe Goat Head was tripped out from smokin' *ganja*."

Or maybe, like they said on the street, the notorious Haiti-to-Jamaica guns-for-*ganja* dope dealer and supreme *ganja* warlord Goat Head Jimmy could summon voodoo sorcery so potent the law could never touch him, no prison could ever hold him. So it wouldn't trouble Goat Head to be sought for a killing. Not a bit.

"Goat Head Jimmy conjure evil *Petro* voodoo," a chubby Haitian *Mambo* had whispered once to the detectives. "Goat Head Jimmy voodoo *Bizango Petro*, most evil. Voodoo this evil make killin' easy. Make a man a mesmerizer who slip through the shadows and do what he please. *Bizango Petro*. Most evil voodoo."

Sure, Harley thought. That probably solves it.

189

Some cops might coast through a gangster-kills-gangster investigation, but Harley worked every murder case hard. So she and Druckett pressed Goat Head's gang members for his whereabouts. They interviewed Russian mobsters expected to track Goat Head in a quest for payback. They staked out his townhouse and visited every other place he'd lived during the past several years. They leaned on their snitches. They checked for airline, train, and long-distance bus travel. They issued Be-On-The-Lookout notices to patrol cops. Nothing. Goat Head Jimmy had vanished, floated away like the wind. Even leaking the story to local TV stations and newspapers didn't turn up any leads.

Harley steered the detectives' unmarked car as they cruised Goat Head's gang territory again. "If he's breathing, we'll find him," she vowed.

"You think maybe the Russians got him?" Druckett asked.

"Unlikely. They'd leave his body someplace public. Make him an example." She continued driving, her hazel eyes searching. A single question nagged her: What had their investigation missed? Something big, she figured. Too many pieces didn't fit.

The following week promised luck but delivered a new riddle.

One of Harley's Haitian snitches got busted holding enough crack cocaine to risk a prison jolt of infinity plus forever, no parole. That's a lot of years, so the snitch figured he'd better make a deal. Harley sat in a cramped interrogation room at the city jail, haggling with the snitch and his attorney, a tired-eyed public defender wearing a blue skirt, an almost matching jacket, and sensible black shoes. The room smelled rank with sweat. So did the snitch.

"Goat Head Jimmy dead and buried long time," the snitch told Harley. "Very long time. I show you where at."

His attorney winced.

"No chance," Harley said to them. "We know Goat Head's good for Korov's ice pick murder. That was six days ago."

"Dead before then," the snitch insisted. He glanced around the room and leaned forward, his voice a cracked whisper. "*Bizango Petro* voodoo allow Goat Head come back, slippin' among us in the shadows. He mesmerize your mind helpless. He go prowlin' and killin' however he please. *Bizango Petro*. Most evil voodoo."

"See you in a thousand years," Harley told him. "If you're out by then."

The public defender shrugged.

Two weeks later, another Russian hoodlum got killed, a vicious 300-pound tattooed enforcer suspected of a dozen mob hits. Patrol cops found him in a littered alley with a pair of bullets in his brain. From the entry wounds, the detectives figured the shooter stood eyeball to eyeball with the massive gangster, shoved the gun straight into his ugly face, and *pop! pop!* twice in the head, the big man's dead. They found the murder weapon, a .22 caliber pocket revolver, next to a pile of cardboard six feet from the body. And Goat Head Jimmy's fingerprints were on the .22, and on the Rolex gracing the Russian's left wrist and the diamond ring on his right pinkie.

And like the Korov ice pick murder, all of this was puzzling.

"Point-blank, powder burns," Harley said. "Stood close enough to this ogre to dance a tango with him and still got the job done."

"And Goat Head left his prints on the gun and the gun with the body?" Druckett wondered aloud. "And if he's so fascinated with the guy's jewelry, why not just take it?"

Soon enough, the street buzz started to echo the snitch's story.

"Goat Head Jimmy dead and buried but he come back," Haitians said on every corner. "Come back prowlin'. Come back killin'. Mesmerize your mind helpless. *Bizango Petro*. Most evil voodoo."

So Druckett got the job of watching crime scene investigators dig up a lonely patch of ground behind a vacant warehouse. Underneath that patch, Harley's snitch insisted, they'd find a long-dead Goat Head Jimmy.

When the CSI crew stopped digging and began retching, Druckett knew they'd found what they came for. He leaned over the hole in the dirt and studied the find before calling Harley.

"We got a dead body here," he told her. "Extra messy."

"But not Goat Head," Harley said.

"Could be him. About the same size. Two gold teeth in front. Dreadlocks down to his shoulders. Forensics will verify an ID."

"How long in the ground?" Harley continued.

"Based on decomp and insects, the techs say at least two months."

"So if we assume the body is Goat Head, our supposed voodoo killer was dead a month before Korov got stabbed? Dead and buried before the two Russian murders happened?"

"Dead and buried at least a month before the murders," Druckett said.

"Medical Examiner?" Harley asked.

"On the way. But there's another thing about the body, whoever the guy is."

"Yeah?"

"Both of his hands are cut off."

"The dead man's dismembered hands were used to leave his fingerprints at both crime scenes," a forensics analyst at the crime lab told Harley the next day.

Harley sat in a waiting room outside the lab, listening and eating a take-out lunch. Pizza, and fries with extra ketchup. Coffee, double cream. She'd brought a slice for the forensics guy too, but he said he wasn't hungry. His white lab smock showed crusty brown specks and wet yellow smears, and carried a slight scent of rotten flesh. He remained standing and continued talking.

"The bloody prints on the Korov ice pick handle show traces of embalming chemicals and industrial alcohol," he said. "Those no doubt came from the missing hands and easily would have kept the fingers in good enough condition to leave prints. We found similar traces on the gun, watch, and ring from the second killing."

"And you just discovered this now?" Harley asked, swirling a fry in a colossal mound of ketchup.

"We weren't looking until now. We already had a positive ID on the prints and the two victims. Why would we test anything for embalming chemicals?"

Harley munched the dripping fry. "Okay, fine. What's the ID on the guy you dug out of the ground?"

"Same as the prints. Goat Head. No doubt."

"Any embalming chemicals in the body?"

"No. He's ripe."

Harley took a bite of pizza. "Medical Examiner give cause and manner of death?"

"No official report yet."

"But?"

"But from what I saw, the guy was poisoned."

"Got it," Harley said.

She thanked him, and after confirming he still wasn't hungry, took the extra pizza slice with her to eat in the car. She phoned Druckett, who was taking a sick day after spending half of yesterday's shift with Goat Head's decomposing body.

"We've been wrong-sided since day one, since the Korov killing," Harley told him, as she drove and ate the pizza.

"How?"

She explained.

"What next?" Druckett asked.

"Find out how many of Goat Head's gang turned up dead in the last month, since the Korov killing. I'll jostle the snitch again."

"He was right about finding Goat Head's body."

"Yeah, that's the other problem."

The next morning, Harley met Druckett in the hall outside the jail interrogation room. The Haitian snitch and his public defender sat inside. Druckett had gotten the information Harley wanted.

"The answer is zero," he told her. "None."

"So the whole world thinks Goat Head is murdering Russian mobsters, but none of Goat Head's people got hit back. No retaliation killings."

"None," Druckett said again.

Harley nodded toward the interrogation room. "And since when did Haitians, not Russians, hustle crack in this town?"

"Since never. Goat Head was devout for *ganja*."

Harley went into the interrogation room. Druckett watched through the two-way mirror. Both the room and the snitch stank worse than last time. The public defender wore an anxious face. She knew what was coming.

Harley sat. "Let's get to it. How'd you know where to find the body?"

"Everybody know," the snitch said. "But I help you find it, see?"

"You just helped yourself into an accessory to murder charge," Harley said.

The public defender put her hand on the snitch's arm, whispered something. He nodded.

"No murder charge," she told Harley. "He'll give you what you want."

"How'd you know where the body was buried?" Harley repeated.

"Everybody know, everybody talk. Goat Head boys talk."

"Same guys you were running crack for?"

"Can't say no names."

"But Goat Head's *ganja* crew is running crack for the Russians now?" Harley asked.

The public defender stopped the snitch from answering. "What's the deal?" she asked.

"He gives me an address," Harley said. "I tell the prosecutor to give him a break."

Five minutes later, Harley and Druckett left the building. The snitch took a deep breath and told the public defender he needed to use a phone.

The two detectives headed toward the address the snitch had given them. Druckett drove while Harley flipped through her notes and reviewed the evidence reports again. She didn't think they'd missed anything.

"The poisoning. That's what led you to ask about the retaliation killings," Druckett said.

"Yeah, the victims were a trio of streetwise thugs who stayed alert and suspicious all the time," Harley said. "But the killers got close enough for a stabbing, a point-blank shooting, and a poisoning."

"Killers?" the junior detective said. "Plural. Insiders maybe?"

"Had to be insiders," Harley said. "Russians killed the two Russians, the Haitians hit Goat Head. Only their own guys could have gotten that close. No retaliations because they're working together."

"To get crack flowing into Haitian gang territory. That would explain killing Goat Head, he'd never approve it. But what about the dead Russians?"

"Probably killed for the same reason as Goat Head. Getting in the way."

"The hands?" Druckett asked.

"I'd guess the Russians made the Haitians take the hands as proof of Goat Head's death and their new loyalty, then left the prints to disguise their own insider killings."

"And to get us chasing Goat Head instead of looking in their direction."

"That too."

Druckett checked a street sign. "Almost there," he said. "Why no backup?"

"Unlikely the snitch gave us anything good," Harley said. "He didn't ask for enough in return. We'll check it out, then prod him again."

They drove the final three blocks in silence.

"Address must be a building or two ahead," Druckett said. "I'll pull over here."

Their car rolled to a stop. The detectives stayed inside, engine running, and took a long, quiet look: Squat brick buildings, empty sidewalks, gutters strewn with busted glass and crushed cigarette butts, and twenty feet beyond the car, a filthy green trash dumpster flush against the curb. Someone had pasted a handbill on the dumpster's side. It read, *GOD FORGIVES YOU* and gave the name of a local church.

"Let's do it," Harley said.

When she and Druckett got out of the car, two men stepped around the corner, half a block ahead across the street. A black man with an automatic pistol, a white man with a shotgun. One Haitian. One Russian. Both killers. They crossed the street diagonally, toward the detectives, walking fast, closing the distance.

The dreadlocked Haitian fired first, a gold-toothed glint in his twisted smile. He held the pistol movie-gangsta style, sideways with his arm extended, spraying bullets everywhere except where he aimed. And then the Russian's shotgun boomed and Druckett went down, blood everywhere. He lay in the street, facing the shooters, eyes open.

Harley fired her service revolver twice at the Russian and twice at the Haitian. Red splotches blossomed on the Russian's chest. His shotgun clattered on the asphalt and he fell, face down next to the dumpster. The Haitian kept coming. Harley dropped to the ground behind the car. She heard the Haitian gunman eject a magazine from his automatic and slap in another. His pistol would hold at least a nine-shot mag, she knew, maybe fifteen shots or more. She emptied her revolver of its four spent casings and two live rounds, and popped a speed-loader into the cylinder. Six bullets.

Harley shifted into position, on her stomach, peering under the car, watching the Haitian's feet as he approached. He'd reached within arms length of the front bumper when Druckett choked out a wet cough. The feet stopped, Harley fired two shots underneath the car, and the Haitian's right foot and left ankle exploded red. Harley leapt up and slid onto the hood of the car as the Haitian hit the ground, took one quick peek-a-boo look, and put four .38 Special hollow-points into his chest. Dead man.

And at that moment, in her peripheral vision, the gritty detective saw what she felt certain was a prelude to her own death. Nothing but blood next to the trash dumpster. No Russian. No shotgun.

She rolled over, still flat on the hood, and looked behind her. The Russian stood on the sidewalk, pointing the shotgun at her midsection. His face had drained to fish-belly white, his clothes slopped blood. The shotgun quivered in his hands. His eyes rolled back in his head and he fell.

Harley slid off the car, pulled away the shotgun, and checked the Russian's pulse. Nothing. She checked Druckett. Weak pulse, still breathing. She tried to slow his bleeding and called it in.

"Code ten thirty-three," she told the dispatcher. "One officer down, emergency medical needed. Two shooters, toes up." She gave her location and kept trying to slow Druckett's bleeding. She heard distant sirens.

The ER doctor told Harley that Druckett was out of surgery, awake and out of danger. The hospital room smelled like disinfectant and Druckett looked like crap. Harley figured she probably didn't look her best either. Twenty-two straight hours waiting in the hospital hallway. Praying for Druckett. Cursing the snitch. Knowing the mistake was hers.

"Taking another sick day already?" she ribbed Druckett. "You need to eat more pizza and fries. Keep you healthy."

"Just tell me the gangsta pistol shooter wasn't Goat Head."

"Wasn't," Harley said. "Had to be one of the guys who double-crossed him. Maybe they'll work out their differences when they meet in hell."

"How'd they find us?" Druckett asked.

"Snitch ratted us out."

"What now?"

"Task force is taking over," Harley said. "Us, the Feds, everybody who's got a badge and a gun."

"Sounds like a bad day to be a gangster."

"Yeah. Good day to be a cop."

This story is an original work of creative fiction. Any resemblance to actual individuals or events is unintended and coincidental. Voodoo, like Catholicism, is a popular and officially recognized religion in Haiti. *Bizango Petro* is an extreme form of the Voodoo religion, roughly analogous to anti-Christ devil worship, and is not representative of mainstream Voodoo religious practices. Rolex is a registered trademark of Rolex and Rolex Watch USA, Inc.

Peter DiChellis concocts sinister tales for anthologies, ezines, and magazines. He is a member of the Short Mystery Fiction Society and an Active (published author) member of the Mystery Writers of America, Private Eye Writers of America, and International Thriller Writers. For more, visit his site Murder and Fries at http://murderandfries.wordpress.com/

BECKY'S FILE

Ruth McCarty

Erin Donnelly had been expecting the call from her sister, Megan, but seeing her number and knowing this could be their mother's last day hit her harder than she thought it would.

Their mother, Mary Catherine Donnelly, had slowly lost herself as Alzheimer's had taken over her mind, and pneumonia had taken over her body.

"Megan..."

"You better come now, Erin. Ma needs you here."

Erin raced across town to the nursing home to be there for her sister. Megan was the one who needed her now—not their mother.

Megan's husband, Charlie, stood outside the room, his cell phone in his hand. His rumpled clothes giving away the fact that he'd been there all night too. "I just called the girls. Katie's on her way from Biddeford, and as soon as Claire gets out of class she'll be here."

"How is Megan holding up?"

"Like she always does. I'm just worried about what she's going to do when your mother is gone."

"I know, Charlie. Megan's done the burden of the work," I said, feeling guilty. But as chief of police, I couldn't be there as much as I wanted to.

The guilt must have shown on my face, because Charlie quickly said, "She knows you couldn't be here, Erin. Besides, with Katie in college and Claire in high school, it gave her something to do."

Erin thanked Charlie, then moved into the room. Megan stood and gave her a hug.

"How's she doing?"

Megan just shook her head. "The home offered to bring us a platter of sandwiches and some coffee."

"That's good. You look so tired. Why don't you and Charlie take a little break? I'll stay here with Ma. It's beautiful outside. The sandwiches can wait."

Megan looked out the window. "Well, I could use a little air, but I hate to leave her."

"Go. It'll be okay."

"You're right." She fussed with the pillows, then leaned in and kissed her mother's cheek. "I won't be long," Megan whispered.

Erin stood listening to the horrible sounds each breath brought and prayed the morphine helped with the pain. She stroked her mother's head. "Ma. It's me, Erin."

Mary Catherine opened her eyes. "I knew you'd come."

And as if her mother knew Megan would be devastated if she died while she was out of the room, she waited until Megan came back to breathe her last breath.

Megan had dropped off the last of their mother's boxes she'd been storing in her basement. She'd taken what she wanted from them, and now it was Erin's turn to go over their mother's stuff. Erin had told Megan she could keep everything, but Megan wouldn't listen. She just didn't get that Erin was fine with memories and didn't need stuff.

It took most of the morning to go through the boxes and Erin was relieved to pick up the last one and slit it open. It took her a few seconds to realize the box contained her father's files. She picked up the top one and read: *Beauregard, Rebecca Jane, Saturday, December 15, 1990.*

A Taser-like shock traveled through her body. It was her father's file on Becky's murder. The one case her father had kept from her even though Becky's murder was the reason Erin had become a police officer.

Erin's mother had hated the idea that she'd have to worry about her daughter as well as her husband so she'd insisted Erin go away to college first, and then if she decided she still wanted to be a law enforcement officer, she wouldn't stop her.

Erin had taken every criminal justice course offered, completed her internship, came home, and started filling in every shift available at the station—of which there weren't many in the small town of Prosperity, Maine. When Erin's father died of a heart attack, not a shooting as her mother imagined, Erin applied for his position and got it.

Becky's file. What she'd call a *Murder Book* today. She walked to the kitchen, opened one of the new blue Bud Light bottles of beer and took it and the file out to the screened in porch.

Her hands shook as she opened it and spotted the Polaroid photo stapled to the inside cover. *Erin and Becky* she read in her mother's handwriting. *Snowball Dance, 1990.*

Her mother had taken the picture right before her father had driven them to the dance. There she was looking like a young Julia Roberts—long wavy hair, thick eyebrows and red lipstick. Her dress was sapphire blue with a thin strap on one shoulder and a huge ruffle on the other. She'd borrowed her mother's silver heels and looked all legs.

Becky's dress was a sparkly purple and she looked like Candace Cameron with her hair dyed blonde and her bangs teased and sprayed with at least a can of Aqua Net. Both of them had a makeup bag in their purse so they could add eyeliner and mascara when they got to the dance.

197

Erin closed the folder. This was getting to her on so many levels. As she finished the bottle of beer, she decided to take a weeks' vacation and hopefully find peace for Becky's family.

Erin cleared the dining room table and took out the extra-large white board and easel she often used while going over a case at home. Across the top she wrote: *Rebecca Jane Beauregard.* And below it: *Saturday, December 15, 1990.*

Then she sat at the table and opened the file and looked at the first page.

Becky's autopsy report.

It took a few minutes for Erin to stop trembling enough for her to read it. She knew Becky had been strangled. It was all over the newspapers. But Erin, seeing it here in black and white, felt like she'd been punched in the chest. *Asphyxia. Petechial hemorrhaging. Consistent with homicidal strangulation. Age: 17.*

Twenty-five years ago. Becky would be forty-three now. *No, she'd be forty-two,* Erin remembered. *Because she had a December birthday that she would have celebrated three days after her death.*

She read and reread the transcripts and the witness interviews, each time making notes for questions she would ask when she conducted her own interviews, ignoring the fact that she knew every witness personally.

Erin knew there was no statute of limitations on murder so first thing in the morning she'd go to the evidence locker and send Becky's clothes out for DNA testing, something her father couldn't have done at the time.

Then she would visit the scene of the crime.

She finally got up the courage to look at the crime scene photos. They were worse than she could have imagined. How had her father investigated this case? Erin vowed to solve it for him—and for Becky. She just had to treat it like any other case.

Ian McDermott, her chief deputy, was at the station when she arrived the next morning. "I thought you were taking the week off. What are you doing here?"

"I'm working on a cold case."

McDermott laughed. "Only you would take a vacation to work on a case."

Erin smiled. He was right. She hated vacations. "I need to get into the lockers."

McDermott raised his eyebrows.

"It's one of my father's cases. Got a minute to go with me?"

"Sure."

The lockers that contained unsolved cases were down in the basement of the police station. Erin signed and dated a sheet, then entered. Newer cases were stored in the front, in actual lockers with keys. The box Erin needed was in the back on a shelf with several others. She checked her case file number against it, showed it to McDermott, then took it off the shelf to the table.

She took out her Swiss army knife and slit the tape. After putting on gloves, she opened the box and took out the items. *Becky's shiny purple dress.*

Erin had to hang onto the table.

McDermott grabbed her elbow. "You okay?"

Erin took a couple of breaths before saying, "My best friend in high school."

"Jeeze, Erin," McDermott said. "I heard about that case when I started here. Why are you doing this now?"

"My sister gave me a box of things that belonged to my father and his copy of this case was in it. It's been twenty-five years, Ian. It's time to give Becky's family some closure."

McDermott watched as she bagged the dress. Then a pair of silver shoes. Finally a padded pushup bra and a pair of bikini panties, each bagged separately. She picked up the locket Becky had been wearing that night. Inside was a photo of Christopher Starks, the boy she'd been dating since her junior year. Starks still lived in town, and Erin had decided that he'd be the first one she would interview.

After boxing and cataloging the evidence bags, she had McDermott sign them, then asked him to get the items to the Maine State Police Lab in Augusta. She knew it could take months to hear back from them, but hopefully she'd have built a case by then.

Now she needed to visit the scene of the crime. She knew she had to go wide and circle in.

Erin parked in front of the long-abandoned high school. Somehow, years after the murder, the town had found the funds to build a new school down by the highway.

Graffiti covered a faded *For Sale* sign stuck in the overgrown lawn. No one wanted the building. The fire department had spray-painted a huge red "X" on all the doors to let their firefighters know the building was unsafe.

Erin looked at the crime scene photos and sketches once more before getting out of her car and walking to the back of the building. The gymnasium, where the dance had taken place, had been added onto the school in the late seventies—a modern design that never fit with the traditional brick building.

A chunky chain threaded through the door handles and a master lock holding them together were supposed to keep trespassers out, but the broken windows allowed anyone to get in. Erin's officers had kicked squatters out many times for their own safety.

Erin peered in one of the windows. Debris covered the floor. A loose beam hung from the ceiling. Nothing to look at there. She followed the path that led to the football and soccer fields. She knew Derek McClintock and Tracy

Silva had gone outside to make out that night and had stumbled upon Becky's body behind the concession stand.

The stand had burned to the ground years ago. Erin found the spot behind it where Becky's body had been found, crouched and picked up a charred plank of wood to look under it. If there had been any evidence here, it was long gone.

After leaving the school, Erin headed to Becky's parents' house. The Beauregards would be in their mid-sixties now. She parked in front of the two story house, walked up to the door and rang the bell. After a minute, Mrs. Beauregard answered.

"Erin Donnelly," she said, pulling Erin into a hug. "It's been too long. What brings you here?"

"I need to talk to you and Mr. Beauregard. Can I come in?"

"Sure. He's right here in the den," she said, then whispered, "he has late stage lung cancer. All that smoking, you know."

Erin saw the frail body tucked into a hospital bed first, then noticed the oxygen tank and heard the labored breathing. "Mr. Beauregard."

He nodded, and Mrs. Beauregard said, "Erin needs to talk to us."

"I won't take long. I just wanted to let you know before it gets all over town that I've reopened Becky's case."

Mrs. Beauregard wobbled and Erin was afraid she was going to faint, but the woman sat down on the bed and grabbed her husband's hand. "Oh, Erin, it would be an answer to our prayers if you could find out who did that horrible thing to our Becky."

Mr. Beauregard took several painful deep breaths and said, "Find the bastard."

Erin felt drained as she drove away. Becky had been their only child. No marriage, no grandkids. She had to solve this case.

Christopher Starks lived outside of town in the only trailer park left. She banged on his door and waited.

"Who is it?" came a gravelly voice from inside.

"Erin Donnelly, Chris. I need to talk to you."

"I ain't done nothing."

"I know. It's not about you. It's about Becky."

The door flung open. Starks stood there in a yellowed stained t-shirt and a dirty pair of jeans. She could see his court-ordered ankle monitor sticking out of his sock. "What about Becky? Did you cops finally find out who killed her so I can live my life in this town?"

"Not yet, but I'm going to. I just have a few questions. Can I come in?"

"I guess."

The inside was as filthy as his clothes. When he offered her a seat, Erin declined. "I won't be staying long. I just need you to tell me what you remember of that night."

Starks sat and put his elbows on his knees and his hands on the side of his head. "I remember I lost the best thing in my life that night."

"Why did you take Becky outside?"

"We just wanted to make out a bit, but it was so cold. So I told Becky I'd go back in and grab her jacket."

It was freezing that night. "Go on."

"Well, when I got back, Mr. Tucker was standing at the door. I guess he realized that kids were sneaking out. So I stood on the side of the building for a few minutes. Mr. Tucker finally disappeared, maybe had to take a whiz. I snuck back in then."

So far his story jibed with his interview. "Then what?"

"Then all hell broke loose. That's when Tracy what's-her-face came running in, screaming and crying and yelling "Becky's dead" over and over. And her jerk of a boyfriend threw up in the pail by the food."

"Derek McClintock?"

"Yeah. That idiot. I tried to go out and get Becky, but they wouldn't let me. You know they wouldn't let any of us out. Then someone yelled that I had Becky's coat and I got tackled by Mr. Tucker."

"I remember."

"Then your old man got there. I'm telling you, like I told him, I loved Becky and she loved me. We was gonna get married."

Erin remembered his photo in the locket. God, he looked awful now. Maybe solving Becky's murder would help him too. She handed him her card. "If you think of anything else, like who you saw outside, give me a call."

"Yeah. Well, it was dark. I didn't see much."

The day had drained her. Erin realized she hadn't had lunch and it was nearly dinner time so she stopped at Romano's to pick up a pizza to go. Once home she'd type up her notes and decide who to call on in the morning.

Maybe Mr. Tucker? She needed to see if he still lived in Prosperity. Mr. Bramhall? The school janitor and his son Jimmy who showed up that night to help with the cleanup? Or should she pop in on Mayor Michael Winslow— her date for the dance. She saw Mike all the time and probably should let him know she was investigating the case since he was the mayor. She decided she'd go see him when town hall opened in the morning.

Then she would visit Mr. Bramhall, who she knew still lived on River Road. She would call on him, and find out where his son lived. Jimmy Bramhall had been two years ahead of her in school, but had dropped out as soon as he'd turned sixteen. She'd seen him around town a few times since, but had never said more than hello to him. She heard he'd married Heather Bates from her class, but three kids later they'd divorced.

Erin worked until she couldn't keep her eyes open and slept fitfully. She woke around three and couldn't get back to sleep, so she tried piecing the dance together in her head.

Her father had dropped her and Becky off at the front of the school and said he'd be back to get them at ten. Mike was already there, talking with a group of kids. He'd always been popular. Seemed to be running for office his whole life.

Becky had said, "Let's go fix our makeup." They'd passed Tracy Silva in the hallway and Erin had guessed her dress had belonged to one of her older sisters. It looked good on Tracy, but the style was too sexy for her age. Tracy's hair was teased and pulled to one side with a gold lamé Scrunchie. She'd smiled and said to Becky, "Love your dress."

Then the music started. Becky had said, "Let's go. The guys are waiting."

Only Chris was waiting when we came out. He'd smiled at Becky and it lit up his face. "Come on, let's dance," he'd said.

Mike came over then and said, "Becky, you look beautiful." She had laughed, grabbed Chris's hand and ran to the dance floor.

Mike had said, "Dance with me."

Right before the band took their first break, Erin had spotted Becky and Chris slipping out the gymnasium door.

Mike had worked up a sweat, so he excused himself and said he'd be back in a minute, and that he'd get them something to drink. Erin remembered standing there alone for a short while, leaning against the wall, waiting for Mike. A couple of girls stopped to talk to her about the band. Then she spotted Mike with two cups in his hands. "Here, take a drink," he'd said.

Erin took a sip and nearly spit it out. It had to be ninety percent alcohol. "Mike, I can't drink this. My father will kill me."

"Come on, Erin. Everyone's drinking."

"How did you get it in here?"

"I just got it out of my car. Walked right in with it. Tucker was clueless."

"Well, you know I can't drink. My father's the chief of police for god sakes."

"You're no fun," he'd slurred. "Hey, where's your little friend?"

Erin had hated when he called Becky "her little friend." Erin was already five-seven and Becky was stuck at five-two. But they were best friends and would be forever. Erin didn't tell Mike that Becky and Chris had snuck out.

She looked at the cup and said, "I'm not going to drink this!"

"Fine," Mike said, grabbing for the cup and spilling some on her dress.

"You jerk." Erin took off to the ladies room to rinse the stain. If she was lucky, her father wouldn't smell it when he picked her up. She didn't want to make up a story about how it got there.

That was the last she remembered of the dance until Tracy came in screaming about Becky, and Derek throwing up in the garbage pail, and Chris standing there, holding Becky's coat.

The band had stopped playing. Mr. Tucker came running into the room and decked Chris. Mr. Bramhall came down the hallway with a mop and pail and Jimmy, his son, was banging on the gymnasium door to be let in. Girls were crying, guys were wringing their hands, and Erin just wanted the nightmare to be over.

Both her mother and father had come that night. Her mother drove her home and her father stayed all night. Erin knew he did because she stayed awake waiting for him. When she heard the door early that morning, she'd gotten up and found her mother and father whispering in the kitchen.

"Becky?" I'd asked. "Is it true?"

Her father had gathered her in his arms and cried. She never asked him about it again.

Erin finally got up and showered. She ate a cold piece of pizza and drank a half glass of orange juice, then headed out to the nearest coffee shop. She felt like hell. And of course there was Mike Winslow sitting at the counter.

"Mayor," she said.

"Erin," he said. "I'm glad you came in. I heard about your investigation."

"Wow. That was fast. I actually had you on my list to talk to today."

Mike laughed. "Guilty."

"That's not funny, Mike."

"I know. Sorry. It seemed like everyone was guilty then."

"Let's go to a booth so I can ask you a few questions."

After they were seated, Erin said, "The main question I have is, did you see anyone when you went out to your car?"

"When I went to my car? Oh, yeah, when I went out to get the vodka. God I was dumb that night."

"Yeah, you were."

"I guess I needed it for courage."

"What?"

"Erin, I wanted for us to you know, change our relationship."

"You mean sleep with you? Ha. You just wanted to get me drunk."

"I was a stupid kid. It all kind of worked out though. We never hooked up and I married Annie and you have your career."

"Yeah, well everything changed that night. Did you see anyone outside?"

"To tell you the truth, I never looked around. I headed for the car and came right back."

"Do you have any idea who could have killed Becky?"

"Not a clue. I suspected Mr. Tucker back then. You know how all the girls thought he was creepy."

She knew all right. He'd made her feel icky a few times. "Well, if you think of anything let me know. Say hi to Annie for me."

After stopping at Mr. Bramhall's house and finding no one home, she found out from a neighbor that he'd been in the hospital and was now a patient at Hilltop Nursing Home.

It felt strange driving there. It had been nearly a month since her mother had passed on and she'd been there to visit. A new receptionist at the desk asked if she could help. Erin told her she wanted to visit Mr. Bramhall and the woman gave Erin his room and floor number.

Erin knocked and waited until she heard someone say to come in. There were two beds in the room, the first one empty and Mr. Bramhall was in the other one.

"Mr. Bramhall, it's me, Erin Donnelly. Do you remember me from school?"

He smiled. "I sure do. You were one of the nice ones. Always said hello."

"Did you know I'm the chief of police now?"

"Ayup. Just like your daddy."

"Right. I hope you don't mind, but I have a couple of questions to ask you."

"Shoot," he said, then laughed at his own joke.

"It's about Becky Beauregard's murder."

The smile left his face. "Poor girl. I remember like it was yesterday."

"Tell me what you remember."

"Well, I got there about an hour after the dance started, and was waiting in my office until it ended. I wasn't feeling well, so I called my son, Jimmy, to see if he could come and help me clean up. Then I heard someone screaming and Miss Davis came running down the hall yelling someone's throwing up."

I'd forgotten about Miss Davis. She'd told my father she hadn't seen anything because she was in the ladies room. Well, she wasn't in the girl's room because I was in there.

"That's when everyone went crazy. Girls crying, parents banging on the doors to get in. I don't know how they got there that fast. Well before cell phones, you know."

"I know."

"I opened the door to let my son and Mayor Winslow in. Course he wasn't mayor then."

"Do you know where Mr. Tucker was?"

"Well, come to think of it, he was coming down the stairs from the second floor when I came out of my office. He said the band was too loud and he had to get away for a little while so he went to the teachers' lounge."

So that's where Mr. Tucker had been.

I called the number listed for Mr. Tucker and was gobsmacked when Mrs. Tucker answered and it turned out to be Miss Davis. They agreed to meet with me at noon.

204

I had to question each of them separately, so Mr. Tucker said he'd take the dog for a short walk. I got right down to it and said, "Miss Davis, sorry, Mrs. Tucker, my father's notes said you were in the ladies room when Becky was murdered. I know you weren't there because I was there."

"Well, you'll hear this from Edward, so I may as well tell you. We were having an affair then. I'm ashamed to say Edward was still married. So we took whatever chance we could to be together."

Miss Davis and Mr. Tucker. Didn't want to go there. Looks like they were each other's alibi. When Mr. Tucker returned, he admitted the truth.

"Did you see anyone else that night?"

"No. Only Michael Winslow. He said he went out to his car to get a jacket. Come to think of it though, he wasn't wearing one when he came back."

Well, I wasn't giving Mike's secret away. I thanked them for their time and headed back to Prosperity.

I pulled up in front of the Park Boarding House on Main where Jimmy Bramhall rented a room. The front door opened as I walked up the stairs and Jimmy said, "Erin, it's good to see you. Dad said you'd be coming by."

He led me to a common living room and motioned for me to sit on the couch across from him. "Can I get you anything? A drink?"

From his shaking hands, I could tell he needed one. "I'm all set, but if you want one go ahead."

"I can wait."

"Jimmy, you got to the school right about the time the murder took place."

He put up his hands and said, "It wasn't me. I was just coming to help my father."

"He said that. Where did you park?"

"In front. Then I walked around back."

"Did you see anyone?"

"Yeah, I saw two kids heading out. I figured they were going somewhere to get lai...um to make out."

"What did they look like?"

"Well, she was tiny. All dressed up with a gold bow in her hair. I only saw that because the light glinted off it."

Tracy. So he got there when she and Derek were heading out. Only moments before they came running back in. "Who let you in?"

"Oh, I didn't go in then. I'd left my cigarettes in the van and went back for them and had a smoke before I came back around."

"Did anyone see you smoking?"

"Umm. Yeah. That kid that you dated, Winslow. That jackass mayor we have now."

"Anybody else? Mr. Tucker?"

"Nope. Just those kids."

205

Erin drove home. Wrote up her notes. Read them over. Who could have done this?

Had Becky's father come early and found her outside? No, he would have gone in the school to look for her, not out to the closed and dark concession stand.

Was it Jimmy? Had he watched as Chris walked her out there? Had he watched as they made out and found an opportunity when Chris went back for her coat? Maybe. Erin would have to ask Mike if he remembered seeing Jimmy that night.

Had Chris lied about leaving her there waiting for his return? Had he already killed Becky? He had the opportunity, but not the motive. It was obvious that he loved Becky then and still did.

Mr. Bramhall had more or less given Mr. Tucker an alibi when he said he saw him coming from the teacher's lounge. Unless Mr. Tucker had left the school, committed the crime, then returned to make love to his mistress. Nope. Didn't seem right.

She read her notes again. The only constant was Mike. Mike went to his car to get the vodka. Jimmy saw him. Mr. Tucker said he went to the car to get a jacket but came back without one. Erin knew Mike went to his car to get the booze because he'd spilled it on her dress.

It all fell into place. Mr. Bramhall said he'd let Jimmy and Mike in after Miss Davis came running to his office.

Her heart sank. Mike had gone back outside when she went to clean her dress.

He picked up on the first ring. "Mike, I need to see you. I have a couple more questions."

"Can't we do this over the phone, Erin? You know the hours I keep."

"I do. It won't take long. Meet me at your office."

Erin called McDermott on her way to town hall and filled him in.

Mike was sitting behind the massive desk in his office. He stood when she entered.

"I only want to know why, Mike."

He collapsed back into his chair. Slowly he pulled open a desk drawer. "I really didn't mean to do it, Erin. I wanted Becky. When she laughed and pushed me away that night, I lost it."

He pulled out a gun and had it under his chin before Erin had time to react.

"Don't do it, Mike. Think of Annie and the kids."

"That's who I'm thinking of."

"Put it down, Mike. Don't let them remember you like this."

"You know, Erin, I was waiting for the day you'd come. I knew you'd never let it go."

"It's over now, Mike. Annie loves you. She'll forgive you. You need to put the gun down."

He lowered the gun to the table.

McDermott stepped into the room.

"Read him his rights, McDermott," Erin said. "I've got to give a dying man his wish."

Ruth McCarty's short mysteries have appeared in Level Best Books anthologies, *Flash Bang Mysteries*, *Kings River Life Magazine* and *Over My Dead Body!* She won the 2009 Derringer for "No Flowers for Stacey" published in *Deadfall: Crime Stories by New England Writers.* She is former editor at Level Best Books, a past president of the New England of Sisters in Crime, and a member of Mystery Writers of America.

NO MULLIGANS

Leone Ciporin

A golf tan doesn't belong on a corpse. I knew that oval tan from my high school summers caddying at the country club. But this golfer would have no more long drives. No more putts. No more Mulligans.

"What's a Mulligan?" Her question warned me I'd been thinking out loud. Dangerous for a detective. My heel dug into the oriental rug as I turned to face her. How do you tell a woman her dead husband has no more second chances, no more "do-overs" of the swing he didn't hit right?

"It's nothing," I said. Her high cheekbones seemed to prop up the rest of her face, wobbly with grief. "I'm sorry for your loss," I added. The props crumbled.

I motioned for the trooper, who escorted her away from the family room crime scene. My cousin, Robert. He'd be professionally sympathetic.

I crouched beside the body. Thirtyish man in a green golf shirt, khakis and loafers, with light brown hair curling over his forehead. Sudden death in a young guy with no apparent health issues had prompted the trooper to call me in.

The remains of a light meal—croissant crumbs, orange juice glasses smeared with pulp, and two coffee mugs, one with a lipstick mark—littered the kitchen table. Given the lack of obvious wounds, any foul play would probably have involved poison in the breakfast. And make the weeping widow a prime suspect.

I headed to the living room to find Barbara Tidwell huddled in a bay window seat. "Mrs. Tidwell? I'm Detective Hal Westridge. Are you up to answering a few questions? Can you tell me what happened?"

She stared out the window, a sunbeam highlighting a mascara smudge on her cheek. "We'd just had breakfast. Jim was saying we should stop by his mother's on the way to Sean's—his brother. I didn't want to go see her." A flicker of resentment crossed her face. "I didn't want her to spoil our weekend."

Her lip trembled and I counted to ten to keep my face a blank slate. Project your own personality and witnesses tailor their story to please you.

I glanced down at a stack of books arranged on a glass table. A glossy art book lay underneath a smaller book on the history of jazz. I barely knew what jazz was before I joined some buddies at a music festival in Litchfield. There, I fell in love with jazz—and with Melanie.

208

Three tissues later, Barbara Tidwell spoke again. "All of a sudden..." Her mouth opened, closed, then opened again, like a fish hanging onto life after being snagged by a hook. "All of a sudden, Jim jumped up and started gasping. I tried to help him. He staggered toward the family room, then he just collapsed. I called 911. I didn't know what to do!" She twisted toward me, grabbing my sleeve. "I watched him choke to death and I didn't know what to do!"

If she was acting, she had talent. I patted her hand while gently extracting it from my sleeve. "You did the right thing, calling 911. Did he have a history of heart trouble? Any health issues?"

She shook her head. "No, not at all. He went to the gym several times a week. And played golf every chance he could." Her hand reached out to straighten the books on the table.

"Did both of you have the same thing for breakfast?"

She gave me a puzzled look. "Yes, croissants. Why?"

"Just asking." I didn't mention the possibility of poison.

I left the widow in Robert's capable hands and went to see Jim Tidwell's mother.

Faye Tidwell lived in a new condominium complex in the wooded Silvermine area straddling the Norwalk-New Canaan border, a line that meant more than a change in zip code. Housing prices doubled once you stepped into New Canaan. The condos stood on the Norwalk side, but the developer had tried to compensate with freshly mulched landscaping and gleaming white trim on the tan siding.

Mrs. Tidwell looked neatly landscaped too, with smooth black slacks, gray silk blouse, and pearls that matched her thick white hair. Only her chafed, red eyes clashed.

"Please come in," she said, her good manners on autopilot. Her hand made a slight flourish as she beckoned me inside. "May I offer you something to drink?"

I accepted. If she thought of me as a guest rather than a policeman, she'd be more likely to open up. After pouring filtered water into a glass, she pulled a bag of bakery cookies out of a cabinet and arranged them on a plate before closing the bag with a crease so hard it acted as a clamp.

The apartment reflected a near-obsessive sense of order, with unmarred cherry furniture, fresh flowers in a blue-and-white vase and a throw carefully tossed on an armchair, as if to deny that the order was deliberate. Silver-framed photographs lined the sofa table, mostly of Jim Tidwell. The only picture of Barbara was a wedding day portrait. Despite the obvious posing, the couple's wide smiles seemed spontaneous, as if they'd just shared a private joke.

I picked up the photo. "Beautiful couple."

She handed me the glass of water and touched his side of the photograph with a shaky finger. "He was a wonderful son." She gave several ragged gulps, as if she had inhaled smoke.

209

I said, "They look happy."

Her face pinched. "They'd have been happier if she could bear children."

Her words rocked me like a fist in my gut. Faye's reaction to her daughter-in-law's infertility was anger. For my family—and Melanie's—it had been despair. Both of us only children, we bore the responsibility for a future generation. At every family gathering, our parents would dart eager glances at Melanie's abdomen, the slimness of her figure draining the hope from their eyes. And then, oh God, the bright, blazing joy of Henry's birth.

I looked away to shift my expression into neutral before facing her again. "They'd been trying awhile?"

Faye pointed a finger at Barbara's wedding gown. "She couldn't have kids. They kept trying, but the doctors finally said she'd never conceive." Faye sucked in air, moving the small lump in her throat up and down. "Now Jim will never have children." She swayed. I flung my water glass and caught her just as her knees buckled.

I eased her onto the sofa, her small frame barely weighing down my arms, then stepped back to let her collect her composure.

"Would you like me to call someone? Can I get you some water?" I glanced at the overturned glass in the middle of a puddle seeping across the carpet.

Faye shook her head. "I'm fine. I'll just be a moment." She wobbled to her feet, steadied herself and stumbled down the hall. A door clicked shut and a faucet turned on.

I found paper towels in the neatly organized cabinet under the kitchen sink, and sopped up the water.

Faye returned wearing a pathetic attempt at a smile. I offered one in return and sat with her awhile before leaving.

As I pulled out of the parking lot, the sun slanted onto my father's badge clipped to my dashboard. As his only son, I'd always known I'd be a cop. I worshipped him the way my cousin Robert worshipped me, especially after my promotion from trooper to detective. At my father's retirement party, he'd presented me his badge with both hands, as if crowning a new king. Someday, I'd present my badge to Henry.

A week later, after some nudging, the lab delivered Tidwell's blood work. Potassium cyanide, a fast acting poison, which meant the breakfast table had held the murder weapon, though I'd have to wait for the next lab results to find out which part of breakfast was fatal.

While Jim Tidwell had lived barely a golf shot from Greenwich, his brother Sean lived in Stamford like me, neither of us rich enough for Greenwich.

Unlike his brother's spacious Colonial and broad stretch of lawn, Sean's small ranch home hugged the curb of a meager yard where grass struggled to grow.

I pressed the doorbell twice before he answered. Shorter and heavier than his brother, Sean Tidwell wore a guarded expression on his round face. "Can I help you?"

Out came my badge. "Detective Westridge. I'm investigating your brother's death. I'd like to talk to you, if you have a moment."

His face flashed sorrow. "Of course. Come in." He stood aside as I walked into a small room decorated in early American bachelor and smelling slightly of hamburger and onions.

Sean sat in a black leather recliner, a stained t-shirt hanging loosely over new jeans. The hair curling across his forehead reminded me of his brother. I sat on a matching sofa opposite him.

"First, let me say how sorry I am about your loss," I told him.

He considered that for a moment. "Thank you."

"They were supposed to have lunch with you that day?"

A slow nod. "Yeah. We met for lunch about once a month. We took turns hosting." His hands fiddled with each other. "When they didn't show up, I knew something was wrong. Jim never forgets an appointment." He spat out that last sentence as if it tasted bad. "Even before Barbara called, I knew something was wrong."

"Do you know anyone who might have wanted to hurt your brother?"

"Jim?" He made a faint huff. "Jim was the perfect guy. He had a happy marriage, just got promoted at work, lots of friends, even a great golf game. Everyone loved Jim." That bad taste again.

"You and he were close?" I wanted to see if he'd lie.

Sean shrugged. "We were brothers. We stayed in touch. But he was always the favorite. I didn't even bother to compete."

The downside of having a sibling, though I'd longed for a brother growing up, to lighten the pressure on me to fulfill the family tradition of police work.

"Did you spend much time with Jim?" I asked.

Sean inspected his fingertips. "I didn't run with his crowd. Not their type." He released his fingers long enough to point at his chest. "I'm divorced, in a dead-end job, not particularly popular."

I waded into another sensitive topic. "Neither you or Jim had kids?"

"No. I'm divorced, like I said. Jim and Barbara tried, but Barbara couldn't have children. Drove my mother crazy. All she ever wanted was grandchildren." He gave a wry laugh. "I couldn't even beat Jim there."

I should've been thinking about the case on the drive home, but I rolled down the window to savor the glory of a Connecticut summer, and I thanked God my son was alive to enjoy it.

The night it happened, it had been my turn to soothe Henry's late-night fussing, but I was exhausted after closing a case and Melanie had to elbow me twice to get out of bed. When I saw the red flush on Henry's cheeks, I knew even before I laid my hand on his head that he burned with fever.

In the hospital waiting room, I'd nearly dropped to my knees, my stomach muscles in spasms from guilt at not going to him sooner. The doctor's reassurance that Henry simply had a virus meant I'd been given a second chance. A Mulligan. I'd promised Henry—and Melanie—I wouldn't waste it.

When I came home after seeing Sean Tidwell, Melanie and Henry were playing on the family room floor. Melanie leaned over Henry, her head nearly hitting the foam stripped corner of the coffee table. I knelt down and hugged them both tight.

"What's wrong, Hal? Did something happen?" She threw me a look that warned against graphic details in front of Henry, though he was at least a year away from talking.

"The body near Greenwich. The golfer."

"Rich," she said. "The rich always get a Mulligan."

"Not this guy."

"Did he have any kids?" Her head stayed close to Henry's.

"No. They tried, but his wife couldn't have children."

Melanie straightened sharply, looked at me wide-eyed and whispered, "Oh, no. That poor woman."

A few days later, Robert appeared at my desk. "Detective Westridge?" He refused to call me Hal, probably thinking coworker was a closer relationship than cousin. "Lab report's in." He put a folder between two piles of paper on my desk.

"Thanks." I smiled. "Trooper."

His lips twitched as he trotted off.

The report revealed that the coffee mug without lipstick had traces of potassium cyanide, as did the bag of decaffeinated coffee in the pantry. The other mug had held poison-free herbal tea. Barbara told me they'd eaten the same breakfast, but she hadn't mentioned the drinks. The widow was the logical suspect, but I had other ideas.

I visited Tidwell's accounting firm in Stamford to learn more about his coffee habits. A receptionist in a buttoned-up blouse informed me Arthur Blaine, Tidwell's boss, was in a meeting, but would be out soon. When I asked for coffee, she brought it in a white mug with the firm's logo on the side. The coffee was strong. I drank it all.

Eventually, the receptionist looked up with a polite smile and escorted me to Blaine's office, a large room with a desk and a conference table. The furniture's mahogany tones emphasized Blaine's pale skin as he crossed the room to greet me. Photos of three toothy grandchildren stood on his credenza. Blaine offered a brief handshake and motioned me to the table. We sat in soft leather chairs. He adjusted his thick glasses and stared expectantly.

"I'm looking into Jim Tidwell's death." My turn to wait. I wanted to get a read on his personality. I suspected he didn't have one.

After a moment, Blaine cleared his throat. "Jim was a good man. Horrible accident." He stared at my face. "Heart attack, was it?"

"We're still investigating. I understand he was promoted recently?"

"He'd just made partner."

"Will you replace him?"

"We'll consider the more experienced associates again to see if one of them is ready." Blaine tilted his head to one side. "You don't think someone here killed Jim for a promotion?"

"Just trying to get to know the victim. I'd like to talk to those who worked closely with him."

Blaine adjusted his glasses again before picking up a pad of paper from the center of the table and scribbling two names. "These two worked with Jim the most." He tore the sheet off the pad and handed it to me. "I hope it's helpful."

I read the names. "It is. Thank you." I closed my fist around the paper. "Did you socialize with the Tidwells? Get together for coffee?"

Blaine stowed the pen in his jacket pocket. "Not really. I host our holiday party. I saw Barbara there, of course, but other than that..." He gave a quick smile with pursed lips. "I'm not much of a golfer."

Back in the lobby, I asked to see both accountants on Blaine's list. The receptionist pointed to the first name. "Jane's out of the country until next week."

"When did she leave?"

"Four weeks ago." Before the murder.

"What about the other one?"

"Fred Naylor's here. One moment." After a quick phone call, she said, "He'll be with you in a minute."

Mere seconds after I sat down, a man loped into the lobby, wisps of dark hair flying, his hand outstretched for a shake. "Fred Naylor, good to meet you." More outgoing than I'd expected from an accountant. "Come on back," he said.

I followed him to a small office. No mahogany here, just a small pine desk and room for one bookshelf. Fred dropped himself behind the desk. "How can I help you?"

"I'm looking into Jim Tidwell's death. I understand you worked with him?"

"Jim was a great guy. I still can't believe he's gone. I keep expecting him to pop his head in and say hi."

"Did you see him much outside the office?"

"No, we talked at work, but that was about it."

213

"So you never went to his house, met for coffee, anything like that?"

"Actually, I tried to get him to cut back on the coffee. Or at least switch to decaf. He was always running at high speed. I told him once he ought to put Valium in his coffee, slow down a little." Fred started to smile before abruptly switching to a frown. "I still can't believe he's gone."

"I understand he was just promoted. What happens to that position now?"

Fred raised his palms. "I'll probably get it. Me or Jane. Hell of a way to get a promotion."

"A promotion means more money, right?"

He didn't rise to the bait. "Sure. I can always use more money. Big mortgage, you know how that is. But I can't match Jim at bringing in clients. He'd get them on the golf course and after eighteen holes, he had their business." His mouth formed a zigzag. "A scratch golfer. But he could lose by a few strokes to a client when he had to."

"He was happily married?"

"Very. He adored Barbara." He sighed. "Jim had it all. Really makes you think."

As I left the building, I mulled Fred's comment about Jim's heavy coffee habit. I felt the tickle at the back of my neck that told me I was getting close.

That night, after we put Henry to bed, I put on a Maynard Ferguson CD and Melanie and I settled on the couch as the trumpet played the first notes of "MacArthur Park." She leaned into me, using my shoulder as a pillow.

"Coffee?" I asked.

She turned to look at my face. "You never have coffee at night. Keeps you up."

"How about decaf?" I disentangled myself and strode into the kitchen, searching the back of our small pantry until I found a bag of coffee.

"That's been there awhile." Melanie had come up behind me. "It probably won't taste good anymore. I should've at least put a clip on it." She opened the bag and sniffed. And the tickle at the back of my neck became a slap.

The next day, I knocked on Barbara Tidwell's door. She answered, looking several years older than she had the day of the murder.

I said, "May I come in?"

"Of course." I followed her down the hall—noting Tidwell's golf bag still leaning against the mudroom door—and into the kitchen where she introduced me to her mother, Mrs. Lakey, sitting at the breakfast table. Barbara sat beside her, pushing aside wisps of hair with shaky fingers.

I waited for the obligatory drink offer. Eventually, Barbara said, "Can I get you something?"

"Let me do it," I said. "I'll make us coffee? Or tea?"

"Please help yourself to coffee. I'll have tea. They're both in the middle cabinet," Barbara said. "Thank you."

"Glad to do it," I said.

I pulled down the decaf coffee and tea. The top of the almost full coffee bag was shut loosely. I held it up. "Is this new?"

Barbara said, "Yes. The police—your people—took the other. I just bought that."

"You drink decaf coffee?"

"I bought that for my mother's visits. I quit caffeine a year ago. Lately, I've been drinking herbal tea instead of decaf coffee." Her hands smoothed the tablecloth.

"So you drank tea the morning your husband died?"

"Yes."

"Why are you asking these questions?" Mrs. Lakey said. "Jim died of a heart attack and you're bothering poor Barbara. Just fill out your forms and leave."

"Ma'am, I'm only trying to get more information." I turned back to Barbara. "When did you start drinking tea?"

"A couple of months ago."

"And Jim? Did he drink decaf coffee?"

"He was trying to cut back on caffeine, just like I had. He said it made him too wired up."

"When did he switch to decaf?"

"Not long before—before it happened." The tablecloth stretched as her hands yanked at it. Mrs. Lakey reached over to smooth Barbara's hair and tuck in a stray piece.

I recalled Fred Naylor's joke about putting Valium in Jim Tidwell's coffee. "Did Jim tell people he was cutting back on caffeine?"

Barbara looked at her mother, who gave a sharp shrug. Barbara said, "Not that I know of."

"Why are you asking all these questions?" Mrs. Lakey's shrill voice sirened through the kitchen.

I sat down next to Barbara. "His coffee was poisoned." I watched her face closely. Her shock seemed real. Her mother's, too.

"Poisoned?" Barbara's voice barely above a whisper. "Who would do that?"

"That's what I'm trying to find out. Who knew you'd stopped drinking decaf coffee?"

"Jim, of course. And my mother." She tilted her head toward Mrs. Lakey, who appeared ready to launch herself at me. "I guess people at my office knew I'd started drinking tea."

215

Mrs. Lakey said, "Are you accusing my daughter of murder? She and Jim loved each other!"

"We're still trying to determine what happened." I turned to Barbara. "Who visited the house recently?"

"No one, really. Just family. Our last party was months ago."

"Family? Your mother," I gestured to Mrs. Lakey. "And your mother-in-law. And Jim's brother?"

Barbara nodded. "That's right."

"Have they all been here recently?"

Barbara stared at me with a trace of anger. "Are you saying someone in our family did this?" For the first time, I saw the resemblance to her mother.

"I'm just trying to gather information. How recent were the visits?"

She relaxed slightly. "Well, my mother-in-law stopped by a week or so before…before. And then, Sean did, for lunch, a couple of weeks earlier than that." She turned to her mother. "You were out of town when Jim died. "

"Do you need to see my plane ticket?" Mrs. Lakey asked.

"I don't think that's necessary." I leaned closer to Barbara. "You mentioned before that you and your mother-in-law don't get along?"

Mrs. Lakey said, "That woman would make ice cubes feel like a warm blanket."

Barbara said, "She never liked me. In college, I planned a romantic getaway on a weekend Jim was supposed to come home. She never forgave me. And there were…other reasons."

"I'm sure you tried to keep the peace." At her nod, I added, "Perhaps you had coffee together the last time she visited?"

"No. She didn't stay long once she realized Jim wasn't here."

Back at the office, I checked the decaf coffee bag in the evidence room. It was loosely closed, but with the imprint of a crease mark running, ruler-straight, across the top. I waited for the sweet rush that came with solving a case, but all I felt was a dull throb. I put the coffee at the bottom of the evidence box and went home.

That night, after Melanie went to bed, I crept into the nursery to watch Henry sleep, his arm curled around Winnie the Pooh. The comforting smell of baby powder hovered over him. The small rise and fall of his chest mesmerized me. I imagined what I'd do to anyone who tried to stop that rhythm. And no law on earth would make any difference.

The next morning, I went to see Faye Tidwell. After quick pleasantries, we took seats and I said softly, "I know what you did."

"Excuse me?" Her bloodshot eyes widened.

I offered an innocent expression. "Your son was poisoned, in his coffee. Decaf coffee, which your daughter-in-law used to drink before she switched to tea. So it looks like someone was trying to kill her." I looked into her eyes. "And killed your son instead."

Her face whitened to match her blouse.

"I won't be satisfied until the killer is punished, I said."

I looked at Faye a long time, then stood and walked slowly toward the door. Her mouth hung open and silent as she stood to watch me leave. I drew the door closed just as she collapsed into a chair. The hiccupping sound of her sobs followed me down the stairs.

As I drove away, I took my father's badge off the dashboard and stowed it in the glove compartment. Henry could choose whatever career he wanted.

That night, over dinner, I told Melanie I wasn't sure I'd make an arrest. She tossed me a glance as she scooted Henry's highchair to the green Formica top table. I laid a hand against its edge to buffer him against the metal strip.

"Any leads?" she asked. "You hate giving up."

Henry's flailing hand deposited a smashed pea on the tip of her small nose. With his baby face, it was too soon to tell, but I hoped Henry had inherited Melanie's classic features instead of my bumpy nose.

"Not much progress so far." I took the spoon from her hand. Henry's mouth opened as the spoon came closer. I held it a moment to extend his experience of anticipation, then his lips closed over the mashed peas. I leaned over and kissed his forehead.

A crease mark wasn't enough to convict, but my lieutenant would expect me to follow the rules. So would Robert. I'd work the case, but it seemed like an empty pursuit. As I watched my son enjoy his meal, I knew punishment had already been delivered, one more terrible than any officer of the law could impose.

Faye Tidwell had swung at her daughter-in-law and struck her son instead. She'd discovered that, in murder, there are no Mulligans.

Leone Ciporin is a mystery writer, animal lover and literary concierge. Her mystery stories have appeared in two Chesapeake Crimes anthologies and she has had four mini-mysteries in Woman's World magazine. She loves animals and walks dogs at her local SPCA; the dogs are excellent personal trainers and listeners. A literary concierge, she enjoys recommending just the right book to friends and colleagues. She golfs badly and needs many Mulligans. Leone lives in Charlottesville, Virginia.

GOLDIE

KM Rockwood

I have the funnest job in the world.

Every day, Sammy comes by the kennel and picks me up for another adventure.

He says, "Hey, there, Goldie. Ready to go to work?" I'm so happy, I dance around in circles while he unlatches the kennel door. Then I jump up and down a few times until he tells me "*Sedni,*" which is Czech for sit down. And I sit.

All the dogs here are trained to use Czech commands. The other dogs, German shepherds and Belgian Malinoises, are already out playing. I'm half golden retriever and, as Sammy says, "half whatever hound dug under the fence."

Sammy's taken me to try the games that the other dogs play, but I'm really not that good at them. I can find people all right, but then I'm so happy I found them, I forget I'm supposed to bark and growl. I usually just lick their hands or, if they're on the ground, their faces. Sammy says if they are ever searching for someone who needs to be licked to death, I'll be the first dog they send.

He puts my leash on and gives me a treat. We're ready for whatever the day brings.

We go over to the sally port entry at the prison across the road from the kennels. A man in civilian clothes—not a corrections officer uniform and not an inmate jumpsuit—comes over to us and talks to Sammy.

I sit down next to Sammy and look around. I hear what the man says to him, but I don't pay much attention. Maybe one of the other people around here would like to pet a dog, and if so, I want to be available to them.

"We've got to get a handle on this Fentanyl," the man says to Sammy. "Seems like every day there's a new supply in here. And it's strong stuff. We've had three ODs in the last week."

"Yes, sir. We'll check the staff at shift change."

The man looks down at me and frowns. "Can that dog detect Fentanyl?"

I stand up and wag my tail. I try to reach over and lick the man's hand, but Sammy pulls me back. "You bet, Warden. He's one of the best drug dogs in the state."

He shakes his head. "I hope so. He's certainly not much of a guard dog."

218

"No, sir." Sammy scratches behind my ears. "He's strictly a detection dog. He can do bombs and drugs. We're thinking about trying him out on cell phones."

"That'd be something." The man turns and walks away.

Two men in uniforms stand on either side of a metal detector in the doorway. Sammy takes me up to them and tells me, "Goldie, *drogy.*" That means I'm supposed to sniff everyone and everything, and if they smell of my targeted scents, I go next to them and sit down.

These men smell of tobacco, and one smells of alcohol, but that's not what I'm supposed to be looking for. So I sniff them politely. They don't seem to want to play, so I step back next to Sammy.

People begin coming in. An entire shift of officers. Maintenance people. Kitchen supervisors. Teachers. Office workers. They all go past me through the metal detector and I sniff them carefully.

We do this a lot, and I hardly ever find anything. Today is no different.

Then Sammy takes me out to the parking lot to sniff around. I always find something there, sometimes on a car, sometimes on the ground. It's the same thing every time, a little cloth bag with some marijuana. Sammy slips it into his pocket, and the next day, it's somewhere out in the parking lot again. I don't know why Sammy keeps losing it, but he's always happy when I find it. We play with my bouncy rubber toy and I get a treat.

Today we go into the mail room.

"We've held this mail for three days," the lady in charge says. "We've got to get it distributed today, or we'll have a riot on our hands. And, of course, we don't have room for any more mail. The delivery'll be here in a few hours."

Sammy turns me loose and I amble past bins of sorted mail. It's got lots of different smells, usually just a faint whiff from something it's been around. Chocolate. Tobacco smoke. Beer.

A few envelopes have been sprayed with perfume and I take a good sniff. Then it really gets in my nose and I sneeze and shake my head.

I climb over a pile of unopened mail sacks. There! One of my target scents! I yip excitedly and start pawing down to find the right sack.

Sammy comes over and lifts the sacks, one by one. I smell them, but turn back to the one on the bottom. When Sammy pulls it out, I sit down next to it.

"He's alerted on this sack," Sammy says.

The lady takes it and empties it on a table. "Can he find the envelope?"

"Sure." Sammy turns to me. "Goldie, *drogy.*" I jump up on the table and nose through the mail. When I find the right envelope, I pick it up in my teeth and shake it.

Sammy trades me a treat for it, and hands it to the lady.

She slits the envelope open and pulls out a few pieces of paper. The she turns the envelope upside down, shakes it, and puts it aside. She unfolds the pieces of paper and flips through them. "I don't see anything." She lifts the pages to her nose and sniffs them. "Maybe a faint marijuana smell, but I'm not sure..."

Meanwhile, I keep watching the envelope. The target scent isn't on the papers. It's still in the envelope.

Sammy picks up the envelope and peers into it. "What's that, down in the inside corner of the envelope? Tiny white pills?"

"Nothing came out when I shook it." The lady takes it from Sammy and looks inside. "Wait. You're right. In the corners. Could be little oxys or something." She turns it upside down and shakes it again. Nothing comes out. "They must have used something sticky to make them stay in the corners like that," the lady says.

They did. A little bit of toothpaste. I can smell that, too.

She runs her fingers over the outside of the envelope. "I guess we're going to have to check in the corners of all the mail when it comes in." She sighs. "Like we didn't have enough to do."

"Well, you could ask the warden to have the dog go over all the mail as it comes in," Sammy says.

"That might be a good idea." The lady shoves the pieces of paper back in the envelope. "We'll give this to the security chief. They're looking for Fentanyl in a powder form, and this isn't that. But it's contraband. He'll follow through on it."

I clamber over the rest of the pile and sniff everything else in the room. No more targeted scents.

Sammy takes me out and we play with my bouncy rubber toy again. Then Sammy and I get in a car and go for a ride.

When we get back, Sammy parks the car next to the administration building near the kennels. But instead of putting me back in my crate, we start walking along the road, away from the prison. It's starting to get dark, but we're far enough out that lights from the banks of floodlights surrounding the prison don't reach us.

We walk quietly along the side of the road, on the edge of the woods. Sammy has a flashlight, but he doesn't turn it on. Underfoot is thick mud.

So many wonderful things to smell! A fox has been here, and several rabbits have used a trail that goes off into the woods. I look at it longingly, but I know I'm not supposed to chase rabbits. An owl swoops overhead. Its feathers make a swooshing sound, not at all like those mechanical thingies that fly over the kennel at night.

Those thingies always reek of my target scents when they fly toward the prison, but only have a trace when they come back. I barked at them the first few times they came over, but no one came to see what I was barking at, and I hadn't been told to search for the scents, so I started ignoring them.

Sammy reaches down and scratches behind my ears. "Goldie, *revir. Drogy.*"

220

Range out and search! Over the whole area.

My ears perk up and my tail whips from side to side. This is my favorite game of all. Especially outdoors. I lift my head up and sniff the evening breeze.

There. The target scents.

I lunge forward, straight through the underbrush. Sammy doesn't want to dash through the blackberry bushes with all their stickers. Or maybe he just isn't holding all that tight to my leash. At any rate, he drops it as I plunge into the woods. That's okay. He can go around and meet me.

I yip excitedly as I push through the brush and into the small clearing.

A pickup truck is parked in the mud, its tailgate down. My target scents are on the tailgate, next to some of those flying thingies. A few cell phones are there, too, but that's not something I'm looking for.

At the sound of my approach, **three men jump** back from the truck. One of them shines a flashlight in my eyes, which confuses me for a minute, but I could still smell all the stuff in the plastic bags and spread out on the tailgate.

"That's a police dog!"

They're so excited. I'm not sure exactly how they play this game, but I know what I'm supposed to do. I jump up on the back of the truck and sit down next to the plastic bags spread around.

One of the men scrambles for the driver's side door of the truck. He slips in the mud and falls down. He has something in his hand, and it goes flying.

One of the other men reaches for the passenger door. He yanks on it, but it won't open.

"What'd ya do with the damn keys?" one of them calls out.

"I dropped them when I fell," says the guy on the ground. "Bring the flashlight over here."

"No time to look for keys! The dog's handler's got to be right behind him. Run for it."

"The dog'll bring you down."

"If he was gonna do that, he'd of done it. He's just a drug dog."

The two men run toward the road. The one on the ground scrambles up and follows them.

I cock my ears and raise my nose to see if I can detect Sammy approaching.

A shot shatters the night. I hear the static of a radio. "Shots fired. Officer down."

The men are running on the blacktop, their feet pounding the hard surface.

Sirens scream into the night. Headlights slice through the darkness. Emergency lights strobe.

I sit in the back of the truck, waiting for Sammy to get there and tell me what to do. He's going to be so proud of me!

He's up next to the tailgate. He's coughing and he smells of blood. I nudge his arm with my nose and whine. He holds onto the wall of the truck bed. "Good dog, Goldie," he says.

The flashing lights get closer. Car doors slam. Several excited dogs bark.

They move down the road, away from us.

Someone comes over to where Sammy is standing next to me. "You hurt?" She shines her flashlight on Sammy.

"Yeah." His voice is garbled and thick. "Shot in the side. But I don't think it's all that serious. Didn't get my heart or my lungs."

"An ambulance is on the way. You'd better lie down."

"My dog…" Sammy coughs.

"We'll take care of your dog."

"Okay. Just shine that light over here so I can see what we got, huh?"

She moves over to the plastic bags and turns her flashlight beam on them. She gives a low whistle.

"Cell phones. And lots of white powder. Maybe China white."

"Powdered Fentanyl?"

"I bet it is. And some drones. That's how they've been getting stuff in."

"Looks like it." Sammy starts to laugh, but it turns into a cough. "And here they banned greeting cards in the mail, 'cause they thought it was coming in on those."

"Yeah, well, some might have been. But this is probably a bigger source."

They're looking at some fine white powder spread out on a piece of plastic wrap. It's definitely one of my target scents.

I bend my head down to sniff at it. It tickles my nose. I sneeze. White powder flies up in our faces.

Sammy and the woman step back, rubbing their noses.

I lick mine.

I feel kind of wobbly and dizzy.

Sammy clutches the side of the truck. He has a coating of the white powder on his face. So does the woman. She sits down abruptly. On the ground. She pulls out her radio.

I can't stay sitting up. I kind of flop down on the truck bed, on top of the flying thingies. I'm very sleepy and I'm having trouble breathing. If I just close my eyes and take a quick nap, I'll feel much better.

Something is stuck up my nose. It wakes me up, and I sneeze again.

Sammy is sitting next to me, patting my side. "That's a good boy, Goldie. Breathe."

I'm too tired to lift up my head, but I thump my tail on the truck bed and look at Sammy. Sammy still smells of blood, but his shirt is off, and he has a big bandage wrapped around his chest. The night air is chilly, and he's shivering.

"Come on, buddy," somebody says, putting his hand on Sammy's shoulder. "We got to get you to the hospital."

222

"Not until I see how my dog's doing." Sammy leans his face down to mine.

I lick his nose. The white powder's gone and he tastes like disinfectant.

"You got more Narcan?" Sammy asks the man. "He may need it."

"Yep. And we already called the vet. He said bring the dog in and they'll monitor him overnight. Now you get in the ambulance."

Sammy gives me a final pat. "Be a good boy, Goldie. We'll be back at it in no time. You done good tonight."

KM Rockwood draws on a varied background for stories, such as working as a laborer in steel fabrication and fiberglass manufacture, and supervising an inmate work crew in a large state prison. These positions, as well as work as a special education teacher in alternative education and a GED instructor in correctional facilities, provide material for numerous short stories and novels, including Abductions and Lies, 6th in the Jesse Damon Crime Novel series.

THE WOMAN IN WHITE

Tracy Falenwolfe

It was Adam's first Beaver Moon as a full-fledged game commission officer, so named by the Native Americans who viewed it as a harbinger of winter, and a reminder to set their beaver traps one last time before the swamps froze over.

It was also Thanksgiving.

As the newbie, Adam got all the crappy shifts. But he didn't care. Being outside on any day was better than being chained to a desk for the rest of his life. He wouldn't have minded being able to eat before being called out, though. His mom roasted a mean turkey, and his grandmother made the best Pennsylvania Dutch filling of anyone. It was better than stuffing, that was for sure. And her made-from-scratch gravy was freakin' awesome. He couldn't say the same for Aunt Susan's pumpkin pie. It was a little soupy, and everyone ate it to be polite.

Aunt Susan had been the one who carried on the most when he'd gotten the call tonight. "Adam Costenbader, where do you think you're going?" she demanded, all put out. "We're just about to sit down to dinner."

"I'm on call," he said. Then he pulled a piece of white meat off the turkey platter and folded it into his mouth. "Sorry."

She swatted him with a cloth napkin as he checked his sidearm and headed toward the door. "At least try to make it back before dessert," she said.

He didn't answer. There weren't very many game commission officers to go around, which meant he covered a large area and didn't have the luxury of working with a partner. If he needed help it was usually quicker to call the staties for back-up. He didn't have to, though. He had the same authority to arrest as they did, just a different focus. So far he hadn't had to use it. Or he hadn't gotten to use it, depending on how you looked at it.

The Thompsons had called about poachers on their land three times this week, but the trespassers were always gone when Adam arrived. This time Mrs. Thompson said her dog, Max, had gotten out and returned with blood on his paws and fur. At first she thought he'd been shot, but after she cleaned him up and saw that he wasn't, she was pissed, and rightly so.

Adam had a feeling either Mrs. Thompson or her husband was planning to confront the poachers. They would be endangering themselves if they did that, so Adam stepped on it. He made it to the Carbon-Lehigh county border in forty minutes. It was dark when he got to the Thompsons' old stone farmhouse, but the moon was bright. Potted mums flanked the front door, interspersed with pumpkins and gourds. Adam knocked and waited.

He heard voices before Mr. Thompson opened the door. "I was giving you ten more minutes," he said. His coat and boots were on, and his shotgun was propped by the door.

"I'm glad you waited," Adam said. "It's dangerous in the woods after dark. Especially if you've got poachers."

Mr. Thompson snorted. "We've always got poachers."

"I understand," Adam said. "Do you know how many there are this time?"

Mr. Thompson shook his head. "No."

Max, a German Shepherd, barked from somewhere in the house and ran to the foyer. He had a bell tied to his collar that made a *ting, ting, ting* as he walked.

Adam held his hand out to let the dog sniff. "How many shots have you heard?"

"None," Mr. Thompson admitted. He came out onto the porch and closed the door behind him. "Look, Officer Costenbader. There's someone out there. Max has been going crazy all day and my Alice has been beside herself since he came back covered in blood."

The dog barked from inside the house.

"I'll take a look," Adam said. "But promise me you'll stay here. And keep Max in too, for now." He didn't mention it, but over Mr. Thompson's shoulder Adam saw a flash of white on the dark mountain. Someone had moved while the two had been standing there on the porch, and judging by the speed, Adam guessed whoever it was knew they weren't supposed to be there. Max knew it too.

"Whatever you say," Mr. Thompson said.

"Great. I'll be back."

The aroma of roast turkey, fresh baked bread, and wood smoke followed Adam into the woods. His stomach growled. Moonlight shone through the trees. He didn't need a flashlight but he turned his on anyway. Catching the poachers and citing them was a goal, but not getting shot at was a bigger one.

Fifty yards from the Thompsons' porch the terrain inclined sharply. Adam knew the area well. It had been his old stomping grounds back in the day, back before the Lehigh Gap Nature Center had been built, before school kids took field trips to the Osprey House, before the reforestation of the mountain had begun.

Once, during his first semester of college, he'd brought a friend here. Pete had been from West Virginia. He'd been impressed enough by the actual channel the rushing waters of the Lehigh River had carved out of the Blue Mountain over the years, but the mountains themselves had made him sad. He said they reminded him of places back home that had been decimated by strip mining. He couldn't see the beauty of the area. It was a barren wasteland to him, and he was more interested in what the nearby zinc smelting plant had taken away than in what nature had given. Adam didn't bring anyone around after that. He didn't want to have his perspective shattered.

Another flash of white caught his eye and he stopped walking. His frozen breath spiraled around his head. He wasn't far enough up the mountain for it to have been what he'd seen from the Thompsons' porch, but it got his heart hammering just the same. He'd probably kicked up a deer and glimpsed the tail as it ran off. He stood in place for a few seconds but didn't hear anything. Odd. There was a lot of loose shale on this mountain, enough that it made it impossible to move without making any noise.

He hiked forward a few paces and stopped. It took a few seconds for the shale to stop tumbling, but after that it was quiet again. Until he heard a low growl off to his left. He put his hand on his sidearm and swiveled toward the sound. A coyote squinted at him and then trotted away. Adam watched it wind through the trees for a few yards and then tracked its movement by sound. It was moving up the mountain, away from him.

He panned his flashlight beam on the ground around the copse of trees where the coyote had been. There was something there. A gut pile, he saw as he got closer. Bear season had ended yesterday, so that wasn't unusual. But this gut pile was steaming. Anything left from yesterday would have been cold.

He crouched down to determine what animal had been illegally killed. There was hardly enough left to make a determination. Weird. If this was a bear or a deer there would have had to have been a whole pack of coyotes feeding on it to leave only this much in such a short amount of time. He didn't doubt there were a lot of coyotes around, but they would have made noise if he'd have scared them off. On the other hand, this find could explain how the Thompsons' dog Max had gotten blood on his fur.

It bothered him that he couldn't tell the species of what he was looking at, though. He pocketed his flashlight and took his phone off his belt. He thought about calling Royer, his supervisor, but it was Thanksgiving so he snapped a few pictures instead. He was crouched down, trying to get a good shot of the hair that was left on the ground when he saw that flash of white again. This time a chill raced up his spine.

Whatever he'd seen couldn't have been a deer or a poacher. It had just grazed the ground and swirled, like a puff of smoke or a wisp of fog. Then it had risen up the mountain in the same direction the coyote had gone.

Adam got to his feet and laughed at himself. He'd been warned about this: psyching himself out, imagining things. Royer said it happened to all rookies at least once. The woods were active at night. And all the things moving around were better equipped to see in the dark than you were. "Trust me," he'd said to Adam's class of cadets, "you will not see a brilliant white stag, your animal spirit guide, or Sasquatch out there. What you will find are drunken idiots, lost hikers, and entrepreneurial stoners who didn't think anyone would ever find the cannabis they planted on public land. Remember, the animals are not the things you need to worry about most."

Fine, fine. So he was the rookie who was seeing things on his first solo call at night. Whatever. He moved up the mountain, still thinking about his teenage years. The Appalachian Trail was only about two hundred yards away from where he was now. He'd been there many times with the scouts. When he got older, he and his friends would tell their parents they were going to camp on the Trail, but really they'd get a six pack and head for Devil's Pulpit.

The pulpit was a flat outcropping of rock, no bigger than his grandmother's dining room table. It jutted out over the Lehigh River, and the view from it was spectacular. The way route 248 wound through the Lehigh Gap reminded him of a model train platform—especially when the actual train came through. There was one spot where it went under the highway and came up on the other side. That had impressed him as a kid, and it still did, especially when he got to see it right around first light when the water below sparkled, and the sun bounced off the gold turbans of the onion church across the highway in Palmerton.

It was actually a Byzantine Catholic church, his friend Pete had pointed out, but to Adam, it would always be the onion church.

He'd spent so much time studying the remains that he thought he'd lost track of the poachers. But then he heard something. The noise started small and got bigger. At first he thought it was tumbling shale from someone moving up the mountain, but when he found himself being pelted in the face, he realized it was sleet. Two seconds later it became a sleet-snow mix that glittered in the moonlight. For a minute he just raised his face to the moon and watched. This. This was the best thing about his job. Being close to nature. One with it. He'd never say it to the other officers, but this is what made him feel alive.

The forecast was for nothing more than flurries, but since it started as sleet it would be slick, and Adam had to be careful not to get himself into any trouble. One wrong step and he could take a tumble. Sprain something. Strand himself. It was up to him to take care of himself since he was working solo, and it was always better to be safe than sorry.

He was about to pack it in and head back to the Thompsons' when he saw whatever he'd seen again. But this time he caught more than a glimpse. He'd seen an arm. Someone darting behind a spruce tree, possibly wearing snow camo. "Game commission!" Adam called. He held his flashlight at eye level and swept it in a downward motion as he gave chase. The figure moved fast— someone knew where they were going.

"Game commission," Adam called again. "Hold up." He'd have lost them already if the moon hadn't been so bright. His quads burned and his lungs were pumping. He slipped, but not on ice—a bushel of apples was scattered at his feet, and judging by the slime and the smell they'd been rotting there for a week. That meant whoever left them had been baiting bear, which was illegal. Unless they'd dumped the apples to bait the deer, which was still illegal since opening day of buck season was on Monday. A raccoon froze in his flashlight beam before scurrying away.

Adam snapped a picture of the bait pile and moved on. The higher he climbed, the stronger the wind became. The sounds changed, too. He heard the river rushing and the cars shushing along the highway below. Coyotes yipped. More than one he was sure, and they were below him now as well. The one he'd

227

seen had probably circled back to the gut pile, bringing the rest of the pack with him. Coyotes were usually very solitary, but if what he'd seen had belonged to a bear, there had been enough to go around.

The snow-sleet mix let up. A few fat flurries floated in the air and the moon seemed like a spotlight, even brighter than it had been when he'd first arrived.

Something above his head fluttered. Probably an owl. He didn't look because the truth was the noise scared him so badly he lurched forward a few steps—okay, he ran—but it didn't matter now, because fifty feet ahead of where he stopped he saw what he'd been chasing.

Not a man in camo. Not a poacher. A girl. A woman. Wearing a white gown, more robe than dress. She was leaning up against a tree, bent at the waist as if she were catching her breath.

For a moment Adam just stood and stared. Everything moved in slow motion—the snow flurries, the heaving of her chest, the thoughts in his head. Moonlight shone on her blonde hair, making it look like she had a halo.

He sensed a presence at his right elbow, but he didn't want to look away. Perhaps if he had, he wouldn't have lost his footing and fell on his ass when the big buck that was standing there snorted a warning. It was so close Adam felt the spray. The distinct whistle few ever got to hear plucked a nerve that tingled all the way down his spine and to the bottoms of his feet. The buck ran off then without incident, but Adam's nerves were jangled, and the woman was gone.

Somehow he'd cracked his flashlight when he fell. And he was going to have one hell of a bruise. He was concerned, too, that he wasn't dealing with poachers, but rather teenagers. The woman in white had been traveling west. Adam had gotten turned around for a minute, but a look over his shoulder at the scenery below told him he was very near Devil's Pulpit.

Back in his high school days, lots of stories and legends and warnings about the pulpit got bandied around. About the haunted house across the way on Marshall's Hill, too. But the ones about the pulpit were the scariest. The most popular was the one that warned of the human sacrifice of a virgin during the full moon. It wasn't enough to stay off the mountain. Supposedly a group of Satan's henchmen selected the virgin and drug her right out of her bedroom to the pulpit on the night of the full moon.

The girls worried. The boys offered to make sure they weren't virgins by the time the full moon came. Sometimes it worked. Most times it didn't. But either way, you could always count on a group of kids to be prowling around the pulpit come the full moon.

He'd hate to have to cite a bunch of teenagers for underage drinking if that were the case tonight, but neither could he ignore it if that's what he found. Maybe back in his day someone in his position could have let it slide, but today if he did that and, god forbid, one of them got hurt or sick or had an accident, he'd end up on the wrong side of a lawsuit. At least maybe then his old friend Pete, who'd gone on to become a lawyer, would be useful for something.

228

The pulpit was a little tricky to get to. It was high up on the mountain, but you actually had to climb down onto it. The loose rocks made it dangerous. Tonight, the barely-there coating of slippery snow made it more so. Adam expected to find a party going on, but as he got closer to the pulpit he only saw the woman. She was standing on the edge, looking down into the icy Lehigh.

"Game commission," Adam said. "Please step back." If she was a potential jumper he needed to call for backup. But he also had to keep her there, keep her talking until they arrived.

He worked his way down to her. His foot slid out from under him, sending a smattering of rocks flying. They bounced off the flat outcropping and went sailing into the abyss. The woman turned to face Adam. She was still too close to the edge, so he didn't dare step out there with her. He dug in there on the rocks to feel her out. "Are you all right? Do you need help?"

She smiled. The moon seemed to glow brighter then. The light coating of flurries on the pulpit looked like a glistening white tablecloth. The woman's hair shone like spun gold, her robe like satin.

"What's your name?" Adam asked.

"It's Gina." Her voice was a song.

"What are you doing out here all alone, Gina?"

She lowered her eyes before turning her head and looking over her shoulder. "It's beautiful here," she said.

"It is," Adam agreed. "But it's also very dangerous. And cold."

She looked at him again.

"Are you cold? Can I give you my coat?" He started taking off his jacket when she moved toward him.

She froze when she saw his sidearm.

"It's okay," he told her. "Here." He held out his jacket. "Take it. Put it on. Let's get you out of here."

Her eyes darkened. "But I love it here," she said.

Okay. She definitely needed a psych consult. Adam took his phone off his belt.

"I love it here," she insisted, taking a step back toward the edge. "Don't you?"

"Gina," he said. "Be careful."

She took another step back. "Don't make me leave."

"Okay." Adam put his phone back on his belt and held his hands up, palms out. "No one's going to make you do anything." He shifted his weight and slid down a few feet, stepping out onto the outcropping with her.

She stepped back once more.

"Gina, please don't move anymore."

She was perched on the edge of the pulpit like a cliff diver. Adam felt a trickle of sweat between his shoulder blades. A pang of fear.

"Look," she said. "Look how beautiful it is here."

Far below, Adam saw the train pass under the highway. He smelled the river, and the cold. He saw the golden turbans on top of the onion church glisten

229

in the moonlight, and the haunted house sitting on top of Marshall's Hill. The scene could have been on a postcard. He felt a warmth in his belly. An overwhelming sense of peace.

The flurries had stopped, and so had the breeze. Something made Adam look down at the pulpit near Gina's feet. She'd moved back and forth, but she'd left no footprints. When he looked at his own feet he saw an oily black splotch quickly spreading into a pool.

Gina raised her arms to the moon and spoke in a language Adam couldn't comprehend. In her hand she held a shiny silver sickle dripping with blood. Adam laid his hand across his stomach. Across the warmth. It got lost in the tangle of entrails spilling out of him onto the pulpit. He shook his head in disbelief. "It's supposed to be a virgin," he said.

Gina smiled her beautiful smile. "You'll do, rookie." She floated away into the night as Adam collapsed into a heap. The last sounds he heard were the frantic yipping of a pack of coyotes, and the *ting, ting, ting* of the Thompsons' dog.

Tracy Falenwolfe is a member of Sisters in Crime, Mystery Writers of America, and the Kiss of Death Chapter of Romance Writers of America. She's been published in several anthologies, and is currently writing a mystery series. She lives in Pennsylvania's Lehigh Valley with her husband and two sons. Learn more at www.tracyfalenwolfe.com

PLAY DEAD

Shawn Reilly Simmons

"He bit me."

Detective Murphy looked at the uniformed officer's slobber-coated hand doubtfully then back at the big brown dog sitting next to the dead body on the lawn.

"You sure? Looks to me like he's smiling at you," Murphy said. He made eye contact with the dog, who froze mid-pant and stared back at him for a moment, then continued his excited breathing. Strands of drool dangled from his jowls and his dark pink tongue lolled from his mouth.

Murphy gazed at the scuffed soles of the man lying in the grass. His legs were splayed open in a V where he had fallen.

"Dog won't let you near the guy," the injured patrolman complained. He squinted up at Murphy from where he sat perched on his car's bumper, holding his hand by the wrist. "I'm putting a call in to Animal Control."

Murphy held up his hand, fending off the suggestion. "He didn't even break the skin, kid. Give me a minute with him first." Murphy thought about Gary Fishman at Animal Control. The man took a little too much pleasure in rounding up the newly-homeless dogs and cats they came across at crime scenes.

Murphy walked back to his partner who stood with her hands on her hips in front of their unmarked car, eyeing the crime scene from behind her aviator sunglasses. Murphy watched two miniature versions of himself talk to her in the reflective frames.

"Dog's guarding his owner's body. Won't let anyone get close," Murphy said.

"I figured as much," Sullivan said. "He's a big one, isn't he?"

Murphy nodded, then turned around to look at the dog again. "Some kind of mastiff, I think." The dog was watching him, had followed his progress to the other side of the lawn. Murphy could see more of the victim's body from this angle. His yellow dress shirt was stained with blood, and the wind fluttered the shirttails up over his belt whenever a stronger gust came through.

"We've got to get to the body," Sullivan mumbled. "Dog or no dog."

Murphy sighed. "Yeah, I know. I'm going in." He relaxed his shoulders and shook out his hands. "Trick is to get him to trust me."

"Luckily he's never played poker with you," Sullivan said. "I'll cover you." She put her hand on the butt of her gun.

"You won't need that," Murphy said. "He's a dog. I've got a way with them." His partner's jaw tightened and he was pretty sure she rolled her eyes at him behind her sunglasses.

Murphy turned away from her and walked up the sloping lawn, his dress shoes slipping on the well-tended grass. The dog pulled his tongue back into his mouth and stared at Murphy, his floppy black ears becoming rigid and riding up to the top of his head. When he got closer, Murphy could hear a deep-throated growl.

"Hey, buddy," Murphy said in a soothing voice as he eased closer. "Good boy. I'm not gonna hurt ya…atta boy…" His eyes flicked down to the man in the grass and he saw that he had been shot at least twice in the chest. The back of his shirt was damp, but the front was dry, so he must have fallen after the rain had stopped just after seven that morning.

Murphy locked eyes with the dog. "Okay, here's what we're going to do. We're going to take…Daddy, or whatever you call him," Murphy said, pointing at the man's body, "and get him some help, okay?"

The dog's growls grew louder in the back of his throat, and his eyes narrowed to slits.

"Easy, big guy," Murphy said, taking another step closer.

The dog tensed, the muscles of his neck tightening under his thick leather collar. Murphy was reminded of the oversized guys at the gym who grunted as they lifted weights in front of the mirror.

Murphy took another tentative step and said, "Come on, I'm just going to—"

The dog sprang off his haunches and lunged toward Murphy, barking loudly, his powerful legs closing the space between them in seconds.

Murphy turned and ran, his shoes slipping on the damp grass. He skidded to the edge of the lawn, tripping on the curb just as he reached Sullivan. His hands slammed down on the hood of their car, breaking his fall. He looked over his shoulder and saw the dog standing at the edge of the lawn, stopping short of crossing onto the sidewalk. After a few more seconds of barking, apparently satisfied the threat had been neutralized, the dog turned and went back to his spot next to his owner's body. He eased back down into a squat, his front leg leaning protectively against the dead man's torso.

Murphy glanced over at the group of patrol officers and saw a few of them snickering at him from behind their hands.

"Jeez, Murphy," Sullivan said. "If that's you having a way with dogs, I'd love to see how you do with the ladies."

"You wish," Murphy said with an open show of irritation.

"Constantly," Sullivan teased.

"Give me a break, will ya, Sully?" Murphy said.

"Excuse me, Detective?" a voice said from behind him.

Murphy turned to see the patrolman with the injured hand, holding up his phone. "What?" he asked loudly.

The officer smiled knowingly and shrugged his shoulders, his carrot-colored hair brightly lit from behind by the sun. "You want me to put that call into Animal Control now?"

Murphy stood up straight and took a step closer to the officer, his eyes flicking down to his name plate. "No, Officer Banes. And lose the attitude. This ain't a comedy show. A man is dead over there."

The smile slipped from Banes's face and he dropped his phone into his front shirt pocket.

"You! Get over here," Murphy shouted, waving at the rest of the uniformed officers. Once the six of them formed a circle around him he said, "What do we know so far?"

"We have a dead body, and the dog is—" someone said from the back of the group.

"Do I look like an idiot? We all know about the dog," Murphy said sharply. He pinched the bridge of his nose and counted to five, reminding himself that sarcasm wasn't usually helpful.

Sullivan took a step forward. "What my partner is asking…are any of you from the neighborhood, anyone know the victim, along those lines," she said. "This is your regular patrol area, right?"

"Who was first on the scene?" Murphy asked.

A tall female officer in the back of the group raised her hand over her head. "We were. That's Mr. Hamlet Papazian. We responded to a call of shots fired at this location…I still can't believe he's dead." Her voice broke at the end and she cleared her throat.

Sullivan motioned for her to move toward the front. "Say his last name again?" She pulled her leather bound notebook from her jacket pocket.

"Papazian," the officer said, recovering her composure. "I went to school with his daughter, we're friends."

"You think she's in the house?" Murphy asked quickly.

The officer shook her head. "No, she's away at school. Stanford."

"Who else lives here with Mr. Papazian?" Sullivan asked, jotting notes.

"Nobody," the female officer responded. She tucked a stray piece of shiny black hair behind her ear. "It was just Milena and her dad when we were growing up. Her mom died when she was little, back in Armenia."

"Big house like this, there might be a maid, gardener, someone taking care of things," Murphy said, looking past the dog at the well appointed home on the hill.

"Yeah, there was a housekeeper. If it's still the same one her name was Miss Thomas, I think," the officer said. "I don't remember them having a dog, but we've been out of school for a while. Milena is graduating from college next year."

"What business is…was…Mr. Papazian in?" Sullivan asked.

"He owns The Diamond House," the officer responded. "The jewelry store up on Main Street." She waved vaguely at the row of buildings behind him.

233

Murphy put his hands on his belt and blew out a sigh. "Okay, that's helpful. Thanks, Officer—"

"Simpkins."

"You still in touch with the daughter?" Murphy asked.

"Yes, sir," Officer Simpkins responded excitedly. "We're Facebook friends."

Murphy nodded tightly. "Find her. See if she's in town, away at school, whatever. Don't notify her on Facebook about her dad's death, though."

"Yes, sir," Simpkins said, eagerly tapping the glass on her phone.

"You two," Murphy said, waving at the officers behind her, "set up a perimeter, keep people off the sidewalk." Murphy glanced across the street, noticing a few onlookers gathered near the corner, shielding the sun with their hands and watching the police activity. "The rest of you start canvassing the neighbors. Split up, hit both sides of the street. Find out if anybody heard or saw anything."

The patrol officers nodded in agreement and hurried away.

"How's your hand?" Murphy asked Banes as he walked past.

He shrugged and said, "Fine, I guess."

"Good. Start knocking on doors then."

"What are we going to do about him?" Sullivan asked after Banes walked away. She jerked an elbow at the dog and flipped through the pages of her notepad.

"I have an idea," Murphy said. "Be right back." He hurried away, crossing the street and heading toward a restaurant on the corner. He deliberately avoided eye contact with the group of onlookers, rushing past them on the sidewalk and pulling open the glass door of the diner, the words *Cypress Grill* etched in blue on the glass.

The diner was brightly lit and relatively clean, and the aroma of bacon hung in the air. Large windows overlooked the sidewalk on three sides, and a row of booths lined the back wall. Several small tables were scattered across the blue and white tiled floor. An old man sat in one of the booths, clutching a newspaper in one fist, his other hand wrapped around a mug of coffee. A girl with long blonde hair and heavy eyeliner sat at one of the tables, gazing intently at her phone and sliding her slender thumb across the screen. Her legs were crossed at the knee, and wrapped back around each other at the ankle. She stirred the ice in her drink distractedly with her straw as she studied her phone.

Murphy made his way to the counter and placed his hand on one of the blue upholstered seats bolted to the floor in front of it. "Excuse me, sir?"

The bulky gentleman facing the flattop grill turned to face him. "Yes?" He wiped his hands on the stained white apron tied around his waist.

"Can I get a couple of burgers to go?" Murphy asked, squinting at the chalkboard menu on the wall behind the register. "And I hate to ask but I need them right away." He pulled open his jacket and flashed the badge on his belt. "I'll pay extra to cut in line. We've got a situation outside." He glanced at the

234

old man sitting in the booth who threw him a dirty look, and slammed his newspaper onto the table.

"*Pes káti,* Stavros!" he shouted in a raspy voice.

"*Skáse,* Savvas!" the cook shouted. "Don't mind my cousin. He can wait, like he always does. How you would like the burgers, Officer? Medium, well-done…?" he asked, trailing off and glancing around distractedly.

Murphy threw an apologetic look over his shoulder at the old man, who huffed and pulled his newspaper angrily back up to his face. "It doesn't matter. Rare is fine. Thanks, Mister—"

"Just Stavros."

"Thanks, Stavros, I appreciate your help," Murphy said, loudly enough for the old man in the booth to hear him. "Say, do you know anything about what happened across the street?"

Stavros began shaking his head before he'd finished the question. "We just opened. I was back there, in the walk-in taking inventory." He hooked his thumb to the left at a swinging door off the kitchen area. "We didn't see nothing."

"You didn't notice anything out of the ordinary? Anyone unfamiliar on the street?" Murphy asked, glancing around the small diner.

"Nope, nothing," Stavros said. "Anyways, let me get your burgers." He turned back to the grill and threw two patties onto the flattop. He cleared his throat and rubbed his hands together as the meat began to sizzle.

Murphy turned around and leaned against the back of the chair, shoving his hands in the pockets of his dress pants. He thought about the dog across the street, obediently protecting Mr. Papazian's body, sadly after he no longer needed protection. He thought about his own rescued mutt at home, and wondered if Peaches would guard his body like that. He thought the little guy probably would. He reminded himself to name the next dog they got, remembering caving too quickly to his young daughter's pleas to name the dog Peaches. He didn't look anything like a Peaches. And he was pretty sure that was a girl's name anyway.

Murphy sighed and his gaze drifted back to the young woman sitting at the table near the counter. He blanched slightly when he saw she was openly staring at him. Their eyes locked, and while his first instinct was to look away, something in her expression made him hold his gaze. She uncrossed her legs and pressed her bony knees together, leaning her forearms onto the table. She smiled and began tonguing the straw in her soda as she stared at him.

Murphy watched her tongue slide around the edge of the straw for a beat longer then looked away. He cleared his throat and spun his wedding band around his finger with his thumb inside his pocket. He wandered to the door, glancing out at the crime scene up the block.

"Oh man," Murphy muttered under his breath. A khaki-colored van lumbered slowly up the street towards the crime scene, a cartoon logo of a bird blazed across the side. He took a few long strides back to the counter and said, "Those burgers almost ready?"

Stavros was folding them inside blue and white checked wrappers, greasy stains already spreading across the paper. "Yes, just a minute." He shook out a white paper bag and pulled a black grease pencil from his front pocket, scribbling something on the side. His head jerked quickly to the left and he put the pencil back in his pocket before stepping in front of the register.

Murphy pulled out his wallet and fingered through the bills inside.

"It's on the house," Stavros said after punching a few buttons on the register.

"No, I insist. And let me pay for his breakfast," Murphy said, waving at the booth behind him.

Stavros laughed nervously. "I don't have any change. Just go. I want to help with whatever is happening."

Murphy stuffed a twenty in the empty tip jar next to the register and grabbed the bag of burgers. He hurried to the door, saying "Thanks" over his shoulder.

Just as he stepped outside, Murphy saw Banes sidling toward the diner. Nodding at the van that had pulled up behind the row of patrol cars he said, "Hey, did you call Animal Control after I told you not to?"

Banes shrugged his thin shoulders and said, "Wasn't me."

Murphy eyed him suspiciously. "Yeah, right. What are you doing now?"

"Canvassing, like you said."

The door of the van groaned open and Gary Fishman rolled out, hoisting himself onto the street with the help of the door. The van noticeably righted itself after being unburdened from his weight.

Murphy threw Banes an irritated glance and hurried toward the van and the large man in the tan uniform standing beside it.

"Hey, Gary!" Murphy shouted, jaywalking across the street to meet him. He looked up at Mr. Papazian's feet, and saw his dog was still in the same spot, watching the police activity around him and guarding his master.

"Oh look, it's Detective Softy," Gary said, smirking at Murphy as he approached.

"Good to see you too, Gary," Murphy said, grasping the paper bag tightly in his fist. "What are you doing here?"

"Heard on the scanner the cops had a vicious dog on a scene. Thought I'd check it out," Gary said. Murphy couldn't see his eyes behind his fingerprint-smudged sunglasses. He did recognize a combination mustard and relish stain on his stitched name tag, the white threads in *GARY* stained yellow and green.

"We're not going to need you on this one," Murphy said quickly.

"We'll see about that," Gary said, reinforcing his smirk. His puffy cheeks were mottled with red splotches. Murphy didn't know from what, maybe from the exertion of getting out of his van or possibly just from standing on his own two feet. Gary scratched his swollen belly between two buttons on his shirt.

236

"Do me a favor and wait in the van. If we need any help, I'll let you know," Murphy said.

"He's a big one," Gary said doubtfully. "Sure you can handle him?"

"Just wait in the van," Murphy said. He turned and walked toward the lawn, making eye contact with his partner as he went.

"I got a tranquilizer gun in the back..." Gary's voice faded into the background as Murphy got closer to Mr. Papazian and the dog.

Sullivan moved in behind him, following his lead and motioning to the uniformed officers to hold their positions on the sidewalk.

The dog watched Murphy approach, beginning his warning growls when he made it halfway up the lawn. Murphy moved forward carefully, opening up the white bag and releasing the scent of hamburger.

"I got something for you, big guy," Murphy said in a gentle voice. "You like burgers, don't you, boy?"

The dog sniffed the air and his expression softened. He didn't move away from Mr. Papazian, but he stopped growling and he allowed them to move in closer. Murphy crouched down and slowly pulled a hamburger from the bag, opening the wrapper.

"This is yours, buddy," Murphy said, extending his arm further. The dog stared at it hungrily then took a bite. Murphy held his arm steady, letting the dog eat from his hand. When he finished the first burger, Murphy offered him the second, which he ate just as quickly.

"Good boy," Murphy said, reaching up slowly to rub behind his ears. The dog pressed his head into Murphy's hand and he rubbed harder, feeling the remaining tension leave the dog's body.

"You're a real charmer, I'll give you that," Sullivan said, pulling on a latex glove and crouching next to Mr. Papazian's body. She pulled out his wallet and flipped it open. "This is definitely Hamlet Papazian."

"And this is Apollo," Murphy said, pointing at the tags on the dog's collar. "Our new friend might know exactly what happened here this morning."

"Signs of a struggle in here," Sullivan said from the doorway of Mr. Papazian's home office. "Looks like it started in here."

Murphy ushered the CSU officers into the foyer and pointed to the blood on the rug leading out the front door and onto the porch. One of them began taking photos while the other set down a large case on the floor out of the way.

"Dust the doorknob, guys," Murphy said. "There's no sign of a break-in...he must have let his killer inside."

Sullivan twisted her mouth into a doubtful line. "You think Mr. Papazian was the habit of just letting people into his house, considering his line of work?"

"Well, the killer didn't fly in through a window," Murphy muttered under his breath as he headed toward the office.

237

"There's no security system for the house," Sullivan said, "but I called the jewelry store's alarm company. It's listed next to the phone on his desk. There's been no one in or out of the store or any alarm activity last night or this morning." Sullivan led the way into the office.

"What a mess," Murphy said, eyeing the papers scattered over the floor. There were bloody drops on several of them.

"Look at this," Sullivan said, gingerly pulling open a section of books on the bookcase. "Almost didn't see it, these are fake, the wood spines make a door to hide the safe. The bloody fingerprint right there caught my eye." She pointed to the spine of *The Thin Man*.

"Anything in the safe?" Murphy asked.

"It's locked," Sullivan said, shrugging.

"So, the killer gets inside somehow, tries to get Papazian to open the safe and what, he refuses?" Murphy asked, trying to set the scene in his mind.

Sullivan shrugged. "That's a possibility."

"Where was Apollo when this was happening?" Murphy asked, looking around the room. "I doubt he'd let his owner get shot without trying to stop it."

Sullivan sighed and put her hands on her hips. "Unless the dog didn't see the killer as a threat until it was too late."

Murphy nodded and stepped carefully through the foyer and onto the front porch. The coroner was zipping Mr. Papazian into a body bag while Apollo sat in the back of their unmarked car, whining through the open window. Murphy sighed and looked at the row buildings across the street, then jogged down the front steps and waved the patrol officers over.

"Where are we?"

Simpkins stepped forward. "I confirmed that Milena is still at school. I called the university to confirm, left a message for her to call me back."

"What about the neighbors? Anyone see or hear anything out of the ordinary this morning?" Murphy asked.

"No, sir," one of the other officers chimed in. "Most of the neighbors were either still asleep or had already left for work. The lady next door said she heard an argument before she went to bed last night, but thought it was coming from the other end of the street, not this direction. Honestly, sir, she couldn't hear me very well and I was in the same room with her, so…"

"Mr. Papazian wasn't shot until this morning, could be something unrelated. It's not much to go on," Murphy said, deflating a bit. "Anything else?"

"She also said Mr. Papazian has a regular housekeeper named Elvira Thomas, but she hasn't seen her around lately. Thinks maybe Mr. Papazian fired her a couple of weeks ago. The last time she saw Miss Thomas from the window she had what looked like all of her personal things and appeared very upset. Miss Thomas used to stop in and ask if she needed anything from the store when she went out shopping. That's how the old lady noticed Miss Thomas hadn't been around."

"Find the housekeeper," Murphy said to him. "Let Miss Thomas know we have some questions. She might be a valuable witness."

"Or if she got fired, maybe she was mad enough to come back and kill her old boss," the officer offered.

Murphy, lost in thought, glanced at the faces of the patrol officers in front of him. "Where's Banes?"

The officers looked at each other without responding.

"Who's partnered with Officer Banes?"

Simpkins raised her hand. "Just for today, sir. My regular partner is out sick. They paired us up at roll call this morning."

Murphy sighed and glanced at the diner. "What's taking him so long? If I find out he ordered breakfast—"

"Murphy," Sullivan yelled from the front door. "You'll want to see this." Sullivan was holding something behind her back in one hand and waving him over with the other.

"What is it?" Murphy asked after he stepped back inside the foyer.

Sullivan held out a piece of a dark purple material in her latex-gloved hand. "What does that look like to you?"

Murphy squinted at the material, trying to place it. "A piece of a raincoat, maybe?"

"It's from a woman's trench coat." She turned it over and pointed to stitched letters on the hem, a label vaguely familiar to him. "Found it behind the desk in the office."

"Maybe it's his daughter's, or the housekeeper's," Murphy mumbled.

Sullivan looked at him doubtfully. "Looks like Apollo took a bite out of it. You think he'd do that to someone he trusted? I'll bet it's the shooter's coat." She handed the ripped fabric to the CSU agent, who nodded and slipped it inside a plastic evidence bag.

Murphy's stomach did a slow turn and he walked back out the front door. He swept his gaze across the lawn, and froze when he saw Gary talking to Apollo through the window of his car. Apollo ignored Gary and continued to stare at the house.

"Simpkins!" Murphy shouted, waving her over.

"Sir?" Simpkins asked, slightly startled as she made her way up the slate path.

"Is Banes back yet?" Murphy demanded.

"Not yet," she said quickly. Her phone buzzed in her hand and she held it up. "It's Milena calling...what should I say?"

"I'd better talk to her," Murphy said, taking the phone from her. "Miss Papazian?" he answered. He turned away and walked to the edge of the lawn, his shoulders hunched as he spoke. After a few minutes he returned, shaking his head. "Milena's on her way home, she's very upset. She confirmed her father let the housekeeper go a couple of weeks ago after he caught her stealing blank checks from the office."

Simpkins stared down at the phone in his hand.

"Show me Milena's Facebook page," Murphy said, holding the phone out to her. She opened it up for him and stepped behind to look at it also.

Murphy tapped on the screen, swiping quickly through her profile. "Jeez, she's got over nine hundred pictures in here," he mumbled. After scrolling through a dozen or so photos of books and plates of food he handed the phone back to her. "Can you find one of her with her dad?"

"Let me see," Simpkins said, flicking quickly through the images. "Here," she said, showing him a picture of Milena and Hamlet standing on the front porch, her arms draped loosely around his waist, both of them smiling. Murphy held the phone closer to his face then swiped to the next picture. A group of teenagers, Milena on one end, smiled at the camera from a sandy white beach. "That's all of us, our group of friends from high school on spring break. There I am," Simpkins pointed to a small image of her younger self in the center.

Murphy studied the photo. "Follow me," he said quietly and hurried away. "Get away from the dog, Gary," he warned as he passed by his car, Simpkins hurrying behind him to keep up.

Gary held his hands up in mock surrender, smiling from behind his smudged glasses. "I'm just getting to know him."

Murphy shot him a warning glance then hurried across the street.

"Follow my lead," Murphy said to Simpkins before pulling open the door of the diner. Simpkins slipped in behind him, her body rigid.

"Stavros," Murphy said.

Stavros spun around from the grill and held his hands in the air, his spatula clanging to the floor between his feet. Two sunny side up eggs bubbled next to a row of bacon on the flattop grill behind him.

Murphy eased open the swinging door over the trash barrel by the door with his fingertips and saw a purple raincoat inside, the bottom hem torn. He darted his gaze around the diner. The old man sat in his booth against the back wall, glaring angrily back at them. "Where's Officer Banes?"

Savvas unwrapped his bony fingers from his coffee mug and pointed behind the counter. Murphy swung his gaze at Stavros, who shook his head nervously.

"He's gone. Left," Stavros said loudly, darting his eyes sharply to the left. "You won't find them here."

A pan clattered on the tile floor and they heard signs of a struggle coming from behind the swinging door.

"Come out now," Murphy demanded loudly, pulling his gun from his belt. "Nobody has to get hurt."

Murphy waved frantically at Stavros to come out from behind the counter, but he stood still and shook his head. Murphy motioned for Simpkins to take a flanking position closer to the cash register. She moved quickly and hardened her expression.

"Come on out!" Murphy shouted.

Murphy watched Simpkins's eyes grow wide with surprise, then turned to see Banes emerge from the stock room behind the counter, his freckled face flushed bright red. A bony arm was wrapped around his neck and the nose of a pistol was pressed against his temple.

"Laura?" Simpkins whispered harshly. "Laura, drop the gun," she said, regaining her voice.

Laura, the girl from the diner with the straw fixation, laughed loudly and tightened her grip around Banes's neck.

"Let him go," Murphy ordered.

Banes shook his head. "Sir, she's crazy! Get her off me!"

Simpkins flicked an uncertain glance at Murphy. "Sir, we're in a hostage situation—"

"I recognized her from Milena's Facebook photo," Murphy said. "A big group of friends from school…looks like your former classmate killed Mr. Papazian."

"Wait, what?" Simpkins said, her confusion deepening.

"Mr. Papazian let you in to his home, didn't he? Milena's childhood friend, he wouldn't turn you away. And you tried to rob him?"

"We're walking out of here now," Laura said calmly. She pulled the gun from Banes's head and waved it around the room. "Get out of the way." She shuffled forward, urging Banes ahead of her.

"Laura, how could you kill Mr. Papazian?" Simpkins asked, struggling to maintain her aim. "He was so nice to all of us."

Laura laughed. "I didn't. I was in the diner the whole time, having breakfast. See? Stavros is making it for me."

"No you weren't," Murphy said. "You shot Mr. Papazian and hid out here when you saw Officers Simpkins and Banes arrive on the scene. You knew she'd recognize you right away. Your plan to rob him didn't work out, so you decided to rob the diner?"

Laura sniffed and smiled at him. "You don't know anything. I love Milena, and her father. He loves me too, and he's got more money than he needs. He doesn't mind giving me a loan when I need one."

"Until today?" Murphy ventured.

Laura's expression faltered, frustration pinched her face. "We had a fight. It's not unusual for a couple to argue over money. He agreed with me eventually."

"What do you mean Mr. Papazian loves you?" Simpkins asked, a look of distaste on her face.

"We're getting married," Laura said with satisfaction. "I'm going to be Milena's stepmother!"

"No!" Savvas shouted from the rear booth. "She a *trelós plisiázon*."

Murphy looked questioningly at Stavros.

"Crazy stalker," he said quickly, then looked at the floor guiltily after catching Laura's glare.

241

"I thought you worked at that insurance office downtown," Simpkins said, pulling Laura's attention away from Stavros.

Laura sniffed. "I did. Not anymore. We're making a new start together. Hamlet is giving me the jewelry store as a wedding gift."

Simpkins looked with pity at her old friend.

"Whatever you think is happening, let's not make things worse now," Murphy said in a gentler tone. "Put the gun down and let's figure this out, Laura."

"How can things get any worse?" Banes choked incredulously, straining against Laura's forearm and ignoring Murphy's warning glance.

"She's had a gun on us the whole time," Stavros spoke up from behind the counter, darting glances at Laura. "Said she'd kill us all if I said anything when you came in. Then this one arrives right after you, asking even more questions. She was about to let us go!"

"Shut up!" Laura said.

Murphy ignored Banes, keeping his eyes on Laura. "Let Officer Banes go," he demanded in a quiet voice.

Laura tightened her grip and led her hostage out from behind the counter. As they got closer to the exit, Simpkins and Murphy closed the distance between them. Banes locked eyes with Murphy just as Laura leaned her back against the door.

Banes suddenly went limp, dropping from her grip and onto the floor. Momentarily confused, Laura looked down, then decided to make a run for it, banging her slender shoulder against the glass.

Simpkins closed the gap between them and grabbed Laura's wrist, pointing her gun up in the air. She squeezed until Laura dropped it, and it clattered across the floor. Banes scrambled to pick it up, then skittered away from Laura, pulling himself upright.

"Look at him go. He moves quick." Laura giggled loudly, leaning into Simpkins.

"Good work, you two," Murphy mumbled.

"Yeah, good work," Laura snorted. "And good luck trying to get me for this. He attacked me, it was self-defense," she said, pointing at Banes. "Police brutality."

"I like our chances," Murphy said, turning her around and handcuffing her. "I have a feeling the fingerprints inside Mr. Papazian's office will match yours."

"Hamlet was my fiancé. My fingerprints and DNA are all over his house," Laura taunted.

"Your bloody fingerprints?" Murphy said. "You'll have a hard time explaining that to a jury."

Laura beamed at him knowingly. "I'll find a way. They probably belong to that nosy housekeeper. Too bad she had to steal those checks, get herself fired."

"No, Hamlet wasn't anything with her!" Stavros shouted from behind them, finding his courage. "This crazy girl showed up at his house all the time, at the store, called him all hours of the night. He didn't want any part of her. He didn't know what to do. He didn't want to get Milena's friend into trouble, a girl he watched grow up, so he didn't tell anybody, except me and Savvas." Stavros took a breath and pointed a finger angrily at Laura. "And I know she's behind Miss Thomas getting fired. That woman would never steal from Hamlet. This crazy girl tricked him somehow."

"Come on, let's go," Murphy said, leading Laura out the door.

As they approached the crowd outside of Mr. Papazian's house, Apollo began to bark loudly from inside the car. When they got to the sidewalk, Apollo tried to squeeze out through the window, his barking becoming insistent and frenzied.

"I have a witness," Murphy said quietly to Laura as they walked past. "Apollo recognizes you."

"Take it easy, big guy," Gary said through the window to Apollo. "I still say this is a vicious dog. Look at him," he said to Murphy.

"Get away from my witness, Gary," Murphy warned as he led Laura past.

"Fine, have it your way. Sure hope he doesn't bite you," Gary said with a smile. "Give me a call if you change your mind." He lumbered back to his van and pulled himself inside.

"Simpkins, you and Banes take her in," Murphy said. "I'll meet you at the station after I make a stop." He pulled out his phone and dialed his wife's number.

Laura laughed and said, "We're getting rid of Apollo after I move in. He doesn't like me."

Murphy shook his head and lowered her into the backseat of Officer Simpkins's patrol car. "Dogs always know who they can trust," he said, closing the door.

He pulled his phone up to his ear after he heard the call connect. "Hi, honey. I'm bringing a friend home. He'll be staying with us for a while."

Shawn Reilly Simmons is the author of the Red Carpet Catering mysteries, published by Henery Press, staring Penelope Sutherland, an on-set movie caterer. Shawn serves on the Board of Malice Domestic, is a member of the Dames of Detection, and an editor & co-publisher at Level Best Books. She's a member of Sisters in Crime, Mystery Writers of America, and the Crime Writers' Association in the UK.

THE MAN WHO WASN'T MISSED

Brenda Seabrooke

I pulled into the parking lot of a strip mall where a woman paced and wrung her hands in front of a lawyer's office. You might think people don't do that in real life but I've seen it many times. They wring their hands or a handkerchief or tissue when they can't process what they've just seen. They aren't ready to cry or scream yet, but as fear
and worry build up inside them, they have to do something to deal with the pressure.

I sized her up: pleasant features settling into middle-age, blue dress size twelve, a little tight under her raincoat, low-heeled shoes, neat brown hair and make-up. She focused on the half-open door of the office as if waiting for someone to come out. I eased the door of my SUV shut with a barely audible click. Her head jerked around.

"Are you the police?"

"Yes, ma'am. I'm Detective Danvers. You're..."

"Lorraine Pollock."

I put my hand out to stop her wringing and to see how she would accept it. Firm shake, cool hand. Functional, then. Used to meeting people. Possibly on autopilot. I parked her in the not-likely category for now. It was too early to chisel her name on a wall of innocents but she wasn't in the red-hot perp category either.

"I'm Jerry's secretary." She retrieved her hand as tears spilled out of the corners of her eyes. She rummaged in a blue leather bag for a tissue and dabbed her cheeks.

"Jerry?"

"Jerry Millbanks, Esquire, the lawyer I work for."

"Tell me what happened."

"I was here as usual by 8:40. I don't have to come in until nine but I like to get things ready for the day."

"Was the door locked?"

"Yes, I'm sure it was. I opened it with my key. Oh. I unlocked it but it was still locked. I had to turn the key again to open the door so I must have locked it when I thought I was unlocking it. I went in. Jerry is always in his office by nine unless he has an appointment. He didn't. I checked his book."

"Which was where?"

"On his desk. It's not like him to take off without telling me."

244

She wrung the tissue into shreds. It was now ten fifty-five. She had waited almost two hours before calling.

"He's just late for now, ma'am. There's probably a good reason for it. Anybody else likely to be in the office?"

"No."

"Wait here." The unlocked door might be a sign of a problem.

The decor was posher than its site might lead one to expect. Persian rugs, possibly imitation Elaine would say, over extra-thick pads to upgrade them. Grandfather clock, or tall case clock, Elaine would say. Leather furniture, antique animal prints on the walls. Repro, Elaine would say, aged with tea. Giant mahogany-finished desk in the inner office. Easy to fake. A bowl of cereal on a stack of law books appeared to be cooked oatmeal with things in it. Lab would have to check, but from the spoon stuck in the hardened mess, I would say somebody changed his mind and went to Krispy Kremes or Muffin Land. I bent over for a sniff and wished I hadn't. It had been here for a while. Maybe since Saturday or Friday. It was now Monday but it smelled like 1984.

I checked closets, the bathroom, and the picture gallery on the desk. Selfies of a solid man, still-handsome despite receding blond hair, with a black-haired woman, well-built and ultra-sultry engaged in activities like skiing, fishing for marlin, and in formal wear at the Winter Snow Ball or Holly Frolic, her left hand flashing a serious diamond. Possibly flawed, Elaine would say, you can't tell without a loup.

Framed awards from civic groups hung on the walls and more photos, more than I'd ever seen in a law office crowded his desk. Millbanks looked like a popular guy with his fingers in a lot of civic pies, service clubs, animal-named clubs and leagues, art, soccer, Little League, and the League of Women Voters. Pancakes featured prominently with Jerry in a comic apron and hat wielding an oversized spatula. What was not there was of more interest: no family pictures or any of kids.

I questioned Lorraine outside. Jerry was newly divorced when he opened his office in Windover seven years earlier. He'd wanted a fresh start away from Brattleboro. She'd been the first applicant for secretary.

Friday her son had a doctor's appointment. Jerry told her to take the whole day.

"He said he was planning to work on some wills and things I could type up today. He said he could handle anything else that might come up. Obviously he couldn't." Her chin quivered.

I powered up my notebook and became impersonally efficient. "So you last saw him Thursday. What time?"

"I left at five. He was on the phone. I don't know who he was talking to."

I'd get his records. "Did you try his home number?"

"He only uses a cell at home. He's usually at his girlfriend's."

245

I got her name and address. She was a buyer for some apparel shops. Nothing more to do here until something turned up. "He probably went somewhere. Judging by the pictures on his desk he likes to travel."

She nodded and hope spurted in her eyes. "He does."

I locked the door and checked for security cameras. None. That would have made this case easier.

"I'll be in touch."

I drove to Millbanks' condo in a smallish building. The super let me in. Two bedrooms, two baths, furnished in minimalist Ikea. Few personal artifacts. Skis, tennis racket, bicycle and helmet hung in the hall. Nothing magnetted to his fridge door. No computer or mail. Correspondence must go to his office. Everything seemed in order. One generic black suitcase and carry-on, well-used. Suits in the bedroom closet. Toiletries in the bathroom, possibly spares. No prescription drugs or contact lenses. Refrigerator held lemons, jars of olives and cocktail onions, a pint of half-and-half, half-gone. Guys don't think about food spoilage. I pour out containers before trips, toss leftovers.

His girlfriend Gina Jacquet, the dark-haired woman in the photos, lived in the fanciest high rise in town, which wasn't saying a lot. For more luxury you had to go to Brattleboro or Boston. She opened the door and the first thing I saw was the headlight diamond on her left ring finger. It could have been fake or flawed, but the wearer wasn't.

I'd introduced myself on the intercom. I showed her the badge. We sat on large leather furniture that seemed to want to massage me. "When did you last see your fiancé?"

"Thursday. We went to dinner Wednesday night and he stayed over. He left early that morning before I got up, and when he didn't come over Thursday night, I went to my sister's in Boston for the weekend." She gazed at me with big dark eyes, fringed with thick lashes that fluttered like dark butterflies landing on a flower. Maybe it was a reflex action. Male on the premises.

"Did he call or give any indication of what his plans were?"

"No to both questions. He texted late Thursday and said he was turning in and would see me when I got back from Boston. He texted Friday morning and said he might drive over that night if he finished something he had to do. He didn't say what."

"He didn't elaborate?"

"No. He never talked about his work except to say he had been in court all day. Maybe that was it."

I'd checked court dockets. No cases for Jerry Millbanks, Esquire, on Thursday, Friday or today. "Anything else you can tell me?"

"He has an ex-wife."

I took out the notebook. "Name and address."

246

"Martha Millbanks. She lives up in Strafford. I don't know the address. Maybe he went up to see his kids."

I got the address from Lorraine. She hadn't mentioned them because they lived so far away. It wasn't that far. Strafford was an easy cruise from Windover. I picked up a burger and was there by three.

The town hall looked like a big white New England church. Signage said it was built in 1700, town population just over 1700. The ex-Mrs. Millbanks lived in a smallish two-story house with a porch north of town. Fake wood, Elaine would say.

I slammed the SUV door and walked to the front entrance. No one answered my knock. I tried the kitchen door. A woman pulled aside the curtain and looked at me. I showed my badge. She stared at it then did something on a cell phone. She talked, hung up and opened the door. "I know this is Vermont, but living out here I can't be too careful."

"I understand."

She offered me coffee and a plate of cranberry cookies that made my knees weak.

"Made with maple syrup," she said. "None of that cancer-causing sugar."

"O-kay."

"What has he done now?"

"Who?"

"Billy. My son, Billy Millbanks."

"He's a problem?"

She rolled her eyes. I noted light lashes. Normal size and batting speed.

"Some might say so. He's just curious. And creative. He took apart a cell phone but couldn't get it back together."

"What boy doesn't do that at least once?"

"He was four. He sneaked another rabbit in to keep the kindergarten rabbit company over the weekend. I don't have to tell you the results of that. Shall I go on?"

"What grade is he in now?"

"Fourth."

I couldn't see a fourth grader driving down to Windover and spiriting his father away.

"Do they get along? Billy and his dad?"

"Of course. Why wouldn't they? Billy doesn't have to pay the rent or buy the food and gas. He doesn't see his dad that much. Jerry's always busy. His clients are usually nubile with long legs and long hair, preferably black." Hers was short and strawberry blond. She raked her fingers through it to make it stay out of her face.

It didn't.

"I take it you pay the bills."

247

"Somebody has to. I teach at the middle school. I'm also an artist. I sell paintings in galleries and online."

"How long have you been divorced?"

"My daughter is seven so it's been seven years. Minimum child support. Daddyhood wasn't for him. Meanwhile he lives the high life while we live the frugal life."

"When did you last see him?"

"I think it was about three years ago at Christmas."

"Do you hear from him?"

"He calls when I'm teaching and leaves messages so he won't have to talk to me. When he comes up, he honks and turns the car around in the driveway and waits for the kids. Same when he brings them back. What's going on? Why all these questions?"

"He hasn't been heard from since Friday."

"Jerry was always taking off. Why are you looking for him, really?"

"He's a prominent lawyer. His secretary is worried about him."

"Is it still Lorraine?"

I nodded.

"Poor Lorraine. If he's taken off, she'll be looking for another job."

"Where were you last Friday?" I had to ask the question, though she didn't seem like a murderer.

"Where I am every weekday. Teaching my classes. You can check with the school."

"Thanks. I will." I stood up.

She handed me a baggie of cookies. "For the road."

The school confirmed she'd been there all day. I munched cookies on the way back to Windover.

This could seem like a waste of time looking for an adult who might jet off somewhere on a whim, but he was a lawyer, an officer of the court. The department was required to look into the case since his secretary was certain something had happened to him. She couldn't believe he would have left without telling her.

"He's never irresponsible," she said.

Except maybe with his kids.

I checked his clients with a list I got from Lorraine. Most were divorce cases. Nobody seemed to blame the lawyer, not even the ex-spouses. All appeared amicable. "Such a sweetheart," one wife said whose husband Jerry represented. "He told me afterward he hated I was getting so little alimony, but he had to go along with the court."

Smooth.

I put together a time line of Millbanks' last known days. He spent Wednesday night with Gina in Windover. Thursday he was in the office all day. Friday he went to his office and microwaved breakfast from packets he kept there while looking over papers on his desk, the wills of a widow and a young couple both typed by Lorraine. He texted Gina, confirmed by cell records, left his breakfast half-eaten and hasn't been seen since. His car was parked in the lot. No odors from the trunk. His safe had been cleaned out. His office door was unlocked, no signs of a break-in. His girlfriend went to Boston Thursday night. His ex-wife was in class all day Friday, too far to dash out during lunch break, kill him and dispose of the body. Why would she want to? Even a pittance of child support is better than what will be paid now unless he's made arrangements for them.

I struck out with cabs and rentals. If he got a lift from a friend, we couldn't find him. Or her. Maybe he bought a bicycle and ditched it.

I called Lorraine. "Oh yes. He had a will. Everything goes to his children."

"Does he have any others besides the two in Strafford?"

"No."

"Was he planning to make a new will?" That was a frequent murder trigger, at least in mystery books. Not as often in real life in my experience, but I hadn't dealt with many rich murder victims.

"I don't know. He hasn't mentioned it. He was talking about marrying Gina at a destination wedding. They hadn't picked one yet. Bali was a strong favorite, though Gina was leaning toward Paris. Shopping."

Not a surprise. Gina dressed couture. Martha dressed thrift shop.

I was late going home. Elaine had eaten out. The cupboard was bare. I was too tired to go out or wait to order in so I made do with half a box of stale donuts while Elaine regaled me with stories of the antique shop she worked in. "Can you believe people think because antiques aren't new they can get used-furniture store prices?"

Mouth full of donuts that required a lot of chewing, I shook my head.

"You have to pay for what you get," she went on.

I fell asleep on the couch and woke up cold in the middle of the night, TV still on, sound off. I crawled into bed with her. She didn't notice.

I went through Jerry's papers in his office the next morning, file by file. I found his will. He left everything to his children with $5,000 a year to his ex-wife for their care until they were of age. According to his checkbook, his wife got more in child support than she would from this will until the kids both reached twenty-two. That made her an unlikely candidate for murder.

It was a difficult case. It might not even be a case. Nobody hated Jerry Millbanks, not his clients or his past girlfriends, his handball team, the guys at the gym, fellow attorneys, his ex-wife, or present girlfriend. Lorraine clearly adored him. Martha had no illusions but didn't appear to hate him.

"He's a bit of a light-weight," his handball partner told me.

"Can you be more specific?"

Bill O'Hara had good muscle tone at thirty-three but he came across as sneery, possibly due to his short upper lip and personality which could be an asset for a trial lawyer. "He was never for the long-haul. He and Gina were going to some distant place to get married, but maybe it was going to be a honeymoon without the wedding, if you know what I mean. Why move into the stable when the mares will come out to play?"

According to gossip they didn't come out to play with him. Jerry was the town catch.

Gina had no reason to kill Jerry. That ring was super-glued to her finger. She gained nothing from his death. Nevertheless, I swung by her condo. An older man answered the door, said he was a friend. Gina introduced him as her financial advisor.

Financial advisor?

I'd heard of Victor deSanto, a Boston stockbroker with his own firm. Urbane, gray hair, years older than Jerry, he exuded success. Was he the replacement boyfriend? Did she go to see him for the weekend instead of her sister? I didn't ask. She wasn't married to Jerry. She had no need to kill him to get him out of her life.

The same didn't go for Victor.

"I was shopping for a bridal gown," she volunteered and showed me a photo on her phone of herself in a tight strapless dress slit to her thigh. I would marry her myself. Any guy would.

I left and went over my list. Everybody on it but Lorraine had a sliver of motive but none were strong enough to hold up in court. Not without a body or evidence or weapon or DNA. The oatmeal proved to be oatmeal, soy milk, dried blueberries and fresh banana. The peel was in the trash can with the empty oatmeal package and a flyer about Bali. Maybe Jerry had decided Paris was worth it.

I looked up male disappearances. One other lawyer had disappeared in Vermont but returned ten years later after living in Mexico. Just wanted to get away, he'd said. His case was suspiciously like Jerry's, whose passport and money were missing. His cellphone had been silent since Friday morning. No activity on email accounts, no charges to credit cards. It seemed Millbanks had taken off. He might be in Bali or Bora Bora or St. Barts. If a man wanted to disappear, it was not the Windover PD's job to find him. He'd committed no crime.

Nobody had strong feelings against Jerry, an okay guy. He was a so-so provider to his children but he was their dad. They seemed to like him. His ex-wife seemed to care only for her children. His girlfriend's sister confirmed Gina had shopped for that bridal gown at Phyllis of Boston, as did the bridal shop. Victor proved to have been sailing with friends, Lorraine home with her sick son. I checked with his doctor. He'd been seen that Friday.

250

I reported my findings. "Want me to bring them in and sweat them a little?" I asked, knowing the answer. This wasn't TV.

Captain Rayles told me to drop it. "It's no case. The man took a powder. Give his ex-wife the name of a private dick if she wants to look for him. Meanwhile she'll have to wait seven years to have him declared dead."

I went shopping for weekend food before going home. Elaine texted she was out with girlfriends, to fend for myself. I was starved for protein and ate a whole roast chicken, with sides of slaw, mac and cheese, and apple pie. I didn't hear her come in.

The next day I took the news to Strafford. Elaine was still sleeping when I left. Martha was digging in the flower bed when I pulled up. She wore an old blue sweatshirt and jeans, and a smear of dirt across her jaw. The kids were hunting tadpoles in the creek.

"Do you have news of Jerry?"

I nodded. She threw down the trowel and invited me in.

Over coffee and banana bread with fresh blueberries in it, I told her we thought her husband had run away.

"Why would he run away from a successful law practice?"

"His girlfriend was pressuring him to marry her and let her spend his money. He was shrewd enough to realize that." I explained what she would have to do to petition the court for relief and prove him dead in seven years.

"So now we don't even have the child support checks." She sighed. "I'd hoped to take the kids to the beach this summer. Guess that will have to wait."

Summer was a month away. A lot could happen by then.

A month later I ran into Lorraine at the drug store picking up her son's asthma prescription. She wore a yellow linen dress and looked slimmer and younger. The frown lines had disappeared. She told me she was moving to Boston to work for Victor. "I'll be making more than my ex-husband."

"What about Victor?"

"What about him?"

"Did he marry Gina?"

She looked surprised. "How did you know?"

"Papers." Victor had married Gina in Paris. I wondered if she'd worn the dress from Boston. I didn't ask.

A man like Victor shouldn't have to knock off Jerry to get his hands on Gina. Just flash a credit card and a ring at her. The penthouse apartment was gravy but maybe he had a Viagra habit and vigorous Jerry didn't.

Other cases came along, a homeless man drowned in a creek, a husband killed his wife. A teenage girl cut school and didn't go home that night. It was August before I thought any more about Jerry Millbanks and the people around him. After three nights with no sighting of Elaine, I realized she was gone. I searched and found a note in the desk drawer. She'd left for a job in Stowe managing a gift shop. How could she give up her antiques?

One Sunday afternoon I drove to Strafford and found Martha unpacking her car. The children ran around hindering as much as helping. Billy showed me the shark's tooth he'd found at the beach.

"In the sand huh?"

"Yeah."

"You know you might find shark teeth in the creek."

He ran off with his sister to look for them.

"He won't stop till he finds one or something equally exciting."

"At his age everything is exciting."

"What brings you to Strafford? It can't be my charms. Must be my baking."

"That, too," I said. "How were you able to go to the beach? You told me you couldn't afford it now."

She flushed a little. "Are you recording this?"

"Should I be?"

"No, but are you?"

"No."

"Lorraine called me. She found some cash behind a drawer when she closed up the office. It was a lot. Jerry must have forgotten it. She wanted me to have it for the children, so didn't report it to the estate. Whatever Jerry had done, we shouldn't have to suffer for it. I used some of the money to take them to Orchard Beach for a week."

She hadn't bought new clothes as Gina would have or a car to replace her clunker. She spent it giving her children a treat. I couldn't find fault with that. And maybe Lorraine really had found the cash. Or maybe it was from Victor.

I took them to supper at Murphy's on the Green in Hanover just across the border in New Hampshire and bought the kids Dartmouth t-shirts. I drove them home and carried Emily to her room.

As I was leaving Martha said, "Will you be coming back?"

"No."

"Was it something I said?"

"No."

"Was it the money?"

"No."

"Then why?"

"You know why."

She did but didn't reveal anything. Her look was unfathomable. She should have been a spy or a secret agent. Or a teacher.

252

She'd left the window down in her car. I got a bottle out of my SUV and sprayed into the car. Nothing. Touched the dashboard. Nothing there either. I reviewed the case as I drove back to Windover.

The reasons people murder, outside of serial killers, people on drugs or alcohol, or with some other disorder, are sex, money, greed, revenge, and jealousy. These can all be filed under the heading of power. Sexual murder is power of one partner over another, money—one wants another's money also a form of power. Jealousy is the same. Ditto revenge. Greed is the power to take what another has.

Of the four people in this case, I excluded Gina. She was a pawn, an outlier, but also maybe the inadvertent catalyst who crossed Victor's path and created desire in him, desire to have her. Maybe Gina didn't want to leave the younger, livelier, sexier fun guy finally ready to marry her. Jerry was the catch of Windover and in Victor's way, so he found Lorraine's weak spot and enticed her to tell Martha Jerry was about to marry and change the old will that left everything to her kids. The new will cut them out except for a token. Maybe Lorraine showed her a will she typed up and said it was waiting for Jerry's signature on Monday.

Lorraine's motive was money and power. Her ex-husband's second family had more than she and her son and maybe that pissed her off. Lorraine was ripe for situational resentment. Secretaries sometimes saw themselves as the other wife. Maybe she resented him marrying Gina.

I went over the way it must have gone down. Lorraine called Jerry to meet her at the office on Thursday night to go over a discrepancy she'd found in the books. Martha drove to the Windover office to talk to Jerry about the children. He got in her car, she shot him. Maybe Lorraine, hiding in the back, tossed something over his head first. Maybe Lorraine shot him. They drove to a secluded spot, tied weights on him and threw him in a river. Or buried him in a shallow grave and disposed of the gun provided by Victor. Lorraine and Martha both had to be in the car because one of them couldn't move Jerry.

Or they drove to a secluded spot where they were met by a boat and Victor spirited the body out to sea for a midnight burial. My money was on Victor and the boat, but however it happened, they returned to the office, staged it with the oatmeal, even having the foresight to imprint the bowl and spoon with fingerprints and saliva from Jerry. Then they texted Gina on his phone. Next morning, Lorraine swung by the office on the way to the doctor and texted Gina with Jerry's cell phone again. Over the weekend she disposed of the phone and the phony will. On Monday Lorraine reported Jerry missing.

I was sure a crime had been committed. Jerry hadn't just taken off. I thought of all the planning this crime involved, research of the previous case of the missing man who turned up, the timing, the risks. Lorraine had left her twelve-year-old son alone. Martha left her children sleeping for several hours. Maybe she even gave them something to help them sleep. She and Lorraine took a chance that nothing would happen to their kids while they were away, no house fires, no break-ins, no unexpected visitors. Martha probably covered the car's seat with plastic for the blood spatter from a head shot. What about the dashboard and door? I found nothing with the Luminol but the dash might be slightly tacky. Martha is an artist used to working with craft materials and she's a baker. Black tape? Non-stick spray? Jerry wouldn't have noticed either in the dark. The inside bulb would've been unscrewed.

It was a tangled web and I had unraveled it, but I had no proof. I was sure of one thing: Jerry would not be coming back. He was not in Mexico or Moorea or Madagascar. I was also sure Victor had set the plot in motion. He was a man who knew how to find the weak spot in people, a prime manipulator. He wound them all up in his desire to secure Gina. Lorraine was an aggrieved single mom who needed money. Victor seduced her with it. He planned the crime with her. She knew everything about Jerry. Maybe Millbanks had refused her the raise she needed. Maybe Jerry decided to move to Bali. She needed that job. Losing her mooring was enough to unhinge her. Victor offered opportunity. She typed the phony will, showed it to Martha to involve her, sent a couple of texts and made phone calls. Victor provided the gun. She could tell herself she was doing the right thing, enabling Martha to hold onto what should be her children's by removing Jerry from the scene. Lorraine and Martha, in their eyes, were protecting their children.

I reported my suspicions to the captain.

"I like Lorraine for the shooter. It would have been easier that way. If Martha pulled out the gun to shoot him, he could've grabbed it in the close quarters of the car's front seat. Blood spatter would be a problem. A shot in the back of the head would be unexpected and neater."

The captain had seen everything on the job but never anything like this case where each of the people involved enabled the others like clockwork figures. When the cog turned, they acted: Gina the lure, Victor the gun and goodies, Lorraine the bogus will, Martha the car, Lorraine the gunshot, Victor the disposal.

"Are you sure they didn't slip up somehow?"

"Not that I can find. I checked all possible traffic cams. They must have known which streets to avoid. If a body ever surfaces and the murder weapon turns up, maybe we can make a case, but for now Jerry Millbanks, Esquire, is a missing person. A person who wasn't missed for almost four days. Not much of an epitaph for a man."

Captain Rayles looked at me for a moment. "Nope, but we're almost always the authors of those epitaphs."

I wondered where those words came from, the job or his personal life. Not my business. I moved on to the next case and noticed I wasn't missing Elaine, but I sure wished I had some of those cranberry cookies. In a gallery I paid cash for one of Martha's paintings of Orchard Beach with children in the foreground playing in the sand. I hung it over the TV where I could look out on the far, wide sea of possibilities beyond the low islands.

Elaine would probably call it fake but she would be wrong.

Brenda Seabrooke is the author of 23 books for young readers including 2016's SCONES AND BONES ON BAKER STREET: SHERLOCK'S DOG (maybe) AND THE DIRT DILEMA and 17 literary and mystery stories. Awards include a grant from the National Endowment for the Arts, and Edgar finalist for CEMETERY STREET, a fellowship from Emerson College, and NCSS honor, Boston Globe-hornbook honor, IRA Children's Choice.

BURNING BRIGHT

Vicki Weisfeld

You couldn't miss those two shiny bikes lying helter-skelter in a grassy patch above the Peshtigo River. I parked the Intrepid and took the path through the thin line of trees. The kids had skidded down the river bank, and I followed. Two kids and a dog.

Though the Peshtigo has some of Wisconsin's best whitewater, along here the greenish-brown water moves slow, heavy with silt and, though the bank is steep, below it a sandy flat makes for easy walking. Excited kid voices and a single bark told me which way to go. I kept clear of the scraggly brush—didn't dare rip my new uniform.

A boy threw a stick into the water, and the dog, some golden lab in him, joyfully returned it. They were twelve or thirteen, faces not yet sealed up by adolescence. One was tall and skinny, the other average size, red hair, aggressive freckles.

"Hey," I said. I smelled tobacco smoke, though the cigarette disappeared before I got close.

"Hey," they said.

The dog clambered onto the bank and showered them with river water before ambling over. I went down on my haunches, rubbed his wet head, and praised him, admiring his friendly brown eyes. "Nice dog."

"He's Jake," the lanky boy said. "We just got him. From the shelter."

"Jake? That's why he looks familiar! I volunteer there. Jake's a sweetheart. Aren't you, boy? I'm glad he's found a home. You ever have a dog before?"

The boy nodded. "My dog died."

"Sorry to hear that." I sat on a rock, awkward with my duty belt. "I'm Deputy Light. You boys have names?"

"Yes, sir," the redhead said, flustered. His pal elbowed him and hissed, "Yes, ma'am."

"Yes, ma'am," the redhead amended. "I'm Mike. He's Ben."

"We know your grandfather," Ben said.

"No kidding." Everyone in Marinette County knows Harry Light. And everyone—even family—calls him Harry.

"Harry fixed my bike. We paid him though."

"Really?" I said.

"Yeah. We weeded his tomatoes."

"Worked off your debt, huh?" That sounded like Harry.

256

"That's right," Ben said.

We sat quietly and watched the lazy water. Jake nudged the stick closer to Ben's leg, and he threw it. A painted turtle crawled onto a thick tree branch poking out of the water.

"I came down here to suggest you boys find a better place for your bikes. Anyone driving River Road can see them and might decide to carry them off."

"Yes, ma'am." Ben ground his sneaker's toe in the dirt, knocking pebbles into the water.

Jake yawned mightily, pink tongue flapping, and settled down between me and the boys. A heron stalked the shallows near the far bank, plunged its long neck into the water and came up, a fish speared on its beak. It flipped that fish right into its gullet.

"Awesome," Mike said.

"Having a good summer?" I asked.

"We came to see the tiger!" Mike blurted.

"A tiger? Here?" Maybe that wasn't cigarette smoke I whiffed.

"No, back there." He pointed behind him. "We've been watching for it through the trees."

Back there was a strip of field, then a trio of ranch houses on two-acre lots. My aunt's best friend lives in one, but she's more the housecat type.

"No kidding!" I said.

"This kid? From school? He lives up there with his brothers, and they're getting a tiger, but first they're building a big pen with a really strong fence, and they have to put a ceiling on it, like, made out of fence stuff, so the tiger can't jump out." Once Mike got going, he was a talker.

"Wow!" I said. "That's exciting!"

"So we want to see if it's there yet," Ben said.

"Why don't you just go to your friend's house and ask?"

"Because," Mike said, displaying the infinite patience needed when explaining the world to adults, "Tay isn't supposed to tell anyone."

"Tay. You mean Taylor Grace? His brothers are Dwayne and Cal?" A bad feeling crept over me.

"Yeah. You won't get him in trouble?"

"Absolutely not. I'd like to see that tiger myself. Beautiful animals." I struggled to my feet. "Let's find a better hiding place for those bikes."

I couldn't believe bureaucratic judgment could lapse so far as to allow the Grace brothers to own an exotic animal. I pulled my Intrepid all the way up their rutted driveway, and there they were, working on that pen. No mistaking these two are brothers. Early twenties, same long greasy hair, same ratty beard, same big and tall wardrobe, but while Cal's eyes betrayed his crafty nature, everything about Dwayne was slow, like the blood in his veins ran too thick.

"Hello, Dwayne. Hello, Cal."

257

For sure they weren't glad to see me. I'd arrested them for cockfighting back in March. Cost them some jail time. Now they were all smiles and shuffling, so naturally I was on my guard.

"Deputy Light. How you doin?" Cal asked.

"Just fine. What're you boys up to?" I nodded at the rolls of chain-link and the pile of eight-foot posts. Corner posts with a few in between marked out a square about twenty feet on a side. A portable cement mixer turned lazily.

"Building a pen for our tiger!" Dwayne said. Cal tries, but hasn't yet squashed the boy out of Dwayne.

"Your tiger? No kidding! That's exciting. Where's your tiger now?"

"It ain't come yet," Dwayne said, avoiding his brother's glare.

"We've got the papers we need," Cal said. "Don't need a license."

"Mind if I take a peek?"

"Them papers are OK," he said, not moving.

"I'm sure. But I've never seen that particular paperwork before. Must be complicated."

"That's for damn sure," Dwayne said.

I smiled at Cal, holding his gaze until he stomped into the house, swearing just loud enough for me to hear it. I turned my smile on Dwayne. "What gave you this idea?"

"We met this dude in a bar said he knows a dude in Green Bay selling a tiger cheap. It'll bring in a lot of money!"

"I'll bet! How so?"

"People will pay good money to see a tiger up close."

"You mean, like admission?"

Cal reappeared, waving a couple of sheets.

"I give you boys credit." I held out my hand. "This project takes imagination!"

A pickup truck rattled up the drive. Its radio blared the Zac Brown Band but shut off quick when the occupants saw my vehicle. Cal hurried over, and out of his view I snapped pictures of the papers with my phone. I went to stand next to Dwayne.

"How much does a tiger eat?" I asked.

"Twenty pounds of meat a day."

"No kidding!"

"They're big."

"How will you feed it and all? I wouldn't want you boys to get hurt."

"See, the pen will have a sliding wall that cuts it in half." He gestured to show me. "We just roll that in place and go in the part the tiger isn't in."

"Clever," I said. Dwayne nodded. "Sounds like you and Cal have thought of everything."

The pickup driver gunned his engine. Scattering gravel, he backed down to River Road.

"Here you go." I handed Cal the papers. "When will you be set up? I'd like to see that tiger myself." I pictured a sad, underfed, under-exercised, moth-eaten old guy. No king of the jungle. Made my heart hurt.

"Four weeks. More or less."

"Very exciting." I climbed into the Intrepid. I had maybe a month to try and stop this.

On my way through town, I turned onto Oconto Avenue, where Harry lives, past the Peshtigo Fire Museum. He was digging in a flower-bed.

"Hold on a minute, Deputy Light." He firmed dirt around a few new perennials. "There. Come inside. I put up a pot of coffee. Help me drink it."

Harry's unfailing hospitality helps explain why friends, neighbors, and his deputy sheriff granddaughter make his place a regular stop. We sat in his bright kitchen enjoying the coffee and a neighbor-lady's corn muffins.

"Harry," I hesitated. "Have you thought about the assisted living place I mentioned?"

"Thought about it. Made my decision." He leaned away from me.

I raised my eyebrows.

"Maybe not never, Carrie, but not now."

"But if you think you might want to move there sometime, you should do it while you've got plenty of health to enjoy it, time to make friends."

"I have friends."

No doubt about that. Harry just had his eighty-fifth birthday, and the hall table was crowded with cards and gifts—gear from his fishing buddies, garden gloves, a CD of John Barry movie themes, and I don't know what-all.

"Yes, and thank goodness you *do* feel great, but this house and the yard…I worry it will get to be too much."

"Keeps me young. I look forward to spring, the garden in the summer, and fall when the leaves turn. It's good. Don't worry."

"The leaves at Acorn Manor change too, you know." I rubbed an invisible spot on the tablecloth.

"They aren't MY leaves on MY trees that your grandmother and I planted sixty years ago."

"Just think about it."

"I will, if you stop pestering me."

I understood that. The whole family digs in when pressured. I'd have to change tactics.

I ran into Chief Deputy Tom Redhail at our ancient coffee machine and told him about the tiger. "The thought of those two idiots managing a six-hundred-pound wild animal sends shivers up my spine."

259

He said he'd register our concerns with the state wildlife office, but if the brothers met the few requirements, that would be that. Those guys didn't know the Graces like we did.

"Then we need stricter requirements," I said. "Is it ignorance or indifference that allows such a thing?"

"I don't know and I don't care," he said, making me laugh out loud. "You're just down on them because they're a couple of pornography-selling, animal-abusing, low-life drunks."

"You saying I'm too fastidious?"

"You don't have to marry them, Carina, just keep them this side of the law." He grinned.

"Has that *ever* happened?"

"Why we call them the Dis-Graces. What's your next move?"

"Chat with their neighbor. A church buddy of my Aunt Joan's."

"OK, Deputy. Just remember, they may be dumb, but they're dangerous. Cal especially. He's a mean s.o.b."

Later, in Redhail's cramped office, I gave him the surprising news my aunt's friend Charlene had shared. She said the Graces had caught a bear, and stashed it somewhere off-premises.

"Are you thinking what I'm thinking?" I asked, studying the awards tacked to the pine paneling.

"Don't like the drift of it, by a damn sight. What're *you* thinking? Specifically?"

"Remember Dwayne described how the pen can be divided in half? What if half is for the tiger and half for the bear? After they're both in there getting on each other's nerves, the boys will slide that divider out and let nature take its course. That's how they'll get the big bucks."

"Make a helluva lot more than cock-fighting."

"That was chickenfeed."

For the next few weeks I kept tabs on the slow progress of the Graces' do-it-yourself construction project from the woods by the river. They weren't skilled workmen, and I figured they'd cut corners, make it only as strong as they thought it needed to be. If I was right about the fight, it would be a one and done. They wouldn't keep a tiger hanging around eating twenty pounds of meat a day. They'd dispose of it. And the bear? They'd just turn him loose. If either animal survived.

I ran into Ben and Mike again too. Mike showed me a picture Tay had sent him, a grinning eight-year-old standing by a cage. The bear inside looked at least five times his weight.

"Tay looks super-excited," I said.

"Yeah. That bear is ginormous."

Aunt Joan was delighted to be "assisting with a police investigation," and she was key to the proposal I had for her friend Charlene. Driving over to Charlene's house, I brought up the subject close to my heart. "You know, Joan, your father isn't getting any younger. I think Harry should move into assisted living where people can look out for him."

"Forget it, Carina. He won't consider it. You or I look in on him all the time. So do people from church and the neighbors. He's fine where he is."

"But what if he fell in the night or something? Getting to the bathroom?" I'd seen what that was like more than once, when our office got called after a couple days.

"Get him one of those emergency call things."

"But what if—"

"Face it. He's not going. Harry does not want to be stuck with a lot of old folks. He wants to be in his own place, with his own stuff. His tools and projects."

"Well, obviously, he'd have his own furniture and pictures on the walls and everything. Acorn Manor is not jail."

"They're not *his* walls. He wouldn't have his workbench. He'd miss his garden. His neighbors. His walks to the store. Leave him be."

"But what if he gets sick?" My voice went up a half-octave.

"Then we'll deal with it. Your grandfather has lived his whole life free and independent. Had his own business, never nine-to-five. He won't change. That's who he is."

We'd arrived, so I let it drop and tucked a brochure for Acorn Manor into Aunt Joan's handbag.

As soon as I'd learned about the bear, Tom and I updated Sheriff Lacy. That wily old lawman saw the potential for disaster at once and had us start some contingency planning with the lieutenant in charge of investigations. At first I had to elbow my way into these strategy sessions, but Tom backed me up. Ultimately, we three shared responsibilities.

The lieutenant arranged for an undercover from the Marinette city police department to hang out in the bars the Dis-Graces favored. He picked up rumors of something big happening in a few weeks, but the regulars clammed up when he tried to get details. Over in Michigan, though, a couple of roadhouse geezers did spill. The fight was real, all right, and scheduled for the last Saturday in August. The tiger might be legal, but the fight was definitely not.

We could warn the Dis-Graces, but we figured that would just force the event further underground. We could raise one technicality after another regarding the tiger, but ultimately state law was on their side. Catching them in the act was our best—and by far the riskiest—option.

Though we're a mostly rural county, our department has sixteen deputies, many with SWAT training. We'd need them all, plus double that number from Marinette and Peshtigo. The sheriff "liaised" with the Wisconsin state troopers—the kind of shoot-the-shit activity he loved—while I put various pieces in place.

We hoped all this was unnecessary, but on the last Friday in August, Charlene called to say a big unmarked truck had arrived at the Graces. Now she'd spend the weekend with Aunt Joan. As to the third family living along there, we were putting them up at a resort in Door County, right on Lake Michigan. No way they'd turn that down. They were ready to go and did.

I promised Charlene I'd take good care of her kitties and was over there early Saturday opening a can of cat food. A roar rolled down from the Graces' yard, an unbelievably powerful roar that ended in a scream, a roar that made my hair stand on end. I had to set the can on the counter until I caught my breath. The tabbies that had been twining themselves around my ankles were long gone, and even the purr of the can opener didn't bring them back.

Mid-afternoon, Sheriff Lacy pulled his car into the double garage alongside mine. With him was Jon Cermak from the state Division of Criminal Investigation. Cermak brought a drone.

"Really? A drone?" I put my hands over my ears.

"Quadcopter," Cermak corrected me. "And this baby? At night? Quieter than the bugs."

Cermak and the sheriff were big boys with a new toy. The drone had a regular camera with an infrared attachment that could look right down in that pen, day or night. When I pointed out Charlene's fondness for her large collection of ceramic cats, they were persuaded not to fly the thing in the living room. They disappeared into the garage.

Another truck rumbled up the Graces' driveway about five. Judging by the racket from their back yard, bear and tiger were not friendly neighbors.

Though we minimized the number of vehicles, Charlene's house was full. We had Sheriff Lacy, Tom Redhail, and me, Cermak and his drone, the lieutenant, three guys from the Department of Natural Resources—the DNR—and two veterinarians from the Milwaukee County Zoo. Plus a county social worker napping in Charlene's guest room.

The vets would anesthetize the animals so they could be taken away safely. We'd have to get the vets right up to the pen so they could do that, but if everything went well, the tiger would go back with them to Milwaukee, and the DNR guys would take charge of the bear.

We also had a perimeter team involving the other county deputies, who would arrest as many spectators as possible. Before dark, they began gathering two miles away in Governor Thompson State Park, closed for the afternoon, thanks to my sweet-talking. We'd borrowed a couple of buses from the Department of Corrections, and they'd transport the arrestees to our temporary processing center. Child and Family Services had a van there too.

"Why bother arresting spectators?" a DNR man asked.

262

"They won't be candidates for Citizen of the Year," I said. "We can probably hold a bunch of them on missed child support, parole violations, outstanding warrants, whatever—at least for a while. Making them mad will guarantee the Graces never try a stunt like this again." That's what I wanted, and I convinced the sheriff to want it too.

The sheriff smiled and folded his hands over his belly. "Cal and Dwayne might even have to relocate out of my county."

There was pile of pizzas in the kitchen, but I couldn't eat. Food would sit in my stomach like a box of bullets. Taking the last slice, the sheriff asked me, "What's your worst-case?"

"Cal fucks up, or Dwayne panics, or their construction is crap and one of these wild animals gets loose and everybody and his brother starts shooting."

The zoo doctor spoke up. "Mine is that my aim is bad and the dart misses or doesn't take effect, and I have to use this." He pointed to a rifle, on the floor by his chair.

"You're not shooting that if there's people around," Sheriff Lacy said.

"Then you'll have to."

My stomach turned over.

"Who'd risk keeping a tiger!" Cermak wondered aloud. A little late to the party, I thought.

"What we say is, more tigers live in U.S. backyards than in the wild," said the zoo man.

"That's nuts."

"Dangerous for people and cruel to the animals. Tigers that have lived in captivity—maybe were born in a cage—can't go back to the wild."

The DNR man spoke up. "But the bear, if he was caught recently, he's still wild and knows how to take care of himself. We can release him where he won't get into trouble. We'll collar and track him awhile to be sure."

Knowing these two dangerous animals were so nearby had everyone on edge. That and the fact that the Graces' acquaintances would almost certainly have guns, since Wisconsin gives a gun license to practically anyone who breathes. With such a high possibility for mayhem, we had to move in force and shut this down fast.

After dark, the guys test drove the drone. Watching the operator's tablet screen, we gasped when the animals came into view. The infrared picked them up clearly—the tiger pacing, unmistakably cat-like on one side of the divided pen, and the bear hunkered in a far corner on the other. Judging by their snarling racket, they were acutely aware of each other.

"The brothers must be in the house. No heat sigs from people," Sheriff Lacy said.

For hours we waited, with only those few lights a widow living alone might keep burning.

The lieutenant emerged from a dark bedroom. "Any reason seven vehicles in three minutes would be creeping down this road, lights off, at"—he checked his watch—"one-forty?"

"Just one," said Sheriff Lacy.

Moonlight revealed more pickup trucks, beds full of men. Someone passed word the Graces' had switched on their floodlights, lighting up their back yard like noon.

As if a spigot had been turned, SUVs and pickup trucks streamed along River Road. We heard gravel crunching and excited shouts.

"Get the drone ready," the sheriff said, and called the park. "Get the Bearcat moving and deploy the perimeter. Have the auxiliaries ready to close the road, but tell them to stay out of sight until my signal. You've got eight minutes to get here."

The Bearcat—an armored personnel carrier our department owned courtesy of the Pentagon—would block the Graces' driveway. A county road crew had recently cleared and deepened the ditch all along there—more of my sweet-talking. Anyone who tried to drive around the Bearcat would be plenty sorry.

The social worker emerged from a bedroom, yawning. "I needed that. I've got a two-month old. My usual bedtime is nine o'clock. What's happening?"

"It's going down," I said.

"My partner and I will take charge of Tay and any other juveniles. Where can I pump my milk?"

I pointed her back to the bedroom.

"God," said DNR. "Who'd bring kids to something like this?" We looked at him. "Right."

When traffic to the Graces' petered out, the sheriff hit the start button. Metaphorically. Before long, we heard the Bearcat rumble. Cermak sent the drone up again and found scores of vehicles parked, their passengers spilling out. A couple hundred people crowded all around the pen. Worst case. We'd hoped one side would stay kind of clear.

The sheriff, the chief deputy, the lieutenant, and I left from Charlene's back porch, the five animal experts tight behind us. As we jogged toward the brightly-lit yard, my adrenaline was pumping so hard I couldn't even feel my feet touch the ground.

The spectators were packed together, their backs to us. Every man of them was bigger than me, and the smell of beer and cigarettes was strong. I put on my meanest face and held my baton as if I was ready to use it, which I was.

When the guys at the back of the crowd realized who we were, a few of them shunted aside, grumbling. Shoulder to shoulder, we carved a swath through the mass of people surrounding us. I turned and edged backwards, watching for drawn weapons. Over the din came one of those massive roars. It sounded like the tiger was right on top of us. I recalled who'd built that fence, and sweat popped out every pore.

"Move it, you crazy fuckers," Tom Redhail yelled. "It's not happening!"

And me following up with "Move it! Move! Go on!" I called out the names of the men I recognized, some I'd known since high school. "What the hell are you thinking?"

Once we reached the fence, we all stood with our backs to it, and the zoo folks got busy. The shot at the tiger must have been right on the money, because I'm told he turned around a couple of times and dropped.

We sidled along the fence to get closer to the bear—a he, as it turned out—and the closer we got, the worse the smell. Fear and bear-funk. "Doesn't want to get close to that tiger," the zoo vet yelled above the din. Moving was a little easier as men headed to their vehicles. They didn't realize it yet, but our deputies and SWAT unit were waiting. I heard later some of them ran across the field toward the woods, and the perimeter guys soon had them cuffed to trees, slapping mosquitoes. I hadn't spotted Cal or Dwayne in all that commotion, which now included a rising tide of sirens and vehicle horns.

The zoo vet's first shot sent the bear into a frenzy, and he charged, which improved the aim of the second attempt. He came at us with such fury I was sure the pen wouldn't hold him, crashing into the fence right behind me. Scared to death, I turned to look as he toppled over.

Eight deputies carried that stinking bear into the tiger's side of the pen, then closed the partition and herded men into the empty half—an impromptu bus shelter. It tickled me to see how they really didn't want to go in there.

Tom and I figured Cal and Dwayne were hiding in the house. Tay was probably there too. Tom signaled me with a tip of his head, and he and I jogged in that direction. He gave me time to run around front, and I flattened myself against the wall next to the door. Tom yelled, "Sheriff!" then kicked in the back door. Sure enough, the front door swung slowly inward, and a shotgun barrel appeared. When Cal's belly followed it, I shoved my gun deep in the soft flesh under his ribs. "Drop it! You need this liver."

Cal gave the matter some thought, taking in the Bearcat and the dozens of police out front, and when I pushed harder, he let his weapon fall. From inside, Dwayne wailed.

"Step into the yard," I ordered, and Cal walked a dozen steps forward. I called to a deputy nearby, and he covered Cal while I cuffed him. Tom came out with Dwayne, hands on top of his head. Cuffed him too.

"Not the buses," I said. "Send them in a cruiser."

Tay stood on the porch, wide-eyed, face crumpling.

I walked over and said, "We have someone to look after you until this gets sorted out."

"They shot my tiger," he wailed.

"Oh, no. That was to make him sleep so they can take him to the zoo. You know what anesthesia is?"

He nodded, tears streaming.

"When he's safe, they'll wake him up again."

Over the cacophony of men yelling, the Bearcat rumbling, the first bus's departure, and the police sirens came the *whack-whack* of a helicopter. It

265

hovered, then descended behind the house. "There's his ride now. Courtesy of the state patrol. Want to watch?"

Deputies hustled the Dis-Grace brothers away, and I walked Tay to the back, where the last of the prisoners was squeezing into the pen. They got a nice blast of grit from the chopper rotors. A medi-vac team brought out a long spine board, and the zoo and wildlife guys secured the tiger to it and loaded it through the helicopter's back bay.

"He's going to a zoo where they'll take good care of him. He'll have the right food to eat and room to run around. He'll be safe. Tigers aren't pets. You know that, don't you?"

Tay sniffed. "The bear?"

I looked behind me, and there was the DNR transport, coming up the drive. The Bearcat must have made way.

"In good hands. You understand this whole thing was a *really* bad idea, right?"

In a tiny voice he said, "Kind of." He let go of my hand and jogged to a card table by the driveway, returning with a Spiderman backpack.

Inside was a pile of $50 and $100 bills—about $25,000, in fact. After some finagling by Sheriff Lacy, the Milwaukee County Zoo received the money, a healthy dent in the bill for the tiger's rescue and rehab. County residents were mighty unhappy about the whole dangerous escapade. Lots of media attention too. Maybe some good will come of it.

Mountains of paperwork later, I found Jake in Harry's back yard, guarding a chipmunk hole. I gave his head a rubdown and located Harry in the basement with the boys, fixing Ben's bicycle headlight. The three of them asked a million questions.

"Sounds like you did a good thing there," Harry concluded. "Proud of you, Deputy."

"I had an excellent tip." I winked at the boys.

"Where's Tay?" Mike asked.

"With his aunt in Green Bay. He's stayed with her before, and she'll try to keep him this time."

They helped Harry return his tools to the pegboard, each one's shape outlined with yellow paint. I wasn't aware my mind was going in this direction until I said, "The tiger can't ever live in the wild, but the bear maybe can. They're working on it."

"Sad," he said. "Living in cages. Regimented. Not like on my birthday CD." He sang the chorus of "Born Free" as he shined the headlamp lens, then gave the cloth a snap. "Like new. Now you boys know your assignment?"

"Yessir," Ben said. "Move five wheelbarrows of mulch."

"Right."

I couldn't quite put my finger on what was bothering me. Was it that I'd wanted Harry to leave all this or that he was so determined to stay? Or was I just exhausted? Whatever, I turned away, said "Coffee," and ran up the basement stairs before he could see me cry. Acorn Manor would just have to wait—forever, I hoped.

Vicki Weisfeld's short stories have appeared in *Ellery Queen Mystery Magazine* (three times), *Betty Fedora*—"kickass women in crime fiction" Yes!—the literary magazine *Big Muddy*, and elsewhere. She's debriding a pair of novels and maintains an active website that includes book, movie, and theater reviews, topics for writers, and grist for the creative mill: www.vweisfeld.com. She's a reviewer for the UK website crimefictionlover.com and thefrontrowcenter.com (theater).

TRUTH, GRACE AND LIES

A.B. Polomski

I worked on an all-male squad, knee-deep in testosterone-fueled male egos. It was no waltz across the dance floor but neither was chasing down old ladies' complaints of prowling rapists. Toms River didn't have much use for detectives, but I hoped the job would be a stepping stone to a more active situation elsewhere. I wanted a gold shield and this town, I guessed, was as good a place to start working for the reward as anywhere.

I sat in a squad car with Bill Lempinen, a career cop content with street patrol, a nine-to-fiver at heart. I'd nicknamed Bill "Officer Love" because he'd once mentioned Lempinen meant "love" in Finnish. Love was forty-two but looked like he'd been living dog years with a balding head, sun-cured face and a hefty paunch.

Love was a talker. Over the course of our shift, I'd learned the life history of Love, his wife Angie, son Billy Junior, daughter Ivy, Love's mother, his father, Love's sister, and what he thought of every hitter for the New York Yankees starting with Joe DiMaggio with leaps back to Tony Lazzeri, Bob Meusel and Earle Comps.

When I tuned in, Love was giving air to his deep-seated philosophical belief that everybody lies.

"Not me," I said. "Not even for the purpose of standard politeness." The truth is meaningful. Not everything in life is.

"Not only the lawbreakers," Love went on. "The vics too. To hide the stupid things they did to get victimized."

"What about witnesses?"

"Come on, Andrews. They lie to cover their butts. No one wants to look stupid. You think I'm lying?"

Before I could answer, the radio burped. "What's your 20?" asked a dispatcher's voice.

I thumbed down the mike and reported we were on thirty-seven eastbound. A response scratched through dead air. I pressed the button that activated the siren and the light bar. Love drove.

It was three minutes past five in the afternoon on an early November day and already dark. Love pulled onto the scene, a busy side street not far from an elementary school. He drew a digital camera from his jacket pocket.

A middle-aged guy, quarterback tall with a military build, jumped out of a Navigator and powered toward us, long legs eating up the space. "The kid ran in front of my vehicle. What the hell was I supposed to do?"

Navigator man reeked of alcohol but sounded lucid. Adrenaline could increase alertness but wouldn't sober up a drunk. Love, roaring like a dinosaur, ordered him back to his vehicle.

I crouched beside the small body, wishing there was someone better equipped to help the victim. Where were the paramedics?

A gangly girl knelt at the other side of the prostrate child. I made her for the older sister. She was dressed in a too small, dirty blue bubble coat and had a cell phone in one hand. Tears skimmed her pale cheeks.

"What's his name?" I asked. She tried to say something and couldn't make it happen. Shock setting in. Where was backup?

The boy, lying in the well-lit street, was perhaps nine. I took his hand and his eyes opened like the weighted lids of a doll and locked on mine. "You're gonna be okay, buddy," I said. A low moan broken by a bubble of blood spilled over the boy's lips. "Don't try to talk." I felt for a pulse. Faint. It fluttered away, as if the pressure from my fingers stilled it. The paramedics arrived and began working. Someone wrapped a blanket around the teenage girl. Love and I watched the boy's small body lifted onto a stretcher and into the ambulance. Everyone did their job as if on automatic pilot, without emotion. Exactly as trained.

Something let go in the girl and she began to heave and moan. "It's my fault. I let him bring that ball!" Her eyes met mine. "How am I going to explain?"

"What's your name?"

"Hannah."

"Hannah, it wasn't your fault," I assured her before the ambulance door closed on her storm of sobbing.

The ambulance that took the victim's sister to the hospital had lights and sirens going. Nicky's ambulance didn't.

"The guy in the Navigator," Love said. "Hugh Cannon, according to his license. Says he wouldn't do a breathalyzer unless I arrested him. I said I'd be happy to and he blew a point one three. We can nail him."

I reassembled myself, became bland, and walked to the Navigator. I pegged the guy for fifty or fifty-five. He was big, health club tanned, and dressed in a tuxedo. His long dark hair was slicked back with something sticky looking. Pathetic and arrogant don't generally go together, but he managed to look both down in the mouth and superior at the same time.

"That kid ran into the street," Cannon said. "Never looked. It could have happened to anyone."

Cannon didn't ask whether the kid was going to make it. "How much have you had to drink, sir," I asked, my voice friendly.

"I'm a diabetic." Cannon took a brown pill bottle off the passenger seat and rattled it. "Low blood sugar."

Too much insulin and not enough sugar in the blood could cause the acetone production in the breath and lead to a false positive. I doubted Cannon suffered from diabetes or hypoglycemia but I kept my face blank and my emotions to myself. "I'm going to administer a field sobriety test, Mr. Cannon," I said, like he'd won a prize.

"I'm sorry," he said, not sounding sorry at all, "but the kid ran out. What was I supposed to do?"

"Mr. Cannon, please exit your vehicle and walk for me." I made it sound like refusing was going to hurt my feelings. "Nine heel-to-toe steps along this line."

He looked at me and smiled ruefully. "For the record, I'm politely refusing the FST which is as accurate as a coin toss. I'll wait for my attorney."

Love told him that passing the field sobriety test would set him free. A lie and all three of us knew it. Again, Cannon politely refused.

"Delivering notification of death in tragic circumstances...it's the toughest job any officer's got to do," our chief-of-police liked to say. Tougher still was being on the receiving end of a "death in tragic circumstances notification." A police officer knocked on my mother's door when I was eleven. Cap pressed to his chest, he told her my brother, Evan, had died.

A minute before he'd arrived, I'd called my brother's cell phone. A nameless morgue technician who answered told me he'd pulled that particular phone out of the pocket of a guy who'd died of a massive head trauma and internal bleeding. "Blood alcohol through the roof." I hadn't understood, thought it was a joke until Officer Dan Mackie showed up at our back door.

Mackie delivered the news that my brother's car hit a tree. Perhaps trying to evade another vehicle. Possibly a drunk driver. We'd never know the whole truth, and he was very sorry for our loss.

He knew Evan and that my brother had been a great kid. "A year of Yale under his belt. Well, how many kids from this town even go to college at all? I'm really sorry, Clara. And you too." He nodded at me.

My brother's death put a wrecking ball through our lives. The lie Mackie told to protect my mother mythologized my brother, and my mother never looked at me the same way.

Evan had been a champion wrestler and an Olympic hopeful. The living room of our house had a wrestling mat instead of a carpet. Before he died, my father had a weight training set installed in the garage. I was eight years younger than my brother. Evan taught me to wrestle before I could walk. I spent my youth body slamming Evan and his friends, full nelsoning most of them, wrenching their arms behind their backs like hairpins, before I was nine. I wonder sometimes if they let me win. I loved my brother.

An hour later, I stood on the doorstep of a modest white Cape Cod and rang the bell. The door was opened by a young woman in a waitress uniform. "Ms. Morris?"

"I'm Melanie Morris." She was dark-haired, oval-faced with straight black hair, bangs, and no makeup. Her shoulders acted like hangers for her gravy-spotted uniform.

270

"May I come in, Ms. Morris? I have some bad news."

She put down a cell phone she'd been fiddling with. "If you're here because I'm using—it's not true." She motioned me inside. "Take a look. I'm not lying. I don't want my son taken away." She glanced at her cell phone. "If I'm late for work, I'll lose my job."

The place smelled of cigarettes and unwashed clothes and faintly of mothballs. It looked like it had been furnished in the late fifties and frozen, then littered with toys. I could see the living room, a cabbage rose sofa and end tables draped in doilies. The kitchen was the size of a large bathtub. The appliances were old, the white enamel chipped and rusting in places, the linoleum floor cracked. "Could you please sit down? I'm here about your son, Nicky."

"What about my son?" Her voice vibrated with the frazzled energy of a single parent. "Nicky's with Hannah. His babysitter."

I touched her shoulder and made her sit. I told her how the ball had gotten away, how Nicky ran off without thinking, how kids his age did that, how the driver of the Navigator couldn't stop.

"That's not possible. Hannah watches him. She's young, I know, but her mother, she helps..." Melanie Morris' body started to shake.

"Hannah stayed with him. She tried to help."

"Is Nicky going to be all right?"

"Your son's skull was fractured upon impact. He died. I'm so sorry."

I watched confusion spread, then her struggle against a tidal wave of anguish.

"I know this is hard, but I'll need you to identify his body. Is there someone who can come with you?"

Sweat broke over Melanie's forehead. She held a hand over her mouth, tore to the sink, and jackknifed to let go of a stream of vomit.

After she rinsed her mouth, she turned to me, glassy eyed and dazed. I offered her a paper napkin. She didn't take it.

"What about the driver?" she asked in a distant voice.

"Under arrest." And out on bail.

"A drunk driver?"

"It looks that way. Is there someone who can come with you?"

She shook her head.

"Nicky's father?"

Melanie clenched her fists and held them in her lap. "I have no one."

Hugh Cannon, the Navigator driver, did have someone. A top-shelf lawyer few people could afford.

"He was legally drunk and he killed a child," I argued. Glenda Walden, the township's chief prosecutor stared at me as if I'd asked her to stand on her head and juggle jelly beans. "Okay, what about the breathalyzer? He blew twice the legal limit. He reeked of alcohol."

"The breath of a person who downs a non-alcoholic beer will smell the same as that of a person who's had an alcoholic one. Also, research has proven that odor strength estimates are unrelated to blood alcohol concentration."

"Right," I said. Glenda, despite her sweet name and good looks, was wickedly intelligent, a trait easy to overlook until she opened her mouth.

"Estimates made by experienced law enforcement officers are no more accurate than random guesses," Glenda said. "And your guy's attorney will argue that a major problem with breath analyzers is that they not only identify the ethanol found in alcoholic beverages, but also other substances of similar molecular structure. Like mouthwash, cough medicines, blood or vomit in the mouth. Tobacco smoke."

"So what? We didn't find any of that on his person."

"Our friend could tell us he whiled away the afternoon spray painting his wine cellar. That could lead to a false positive."

"He's not going to do that," I said.

Glenda agreed. "Mr. Cannon has an airtight diabetes defense. I could take him to court, but he'll bury me in a biblical rain of expert witnesses. I don't have those kinds of resources, Grace. He'll win. He's won before."

"What are you talking about?"

"Vehicular homicide. He went through a highway median, blood alcohol twice the legal limit. His fiancée died in the crash. He got away with a few cuts and bruises. Her family sued. They got themselves a decent lawyer who brought the case before a jury. They awarded the fiancée's family a judgment of half a million dollars."

"So Cannon lost."

"And the plaintiffs can't collect a cent."

"Why not? Cannon's a wealthy guy. A hot shot executive in a financial firm with a top floor office with bomb-resistant glass and access to a corporate jet." I thought what it would take to kill a man like him. A jihadi terrorist with a bomb launcher? Even then I'd give Cannon better odds.

"Everything he owns is tied up in corporations and trusts. It could take years to unravel and trace, and by that time the whole settlement would be eaten up in legal fees."

"So what happens? Nothing?"

"He's pled 'not guilty.' We're going to accept his plea and hit him with a stiff fine which he'll probably wiggle out of paying and that's it. The mother can file a complaint in civil court."

"Have you met the mother? She's in no condition to file her nails."

The next time I laid eyes upon Hugh Cannon, he came by the police station to see me. Since he didn't remember my name, he asked to speak to "the uniform who looks like a cross between Scarlett Johansson and a teamster and is probably a lesbian."

"Make her leave me alone," he said. "I'm a tax-paying citizen."

272

Somehow I doubted that. "Who are you talking about?"

"That woman. Melanie Morris."

"The mother of the child you ran down?"

"If your medical people had gotten there faster, the damn kid would have lived. I hate what happened, but it's over. Why can't she get that?"

Because her child is dead. I thought of my mother and her shrine to Evan. A bedroom we never entered. A museum to a boyhood, a son and a brother. "And the problem is?"

"She's stalking me. And she's got some other bitch helping her. I can't go to a restaurant, the theater, not even a ball game." He started to run his hand through his sticky looking black hair and thought better of it. "Everywhere I go, I see her. In the morning, she's parked outside my health club. How am I supposed to live seeing her stupid face all the time? Stalking is a crime. Do your job."

"Stalking is conduct that would cause a reasonable person to fear bodily injury or death. You're afraid she's going to hurt you?"

"She's a known drug addict. Would you trust her?"

"Former drug addict. She's turned her life around." Because of her son.

"I don't care about any of that. I want her out of my sight."

"Get a restraining order," I said, "though a judge may rule that she's only exercising her right to free speech." Because Cannon and Melanie didn't have a previous relationship, there technically was no history of abuse. "Or spring for domestic security. Someone who can drive you around. Safer for everyone."

"Listen to me. I want her stopped." He pointed a finger pistol at my face and dropped the hammer. "I'm only going to ask you once."

"Before you go, Mr. Cannon, can I ask you something?"

He tried to think of a reason to say no.

"What's my name?"

He glanced at the block letters on my gold name plate and said, "I couldn't care less."

I didn't file a report or talk to Melanie.

The next time I saw Hugh Cannon, he was dead. When I heard he'd died in the bathroom of his Hoboken apartment, I offered to help with background.

Across the street from Cannon's place, the apartments were identical and old. Police barricades had been erected and half a dozen uniforms kept things under control. I got out of the way for EMTs who were taking the body to a waiting ambulance.

An elevator from the Jurassic period brought me to the seventh floor. Cannon had lived in a forties-style apartment with plaster arches between rooms and hardwood flooring. The place was vast by New York City standards. The windowless, white-tiled bathroom was about the size of a walk-in closet.

273

The detective on the scene, Jack Spence, was less than thrilled to see me. He had a reputation for closing cases, the faster the better, nice and neat with minimum outside interference and scant paperwork. "Including you in this party, what's in it for me?"

"The Ocean County Sheriff's Department has the finest CSI lab in the country, and I have friends who work there."

"I thought you were going to threaten me with bodily harm." He screamed like a Ninja on crack and karate chopped the air. "I spend a few nights heart-punching the heavy bag at the officer's gym."

"Good for you," I said and looked around, taking in the details of Cannon's bathroom which reeked of bleach and sour vomit. A heated towel rack with one empty rod looked odd. "Towel's missing. Was it on his body?"

"Nope. Naked as a worm, his back on the cold marble floor, feet facing the door."

"Any idea how it happened?" I asked.

"Looks as though he slipped and cracked his head sometime this morning. We'll know more when we get a lab report. Maybe a heart attack, poor bastard. Those three-hundred dollar steak power lunches washed down with top shelf scotch finally caught up with him."

"Women are more likely to vomit before a heart attack."

"That's not Cannon's puke. The cleaning woman's," he said, consulting a small notebook. "One Olga Prochorov hurled when the super finally got the door open. Olga kept wailing it was her fault. If only she'd found him sooner, blah, blah."

"Did she not know he was home?"

"Said she called out and there was no answer, so she went about her business, dusting, vacuuming and polishing."

"Why'd she call the super?"

"She has this regimen. Cleans the bathroom last. She tried the door and it wouldn't open. Maintenance jimmied it."

I took a tissue and turned the crystal knob. It went all the way around without catching. "Maintenance guy break the lock?" I asked.

"Super says he found it that way. Cleaning woman agrees." The detective blew an impressive honk into a dirty tissue. "I'm guessing heart attack. Fractured his skull on the marble floor. Case closed."

"With Cannon gone, who gets his money?"

The detective shrugged. "Not me or you so who cares?"

There was a foundation set up to liquidate and dole out Cannon's estate to a family trust and a few charities, none of which I'd have given an eyelash to, but hey, I'm not into Scientology or Cryopreservation. He also left a few thousand to a support group for people abducted by aliens. A joke. Probably.

A week later, I stared at a copy of a preliminary autopsy report. "Fatality shows sloughing of the bronchial columnar epithelium, purulent intraluminal exudate, hyaline membranes in the alveolar spaces, thrombi in the pulmonary vessels, and interstitial and alveolar pulmonary edema."

"What does all this mean?" Love asked. He'd been reading over my shoulder.

"Come on, Love. You went to nursing school."

"For about a month until I met my wife. What's it mean?"

"It's what happens to your respiratory system when you inhale chlorine gas. The gas shreds your nasal passages, trachea, and lungs by causing massive cellular damage. It's a painful death."

"The head trauma didn't kill him?"

"It's inconclusive. But it certainly wasn't a heart attack."

"How does someone pump chlorine gas into a windowless bathroom?"

"The doorman said he'd had no visitors."

"What about the cleaning woman?" Love asked.

"She has a key and lets herself in and out. Olga Prochorov. Dresses in layers like a homeless woman with dark glasses and a big felt hat. Says she's sensitive to the sun."

"Did Olga like her boss?"

"No, I'm guessing. He barely spoke to her. Scribbled his complaints on post-its and docked her pay when he found a crumb under the toaster, stuff like that, but mostly she tried to stay out of his way."

"So while she's running the vacuum, Cannon strips, walks into his bathroom to take a shower and falls dead from chlorine fumes?"

An idea took shape in my mind and quivered just outside my senses. "The building's old, historic. The pin holding the latch in the knob slipped. Forensics found it on the floor."

"So Cannon closed the door and couldn't get out. He was loaded and slipped, hit his head and what?"

I shook my head. "This was no accident. He was poisoned. What we don't know for sure is how the poison gas got in there."

"I'll talk to Melanie Morris. She might know something."

"And I'm gonna take a ride to Hoboken," I said. "I want to talk to Helen Laird. Melanie's mother."

Melanie's mother was a tall, elegant, well-dressed woman. I put her in her late fifties, but she could have been older. She wore a cream-colored blouse and ivory pants.

"I've already talked to the detectives."

"I'm assisting the investigation."

She hesitated, then led the way to a formal sitting area decorated in restful shades of green. She arranged herself on a plush sofa and I sat across from her in a hard, upholstered chair. For a moment, we stared at one another. I tried to read her face for clues but it was composed, a mild and friendly mask that revealed nothing. "I'm sorry about what happened to your grandson. Were you close?"

A shadow crossed her face. Quickly it was gone. "Melanie's adopted. Did you know that? The worst thing we did is to tell her. She's struggled with abandonment issues ever since. Acting out, running away, drug and alcohol abuse. She put us through our paces, I can tell you. Then she found herself pregnant. The father-to-be learned about the baby and disappeared. Melanie blamed me for ruining her life. A recurring theme."

"And then her son was born."

"Nicky was adorable. I wasn't allowed to see him, but I did talk to him in the park when he was with one sitter or another, some so-called friends of Melanie's." Helen's voice thickened. "I sound terribly judgmental, don't I?" She shook her head as if she'd stepped through a cobweb. "I'll admit that Melanie was not the daughter I'd hoped for, but she loved her son and had worked hard to get her life together. I thought she'd relapse after Nicky's death but she didn't."

"She'd found some purpose in her life."

"Yes. Bringing Cannon to justice."

"That's why she was stalking Cannon. Did you help her with that?"

"I told Melanie it was senseless following that monster around, but she'd developed an obsessive attachment. There was nothing I could do or say."

"Cannon is dead. Is she happy?"

"Happy? I don't think so. Two nights ago she was raped and sodomized with..." she cleared her throat, "with the business end of a broken broom handle."

So, Cannon had sprung for domestic security. Not a big, humorless ex-navy SEAL who carried a Taser, handgun and plastic handcuffs. Too pricey. He'd hired a thug to do unspeakable things to a young woman who missed her dead boy.

"Have you—"

"Contacted the police? No. I didn't report the assault. Melanie is being taken care of privately. If that's all, I need to be alone."

This was my cue to leave. To take my suspicions and let this poor woman live with what would pass for happily ever after. That had been Officer Dan's well-intentioned strategy, that ignorance would bring bliss.

"You can't understand," she said when I made no move to leave. "I once thought there was nothing worse than losing a child. That's difficult to bear. The thought of my child suffering? That's unbearable."

"You still have your child, Mrs. Laird. Melanie's alive." My brother was dead. He'd caused his own death, there was no one else to blame. Accidents happen, people make mistakes. Sometimes we are called to pay and the cost is dearer to the ones who love us than we can imagine. A lie doesn't mitigate the pain. It only hides the truth. And truth is meaningful. "Just one more thing. You know Mr. Cannon's cleaning woman?"

276

"Yes."

"Because she cleans for you?"

She said nothing.

"You hired Olga Prochorov after the accident."

"Is that what we're calling Nicky's death now? An accident?" The words were sharp, but her face wore a patient expression.

"You hired Olga Prochorov after learning that she cleaned for Cannon. You watched her go in and out of his building. You knew Olga had a key."

Her face held in a neutral mask, Helen rose. I was certain the interview was over, but she said, "I'll make us some tea."

I trailed her to a surgically-clean kitchen. No dish towels in sight. My mother always hung hers over the sink. I use the oven door.

"I don't see how our having a cleaning person in common has any bearing on anything." She turned on a burner under the kettle.

We smiled serpent smiles at one another. Nothing tripped in her eyes, but I knew the truth. And I was certain she didn't want to hear it. "Cannon is dead and you had access to the key to his apartment."

"I hated the man. He was evil and caused many people a great deal of pain, but what could someone like me do? I'm not rich."

"Yet you're paying your cleaning woman twice her going rate."

The tea kettle screamed and she snapped off the burner. The whistle died. Helen didn't make tea.

"If there's nothing else, Officer, please leave."

"One more question. You were a school teacher?"

"Yes. A long time ago."

I waited and this time Helen broke the strained silence. "I want to talk to my attorney."

"You nailed her because she taught high school chemistry?" Love asked.

"She fit. She accompanied Melanie a couple of times to persuade her daughter that stalking Cannon was an exercise in futility. Helen watched Olga leave the building and later, offered her a job. She didn't have a plan until after her daughter's assault. She made a copy of Cannon's key and used it to enter his apartment before he was due to get back from the gym. An hour before Olga showed up to clean."

"Cannon was a creature of habit?"

"Highly disciplined. Had a fear of chaos. Every hour was scheduled."

"So Helen, dressed like the cleaning woman, strolls into Cannon's building."

"Hauling a couple of plastic shopping bags, she entered the apartment and in the master bath, turned off the water at the main tap. Then she took the top off the toilet tank and flushed. When the tank and bowl emptied, she poured in a couple of gallons of ammonia and replaced the cover. Then she took the exact amount of bleach and poured it into the bowl."

277

"And no one saw her go in or out."

"Nope."

"What about Cannon? He didn't see her in the apartment?"

"If he did, he ignored her like everyone else. Maybe he noticed the smell of bleach and didn't think anything of it. He closed the bathroom door to take a leak, flushed the toilet and took off his clothes while the chlorine bleach and ammonia combined to create a deadly gas."

"And any high school chemistry teacher would know that," Love said.

"I'm betting she rolled up a towel to place under the door to keep the deadly fumes in. I'll also bet she took the towel with her and dumped it along with the empty bleach and ammonia bottles."

Love nodded.

"Helen Laird left and Olga arrived. As usual, Olga started her cleaning routine in the kitchen, then polished, dusted and vacuumed her way through the apartment. It's a routine Olga sticks to, no matter what."

"And the kicker is," Love said, "Olga dusted, wiped and vacuumed away any evidence of Helen Laird's presence in Cannon's apartment."

"Yup. She emptied the contents of the canister down the trash chute and was ready to start on the bathroom. When she couldn't get in, she called the super and you know the rest."

"It's a good story, but we don't have any proof," Love said.

"I told her we had all the evidence we needed on the apartment building's closed circuit cameras."

"There are no cameras. The whole block is historic buildings."

"You said it yourself, Love. Everyone lies."

Love looked pleased. "Great apes and humans."

"What?"

"The only ones able to lie. Congrats and welcome to the human race soon-to-be Detective Andrews."

"Thanks." I arched an eyebrow. "By the way, does Lempinen really mean 'love' in Finnish?"

Love grinned at me with all his teeth. "Nah. I lied."

A.B. Polomski lives and works in New Jersey. She has over twenty Solve-It-Yourself Mysteries published in Woman's World. When not writing, A.B. works as a mediator for the Ocean County Court.

PET PEEVE

Kari Wainwright

The weary policeman sped through the streets—not lights-and-siren fast—but still over the speed limit. The homicide that had been called in wasn't going anywhere, but Detective Martin Lynch felt that driving fast would work off some of his frustration. In a few hours, he was supposed to start his vacation. He was supposed to spend the next few days holding a fishing rod, not a badge, and trying to catch trout, not a murderer.

He slowed down when he saw the black-and-whites scattered across the road, the yellow crime scene tape strung around a neglected yard, and a bruised teenager leaning against the back of a cop car.

Lynch pulled to the side of the road. This neighborhood wasn't his favorite in Albuquerque. Actually, there weren't many areas he liked in town anymore. He much preferred his mountain cabin near Chama, New Mexico.

He parked his car, got out, hitched up his pants and ducked under the tape. A uniformed brunette woman stood sentry outside the front door on the cracked and crumbling sidewalk. She ignored her partner throwing up near an overgrown pyracantha bush.

"Bad in there, Delores?" Lynch asked.

She flicked a thumb in the other guy's direction. "He thinks so. It's his first dead guy and it doesn't help that it's a messy scene."

The cop they were discussing rose from his bent-over position, removed his cap and rubbed his forehead. "Sorry," he rasped.

Delores seemed to take pity on him. "Drink some water and take a break. Just keep an eye on the kid while I show Detective Lynch our victim."

She led the way through a living room rife with bad smells—stale pizza, sour beer, but worst of all, the evacuated bowel of a dead body. Lynch rubbed a finger under his nose. He used to use Vicks to keep the crime scene stench at bay, but found that Vicks often captured and held those smells to torment him later. These days, he just dealt with the stink as another everyday aspect of his job.

The room might have looked decent once, but now was trashed. An overturned, broken coffee table dominated the area, while a shattered glass lamp littered the dark carpet with sparkling green shards.

When Delores reached the kitchen door, she stopped and pulled out a notebook from a shirt pocket. "The house is owned by one Michael Cadwallader. The kid outside is Keith Hunter. Says he and his mom used to live with Cadwallader, but moved out a few days ago. She sent Keith to get some of

279

her stuff."

"And Cadwallader didn't approve?" he asked, thinking of the kid's fresh bruises.

Delores shrugged. "You want to talk to him here or down at the station?"

What would get this case solved the fastest? All he really wanted to do was throw his suitcase, a beer cooler, and his fishing gear into the back of his SUV and take off for the fresh scent of pine trees and the smoke from a campfire. "Leave the kid here with your partner while I take a look around. Then I'll talk with him. Send in the medical investigator when he gets here."

"He should arrive soon," she said. "There was a multiple car accident a few hours ago, so for now," she waved toward the kitchen, "it's all yours."

"Chicken, Delores?" he asked.

"Hey, I've already seen it. And I managed to keep my breakfast burrito down." She went back outside.

He took a shallow breath before stepping into the room with the body sprawled across the linoleum floor. The stench grew stronger. All he could see of the victim initially was his lower body, so Lynch's first thought was that the orange and brown pattern on the linoleum was one of the ugliest things he'd ever seen. That is, until he stepped past a counter and saw the man's face. Or the place where his face used to be. His features were gone or so wildly distorted that his face resembled raw, red ground beef more than human flesh. Now Lynch understood the rookie's gut reaction. He swallowed hard. It'd been a damn long time since he'd thrown up at a crime scene.

What in the world had attacked this guy? He saw what looked like paw prints painted red and growing lighter as they stretched across the floor toward the open back door. If the prints were bigger, he might have thought mountain lion, but these looked more the size of an ordinary household pet. The detective wished the medical investigator would hurry up so he could look at the man's wounds and come up with a theory.

Lynch carefully stepped over the blood pooled around Cadwallader's head and studied the rest of the room. Awkward stacks of dirty dishes were piled on the countertops. Two lonely bowls sat empty on the floor near the back door. Beer bottles were scattered about the kitchen like forgotten refugees.

He pushed opened a partially closed door in the wall opposite the body and discovered a laundry room with a basket overflowing with dirty clothes. A depressed area in the middle of it made Lynch think of a nest. An overturned box of detergent created a chaos of white powder interspersed with more paw prints. Urine puddles and fecal piles added another layer of stench to the crime scene.

Enough with the stink. The detective decided to explore some less smelly parts of the house. He went back into the living room and down the hallway to a bedroom. He found women's clothes strewn about the bed, sliced into colorful ribbons of cloth. Keith's mother probably wasn't going to be very happy about that.

280

Time to talk to the young man. Lynch went outside, strode over to the teenager, and introduced himself.

He noticed skinned and bloodied knuckles on the kid's hand when he went to shake with him.

"I'm Keith," the kid muttered.

Lynch tried to look casual as he studied the purple and yellow swirls surrounding one of the boy's eyes. He didn't want to spook the kid with his usual intensity at a homicide scene. "You're the one who called 911?"

Keith nodded.

"Do you know the deceased?"

The boy's Adam's apple bobbed up and down. "I think so. I couldn't tell by his face, though. God, he looked effing awful."

"Then how could you tell who it was?"

"His clothes. He was wearing that same plaid shirt last night. And the ring on his finger. Plus, his big ugly shoes. That's Mike The Cad, alright."

"The Cad?"

"Yeah, that's what me and Mom call him now."

"You and your mother used to live here?"

The boy nodded again.

"But you've moved out?"

"Yeah."

Not a young man of many words. "Did The Cad—Mr. Cadwallader— ever hurt your mom or you?"

The boy glanced down. He avoided looking at the detective. "Yeah, he beat her. If he didn't like what she fixed for supper, he'd throw the food against the wall, then make her clean up the mess. I hated him."

"I can understand that." Lynch paused. "Did he hurt you?"

Keith shook his head. The kid wasn't burly, but he was probably almost as tall as The Cad and had some muscle tone to his upper body. That and his youthful strength probably protected him. At least until recently.

"How'd you get the bruises, Keith?"

The boy took a deep breath, as if gathering the strength to tell his tale. "I came over last night to get some of my mom's stuff. Usually The Cad is gone on Friday nights. He gets his paycheck and hits Rosie's, a bar near here."

"But last night was different?"

"Yeah. I'd just discovered what he'd done to Mom's clothes and was looking for—"

A van parked behind the detective's car, interrupting Keith's story. The medical investigator had arrived. A bigger van pulled up, with the forensics team ready to gather their bloody clues.

Lynch wished them luck, then turned back to the kid. "So, what happened?"

"He saw my mom's car out front and came in all mad and stuff."

"Were you angry, too?"

"For damn sure, I was. He'd ruined my mom's clothes. And I couldn't

281

find Cupcake."

"Cupcake?"

"My mom's cat. We couldn't find her the night we left, so Mom worried about her something fierce."

"We'll keep an eye out for her," Lynch said, not even sure he really meant it. He just wanted the kid to get on with his story about The Cad. "So, did you and Cadwallader get into a fight? Did it go too far?"

Keith pointed to the house, his arm outstretched. "He was alive when I left. I swear."

"But you fought."

"Yeah."

"Details, son, I need details."

"I heard him cussing when he came in. We met up in the living room. He threw a lamp at me. I ducked. Then he tackled me, and we both went down. I think that's when we broke the coffee table. It knocked the wind out of me."

He stopped talking, as if his thoughts took him back to last night for real.

"How'd the two of you wind up in the kitchen?" Lynch asked.

"After he punched me a few times and I couldn't fight back, he lost interest. Just told me to get the hell out of his house and went to the kitchen to get a beer. As if he needed another."

"He'd been drinking?"

"Sure smelled like it."

"You followed him into the kitchen?"

Keith grimaced. "I wasn't gonna, but that sonofabitch said he had somethin' for me."

"What was it?"

"Cupcake. He said she'd been shut up in the laundry room since we left 'cause he wanted no part of her. Then he opened the laundry room door and grabbed her. She managed to scratch him a few times before he could get the back door open to throw her out into the yard." Pride in the cat reverberated in Keith's voice.

"What did you do?"

"Shoved him. He wouldn't get out of the way so I could go after her. That's when he fell. He hit his head on the counter."

"Is that how he died?"

"No, sir! He was alive when I left. I went out the back door after Cupcake. I musta looked for fifteen, twenty minutes, but I couldn't find her in the dark. I peeked back in the kitchen 'fore I went home. The Cad was lying on the floor, but he could still cuss me out."

The kid sounds like he's telling the truth. But there's still a dead man in that kitchen.

Delores tapped him on the shoulder. "The M. I. wants you."

Lynch acknowledged her, then turned back to Keith. "Just one last question for now. Why'd you come back this morning?"

282

"To find Cupcake. Mom said don't come back without her. She was real upset when I told her what The Cad had done."

Lynch told Keith to stay put. A heavy sigh escaped the young man's mouth as he leaned back against the car again.

The detective didn't pause at the front door, just strode in as if he meant business. The kitchen didn't smell or look any better the second time around. "Hey, Danny, what do you have for me?"

The M. I. straightened out of his kneeling position next to the victim, or The Cad, as the detective now thought of him, too. Danny wore the look of a tired bloodhound. "It's been a long night, Marty. A really long night."

"Then let's wrap this one up and you can join me at my cabin."

"You have a cabin?"

"Near Chama. Good fishing there."

Danny's brown eyes sparked brightly. "Sounds like a plan. Wish I could join you. But maybe I can help *you* get there faster."

Now it was Lynch's turn to brighten. "You telling me you solved the case?"

"If the autopsy backs up my educated guess."

"I thought medical investigators weren't supposed to guess."

"Only if they're *un*-educated."

"Okay, okay, tell me what you think you know."

"Judging from the fact that rigor mortis is just starting to set in, he died sometime in the early morning hours. Only an hour or two ago."

Lynch told him the kid's story and pointed to the corner of the countertop. "Could that blow to the head have killed him?"

"Of course, I'll check that out, but it does seem that the guy was still alive last night."

Have to check the kid's alibi. Of course, it's likely his mother will cover for him, no matter what.

The M. I. indicated the pool of blood. "As for cause of death, I'm guessing he bled out—from all these facial and scalp wounds."

"Any idea what caused these injuries?"

"Sure enough. I've seen something like this once before. On the rez."

Lynch wondered what had happened on the Indian reservation similar to this.

A loud, plaintive yowl erupted from the back yard. *Cupcake?*

The detective went to the back door, which was ajar, and pulled it all the way open. Sitting a few feet away, a Siamese cat, all tan and cinnamon, licked the red off one of her front paws. Crimson surrounded her mouth, like lipstick gone totally awry.

"Just like at the rez," Danny said. "An old woman died and wasn't found for several days. Her pet must have gotten real hungry. Or really peeved. When the old lady was finally discovered, she had no face left either."

"But do you think Cadwallader was dead when the cat ate his face?"

"Nope. I'm thinking unconscious. There wouldn't be so much bleeding

283

if he'd already been dead. Blood doesn't pump in a corpse."

Sounded plausible to the detective. But then he didn't know much about cats. "How do we prove she made the fatal wounds? She could have just caught a mouse or something."

"She has to shit sometime. And my assistant will be there. Plus, we can get DNA from the blood on her face."

The detective stood in silence for a moment. Stunned. The cat stared at the men through enigmatic eyes, licked her lips, and started strolling off across the back yard.

Lynch realized Cupcake might be the key to solving this crime. The sooner it was solved, the sooner he could go fishing. He couldn't let her get away. "Someone, catch that cat," he yelled. "She's destroying evidence."

Delores arrived at the back yard gate. "I'm not going near that animal. I'm allergic to the dang things."

"Then call the kid," Lynch ordered.

Keith was summoned. Armed with Cupcake's favorite treats, he caught her after only a brief chase and a few scratches. Cradling the blood-stained animal in his arms, he said, "Mom will be a lot happier now."

"Sorry, son," Detective Lynch said. "We need to take Cupcake into custody for a while. We think she caused Mr. Cadwallader's death."

"You mean she ate his face?"

Lynch nodded.

The kid held the cat away from his body, studying her red-stained fur. "Cool! Good kitty."

"More like bad kitty, son," the detective said.

"Pretty much," Danny agreed. "If my theory is correct, looks like the cause of death was a serious case of cat nips."

The detective groaned. Maybe it was time to retire, take up life full-time at his cabin, where the only blood he'd have to deal with would be from the fish he gutted.

No cats allowed.

Kari Wainwright divides her time between her Colorado mountain home and her Arizona desert residence. She tries to spend the seasons in the place with the best weather, but doesn't always succeed. Wherever she is, she shares her life with husband Tom, son Travis and Shih Tzu Oscar Wilde. She has short stories published in *Desert Sleuth* anthologies as well as *That Mysterious Woman* and is a member of Sisters in Crime.

BAD FRIDAY

Martin Edwards

"I want you out of my life! I just wish you would die!"

Like a chisel ripping through flesh, the woman's voice pierces the hubbub in Coach U. I'm wedged in the carriage entrance behind a morbidly obese businessman who blocks the aisle while trying to squeeze a bulging suitcase between two seats. The woman swears and I wince as hot rage pours from an unseen mouth into the sweaty air.

The first off-peak train on a Friday evening from Euston to Liverpool Lime Street is always jam-packed. To make matters worse, the previous train has been cancelled—leaves on the line, or the wrong kind of rain, or some other excuse, I don't know—and this one teems with specimens of exhausted humanity desperately seeking unreserved seats.

The fat bloke abandons the unequal struggle and disappears down the train, matching fat suitcase in hand. As people push forward, I lean against a luggage rack and catch my breath. I've not felt so exhausted since the last weeks of my pregnancy. There is nowhere to stash my bag, but at least I can keep hold of it. Anything rather than the embarrassment of finding I'm the victim of a thief.

The train lurches forward and I catch sight of the woman who wants someone dead. She's lucky enough to have bagged a seat, but is staring at her iPhone with the sort of concentrated disgust that only a faithless lover can inspire. I can't tell whether she's hung up on him, or he's hung up on her. She is in her mid-twenties, with luxuriant dark hair and lips whose default expression is a spoiled-brat's pout. Because she has over-indulged in fake tan, and under-dressed for an October evening, a great deal of orange flesh is on display. If Josh were here, he'd be ogling like mad. But Josh and I aren't together anymore.

The orange-skinned woman stabs the dialling pad with a purple fingernail and screeches "It's me!" at precisely the moment we enter the tunnel outside Euston. Losing the connection provokes her into a lurid bout of swearing, and this prompts the old chap sitting next to her to bury his head in the *Evening Standard*. I read the headlines on the other side of the paper—*Brexit negotiations falter. Celebrity couple split. Hoxton minimart stabbings: "No arrest imminent." Chelsea striker suspended.*—and, shuddering, avert my eyes. A young couple in the seats opposite Ms Orange murmur to each other in a foreign language I can't identify. I find myself hoping their command of English isn't good enough to enable them to understand what she is saying.

285

As we emerge from the tunnel into the evening gloom, the train manager announces that the shop and buffet car are open, and after apologising for the overcrowded conditions, he offers a sweetener: a few free seats in the first class carriages are being made available for the common herd. Those of the common herd (sorry, customers) who still haven't found seats stampede towards the rear of the train, and they are joined by the elderly man next to Ms Orange, who grabs his ancient bag and dashes for freedom with an unexpected turn of speed.

Without thinking, I thrust my own case into the newly created space on the luggage rack, and plonk myself down right next to Ms Orange, where I can keep an eye on it. At once I discover that her perfume is as pungent as her voice is loud and her manners vile. Never mind; after a long and dispiriting day of foot-slogging around Hackney, I'd rather endure an unpleasantly close encounter for two and a quarter hours than stand any longer.

I glance at the *Evening Standard* the man abandoned in his haste to escape. Opinion pieces about the quest for a kinder, gentler politics—good luck with that—and the fact that our police are no longer wonderful. I'm not tempted to read them. It's been a bad, bad Friday—and it's the 13th of the month. Perhaps there's something in the old superstition. The weekend offers minimal prospect of rest and recuperation. I'm dying to sweep Barnaby up in my arms, of course, and at least the sight of his tousled hair and big brown eyes will more than compensate for the pain of encountering Josh and Erica again. I have a recurrent nightmare that one day I'll go back to Aigburth to see my son and he won't recognise me. Mum says it's my own fault, and I hate to admit it, but she's right. She's even hinted that he's starting to care more for Erica than for me.

I'm ashamed I'm not looking forward to staying with Mum, and not simply because Archie is an old bore. I'm the child of a broken marriage, perhaps it's in the genes, and I'm destined to see my own relationships forever falling apart. Or perhaps Mum's also right when she says I love my work more than any of the men who have flitted through my life. Archie is a tedious old sexist who treats Mum like a servant, but at least he's hung around for the past ten years, and grows tasty vegetables in his allotment for her to cook.

Ms Orange indicates with a graceless shuffle of her body that she wants to get out of her seat, and I stand up and move aside to let her pass. Neither of us speak. Is she, too, destined for the first class coaches? Somehow I doubt I'm going to be so lucky. I offer a politely conspiratorial smile to the foreign couple opposite, but they are wholly preoccupied with each other, their mutual devotion a stinging reminder of what I've thrown away. I close my eyes, but I can't get Josh's sad face out of my mind. The expression he wore when he said enough was enough will haunt me to the grave. How could I not have realised I'd made such a mess of everything?

I'm still scarifying myself mentally when a loud noise rouses me. Ms Orange is back, bearing a paper bag crammed with smelly train food. I'm betting her knack of conveying impatience and bad temper is the product of years of practice. I haul myself to my feet with an insincere smile of apology, and resist the temptation to stamp on her toes as she shoves past me. I regret my self-restraint instantly as she pokes a sharp elbow into my midriff in the process of sitting down.

After watching her take out of the bag a burger with onions, a Kit Kat, and a small bottle of Shiraz, I resort to eye-closing once more, trying in vain neither to inhale nor visualise her chomping away with her mouth open. The sound effects alone are graphic enough to demand a health warning.

She's just started slurping down the wine when a rap music ringtone hits me like a cannonball. My eyes are forced open as she starts bellowing into the iPhone to someone called Sheena about the awfulness of her ex. But my attention isn't really roused until, ten minutes into a rant studded with obscenities, she mentions his name.

"I told him, I'm never going to help you out again, no matter what. You treat me like a slave, Josh, I said, and I'm not standing for it no more."

For a wild, fantastic moment, I wonder if she's talking about my Josh. Or at least, the Josh who used to be mine. Could he be two-timing Erica? Suppose he'd met Ms Orange on the rebound, and decided he wanted someone crude and curvy as a replacement for a tall, thin, twitchy workaholic. Might he have an unsuspected craving for implants and neck tattoos? You can't put anything past a man, that's one thing I know for sure. But it makes no sense—the world is full of Joshes. Including that other Josh, the one who these past few days has crowded even my ex-husband out of my thoughts. I'm still not sure whether that's a good thing, or bad.

A brief period of respite follows. Ms Orange's complacent smile tells me that Sheena is reassuring her that she was wasted on Josh anyway. But then we enter another tunnel, and she bangs the iPhone down on the table separating us from the foreign couple. Predictably, this cracks the screen, prompting another fusillade of obscenities as she inspects the damage. The pair sitting opposite don't turn a hair.

The rapper returns as we speed through the Midlands, giving me my cue to get up and amble off in search of a cup of coffee. I take my time, only to find on my return that Ms Orange is deep in conversation with yet another friend. This time it's Kayleigh who is being treated to an exhaustive account of Josh's offensive habits and profound unworthiness. Unfortunately, it seems that in happier times Ms Orange acquired a Josh-related tattoo on an intimate part of her anatomy. Kayleigh once had a similar problem, apparently, and they debate the drawbacks of laser treatment.

Why do people talk so loudly about personal stuff on train journeys? I suppose they think it doesn't matter—people within earshot don't know them, and their paths won't ever cross in future. I try to shut out her furious East End tones, but it isn't easy. There's no escape; on my foray to carriage C for coffee, I passed several people sitting on suitcases, who no doubt presumed that those spare first class seats would all be filled by the time they made their way to the other end of the train. At least we're not far from Stafford now. Anyway, by profession, I suppose I'm a nosey parker.

287

The foreign couple are stroking each other's hands. It's sweet, but also excruciating, if you've messed up pretty much every relationship you've ever had. I take refuge in the Closed Eye Ploy, fantasising that the train will get stuck in an unexpected snowdrift in the middle of nowhere, and that Ms Orange's ranting will provoke all her fellow passengers (sorry, customers) into a joint enterprise murder plot. But before long, images from a different movie, that old black and white thriller about strangers on a train, start floating through my head. How about offering Ms Orange a deal—I'll kill your Josh if you kill mine?

But no. Not a good idea. Apart from anything else, I wouldn't trust her not to mess up. She might even try a spot of blackmail, in preference to murder. Besides, I don't really want Josh to die. He's not a bad man, even if he did move in with my sister a matter of weeks after our marriage finally broke down. I suspect most people blame me and my obsession with work for our break-up, and even I reckon Erica chased him rather than the other way around. All the same, the day he left me in London to go back to Aigburth, taking Barnaby with him, I could have killed him—possibly with my bare hands. If I hadn't been out on a job, that is. Call me a lousy mother—plenty of people have—but I'm still not confident that I'm ready to look after our son on my own, two hundred miles away from domestic back-up. I'd have to ask Mum to be there for him when I'm working away. Or, even worse, beg Erica for help. I don't wish her dead, either, but we're not on speaking terms right now. She's always been a predator, but I never expected her to catch my husband.

A patch of countryside with poor mobile coverage kills Ms Orange's latest conversation, and the moment her signal is restored, the rapper heralds a call from someone wanting to make an appointment with her. Apparently, Ms Orange is a mobile hair stylist. There are plenty of them around, of course, just as there are plenty of Joshes. Even so, my ears prick up as Ms Orange takes careful note of the new client's address in Hackney, and when she gives her own email address, I commit it to memory. No longer am I quite so desperate for her to pipe down.

The appointment fixed, we arrive at Stafford, and Ms Orange rings another friend, Pixie. From the frequent references to an ailing Mam—evidently in hospital at Arrowe Park at the moment—you don't need to be Stella Gibson or Sarah Lund to deduce that Pixie is her sister. I suppose it's a point in their favour that she and Pixie seem much closer than Erica and me. Their mother had a heart attack, I gather, while on a pilgrimage to Liverpool to visit John Lennon's birthplace. As for Pixie, far from wanting to snare Josh for herself, she seems to be egging Ms Orange on in her denunciation of her ex. Not like Erica at all; after dumping her own husband, she never made any secret of her interest in mine. Do I believe that they only got together after Josh and I split? Maybe it's true, and anyway, who cares? I never thought Erica was Josh's type, one more mistake in a long line. Water under the bridge.

"I lied for him," Ms Orange says. My eyes remain shut, but now I'm agog. "I risked my own neck, when Mam was hovering between life and death. And you know what? He didn't even say thank you."

The diatribe goes on and on, giving me plenty of time to reflect on human nature's oddities. Ms Orange complaining about discourtesy? Pot, meet kettle. But for all her loudness, rudeness, and sheer unpleasantness, I'm starting to warm to her. Is it possible she could improve my day?

"You're right," she tells Pixie. "He deserves what's coming to him."

I send a text to Andrew, asking him to remind me of a name. Within a minute a reply pings, and I sneak a glance.

Daniella Blyth.

All the way to Crewe and beyond, I keep willing Ms Orange to explain herself in words of one syllable. But she enjoys insulting her ex too much to say anything worthwhile. Not to worry. Instinct tells me I'm on to something. And then I remind myself that my instinct is hardly infallible.

This is different, though. It's business, not personal. I'm hoping for more information, but by the time we reach Runcorn, she's announced that she never wants to think about him again. She just wants him out of her life. As she said before.

Well, it might just be I could play Fairy Godmother, and grant her wish.

We're slowing down on the approach to Edge Hill, close to our destination in the heart of Liverpool, when I steal another look at Andrew's text. This time, I put my phone down on a small patch of the table untouched by the mess made by Ms Orange's meal. It catches her eye.

She turns her head, and stares at me. Something flickers in her expression. Yes, there is outrage, but also I recognise fear.

"What's going on?" she demands.

I gaze straight back at her. "Daniella Blyth?"

She squints at the foreign couple, as if suspecting them of working undercover. "Who wants to know?"

The train slows. In a few moments we'll pull in to Lime Street. Like a conjuror plucking a pigeon from his sleeve, I take out my warrant card.

"Detective Sergeant Leanne Wood, Metropolitan Police."

The orange cheeks redden as the horror of what she's said begins to dawn. "You've been earwigging, you nosey bitch."

"Hard to avoid hearing what you've had to say, Daniella."

She launches into another volley of obscenities, but I see in her fuddled eyes that she can't recall exactly what she's said out loud. Probably she thinks she's given more away than she did. That's the trouble with a guilty conscience. It's not compatible with having a big mouth.

I soak up the abuse for half a minute before saying, "It's not you we're after. It's Josh."

And then I watch as dismay gives way to calculation. She's been caught out, and she knows as well as I do that she's facing a charge of perverting the course of justice in a double murder case. But she's also streetwise enough to realise the advantage of playing a get out of jail card. So often doing justice depends on changing loyalties. If Daniella wants Josh to die, she may be more than happy to help us to arrest him on suspicion of murdering Saeed Anwar and Begum Anwar at Hoxton in London seven days ago. All she needs to do is to withdraw the alibi she gave him when Andrew interviewed her.

The story was that the pair of them had been occupying each other in bed in Daniella's flat at the time a man in a crash helmet tried to rob Anwar's Minimart in Hoxton. When the owner and his daughter refused to hand over the takings and rang an alarm, he stabbed them both in a panic both before fleeing the store. Saeed suffered a ruptured liver, and died at the scene. Begum's throat was cut, and she only lived forty-eight hours. The incident took less than two minutes from start to finish, and was captured on an ancient CCTV, but the images were too blurry for us to identify the killer beyond doubt. Our top five suspects included local petty criminal Joshua Hughes, but Andrew couldn't crack his alibi, and our attention turned elsewhere. Not that I or my colleagues have got very far. My own inquiries have amounted to one dead end after another. So it's been a tough old week, though a thousand times harder for the grieving widow and mother.

"All right," Daniella says as we pull into the station. "But you'll have to do me a deal. I'll want to call a lawyer. You lot aren't to be trusted."

I stand up, and pull out my case, trying to disguise my exultation. I've even figured out why I didn't recognise her from the photo pinned to the whiteboard in the incident room. She's changed her hairstyle and colour, as well as going overboard on the fake tan.

"I trust you to co-operate, Daniella. After all you've said about him."

She glares before giving an *easy-come-easy-go* shrug. We get out of the train together. I don't want to let her out of my sight, but I doubt she'll try making a run for it. She probably thinks I've recorded everything she's said, all the way up from Euston.

We walk along the platform, side by side. At the barrier, I glimpse two familiar faces. Josh—*my* Josh—and Barnaby. What are they doing here? It wasn't in the script. Barnaby's waving excitedly, and Josh is wearing the bashful grin that I recall from our earliest days together. No sign of Erica.

Don't tell me that he's dumped her?

For a mad moment, I forget that I'm a police officer, just as Josh has so often wanted me to. I drop my suitcase and run to the barrier, arms outstretched. For a moment, I even forget about Daniella.

I want you back in my life. I'm so glad you're alive.

He's the opposite of Josh Hughes, and I'm a fool not to have seen it until now.

Who would have believed? It's finally a Good Friday.

MARTIN EDWARDS' eighteen novels include the Lake District Mysteries and the Harry Devlin series. The Coffin Trail was shortlisted for the Theakston's Prize for Crime Novel of the Year, while All the Lonely People was nominated for the John Creasey Memorial Dagger for best first crime novel. His genre study The Golden Age of Murder has won the Edgar®, Agatha, H.R.F. Keating and Macavity awards. He has edited thirty crime anthologies, has won the CWA Short Story Dagger, the CWA Margery Allingham Prize, and the Red Herring award, and is series consultant for the British Library's very successful series of Crime Classics. In 2015, he was elected eighth President of the Detection Club, and he is currently also Chair of the Crime Writers' Association.

Made in the USA
Columbia, SC
21 May 2017